IRON KISSED

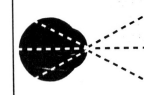

This Large Print Book carries the
Seal of Approval of N.A V.H.

A MERCY THOMPSON NOVEL, BOOK 3

IRON KISSED

PATRICIA BRIGGS

WHEELER PUBLISHING
A part of Gale, Cengage Learning

GALE
CENGAGE Learning

Detroit • New York • San Francisco • New Haven, Conn • Waterville, Maine • London

GALE
CENGAGE Learning

Copyright © 2007 by Hurog, Inc.
A Mercy Thompson Novel #3.
Map Illustrations by Michael Enzweller.
Wheeler Publishing, a part of Gale, Cengage Learning.

Wheeler Publishing Large Print Softcover.
The text of this Large Print edition is unabridged.
Other aspects of the book may vary from the original edition.
Set in 16 pt. Plantin.
Printed on permanent paper.

LIBRARY OF CONGRESS CATALOGING-IN-PUBLICATION DATA

Briggs, Patricia.
  Iron kissed / by Patricia Briggs.
    p. cm.
  "A Mercy Thompson novel #3"—T.p. verso.
  ISBN-13: 978-1-59722-867-1 (pbk. : alk. paper)
  ISBN-10: 1-59722-867-2 (pbk. : alk. paper)
  1. Thompson, Mercy (Fictitious character)—Fiction. 2. Werewolves—Fiction. 3. Vampires—Fiction. 4. Large type books. I. Title.
PS3602.R53165I76 2008
813'.6—dc22   2008035045

Published in 2008 by arrangement with The Berkley Publishing Group, a member of Penguin Group (USA) Inc.

Printed in the United States of America
1 2 3 4 5 6 7 12 11 10 09 08

For Collin:
Collector of all that is Sharp and Pointy
Dragon Slayer

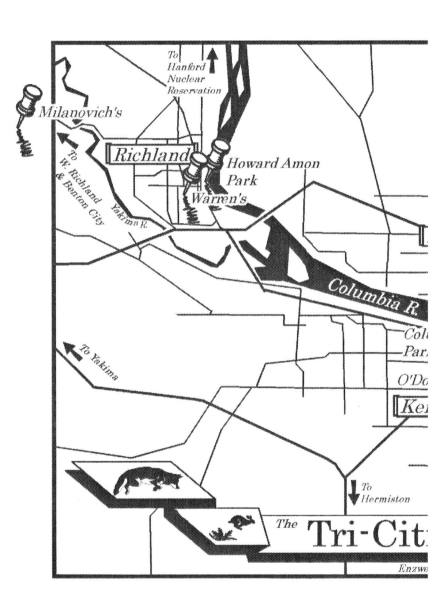

To
Hanford
Nuclear
Reservation

Milanovich's

Richland

To
W. Richland
& Benton City

Yakima R.

Howard Amon
Park

Warren's

Columbia R.

To Yakima

Col
Par.

O'Do

Ke

To
Hermiston

The Tri-Cit

Enzw

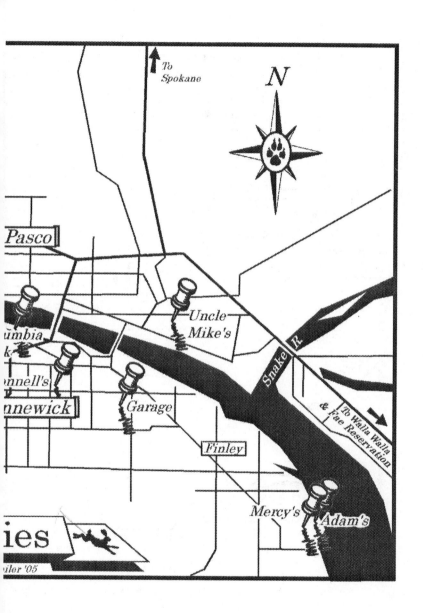

ACKNOWLEDGMENTS

Editing: Anne Sowards, of course, but also Mike and Collin Briggs, Dave, Katharine, and Caroline Carson, Jean Matteucci, Ann (Sparky) Peters, Kaye and Kyle Roberson, and Gene Walker — brave folk who all read this book or parts of it in various stages of disrepair and did their best to help me shore up foundations.

German: Michael and Susann Bock of Hamburg — for their gallant efforts, Zee is truly grateful. *Danke.*

Research: Jana and Dean of the Butte Silver Bow Arts Foundation, George Bowen and the Kennewick Police Department, Cthulu Bob Lovely, and Dr. Ginny Mohl.

Map: Michael Enzweiler.

The author is especially grateful to Jesse Robison, who volunteered to step in when Mercy needed a bookstore and someone who knows his books.

And, of course, the dedicated folks of the

Three Rivers Folklife Society and the many talented musicians who put on the Tumbleweed Music Festival every Labor Day weekend so that we should have music.

Despite the valiant efforts (and struggles) of these many talented people, I expect that there are still mistakes herein, and I accept full responsibility for them.

CHAPTER 1

"A cowboy, a lawyer, and a mechanic watched *Queen of the Damned*," I murmured.

Warren — who had once, a long time ago, been a cowboy — snickered and wiggled his bare feet. "It could be the beginning of either a bad joke or a horror story."

"No," said Kyle, the lawyer, whose head was propped up on my thigh. "If you want a horror story, you have to start out with a werewolf, his gorgeous lover, and a walker . . ."

Warren, the werewolf, laughed and shook his head. "Too confusing. Not many people still remember what a walker is."

Mostly they just confused us with skinwalkers. Since walkers and skinwalkers are both Native American shapeshifters, I can sort of understand it. Especially since I'm pretty sure the walker label came from some dumb white person who couldn't tell the difference.

But I'm not a skinwalker. First of all, I'm from the wrong tribe. My father had been Blackfoot, from a northern Montana tribe, and skinwalkers come from the Southwestern tribes, mostly Hopi or Navajo.

Second, skinwalkers have to wear the skin of the animal they change into, usually a coyote or wolf, but they cannot change their eyes. They are evil mages who bring disease and death wherever they go.

When I change into a coyote, I don't need a skin or — I glanced down at Warren, once a cowboy and now a werewolf — the moon. When I am a coyote, I look just like every other coyote. Pretty much harmless, really, as far down the power scale of the magical critters that lived in the state of Washington as it was possible to get. Which is one of the things that used to help keep me safe. I just wasn't worth bothering about. That had been changing over the past year. Not that I'd grown any more powerful, but I'd started doing things that drew attention. When the vampires figured out that I'd killed not one, but two of their own . . .

As if called by my thoughts, a vampire walked across the screen of the TV, a TV so big it wouldn't have fit in my trailer's living room. He was shirtless and his pants clung inches below his sexy hipbones.

I resented the shiver of fear that surged through my body instead of lust. Funny how killing them had only made the vampires more frightening. I dreamed of vampires crawling out of holes in the floor and whispering to me from shadows. I dreamed of the feel of a stake sliding through flesh and fangs digging into my arm.

If it had been Warren with his head on my lap instead of Kyle, he would have noticed my reaction. But Warren was stretched out on the floor and firmly focused on the screen.

"You know," I snuggled deeper into the obscenely comfortable leather couch in the upstairs TV room of Kyle's huge house and tried to sound casual, "I wondered why Kyle picked this movie. Somehow I didn't think there would be quite so many bare manly chests in a movie called *Queen of the Damned*."

Warren snickered, ate a handful of popcorn from the bowl on his flat stomach, then said with more than a hint of a Texas drawl in his rough voice, "You expected more naked women and fewer half-clothed men, did you, Mercy? You oughtta know Kyle better than that." He laughed quietly again and pointed at the screen. "Hey, I didn't think vampires were immune to gravity. Have you ever seen one dangle from the ceiling?"

I shook my head and watched as the vampire dropped on top of his two groupie victims. "I wouldn't put it past them, though. I haven't seen them eat people yet either. Ick."

"Shut up. I like this movie." Kyle, the lawyer, defended his choice. "Lots of pretty boys writhing in sheets and running around with low-cut pants and no shirts. I thought you might enjoy it, too, Mercy."

I looked down at him — every lovely, solar-flexed inch of him — and thought that he was more interesting than any of the pretty men on the screen, more real.

In appearance he was almost a stereotype of a gay man, from the hair gel in his weekly cut dark brown hair to the tastefully expensive clothes he wore. If people weren't careful, they missed the sharp intelligence that hid beneath the pretty exterior. Which was, because it was Kyle, the point of the facade.

"This really isn't bad enough for bad movie night," Kyle continued, not worried about interrupting the movie: none of us were watching it for its scintillating dialogue. "I'd have gotten *Blade III,* but oddly enough, it was already checked out."

"Any movie with Wesley Snipes is worth

watching, even if you have to turn off the sound." I twisted and bent so I could snitch a handful of popcorn from Warren's bowl. He was too thin still; that and a limp were reminders that only a month ago he'd been so badly hurt I'd thought he would die. Werewolves are tough, bless 'em, or we'd have lost him to a demon-bearing vampire. That one had been the first vampire I'd killed — with the full knowledge and permission of the local vampire mistress. That she hadn't actually intended me to kill him didn't negate that I'd done it with her blessing. She couldn't do anything to me for his death — and she didn't know I was responsible for the other.

"As long as he's not dressed in drag," drawled Warren.

Kyle snorted agreement. "Wesley Snipes may be a beautiful man, but he makes a butt-ugly woman."

"Hey," I objected, pulling my mind back to the conversation. "*To Wong Foo* was a good movie." We'd watched it last week at my house.

A faint buzzing noise drifted up the stairs and Kyle rolled off the couch and onto his feet in a graceful, dancelike move that was wasted on Warren. He was still focused on the movie, though his grin probably wasn't the reaction the moviemakers had intended for their bloodfest scene. My feelings were much more in line with the desired result. It was all too easy to imagine myself as the victim.

"Brownies are done, my sweets," said Kyle. "Anyone want something more to drink?"

"No, thank you." It was just make-believe, I thought, watching the vampire feed.

"Warren?"

His name finally drew Warren's gaze off the TV screen. "Water would be nice."

Warren wasn't as pretty as Kyle, but he had the rugged-man look down pat. He watched Kyle walk down the stairs with hungry eyes.

I smiled to myself. It was good to see Warren happy at last. But the eyes he turned to me as soon as Kyle was out of sight were serious. He used the remote to raise the volume, then sat up and faced me, knowing Kyle wouldn't hear us over the movie.

"You need to choose," he told me intently. "Adam or Samuel or neither. But you can't keep them dangling."

Adam was the Alpha of the local werewolf pack, my neighbor, and sometimes my date. Samuel was my first love, my first heartbreak, and currently my roommate. Just my roommate — though he'd like to be more.

I didn't trust either of them. Samuel's easygoing exterior masked a patient and ruthless predator. And Adam . . . well, Adam just flat scared me. And I was very much afraid that I loved them both.

"I know."

Warren dropped his eyes from mine, a sure sign he was uncomfortable. "I didn't brush my teeth with gunpowder this morning so I could go shooting my mouth off, Mercy, but this is serious. I know it's been difficult, but you can't have two dominant werewolves after the same woman without bloodshed. I don't know any other wolves who could have allowed you as much leeway as they have, but one of them is going to break soon."

My cell phone began playing "The Baby Elephant Walk." I dug it out of my hip pocket and looked at the caller ID.

"I believe you," I told Warren. "I just don't know what to do about any of it." There was more wrong with Samuel than undying love of me, but that was between him and me and none of Warren's business. And Adam . . . for the first time I wondered if it wouldn't just be easier if I pulled up stakes and moved.

The phone continued to sing.

"It's Zee," I said. "I have to take this."

Zee was my former boss and mentor. He'd taught me how to rebuild an engine from the ground up — and he'd given me the means to kill the vampires responsible for Warren's limp and the nightmares that were leaving fine lines around his eyes. I figured that gave Zee the right to interrupt *Friday Night at the Movies*.

"Just think about it."

I gave him a faint smile and flipped open my phone. "Hey, Zee."

There was a pause on the other end. "Mercedes," he said, and not even his thick German accent could disguise the hesitant tone of his voice. Something was wrong.

"What do you need?" I asked, sitting up straighter and putting my feet on the floor. "Warren's here," I added so Zee would know we had an audience. Werewolves make having a private conversation difficult.

"Would you drive out to the reservation with me?"

He could have been speaking of the Umatilla Reservation, which was a short drive from the Tri-Cities. But it was Zee, so he was talking about the Ronald Wilson Reagan Fae Reservation just this side of Walla Walla, better known around here as Fairyland.

18

"Now?" I asked.

Besides . . . I glanced at the vampire on the big-screen TV. They hadn't gotten it quite right, hadn't captured the real *evil* — but it was too close for comfort anyway. Somehow I couldn't work up too much sorrow at missing the rest of the movie — or more conversation about my love life either.

"No," Zee groused irritably. "Next week. *Jetzt.* Of course, *now.* Where are you? I will pick you up."

"Do you know where Kyle's house is?" I asked.

"Kyle?"

"Warren's boyfriend." Zee knew Warren; I hadn't realized he hadn't met Kyle. "We're out in West Richland."

"Give me the address. I will find it."

Zee's truck purred down the highway even though it was older than I was. Too bad the upholstery wasn't in as good a shape as the engine — I shifted my rump over a few inches to keep a wayward spring from digging in too deeply.

The dash lights illuminated the craggy face that Zee presented to the world. His fine white hair was mussed a little, as if he'd been rubbing his hands over it.

Warren hadn't said more about Adam or

Samuel after I'd hung up because Kyle, thank goodness, had arrived with brownies. It wasn't that I was bothered by Warren's interference — I'd done enough interfering in his love life that I figured he had a right. I just didn't want to think about it anymore.

Zee and I rode mostly in silence from West Richland, all the way past Richland and on through Pasco. I knew better than to try to get something out of the old gremlin until he was ready to talk, so I let him alone until he decided to speak — at least after the first ten or fifteen questions he hadn't answered.

"Have you been to the reservation before?" he asked abruptly as we crossed the river just outside Pasco on the highway to Walla Walla.

"No." The fae reservation in Nevada welcomed visitors. They had built a casino and small theme park to attract tourists. The Walla Walla reservation, however, actively discouraged anyone who wasn't fae from entering. I wasn't quite certain if it was the Feds or the fae themselves responsible for the unfriendly reputation.

Zee tapped unhappily on his steering wheel with hands that belonged to a man who'd spent his lifetime repairing cars, tough and scarred with oil so ingrained not even pumice soap would remove it.

They were the right hands for the human that Zee had pretended to be. When the Gray Lords, the powerful and ruthless beings who ruled the fae in secret, forced him to admit what he was to the public a few years ago, a decade or more after the first fae had come out, Zee hadn't bothered to change his outward appearance at all.

I'd known him for a little over ten years, and the sour old man face was the only one I'd ever seen. He had another; I knew that. Most fae lived among humans under their glamour, even if they admitted what they were. People are just not ready to deal with the fae's true appearance. Sure, some of them looked human enough, but they also don't age. The thinning hair and the wrinkled, age-spotted skin were sure signs that Zee wasn't wearing his true face. His sour expression, though, was no disguise.

"Don't eat or drink anything," he said abruptly.

"I've read all the fairy tales," I reminded him. "No food, no drink. No favors. No thanking anyone."

He grunted. "Fairy tales. Damned children's stories."

"I've read Katherine Briggs, too," I offered. "And the original Grimm's." Mostly looking for some mention of a fae who

21

could have been Zee. He wouldn't talk about it, though I think he'd been Someone. So finding out who he'd been had become something of a hobby of mine.

"Better. Better, but not much." He tapped his fingers on the wheel. "Briggs was an archivist. Her books are only as correct as her sources and mostly they are dangerously incomplete. The stories of the Brothers Grimm are more concerned with entertainment than reality. Both of them are *nur Schatten* . . . only shadows of reality." He looked at me, a quick searching glance. "Uncle Mike suggested you might be useful here. I thought it was a better repayment than might otherwise come your way."

To kill the sorcerer vampire, who was gradually being taken over by the demon that made him a sorcerer, Zee'd risked the wrath of the Gray Lords to loan me a couple of the treasures of the fae. I'd killed that vampire all right, and then I'd killed the one who'd made him. As in the stories, if you use a fairy gift once more than you have permission for, there are consequences.

If I'd known this was going to be repayment for favors rendered, I'd have been more apprehensive from the start: the last time I'd had to repay a favor hadn't ended well.

"I'll be all right," I told him despite the cold knot of dread in my stomach.

He gave me a sour look. "I had not thought about what it might mean to bring you into the reservation after dark."

"People do go to the reservation," I said, though I wasn't really sure of it.

"Not people like you, and no visitors after dark." He shook his head. "A human comes in and sees what he should, especially by daylight, when their eyes are easier to fool. But you . . . The Gray Lords have forbidden hunting humans, but we have our share of predators and it is hard to deny nature. Especially when the Gray Lords who make our rules are not here — there is only I. And if you see what you should not, there are those who will say they are only protecting what they have to . . ."

It was only when he switched into German that I realized that he had been talking to himself for the last half of it. Thanks to Zee, my German was better than two requisite years of college classes had left it, but not good enough to follow him when he got going.

It was after eight at night, but the sun still cast her warm gaze on the trees in the foothills beside us. The larger trees were green still, but some of the smaller bushes were giving hints of the glorious colors of fall.

Near the Tri-Cities, the only trees were in town, where people kept them watered through the brutal summers or along one of the rivers. But as we drove toward Walla Walla, where the Blue Mountains helped wring a little more moisture out of the air, the countryside got slowly greener.

"The worst of it is," Zee said, finally switching to English, "I don't think you'll be able to tell us anything we don't already know."

"About what?"

He gave me a sheepish look, which sat oddly on his face. "*Ja,* I am mixing this up. Let me start again." He drew in a breath and let it out with a sigh. "Within the reservation, we do our own law enforcement — we have that right. We do it quietly because the human world is not ready for the ways we have to enforce the law. It is not so easy to imprison one of us, eh?"

"The werewolves have the same problem," I told him.

"*Ja,* I bet." He nodded, a quick jerk of a nod. "So. There have been deaths in the reservation lately. We think it is the same person in each case."

"You're on the reservation police force?" I asked.

He shook his head. "We don't have such a thing. Not as such. But Uncle Mike is on the Council. He thought that your accurate nose might be useful and sent me to get you."

Uncle Mike ran a bar in Pasco that served fae and some of the other magical people who lived in town. That he was powerful, I'd always known — how else could he keep a lid on so many fae? I hadn't realized he was on the Council. Maybe if I'd known there was a council to be on, I might have suspected it.

"Can't one of you do as much as I can?" I held up a hand to keep him from answering right away. "It's not that I mind. I can imagine a lot worse ways to pay off my debt. But why me? Didn't Jack's giant smell the blood of an Englishman for Pete's sake? What about magic? Couldn't one of you find the killer with magic?"

I don't know much about magic, but I would think that a reservation of fae would have someone whose magic would be more useful than my nose.

"Maybe the Gray Lords could make magic do their bidding to show them the guilty party," Zee said. "But we do not want to call their attention — it is too chancy. Outside of the Gray Lords . . ." He shrugged. "The murderer is proving surprisingly elusive. As far as scent goes, most of us aren't gifted in that way — it was a talent largely given only to the beast-minded. Once they determined it would be safer for all of us to blend in with humans rather than live apart, the Gray Lords killed most of the beasts among us that had survived the coming of Christ and cold iron. There are maybe one or two here with the ability to sniff people out, but they are so powerless that they cannot be trusted."

"What do you mean?"

He gave me a grim look. "Our ways are not yours. If one has no power to protect himself, he cannot afford to offend anyone. If the murderer is powerful or well connected, none of the fae who could scent him would be willing to accuse him."

He smiled, a sour little quirk of his lips. "We may not be able to lie . . . but truth and honesty are rather different."

I'd been raised by werewolves who could, mostly, smell a lie at a hundred yards. I knew all about the difference between truth and honesty.

Something about what he said . . . "Uhm. I'm not powerful. What happens if I say something to offend?"

He smiled. "You will be here as my guest. It might not keep you safe if you see too much — as our laws are clear on how to deal with mortals who stray Underhill and see more than they ought. That you were invited by the Council, knowing what you are — and that you are not quite human — should provide some immunity. But anyone who is offended when you speak the truth must, by our guesting laws, come after me rather than you. And *I* can protect myself."

I believed it. Zee calls himself a gremlin, which is probably more accurate than not — except that the word *gremlin* is a lot newer than Zee. He is one of the few kinds of fae with an affinity for iron, which gives him all sorts of advantages over the other fae. Iron is fatal to most of them.

There wasn't any sign that marked the well-maintained county road where we turned off the highway. The road wove through small, wooded hills that reminded me more of Montana than the barren, cheat-grass and sagebrush covered land around the Tri-Cities.

We turned a corner, drove through a patch of thick-growing poplar, and emerged with twin walls of cinnamon-colored concrete block rising on either side of us, sixteen feet tall with concertina wire along the top to make guests feel even more welcome.

"It looks like a prison," I said. The combination of narrow road and tall walls made me claustrophobic.

"Yes," agreed Zee a bit grimly. "I forgot to ask, do you have your driver's license with you?"

"Yes."

"Good. I want you to remember, Mercy, there are a lot of creatures in the reservation who are not fond of humans — and you are close enough to human that they will bear you no goodwill. If you step too far out-of-bounds, they will have you dead first and leave me to seek justice later."

"I'll mind my tongue," I told him.

He snorted with uncomplimentary amusement. "I'll believe that when I see it. I wish Uncle Mike were here, too. They wouldn't dare bother you then."

"I thought this was Uncle Mike's idea."

"It is, but he is working and cannot leave his tavern tonight."

We must have traveled half a mile when the road finally made an abrupt right turn to reveal a guardhouse and gate. Zee stopped his truck and rolled down the window.

The guard wore a military uniform with a

large BFA patch on his arm. I wasn't familiar enough with the BFA (Bureau of Fae Affairs) to know what branch of the military was associated with them — if any. The guard had that "Rent-a-Cop" feel, as if he felt a little out of place in the uniform even as he relished the power it gave him. The badge on his chest read O'DONNELL.

He leaned forward and I got a whiff of garlic and sweat, though he didn't smell unwashed. My nose is just more sensitive than most people's.

"ID," he said.

Despite his Irish name, he looked more Italian or French than Irish. His features were bold and his hair was receding.

Zee opened his wallet and handed over his driver's license. The guard made a big deal of scrutinizing the picture and looking at Zee. Then he nodded and grunted, "Hers, too."

I had already grabbed my wallet out of my purse. I handed Zee my license to pass over to the guard.

"No designation," O'Donnell said, flicking the corner of my license with his thumb.

"She's not fae, sir," said Zee in a deferential tone I'd never heard from him before.

"Really? What business does she have here?"

"She's my guest," Zee said, speaking quickly as if he knew I was about to tell the moron it was none of his business.

And he was a moron, he and whoever was in charge of security here. Picture IDs for fae? The only thing all fae have in common is glamour, the ability to change their appearance. The illusion is so good that it affects not only human senses, but physical reality. That's why a 500-pound, ten-foot-tall ogre can wear a size-six dress and drive a Miata. It's not shapeshifting, I am told. But as far as I'm concerned, it's as close as makes no never mind.

I don't know what kind of ID I would have had them use, but a picture ID was worthless. Of course, the fae tried really hard to pretend that they could only take one human form without ever saying exactly that. Maybe they'd convinced some bureaucrat to believe it.

"Will you please get out of the truck, ma'am," the moron said, stepping out of the guardhouse and crossing in front of the truck until he was on my side of the vehicle.

Zee nodded. I got out of the car.

The guard walked all the way around me, and I had to restrain my growl. I don't like people I don't know walking behind me. He wasn't quite as dumb as he first appeared because he figured it out and walked around me again.

"Brass doesn't like civilian visitors, especially after dark," he said to Zee, who had gotten out to stand next to me.

"I am allowed, sir," Zee replied, still in that deferential tone.

The guard snorted and flipped through a few pages on his clipboard, though I don't think he actually was reading anything. "Siebold Adelbertsmiter." He pronounced it wrong, making Zee's name sound like Seabold instead of Zeebolt. "Michael McNellis, and Olwen Jones." Michael McNellis could be Uncle Mike — or not. I didn't know any fae named Olwen, but I could count the fae I knew by any name on one hand with fingers left over. Mostly the fae kept to themselves.

"That's right," Zee said with false patience that sounded genuine; I only knew it was false because Zee had no patience with fools — or anyone else for that matter. "I am Siebold." He said it the same way O'Donnell had.

The petty tyrant kept my license and walked back to his little office. I stayed where I was, so I couldn't see exactly what he did, though I could hear the sound of computer keys being tapped. He came back

31

after a couple of minutes and returned my license to me.

"Stay out of trouble, Mercedes Thompson. Fairyland is no place for good little girls."

Obviously O'Donnell had been sick the day they'd had sensitivity training. I wasn't usually a hard-core stickler, but something about the way he said "little girl" made it an insult. Mindful of Zee's wary gaze, I took my license and slipped it into my pocket and tried to keep what I was thinking to myself.

I don't think my expression was bland enough, because he shoved his face into mine. "Did you hear me, girl?"

I could smell the honey ham and mustard he'd had on his dinner sandwich. The garlic he'd probably eaten last night. Maybe he'd had a pizza or lasagna.

"I heard you," I said in as neutral a tone as I could manage, which wasn't, admittedly, very good.

He fingered the gun on his hip. He looked at Zee. "She can stay two hours. If she's not back out by then, we'll come looking for her."

Zee bowed his head like combatants do in karate movies, without letting his eyes leave the guard's face. He waited until the guard walked back to his office before he got back in the car, and I followed his lead.

The metal gate slid open with a reluctance that mirrored O'Donnell's attitude. The steel it was built of was the first sign of competence I'd seen. Unless there was rebar in the walls, the concrete might keep people like me out, but it would never keep fae in. The concertina wire was too shiny to be anything but aluminum, and aluminum doesn't bother the fae in the slightest. Of course, ostensibly, the reservation was set up to restrict where the fae lived and to protect them, so it shouldn't matter that they could come and go as they pleased, guarded gate or not.

Zee drove through the gates and into Fairyland.

I don't know what I expected of the reservation; military housing of some sort, maybe, or English cottages. Instead, there were row after row of neat, well-kept ranch houses with attached one-car garages laid out in identical-sized yards with identical fences, chain link around the front yard, six-foot cedar around the backyard.

The only difference from one house to the next was in color of paint and foliage in the yards. I knew the reservation had been here since the eighties, but it looked as though it might have been built a year ago.

There were cars scattered here and there, mostly SUVs and trucks, but I didn't see any people at all. The only sign of life, aside from Zee and me, was a big black dog that watched us with intelligent eyes from the front yard of a pale yellow house.

The dog pushed the Stepford effect up to übercreepy.

I turned to comment about it to Zee when I realized that my nose was telling me some odd things.

"Where's the water?" I asked.

"What water?" He raised an eyebrow.

"I smell swamp: water and rot and growing things."

He gave me a look I couldn't decipher. "That's what I told Uncle Mike. Our glamour works best for sight and touch, very good for taste and hearing, but not as well for scent. Most people can't smell well enough for scent to be a problem. You smelled that I was fae the first time you met me."

Actually he was wrong. I've never met two people who smell exactly alike — I'd thought that earthy scent that he and his son Tad shared was just part of their own individual essences. It wasn't until a long time later that I learned to distinguish between fae and human. Unless you live within an hour's drive of one of the four fae reservations in the U.S., the chances of running into one just weren't that high. Until I'd moved to the Tri-Cities and started working for Zee, I'd never knowingly met a fae.

"So where is the swamp?" I asked.

He shook his head. "I hope that you will be able to see through whatever means our murderer has used to disguise himself. But for your own sake, *Liebling,* I would hope that you would leave the reservation its secrets if you can."

He turned down a street that looked just like the first four we'd passed — except that there was a young girl of about eight or nine playing with a yo-yo in one of the yards. She watched the spinning, swinging toy with solemn attention that didn't change when Zee parked the car in front of her house. When Zee opened the gate, she caught the yo-yo in one hand and looked at us with adult eyes.

"No one has entered," she said.

Zee nodded. "This is the latest murder scene," he told me. "We found it this morning. There are six others. The rest have had a lot of people in and out, but except for this one" — he indicated the girl with a tip of his head — "who is a Council member, and Uncle Mike, there have been no other trespassers since his death."

I looked at the child who was one of the Council and she gave me a smile and popped her bubblegum.

I decided it was safest to ignore her. "You want me to see if I can smell someone who was in all the houses?"

"If you can."

"There's not exactly a database where scents are stored like fingerprints. Even if I scent him out, I'll have no idea who it is — unless it's you, Uncle Mike, or your Council member here." I nodded my head toward Yo-yo Girl.

Zee smiled without humor. "If you can find one scent that is in every house, I will personally escort you around the reservation or the entire state of Washington until you find the murdering son of a bitch."

That's when I knew this was personal. Zee didn't swear much and never in English. *Bitch,* in particular, was a word he'd never used in my presence.

"It will be better if I do this alone then," I told him. "So the scents you're carrying don't contaminate what is already there. Do you mind if I use the truck to change?"

"Nein, nein," he said. "Go change."

36

I returned to the truck and felt the girl's gaze on the back of my neck all the way. She looked too innocent and helpless to be anything but a serious nasty.

I got into the truck, on the passenger side to get as much room as possible, and stripped out of all my clothes. For werewolves, the change is very painful, especially if they wait too long to change at a full moon and the moon pulls the change from them.

Shifting doesn't hurt me at all — actually it feels good, like a thorough stretch after a workout. I get hungry, though, and if I hop from one form to the other too often, it makes me tired.

I closed my eyes and slid from human into my coyote form. I scratched the last tingle out of one ear with my hind paw, then hopped out the window I'd left open.

My senses as a human are sharp. When I switch forms, they get a little better, but it's more than that. Being in coyote form focuses the information that my ears and nose are telling me better than I can do as a human.

I started casting about on the sidewalk just inside the gate, trying to get a feel for the smells of the house. By the time I made it to the porch, I knew the scent of the male (he certainly wasn't a man, though I couldn't quite pinpoint what he was) who had made this his home. I could also pick out the scents of the people who visited most often, people like the girl, who had returned to her spinning, snapping yo-yo — though she watched me rather than her toy.

Except for her very first statement, she and Zee hadn't exchanged a word that I had heard. It might have meant they didn't like each other, but their body language wasn't stiff or antagonistic. Perhaps they just didn't have anything to say.

Zee opened the door when I stopped in front of it, and a wave of death billowed out.

I couldn't help but take a step back. Even a fae, it seemed, was not immune to the indignities of death. There was no need for the caution that made me creep over the threshold into the entryway, but some things, especially in coyote form, are instinctive.

CHAPTER 2

It wasn't hard to follow the scent of blood to the living room, where the fae had been killed. Blood was splattered generously over various pieces of furniture and the carpet, with a larger stain where the body had evidently come to rest at last. His remains had been removed, but no further effort had been made to clean it up.

To my inexpert eyes, it didn't look like he'd struggled much because nothing was broken or overturned. It was more as if someone had enjoyed ripping him apart.

It had been a violent death, perfect for creating ghosts.

I wasn't sure Zee or Uncle Mike knew about the ghosts. Though I'd never tried to hide it — for a long time, I hadn't realized that it wasn't something everyone could do.

That was how I'd killed the second vampire. Vampires can hide their daytime resting places, even from the nose of a werewolf

— or coyote. Not even good magic users can break their protection spells.

But I can find them. Because the victims of traumatic deaths tend to linger as ghosts — and vampires have plenty of traumatized victims.

That's why there aren't many walkers (I've never met another) — the vampires killed them all.

If the fae whose blood painted the floors and walls had left a ghost, though, it had no desire to see me. Not yet.

I crouched down in the doorway between the entryway and the living room and closed my eyes, the better to concentrate on what I smelled. The murder victim's scent, I put aside. Every house, like every person, has a scent. I'd start with that and work out to the scents that didn't belong. I found the base scent of the room, in this case mostly pipe smoke, wood smoke, and wool. The wood smoke was odd.

I opened my eyes and looked around just in case, but there was no sign of a fireplace. If the scent had been fainter, I would have assumed someone had come in with it on their clothes — but the scent was prevalent. Maybe he'd found some incense or something that smelled like a fire.

Since discovering the mysterious cause of

the burnt-wood smell was unlikely to be useful, I put my chin back on my front paws and shut my eyes again.

Once I knew what the house smelled like, I could better separate the surface scents that would be the living things that came and went. As promised, I found that Uncle Mike had been here. I also found the spicy scent of Yo-Yo Girl both recent and old. She had been here often.

All the scents that were left I absorbed until I felt I could recall them upon command. My memory for scent is somewhat better than for sight. I might forget someone's face, but I seldom forget their scent — or their voice, for that matter.

I opened my eyes to head back to search the house further and . . . everything had changed.

The living room had been smallish, tidy, and every bit as bland as the outside of the house. The room I found myself standing in now was nearly twice as big. Instead of drywall, polished oak panels lined the walls, laden with small intricate tapestries of forest scenes. The victim's blood, which I'd just seen splattered over an oatmeal-colored carpet, coated, instead, a rag rug and spilled over onto the glossy wood floor.

A fireplace of river stone stood against the

front wall where a window had looked out over the street. There were no windows on that side of the room now, but there were lots of windows on the other side, and through the glass, I could see a forest that had never grown in the dry climate of Eastern Washington. It was much, much too large to be contained in the small backyard that had been enclosed in a six-foot cedar fence.

I put my paws on the window ledge and stared out at the woods beyond, and wonder replaced the childish disappointment of discovering the reservation to be a particularly unimaginative suburbia.

The coyote wanted to go explore the secrets that we just knew lay within the deep green forest. But we had a job to do. So I pulled my nose away from the glass and hop-scotched on the dry places on the floor until I was back out in the hallway — which looked just as it always had.

There were two bedrooms, two bathrooms, and a kitchen. My job was made easier because I was only interested in fresh scents, so the search didn't take me long.

When I looked back into the living room, on my way out of the house, its windows still looked out to forest rather than backyard. My eyes lingered for a moment on the easy chair which was positioned to look out at the trees. I could almost see him sitting there, enjoying the wild as he smoked his pipe in a haze of rich-smelling smoke.

But I didn't see him, not really. He wasn't a ghost, just a figment of my imagination and the scent of pipe smoke and forest. I still didn't know what he'd been, other than powerful. This house would remember him for a long time, but it held no unquiet ghosts.

I walked out the open front door and back into the bland little world the humans had built for the fae to keep them out of their cities. I wondered how many of those opaque cedar fences hid forests — or swamps — and I was grateful that my coyote form kept me from being able to ask questions. I doubt I'd have had the will-power to keep my mouth shut otherwise, and I thought the forest was one of those things I wasn't supposed to see.

Zee opened the truck door for me and I hopped in so he could drive me to the next place. The girl watched us drive off, still not speaking. I couldn't read the expression on her face.

The second house we stopped at was a clone of the first, right down to the color of the trim around the windows. The only difference was that the front yard had a small lilac tree and a flower bed on one side of the sidewalk, one of the few flower beds I had seen since I came in here. The flowers were all dead and the lawn was yellowed and in desperate need of a lawn mower.

There was no guardian at this porch. Zee put his hand on the door and paused without opening it. "The house you were in was the last one who was killed. This house belongs to the first and I imagine that there have been a lot of people in and out since."

I sat down and stared up into his face: he cared about this one.

"She was a friend," he said slowly as his hand on the door curled into a fist. "Her name was Connora. She had human blood like Tad. Hers was further back, but left her weak." Tad was his son, half-human and currently at college. His human blood hadn't, as far as I could see, lessened the affinity for metals he shared with his father. I don't know whether he'd gotten his father's immortality: he was nineteen and looked it.

"She was our librarian, our keeper of records, and collector of stories. She knew every tale, every power that cold iron and Christianity robbed us of. She hated being weak; hated and despised humans even more. But she was kind to Tad."

Zee turned his face so I couldn't see it and abruptly, angrily, opened the front door.

Once again I entered the house alone. If Zee hadn't told me Connora had been a librarian, I might have guessed. Books were stacked everywhere. On shelves, on floors, on chairs and tables. Most of them weren't the kind of books that had been made in the last century — and none of the titles I saw were written in English.

As in the last house, the smell of death was present, though, as Zee had promised, it was old. The house mostly just smelled musty with a faint chaser of rotten food and cleaning fluids.

He hadn't said when she died, but I could guess that there hadn't been anyone here for a month or more.

About a month ago, the demon had been causing all sorts of violence by its very presence. I was pretty sure that the fae had considered that, and was reasonably certain the reservation was far enough away to have escaped that influence. Even so, when I regained my human form, I thought I might ask Zee about it.

Connora's bedroom was soft and feminine in an English cottage way. The floor was pine or some other softwood covered with scattered handwoven rugs. Her bedspread

45

was that thin white stuff with knots that I always have associated with bed-and-breakfasts or grandmothers. Which is odd, since I've never met any of my grandparents — or slept in a bed-and-breakfast.

A dead rose in a bud vase was on a small table next to the bed — and there wasn't a book to be found.

The second bedroom was her office. When Zee said she was collecting stories, I'd somehow expected notebooks and paper, but there was only a small bookcase with an unopened package of burnable discs. The rest of the shelves were empty. Someone had taken her computer — though they'd left her printer and monitor; maybe they'd taken whatever had been on the shelves as well.

I left the office and continued exploring.

The kitchen had been recently scrubbed with ammonia, though there was still something rotting in the fridge. Maybe that was why there was one of those obnoxious air fresheners on the counter. I sneezed and backed out. I wasn't going to get any scents from that room — all that trying would do was deaden my nose with the air freshener.

I toured the rest of the house, and by process of elimination deduced that she'd died in the kitchen. Since the kitchen had a door and a pair of windows, the killer could certainly have entered and left without leaving scent anywhere else. I made a mental note of that, but made a second round of the house anyway. I caught Zee's scent, and more faintly Tad's as well. There were three or four people who had visited here often, and a few who were less frequent visitors.

If this house held secrets like the last one, I wasn't able to trigger them.

When I came out of the front door, the last of the daylight was nearly gone. Zee waited on the porch with his eyes closed, his face turned slightly to the last, fading light. I had to yip to get his attention.

"Finished?" he asked in a voice that was a little darker, a little more *other* than usual. "Since Connora's was the first murder, why don't we hit the murder scenes in order from here on out?" he suggested.

The scene of the second murder didn't smell of death at all. If someone had died here, it had been so well cleaned that I couldn't smell it — or the fae who had lived here was so far from humanity that his death didn't leave any of the familiar scent markers.

There were, however, a number of visitors shared between this house and the first two and a few I'd found only in the first and third house. I kept them on the suspect list because I hadn't been able to get a good scent in Connora the librarian's kitchen. Also, since this house was so clean, I couldn't entirely eliminate anyone who had been only in the first house. It would be handy to be able to keep track of where I'd scented whom, but I'd never figured out any way to record a scent with pen and paper. I'd just have to do the best I could.

The fourth house Zee took me to looked no more remarkable than any of the others had appeared. A beige house trimmed unimaginatively in white with nothing but dead and dying grass in the yard.

"This one hasn't been cleaned," he said sourly as he opened the door. "Once we had a third victim, the focus of effort changed from concealing the crime from the humans to figuring out who the murderer is."

He wasn't kidding when he said it hadn't been cleaned. I hopped over old newspapers and scattered clothing that had been left lying in the entryway.

This fae had not been killed in the living room or kitchen. Or in the master bedroom where a family of mice had taken up residence. They scurried away as I stepped inside.

The master bathroom, for no reason I

could see, smelled like the ocean rather than mouse like the rest of this corner of the house. Impulsively, I closed my eyes, as I had in the first house, and concentrated on what my other senses had to tell me.

I heard it first, the sound of surf and wind. Then a chill breeze stirred my fur. I took two steps forward and the cool tile softened into sand. When I opened my eyes, I stood at the top of a sandy dune at the edge of a sea.

Sand blew in the wind, stinging my nose and eyes and catching in my fur as I stared dumbfounded at the water while my skin hummed with the magic of the place. It was sunset here, too, and the light turned the sea a thousand shades of orange, red, and pink.

I slipped down through the sharp-edged salt grass until I stood on the hard-packed beach. Still I could see no end of the water whose waves swelled and gentled to wash up on shore. I watched the waves for long enough to allow the tide to come in and touch my toes.

The icy water reminded me that I was here to work, and as beautiful and impossible as this was, I was unlikely to find the murderer here. I could smell nothing but sea and sand. I turned to leave the way I'd come before true night fell, but behind me all I could see were endless sand dunes with gentle hills rising behind them.

Either the wind in the sand had erased my paw prints while I'd been watching — or else they had never been there at all. I couldn't even be sure which hill I'd come down.

I froze where I stood, somehow convinced that if I moved so much as a step from where I was, I'd never find my way back. The peaceful spell of the ocean was entirely dispelled, and the landscape, still beautiful, held shadows and menace.

Slowly I sat down, shivering in the breeze. All I could do was hope that Zee found me, or that this landscape would fade away as quickly as it had come. To that end I lowered myself until my belly was on the sand with the ocean to my back.

I put my chin on my paws, closed my eyes, and thought *bathroom* and how it ought to smell of mouse, trying to ignore the salt-sea and the wind that ruffled my fur. But it didn't go away.

"Well, now," said a male voice, "what have we here? I've never heard of a coyote blundering Underhill."

I opened my eyes and spun around, crouching in preparation to run or attack as seemed appropriate. About ten feet away, between me and the ocean, a man watched me. At least he looked mostly like a man. His voice had sounded so normal, sort of Harvard professorial, that it took me a moment to realize just how far from normal this man was.

His eyes were greener than the Lincoln green that Uncle Mike had his waitstaff wear, so green that not even the growing gloom of night dimmed their color. Long pale hair, damp with saltwater and tangled with bits of sea plants, reached the back of his knees. He was stark naked, and comfortable with it.

I could see no weapons. There was no aggression in his posture or voice, but my instincts were screaming. I lowered my head, keeping eye contact, and managed not to growl.

Staying in coyote form seemed the safest thing. He might think me simply a coyote . . . who had wandered into the bathroom of a dead fae and from there to wherever here was. Not likely, I had to admit. Maybe there were other paths to get here. I'd seen no hint of another living thing, but maybe he'd believe I was exactly what I looked like.

We stared at each other for a long time,

neither of us moving. His skin was several shades paler than his hair. I could see the bluish cast of veins just below his skin.

His nostrils fluttered as he drew in my scent, but I knew I smelled like a coyote.

Why hadn't Zee used him? Obviously this fae used his nose, and he didn't seem powerless to me.

Maybe it was because they thought he might be the murderer.

I shuffled through folklore as he watched me, trying to think of all the human-seeming fae who dwelt in or about the sea. There were a lot of them, but only a few I knew much about.

Selkies were the only ones I could remember that were even neutral. I didn't think he was a selkie — mostly because I couldn't be that lucky — and he didn't smell like something that would turn into a mammal. He smelled cold and fishlike. There were kinder things in lakes and lochs, but the sea spawns mostly horror stories, not gentle brownies who keep houses clean.

"You smell like a coyote," he said finally. "You look like a coyote. But no coyote ever wandered Underhill to the Sea King's Realm. What are you?"

"Gnädiger Herr," said Zee cautiously from somewhere just behind me. "This one is

working for us and got lost."

Sometimes I loved that old man as much as I loved anyone, but I'd never been so happy to hear his voice.

The sea fae didn't move except to raise his eyes until I was pretty sure he was looking Zee in the face. I didn't want to look away, but I took a step back until my hip hit Zee's leg to reassure myself that he wasn't just a figment of my imagination.

"She is not fae," said the fae.

"Neither is she human." There was something in Zee's voice that was awfully close to deference, and I knew I'd been right to be afraid.

The stranger abruptly strode forward and dropped to one knee in front of me. He grabbed my muzzle without so much as a by-your-leave and ran his free hand over my eyes and ears. His icy hands weren't ungentle, but even so, without Zee's nudge I might have objected. He dropped my head abruptly and stood again.

"She wears no elf-salve, nor does she stink of the drugs that occasionally drop a lost one here to wander and die. Last I knew, rare though it is, your magic was not such as could do this. So how did she get here?"

As he spoke, I realized that it wasn't Harvard I heard in his voice, but Merrie Old

England.

"I don't know, *mein Herr*. I suspect that she doesn't know either. You of all people know that the Underhill is fickle and lonely. If my friend broke the glamour that hides the entrances, it would never keep her out."

The sea creature grew very still — and the waves of the ocean subsided like a cat gathering itself to pounce. The wisps of clouds in the sky darkened.

"And how," he said very quietly, "would she break our glamour?"

"I brought her to help us discover a murderer because she has a very good nose," Zee said. "If glamour has a weakness, it is scent. Once she broke that part of the illusion, the rest followed. She is not powerful or a threat."

The ocean struck without warning. A giant wave slapped me, robbing me of my footing and my sight. In one bare instant it stole the heat of my body so I don't think I could have breathed even if my nose wasn't buried in water.

A strong hand grabbed my tail and yanked hard. It hurt, but I didn't protest because the water was retreating, and without that grip, it would have carried me out with it. As soon as the water had subsided to my knees, Zee released his hold.

Like me, he was drenched, though he wasn't shivering. I coughed to get out the saltwater I'd swallowed, shook my fur off, then looked around, but the sea fae was gone.

Zee touched my back. "I'll have to carry you to take you back." He didn't wait for a response, just picked me up. There was a nauseating moment when all my senses swam around me, and then he set me down on the tile of the bathroom floor. The room was dark as pitch.

Zee turned on the light, which looked yellow and artificial after the colors of the sunset.

"Can you continue?" he asked me.

I looked at him, but he gave his head a sharp shake. He didn't want to talk about what happened. It irked me, but I'd read enough fairy tales to know that sometimes talking about the fae too directly lets them listen in. When I got him out of the reservation, I would get answers if I had to sit on him.

Until then, I put my curiosity aside to consider his question. I sneezed twice to clear my nose and then put it down on the floor to collect more people from this house.

This time Zee came with me, staying back so as not to interfere, but close on my heels.

He didn't say anything more and I ignored him as I struggled for an explanation of what had just happened to me. Was this house real? Zee told the other fae that I had broken the glamour — wouldn't that mean that it was the other landscape that was real? But that would mean that there was an entire ocean here, which seemed really unlikely — though I could still smell it if I tried. I knew that Underhill was the fairy realm, but the stories about it were pretty vague where they weren't outright contradictory.

The sun had truly set and Zee turned on lights as we went. Though I could see fine in the dark, I was grateful for the light. My heart was still certain that we were going to be eaten, and it pounded away at twice its usual speed.

Death's unlovely perfume drew my attention to a closed door. If I'd been on my own, I could have opened the door easily enough, but I believe in making use of others. I whined (coyotes can't bark, not like a dog) and Zee obediently opened the door and revealed the stairs going down into a basement. It was the first of the houses that had had a basement — unless they'd been hidden somehow.

I bounded down the stairs. Zee turned on

the lights and followed me down. Most of the basement looked like basements look: junk stored without rhyme or reason, unfinished walls and cement floor. I padded across the floor, following death to a door, shut tight. Zee opened that one without me asking and I found, at last, the place where the fae who had lived here was murdered.

Unlike the rest of the house, this room had been immaculate before the resident had been murdered. Underneath the rust-colored stains of the fae's blood, the tile floor gleamed. Cracked leather-bound tomes with the authentic lumpiness of pre–printing press books sat intermingled with battered paperbacks and college math and biology texts in bookcases that lined the walls.

This room was the bloodiest I'd seen so far — and given the first murder, that was saying something. Even dried and old, the blood was overwhelming. It had pooled, stained, and sprayed as the fae had fought with his attacker. The lower shelves of three bookcases were dotted with it. Tables had been knocked over and a lamp was broken on the floor.

Maybe I wouldn't have realized it if I hadn't just been thinking about them, but the fae here had been a selkie. I had never met one before that I knew, but I'd been to zoos and I knew what seals smelled like.

I didn't want to walk into the room. I wasn't usually squeamish, but lately I'd been walking in enough blood. Where the blood had pooled — in the grout between tiles, on a book lying open, and against the base of one of the bookcases where the floor wasn't quite level — it had rotted instead of dried. The room smelled of blood, seal, and decaying fish.

I avoided the worst of the mess where I could and tried not to think too much about what I couldn't avoid. Gradually what my nose told me distracted me from the unpleasantness of my task. I quartered the room, while Zee waited just outside it.

As I started for the door, I caught *something.* Most of the blood here belonged to the fae, but on the floor, just in front of the door, were a few drops of blood that did not.

If Zee had been a police officer, I'd have shifted then and there to tell him what I'd found. But if I pointed my finger toward a suspect, I was pretty sure I knew what would happen to the person I pointed it at.

Werewolves dealt with their criminals the same way. I don't have any quarrel with killing murderers, but if I'm the one doing the accusing, I'd like to be absolutely certain, given the consequences. And the person I'd be accusing was an unlikely choice for killing this many fae.

Zee followed me up the stairs, turning off lights and closing doors as we went. I didn't bother looking further. There had only been two scents in the basement room besides Uncle Mike's. Either the selkie didn't bring guests into his library, or he had cleaned since the last time. Most damning of all was the blood.

Zee opened the front door and I stepped out into full night where the silvered moon had fully risen. How long had I sat staring at the impossible sea?

A shadow stirred on the porch and became Uncle Mike. He smelled of malt and hot wings, and I could see that he was still dressed in his tavern-keeper clothes: loose ivory-colored khakis and green T-shirt with his own name in the possessive across his chest in sparkling white letters. It wasn't egocentrism; Uncle Mike's was the name of his tavern.

"She's wet," he said, his Irish thicker than Zee's German.

"Seawater," Zee told him. "She'll be all right."

Uncle Mike's handsome face tightened.

"Seawater."

"I thought you were working tonight?" There was a warning in Zee's voice as he changed the topic. I wasn't sure whether he didn't want to talk about my encounter with the sea fae, or if he was protecting me — or both.

"BFA was out patrolling looking for you two. Cobweb called me because she was worried they'd interfere. I sent the BFA off with a flea in their ear — they have no authority to tell you how long you can keep a visitor — but I'm afraid we've drawn their attention to you, Mercy. They might cause you trouble."

His words were nothing out of the ordinary, but there was something darker about his voice that had nothing to do with the night and everything to do with power.

He looked back at Zee. "Any luck?"

Zee shrugged. "We'll have to wait until she changes back." He looked at me. "I think it is time to bring this to an end. You see too much, Mercy, when it isn't safe."

The hair on the back of my neck told me something was watching us from the shadows. I drew the wind in my nose and knew it was more than two or three. I looked around and growled, letting my nose wrinkle up to display my fangs.

Uncle Mike raised his eyebrows at me, then took a look around himself. He tipped up his chin and said, his eyes on me, "You will all go home *now.*" He waited and then said something sharp in Gaelic. I heard a crash and someone took off down the sidewalk in a clatter of hooves.

"We're alone now," he told me. "You can go ahead and change."

I gave him a look, then glanced at Zee. Satisfied I had his attention, I hopped off the porch and trotted toward the truck.

Uncle Mike's presence raised the stakes. I might have been able to talk Zee into waiting for some other evidence to confirm my suspicions — but I didn't know Uncle Mike as well.

I thought furiously, but by the time I made it to the truck, I was as certain as I could be without seeing him kill that the blood I'd found belonged to the murderer. I'd been suspicious of him even before I'd found blood. His scent had been all over the other houses, even the one that had been mostly scrubbed clean — as if he'd been searching the houses for something.

Zee followed me to the truck. He opened my door, then closed it behind me before rejoining Uncle Mike on the porch. I shifted into human form and dove into my warm clothes. The night air was warm, but my wet hair was still cold against my damp skin. I didn't bother putting my tennis shoes back on, but got out of the truck barefoot.

On the porch, they waited patiently, reminding me of my cat, who could watch a mouse's hole for hours without moving.

"Is there any reason for BFA to have sent someone into all the murder scenes?" I asked.

"The BFA can do random searches," Zee told me. "But they were not called in here."

"You mean there was a Beefa in each house?" Uncle Mike asked. "Who, and how do you know him?"

Zee's eyes narrowed suddenly. "There's only one BFA agent she would know. O'Donnell was at the gate when I brought her in."

I nodded. "His scent was in every house and his blood was on the floor in the library inside here." I tipped my head at the house. "His was the only scent in the library besides the selkie's and yours, Uncle Mike."

He smiled at me. "It wasn't me." Still with that charming smile he looked at Zee. "I'd like to talk to you alone."

"Mercy, why don't you take my truck. Just leave it at your friend's house and I'll pick it up tomorrow."

I took a step off the porch before I turned around. "The one I met in there . . ." I tipped my head at the selkie's house.

Zee sighed. "I did not bring you here to risk your life. The debt you owe us is not so large."

"Is she in trouble?" asked Uncle Mike.

"Bringing a walker into the reservation might not have been as good an idea as you thought," Zee said dryly. "But I think matters are settled — unless we keep talking about it."

Uncle Mike's face took on that pleasant blankness he used to conceal his thoughts.

Zee looked at me. "No more, Mercy. This one time be content with not knowing."

I wasn't, of course. But Zee had no intention of telling me more.

I started back to the truck and Zee cleared his throat very quietly. I looked at him, but he just stared back. Just as he had when he was teaching me to put together a car and I'd forgotten a step. Forgotten a step . . . right.

I met Uncle Mike's gaze. "This ends my debt to you and yours for killing the second vampire with your artifacts. Paid in full."

He gave me a slow, sly smile that made me glad Zee had reminded me. "Of course."

■ ■ ■ ■

According to my wristwatch, I'd spent six hours at the reservation, assuming, of course, that a whole day hadn't passed by. Or a hundred years. Visions of Washington Irving aside, presumably if I had been there a whole day — or longer — either Uncle Mike or Zee would have told me. I must have spent more time staring at the ocean than I'd thought.

At any rate, it was very late. There were no lights on at Kyle's house when I arrived, so I decided not to knock. There was an empty spot in Kyle's driveway, but Zee's truck was old and I worried about leaving oil stains on the pristine concrete (which was why my Rabbit was parked on the blacktop). So I pulled in and parked it on the street behind my car. I must have been tired, because it wasn't until I'd already turned off the truck and gotten out that I realized any vehicle belonging to Zee would never drip anything.

I paused to pat the truck's hood gently in apology when someone put his hand on my shoulder.

I grabbed the hand and rotated it into a nice wrist lock. Using that as a convenient handle, I spun him a few degrees to the outside, and locked his elbow with my other hand. A little more rotation, and his shoulder joint was also mine. He was ready to be pulverized.

"Damn it, Mercy, that is enough!"

Or apologized to.

I let Warren go and sucked in a deep breath. "Next time, say something." I should have apologized, really. But I wouldn't have meant it. It was his own darn fault he'd surprised me.

He rubbed his shoulder ruefully and said, "I will." I gave him a dirty look. I hadn't hurt him — even if he'd been human, I wouldn't have done any real hurt.

He stopped faking and grinned. "Okay. Okay. I heard you drive up and wanted to make sure everything was all right."

"And you couldn't resist sneaking up on me."

He shook his head. "I wasn't sneaking. You need to be more alert. What was up?"

"No demon-possessed vampires this time," I told him. "Just a little sleuthing." And a trip to the seashore.

A second-floor window opened, and Kyle stuck his head and shoulders out so he could look down at us. "If you two are finished playing Cowboy and Indian out

65

there, some of us would like to get their beauty sleep."

I looked at Warren. "You heard 'um, Kemo Sabe. Me go to my little wigwam and get 'um shut-eye."

"How come you always get to play the Indian?" whined Warren, deadpan.

" 'Cause she's the Indian, white boy," said Kyle. He pushed the window up all the way and set a hip on the casement. He was wearing little more than most of the men in the movie we'd been watching, and it looked better on him.

Warren snorted and ruffled my hair. "She's only half — and I've known more Indians than she has."

Kyle grinned wickedly and said, in his best Mae West voice, "Just how many Indians have you known, big boy?"

"Stop right there." I made a play at plugging my ears. "Lalalala. Wait until I hop in my faithful Rabbit and ride off into the sunrise." I stood on my tiptoes and kissed Warren somewhere in the region of his chin.

"It is pretty late," Warren said. "Do you still want to meet us at Tumbleweed tomorrow?"

Tumbleweed was the yearly folk music festival held on Labor Day weekend. The Tri-Cities were close enough to the coast that the cream of the Seattle and Portland music scene usually showed up in force: blues singers, jazz, Celtic, and everything in between. Cheap, good entertainment.

"I wouldn't miss it. Samuel still hasn't managed to wiggle out of performing and I have to be there to heckle him."

"Ten a.m. by the River Stage, then," Warren said.

"I'll be there."

CHAPTER 3

Tumbleweed was held in Howard Amon Park, right off the Columbia River in Richland. The stages were scattered as far apart as could be managed to minimize interference between performances. The River Stage, where Samuel was to perform, was about as far from available parking as it was possible to get. Normally that wouldn't have bothered me, but karate practice this morning hadn't gone so well. Grumbling to myself, I limped slowly across the grass.

The park was still mostly empty of anyone except musicians toting various instrument cases as they trudged across the vast green fields on their way to whatever stage they were performing on. Okay, the park isn't really that huge, but when your leg hurts — or when you're hauling a string bass from one end to the other — it's big enough.

The bassist in question and I exchanged weary nods of mutual misery as we passed each other.

Warren and Kyle were already seated on the grass in front of the stage and Samuel was arranging his instruments on various stands, when I finally made it.

"Something wrong?" Kyle asked with a frown as I sat down next to him. "You weren't limping last night."

I wiggled on the lumpy, dew-dampened grass until I was comfortable. "Nothing important. Someone caught me a good one on my thigh at karate practice this morning. It'll settle down in a bit. I see the button men found you already."

Tumbleweed was nominally free, but you could show your support by purchasing a button for two dollars . . . and the button men were relentless.

"We got one for you, too." Warren reached across Kyle and handed a button to me.

I pinned it on my shoe, where it wouldn't be immediately obvious. "I bet I can attract four button men before lunch," I told Kyle.

He laughed. "Do I look like a newbie? Four before lunch is too easy."

More people gathered in front of Samuel's stage than I'd expected, given that his was one of the first performances.

I recognized some of the emergency room personnel who Samuel worked with near the center of the audience with a larger group. They were setting up lawn chairs and chattering together in such a fashion that I was pretty sure they all worked at Samuel's hospital.

Then there were the werewolves.

Unlike the medical personnel, they didn't sit together, but scattered themselves here and there around the fringes. All of the Tri-City werewolves, except for Adam, the Alpha, were still pretending to be human — so they mostly avoided hanging out together in public. They'd all have heard Samuel sing before, but probably not at a real performance because he didn't do them often.

A cool breeze came off the Columbia River, just a hop, skip, and a jump over a narrow footpath away — which was why the stage was the River Stage. The morning was warm, as early fall mornings in the Tri-Cities often are, so the slight edge to the wind was more welcome than not.

One of the festival volunteers, wearing a painter's apron covered with Tumbleweed buttons from this and previous years, welcomed us to this year's festival and thanked us all for coming. He spent a few minutes talking about sponsors and raffles while the audience shifted restlessly before he introduced Samuel as the Tri-Cities' own folksinging physician.

We clapped and whistled as the announcer bounced down the stairs and back to the sound station where he would keep the speakers behaving properly. Someone settled in behind me, but I didn't look around, because Samuel walked to center stage with his violin dangling almost carelessly from one hand.

He was wearing a cobalt blue dress shirt that set off his eyes, tipping the balance from gray to blue. He'd tucked the shirt into new black jeans that were tight enough to show off the muscle in his legs.

I had seen him just this morning as he drank his coffee and I ran out the door. There was no reason that he should still affect me like this.

Most werewolves are attractive; it goes with the permanently young-and-muscled look. Samuel had more, though. And it wasn't only that extra zap that the more dominant wolves have.

Samuel looked like a person you could trust — something about the hint of humor that lurked in the back of his deep-set eyes and the corner of his mouth. It was part of what made him such a good doctor. When he told his patients they were going to be fine, they believed him.

His eyes locked on mine for a moment and the quirk of his mouth powered up to a smile.

It warmed me to my toes, that smile: reminded me of a time when Samuel was my whole world, a time when I believed in a knight in shining armor who could make me happy and safe.

Samuel knew it, too, because the smile changed to a grin — until he looked behind me. The pleasure cooled in his eyes, but he kept the grin, turning it on the rest of his audience. That's how I knew for certain that the man who'd sat behind me was Adam.

Not that I'd been in much doubt. The wind was coming from the wrong direction to give me a good scent, but dominant wolves exude power, and Adam — all apart from him being the Alpha — was nearly as dominant as they come. It was like having a car battery sitting behind me and being hooked up with a pair of wires.

I kept my eyes forward, knowing that as long as my attention was on him, Samuel wouldn't get too upset. I wished Adam had chosen to sit somewhere else. But if he'd been that kind of a person, he wouldn't be an Alpha — the most dominant wolf in his pack. Almost as dominant as Samuel.

The reason Samuel wasn't the pack Alpha

was complicated. First, Adam had been Alpha here as long as there had been a pack in the Tri-Cities (which was before my time). Even if a wolf is more dominant, it is not an easy matter to oust an Alpha — and in North America, that never happens without the consent of the Marrok, the wolf who rules here. Since the Marrok was Samuel's father, presumably he could have gained permission — except that Samuel had no desire to be Alpha. He said that being a doctor gave him more than enough people to take care of. So he was officially a lone wolf, a wolf outside of pack protection. He lived in my trailer, not a hundred yards from Adam's house. I don't know why he chose to live there, but I know why I let him: because otherwise he'd still be sleeping on my front porch.

Samuel had a way of making sure people did what he wanted them to.

Testing the violin's temperament, Samuel's bow danced across the strings with a delicate precision won through years . . . probably centuries of practice. I'd known him all my life, but it wasn't until less than a year ago that I'd found out about those "centuries."

He just didn't act like an old werewolf. Old werewolves were uptight, easy to anger, and especially in this last hundred years of rapid changes (I'm told), were more likely to be hermits than doctors in busy emergency rooms with all that new technology. He was one of the few werewolves I knew who really liked people, human people or werewolf people. He even liked them in crowds.

Not that he would have gone out of his way to perform at a folk music festival. That took a little creative blackmail.

It wasn't me. Not this time.

The stresses of working in an emergency room — especially since he was a werewolf and his reaction to blood and death could be a little unpredictable — meant that he took his guitar or violin to work and played when he had a chance.

One of his nurses heard him play and had him signed up for the festival before he could figure out how to get out of it. Not that he tried very hard. Oh, he made a lot of noise, but I know Samuel. If he really hadn't wanted to do it, a bulldozer wouldn't have gotten him up there.

He tuned the violin with one hand while he held it under his chin and plucked with the other. A few measures of a song and the crowd sat forward in anticipation, but I knew better. He was still warming up. When he really started playing, everyone would know it: he came alive in front of an audience.

Sometimes watching Samuel perform was more like a stand-up comedy act than a concert. It all depended on how he was feeling at the moment.

It happened at last, the magic moment when Samuel sucked his audience in. The old violin made a shivering sound, like an old hoot owl in the night, and I knew he'd decided to be a musician today. All the quiet whispers stopped and every eye lifted to the man on the stage. Centuries of practice and being a werewolf might give him speed and dexterity, but the music came from his Welshman's soul. He gave the audience a shy smile and the mournful sound became song.

While getting my history degree, I'd lost any romantic notions about Bonnie Prince Charlie, whose attempt to regain the throne of England had brought Scotland to its knees. Samuel's rendition of "Over the Sea to Skye" brought tears to my eyes anyway. There were words to that song, and Samuel could sing them, but for now, he let the violin speak for him.

As he played the last notes softly, over the top of it he began singing "Barbara Allen," as close to a universally known song among folksingers as "Stairway to Heaven" is to guitarists. After the first few measures, he sang the rest of the first verse a capella. When he hit the chorus, he brought in the violin in eerie descant. By the second verse, invited by his smile, the audience was singing the chorus, too. The singing was tentative until one of the other professional groups who had been walking by on the black-top path stopped and sang, too.

He gave them a nod at the last verse and stopped singing, letting the other group showcase the tight harmony that was their trademark. When the song ended, we cheered and clapped as he thanked his "guest performers." The audience had been filling in as he played and we all scooted a little closer together.

He set the violin down and picked up his guitar to play a Simon and Garfunkel piece. Not even the stupid Jet Ski that kept roaring past along the river a hundred yards away detracted much from his performance. He launched into a silly pirate song then put his guitar down and took up a bodhran — a wide flat drum played with a double-ended stick — and broke into a sea chantey.

I noticed the Cathers, the elderly couple who lived next door to me, sitting on a pair of camp chairs on the other side of the crowd.

"I hope it doesn't rain. We wouldn't want to miss seeing Samuel play," she'd told me yesterday morning when I'd found her tending her flowers. "He's such a *nice* man."

Of course she didn't have to live with him, I thought, chin on my knee as I watched him play. Not that Samuel wasn't "a nice man," but he was also stubborn, controlling, and pushy. I was stubborn and meaner than he was, though.

Someone whispered a polite "excuse me" and sat in the small square of grass in front of me. I found it a little too close for someone I didn't know, so I scooted away a few inches, until my back rested firmly against Adam's leg.

"I'm glad you talked him into playing," murmured the Alpha werewolf. "He's really in his element in front of a crowd, isn't he?"

"I didn't talk him into it," I said. "It was one of the nurses he works with."

"I once heard the Marrok and both of his sons, Samuel and Charles, sing together," murmured Warren, so softly I doubt anyone else heard him. "It was . . ." He turned away from the stage and caught Adam's gaze over the top of Kyle's head to shrug his inability to find the words.

"I've heard them," Adam said. "It's not something you forget."

Samuel had picked up his old Welsh harp while we were talking. He played a few notes to give the tech time to rush around and adjust the sound system for the softer tones of the new instrument. He ran his eyes over the crowd and his gaze stopped on me. If I could have scooted away from Adam without sitting on top of a stranger, I would have. Adam saw Samuel's gaze, too, and put a possessive hand on my shoulder.

"Stop that," I snapped.

Kyle saw what was happening and put his arm around my shoulders in a hug, knocking Adam's hand away in the process. Adam snarled softly, but he moved back a few inches. He liked Kyle — and better yet, since Kyle was gay and human, he didn't view him as any kind of threat.

Samuel took a deep breath and smiled, a little stiffly, as he introduced his last piece. I relaxed against Kyle as harp and harper made an old Welsh tune come to life. Welsh was Samuel's first language — when he was upset, you could still hear it in his voice. It was a language made for music: soft, lilting, and magical.

The wind picked up a little, making the green leaves rustle an accompaniment to

Samuel's music. When he finished, the sound of the leaves was the only noise for a few heartbeats. Then the jerk on the stupid Jet Ski came buzzing by, breaking the spell. The crowd rose to their feet and broke into thunderous applause.

My cell phone had been vibrating in my pocket off and on for most of the song, so I slipped away while Samuel packed away his instruments and vacated the stage for the next performer.

When I found a relatively quiet place, I pulled out the phone to find that I had missed five calls — all of them from a number I wasn't familiar with. I dialed it anyway. Anyone who called five times in as many minutes was in quite a lather.

It was answered on the first ring.

"Mercy, there is trouble."

"Uncle Mike?" It was his voice, and I didn't know anyone else who spoke with such a thick Irish accent. But I'd never heard him sound like this.

"The human police have Zee," he said.

What? But I knew. I had known what would happen to someone who was killing fae. Old creatures revert to older laws when push comes to shove. I'd known when I told them who the killer was that I was signing O'Donnell's death warrant — but I had been pretty sure that they would do it in such a way that blame would not have fallen anywhere. Something that looked accidental or like a suicide.

I hadn't expected them to be clumsy enough to attract the attention of the police. My phone buzzed, telling me that there was another call coming in, but I ignored it. Zee had murdered a man and gotten caught.

"How did it happen?"

"We were surprised," Uncle Mike said. "He and I went to talk to O'Donnell."

"Talk?" Disbelief was sharp in my voice. They had not gone to his house to talk.

He gave a short laugh. "We would have talked first, whatever you think of us. We drove to O'Donnell's house after you left. We rang the bell, but no one came to the door, though there was a light on. After we rang a third time, Zee opened the door and we entered. We found O'Donnell in the living room. Someone had beaten us to him, ripped his head from his body, a wounding such as I have not seen since the giants roamed the earth, Mercedes."

"You didn't kill him." I could breathe again. If Zee hadn't killed O'Donnell, there was still a chance for him.

"No. And as we stood there dumb and still, the police came with their lights and *bean sí* cries." He paused and I heard a noise. I recognized the sound from my karate. He'd hit something wooden and it had broken.

"He told me to hide myself. His talents aren't up to hiding from the police. So I watched as they put him into their car and drove away."

There was a pause. "I could have stopped them," he said in a guttural voice. "I could have stopped them all, but I let the humans take Siebold Adelbertskrieger (the German version of the name, Adelbertsmiter, Zee was using), the Dark Smith, to *jail*." Outrage didn't completely mask the fear in his voice.

"No, no," I told him. "Killing police officers is always a bad plan."

I don't think he heard me; he just kept talking. "I did as he said and now I find that no matter how I look at it, my help will only make his position worse. This is not a good time to be fae, Mercy. If we rally to Zee's defense, it could turn into a blood bath."

He was right. A rash of deaths and violence not a month past had left the Tri-Cities raw and bleeding. The tide of escalated crime had stopped with the breaking of a heat wave that had been tormenting us all at the same time. The cooler weather was a fine reason for the cessation of the pall of anger that had hung in the air. Driving the demon that was causing the violence back to the outer limits by killing its host vampire was an even better one, though not for the consumption of the public. They only knew about a few werewolves and the nicer side of the fae. Everyone was safer as long as the general population didn't know about things like vampires and demons — especially the general population.

However, there was a strong minority who were murmuring that there had been too much violence to be explained by a heat wave. After all, heat came every summer, and we'd never had a rash of murders and assaults like that. Some of those people were looking pretty hard at blaming the fae. Only last week there had been a group of demonstrators outside the Richland Courthouse.

That the werewolves had, just this year, admitted their existence wasn't helping matters much. The whole issue had gone as smoothly as anyone could have hoped, but nothing was perfect. The whole ugly anti-fae thing, which had subsided after the fae had voluntarily retired to the reservations, had been getting stronger again through the whole country. The hate groups were eager to widen their target to include werewolves and any other "godless" creatures, human or not.

In Oklahoma, there had been a witch burning last month. The ironic thing was that the woman who burned hadn't, it turned out, been a witch, a practitioner, or even Wiccan — which are three different things, though one person might be all three.

She'd been a good Catholic girl who liked tattoos, piercings, and wearing black clothing.

In the Tri-Cities, a place not noted for political activism or hate groups, the local anti-fae, anti-werewolf groups had been getting noticeably stronger.

That didn't mean spray-painted walls or broken windows and rioting. This was the Tri-Cities, after all, not Eugene or Seattle. At last week's Arts Festival, they'd had an information booth and I'd seen at least two different flyers they'd sent out in the mail this past month. Tri-City hate groups are civilized like that — so far.

O'Donnell could change that. If his death was as dramatic as Uncle Mike indicated, O'Donnell's murder would make every paper in the country. I tried to quell my panic.

I wasn't worried about the law — I was

pretty sure that Zee could walk out of any jail cell, anytime he wanted. With glamour he could change his appearance until even I wouldn't know him. But it wouldn't be enough to save him. I wasn't sure innocence would be enough to save him.

"Do you have a lawyer?" Our local werewolf pack didn't have one officially, though I think Adam had a lawyer he kept on the payroll for his security business. But there weren't nearly as many werewolves as there were fae.

"No. The Gray Lords own several firms on the East Coast, but it was deemed unnecessary for our reservation here. We are low-key." He hesitated. "Fae who are suspected of crimes tend not to survive to need lawyers."

"I know," I replied, swallowing around the knot in my throat.

The Gray Lords, like the werewolves' Marrok, were driven to preserve their species. Bran, the Marrok, was scrupulously fair, though brutal. The Gray Lords' methods had a strong tendency to be more expedient than fair. With prejudice so loud and strong, they'd want to hush this up as soon as possible.

"How much danger is Zee in?" I asked.

Uncle Mike sighed. "I don't know. This

crime is about to become very public. I do not see how his death would benefit the fae more than his survival right now — especially since he is innocent. I have called and told Them that this death is not on his head." *Them* was the Gray Lords. "If we can prove his innocence . . . I don't know, Mercy. It depends upon who actually did kill O'Donnell. It wasn't a human — maybe a troll could have done this — or a werewolf. A vampire could have, but O'Donnell was not killed for food. Someone was very, very angry with him. If it is a fae, the Gray Lords will not care who it was, just that the case is solved quickly and finally."

Quickly, like before a trial could call more attention to the crime. Quickly, like a suicide with a note admitting guilt.

My phone beeped politely, telling me I had a second call.

"I assume you think that I can be a help?" I asked — otherwise he'd never have called me.

"We cannot come to his aid. He needs a good lawyer, and someone to find out who killed O'Donnell. Someone needs to talk to the police and tell them that Zee did not kill this scum. Someone they will believe. You have a friend on the Kennewick police force."

"O'Donnell died in Kennewick?"

"Yes."

"I'll find a lawyer," I told Uncle Mike. Kyle was a divorce attorney, but he would know a good criminal defense lawyer. "Maybe the police will keep the worst of the details out of their press releases. They're not going to be all that interested in having the press of the world descend upon them. Even if they just tell people he was beheaded, it doesn't sound so bad, does it? Maybe we can buy a little time with the Gray Lords if it stays out of the major papers. I'll talk to the policeman I know, but he might not listen."

"If you need money," he said, "let me know. Zee doesn't have much, I don't think, though you can never tell with him. I do, and I can get more if we need it. But it will have to go through you. The fae cannot be more involved with this than we already are. So you hire a lawyer and we will pay you whatever it costs."

"All right," I said.

I hung up, my stomach in knots. My phone said I'd missed two calls. Both of them were from my friend Tony the cop's cell phone. I sat down on the knob of a tree root and called him back.

"Montenegro here," he said.

"I know about Zee," I told him. "He didn't kill anyone."

There was a little pause.

"Is it that you don't think he could do something like this, or do you know something specifically about the crime?"

"Zee's perfectly capable of killing," I told him. "However, I have it on very good authority that he didn't kill this person." I didn't tell him that if Zee had found O'Donnell alive, he *would* most likely have killed him. Somehow, that didn't seem helpful.

"Who is your very good authority — and did they happen to mention who did kill our victim?"

I pinched the top of my nose. "I can't tell you — and they don't know — just that the killer was not Zee. He found O'Donnell dead."

"Can you give me something more substantial? He was found kneeling over the body with blood on his hands and the blood was still warm. Mr. Adelbertsmiter is a fae, registered with the BFA for the past seven years. Nothing human did this, Mercy. I can't talk about the specifics, but nothing human did this."

I cleared my throat. "I don't suppose you could keep that last bit out of the official report, eh? Until you catch the real killer, it would be a very good idea not to have people stirred up against the fae."

Tony was a subtle person, and he caught what I wasn't saying. "Is this like when you said it would be very good if the police didn't go looking for the fae as a cause of the rise in violent crime this summer?"

"Exactly like that." Well, not quite, and honesty impelled me to correct myself. "This time, though, the police themselves won't be in danger. But Zee will, and the real killer will be free to kill elsewhere."

"I need more than your word," he said finally. "Our expert consultant is convinced that Zee is our culprit, and her word carries a lot of weight."

"Your expert consultant?" I asked. As far as I knew, *I* was the closest thing to an expert consultant on fae that the Tri-Cities police forces had.

"Dr. Stacy Altman, a folklore specialist from the University of Oregon, flew in this morning. She is paid a lot, which means my bosses think we ought to listen to her advice."

"Maybe I should charge more when I consult for you," I told him.

"I'll double your paycheck next time," he promised.

I got paid exactly nothing for my advice, which was fine with me. I was liable to be in enough trouble without the local supernatural community thinking I was narking to the police.

"Look," I told him. "This is unofficial." Zee hadn't told me not to say anything about the deaths on the reservation — because he hadn't thought he would have to. It was something I already knew.

However, if I spoke fast, maybe I could get it all out before I thought about how unhappy they might be with me for telling the police. "There have been some deaths among the fae — and good evidence that O'Donnell was the killer. Which was why Zee went to O'Donnell's house. If someone found out before Zee, they might have killed O'Donnell."

If that were true, it might save Zee (at least from the local justice system), but the political consequences could be horrific. I'd been just a kid when the fae had first come out, but I remembered the KKK burning a house with its fae occupants still in it and the riots in the streets of Houston and Baltimore that provided the impetus to confine the fae on reservations.

But it was Zee who mattered. The rest of the fae could rot as long as Zee was safe.

"I haven't heard anything about people dying in Fairyland."

"Why would you?" I asked. "They don't bring in outsiders."

"Then how do you know about it?"

I'd told him I wasn't a fae or a werewolf — but some things bear repeating so eventually they believe you. That's the theory I was working with. "I told you I'm not fae," I said. "I'm not. But I know some things and they thought I might be able to help." That sounded really lame.

"That's lame, Mercy."

"Someday," I told him, "I'll tell you all about it. Right now, I can't. I don't think I'm supposed to be telling you about this either, but it's important. I believe O'Donnell has killed" — I had to go over it in my head — "seven fae in the past month." Zee hadn't taken me to the other murder scenes. "You aren't looking at a law enforcement agent who was killed by the bad guys. You are looking at a bad guy who was killed by —" Whom? Good guys? More bad guys? "Someone."

"Someone strong enough to rip a grown man's head off, Mercy. Both of his collarbones were broken by the force of whatever did it. Our high-paid consultant seems to think Zee could have done it."

Oh? I frowned at my cell phone.

"What kind of fae does she say that Zee is? How much does she know about them?" I figured if Zee hadn't told me any of the stories about his past, and I had looked for them, this consultant could not possibly know any more than I did.

"She said he's a gremlin — so does he, for that matter. At least on his registration papers. He's not said a word since we picked him up."

I had to think for a minute on how to best help Zee. Finally I decided that since he was actually innocent, the more truth that came to light, the better off he would be.

"You're consultant isn't worth squat," I told Tony. "Either she doesn't know as much as she says she does, or she's got her own agenda."

"Why do you say that?"

"There are no such things as gremlins," I told him. "It's a term made up by British pilots in the Great War as an explanation for odd things that kept their planes from working. Zee is a gremlin only because he claims he is."

"Then what is he?"

"A Mettalzauber, one of the metalworking fae. Which is a very broad category that contains very few members. Since I met him, I've done a lot of research on German fae out of sheer curiosity, but I've never found anything quite like him. I know he works metal because I've seen him do it. I don't know if he'd have had the strength to rip someone's head off, but I do know that there is no way that your consultant would know one way or another. Especially if she's calling him a gremlin and acting like that is a real designation."

"World War One?" asked Tony thoughtfully.

"You can look it up on the Internet," I assured him. "By the Second World War, Disney was using them in cartoons."

"Maybe that's when he was born. Maybe he's where the legends come from. I could see a German fae tampering with the enemy's planes."

"Zee is a lot older than World War One."

"How do you know?"

It was a good question, and I didn't have a proper answer for it. He'd never really told me how old he was.

"When he is angry," I said slowly, "he swears in German. Not modern German, which I can mostly understand. I had an English prof who read us *Beowulf* in the original language — Zee sounds like that."

"I thought *Beowulf* was written in an old

version of English, not German."

Here I was on firmer ground. History degrees aren't entirely useless. "English and German both come from the same roots. The differences between medieval English and German are a lot smaller than the modern languages."

Tony made an unhappy noise. "Damn it, Mercy. I have a brutal murder and the brass wants it solved yesterday. Especially as we have a suspect caught red-handed. Now you're telling me that he didn't do it and that our high-paid, expert consultant is lying to us or doesn't know as much as she says she does. That O'Donnell was a murderer — though the fae will probably deny that any murders ever took place — but if I so much as ask about it, we're going to have the Feds breathing down our necks because now this crime involves Fairyland. All this without one hard, cold piece of evidence."

"Yes."

He swore nastily. "The hell of it is that I believe you, but I'll be damned if I can figure out how I'm going to tell any of this to my boss — especially as I'm not really in charge of this case."

There was a long silence on both our parts.

"You need to get him a lawyer," he said.

93

"He's not talking, which is wise of him. But he needs to have a lawyer. Even if you are sure he is innocent, especially if he is innocent, he needs a very good lawyer."

"All right," I agreed. "I don't suppose I could get in to get a look" — a sniff, actually — "at the crime scene?" Maybe I'd be able to find out something that modern science could not — like someone who'd been at one of the other murder sites.

He sighed. "Get a lawyer and ask him. I don't think I'm going to be able to help you with that. Even if he gets you in, you'll have to wait until our crime scene people are through with it. You'd do better to hire a private investigator, though, someone who knows how to look at a crime scene."

"All right," I said. "I'll find a lawyer." Hiring a human investigator would either be a waste of money — or a death sentence for the investigator if he happened upon some secret or other that the Gray Lords didn't want made public. Tony didn't need to know that.

"Tony, make sure you are looking farther than the length of your nose for a killer. It wasn't Zee."

He sighed. "All right. All right. I'm not assigned to this case, but I'll talk to some of the guys who are."

We said our good-byes and I looked around for Kyle.

I found him standing in a small crowd a little ways away, far enough from the stage that their conversation didn't interfere with the next performer's music. Samuel and his instrument cases were in the center of the group.

I put my cell phone in my back pocket (a habit that has destroyed two phones so far) and tried to blank my face. It wouldn't help with the werewolves, who would be able to smell my distress, but at least I wouldn't have complete strangers stop and ask me what was wrong.

There was an earnest-looking young man wearing a tie-dyed shirt talking at Samuel, who was watching him with amusement apparent only to people who knew him very well.

"I haven't ever heard that version of the last song you played," the young man was saying. "That's not the usual melody used with it. I wanted to find out where you heard it. You did an excellent job — except for the pronunciation of the third word in the first verse. This" — he said something that sounded vaguely Welsh — "is how you said it, but it should really be" — another unpronounceable word that sounded just like the first one he'd uttered. I may have grown up in a werewolf pack led by a Welshman, but English was the common language and neither the Marrok nor Samuel his son used Welsh often enough to give me an ear for it. "I just thought that since everything else was so well done, you should know."

Samuel gave him a little bow and said about fifteen or twenty Welsh-sounding words.

The tie-dyed man frowned. "If that's where you looked for pronunciation, it is no wonder you had a problem. Tolkien *based* his Elvish on Welsh and *Finnish*."

"You understood what he said?" Adam asked.

"Oh, please. It was the inscription on the One Ring, you know, *One Ring to Rule Them All* . . . everyone knows that much."

I stopped where I was, bemused despite the urgency of my need. A folk song nerd, who would have thought?

Samuel grinned. "Very good. I don't speak any more Elvish than that, but I couldn't resist playing with you a little. An old Welshman taught me the song. I'm Samuel Cornick, by the way. You are?"

"Tim Milanovich."

"Very good to meet you, Tim. Are you performing later?"

"I'm doing a workshop with a friend." He smiled shyly. "You might like to attend it: Celtic folk music. Two o'clock Sunday in the Community Center. You play very well, but if you want to make it in the music business, you need to organize your songs better, get a theme — like Celtic folk songs. Come to my class, and I'll give you a few ideas."

Samuel gave him a grave smile, though I knew the chances of Samuel "organizing" his music was about an icicle's chance in Hell. But he lied, politely enough. "I'll try to catch it. Thank you."

Tim Milanovich shook Samuel's hand and then wandered off, leaving only the werewolves and Kyle behind.

As soon as he was out of earshot, Samuel's eyes focused on me. "What's wrong, Mercy?"

CHAPTER 4

Kyle found a lawyer for me. He assured me that she was expensive, a pain in the neck, and the best criminal defense attorney this side of Seattle. She wasn't happy to be defending a fae, but, Kyle told me, that wouldn't affect her performance, only her price. She lived in Spokane, but she agreed that time was of the essence. By three that afternoon she was in Kennewick.

Once assured that Zee wasn't talking to the police, she'd demanded to meet with me in Kyle's office first, before she went to the police station. To hear the story from me, she told Kyle, before she spoke to Zee or the police.

Since it was a Saturday, Kyle's efficient staff and the other two lawyers who worked with him were gone, and we had his luxurious office suite to ourselves.

Jean Ryan was a fifty-something woman who had kept her figure with hard work that left taut muscles beneath the light linen suit she wore. Her pale, pale blond hair could only have come from a salon, but the surprisingly soft blue eyes owed nothing to contact lenses.

I don't know what she thought when she looked at me, though I saw her eyes take in my broken nails and the ingrained dirt on my knuckles.

The check I wrote to her made me swallow hard and hope that Uncle Mike would be as good as his word and cover the amount — and this was for only the initial consultation. Maybe my mother had been right, and I should have been a lawyer. She always maintained that at least as a lawyer my contrary nature would be an asset.

Ms. Ryan tucked my check into her purse, then folded her hands on the top of the table in the smaller of Kyle's two conference rooms. "Tell me what happened," she said.

I had just started when Kyle cleared his throat. I stopped to look at him.

"Zee can't afford for Jean to know just the safest part," he told me. "You have to tell her everything. No one knows how to sniff out a lie like a criminal defense lawyer."

"Everything?" I asked him, wide-eyed.

He patted my shoulder. "Jean can keep

secrets. If she doesn't know everything, then she's defending your friend with one hand tied behind her back."

I folded my arms across my chest and gave her a long, level look. There was nothing about her that inspired me to trust her with my secrets. A less motherly looking woman I'd seldom seen — except for those eyes.

Her expression was cool and vaguely unhappy — whether it was caused by driving a hundred and fifty miles on a Saturday, defending a fae, defending a murderer, or all three, I couldn't tell.

I took a deep breath and sighed. "All right."

"Start with the reason why Mr. Adelbertsmiter would feel the need to call in a mechanic to examine a murder scene," she said without tripping on Zee's name. I wondered uncharitably if she'd practiced it on the drive over. "It should begin, 'Because I'm not just a mechanic, I'm a —' "

I narrowed my eyes at her; the vague dislike her appearance had instilled in me blossomed at her patronizing tone. Being raised among werewolves left me with a hearty dislike of patronizing tones. I didn't like her, didn't trust her to defend Zee — and only defending Zee would be worth exposing my secrets to her.

Kyle read my face. "She's a bitch, Mercy. That's what makes her so good. She'll get your friend off if she can."

One of her elegant eyebrows rose. "Thank you so very much for the character assessment, Kyle."

Kyle smiled at her, a relaxed, full-faced smile. Whatever I thought of her, Kyle liked her. Since it couldn't be her warm manner, it must mean she was good people.

I'd have felt better if she'd had pets. A dog or even a cat would have hinted at a warmth that I couldn't see in her, but she only smelled of Chanel No. 5 and dry-cleaning fluid.

"Mercy," coaxed Kyle in a tone he must have perfected with the women whose divorces he handled. "You have to tell her."

I don't go around telling people I'm a walker. Outside of my family, Kyle is the only human who knows.

"Freeing your friend might mean that you have to take the stand and tell a whole courtroom of people what you are," said Ms. Ryan. "How much do you care about what happens to Mr. Adelbertsmiter?"

She thought I was a fae of some kind.

"Fine." I got out of the sinfully comfortable chair and walked over to the window to look down at the traffic on Clearwater

Avenue for a moment. I could see only one way to get this over with quickly.

"I'm not just a mechanic," I told her, using her words, "I'm Zee's friend." I spun abruptly on my heel so that I faced her and pulled my T-shirt over my head, using my toes to push off my tennis shoes and socks at the same time.

"Are you trying to tell me you're a stripper, too?" she asked, as I took off my bra and dropped it on top of my shirt on the floor. From her tone of voice, I could have been doing sit-ups instead of undressing.

I unsnapped my jeans and pushed them off my hips along with my underwear. When I stood wearing nothing but my tattoos, I called the coyote to me and sank into her shape. It was over in moments.

"Werewolf?" Ms. Ryan had scrambled out of her chair and was backing slowly to the door.

She couldn't tell a coyote from a werewolf? That was like looking at a Geo Metro and calling it a Hum-Vee.

I could smell her fear and it satisfied something deep inside me that had been writhing under her cool, superior expression. I curled my upper lip so she could get a good look at my teeth. I might weigh only thirty or so pounds in my coyote shape, but

I was a predator and could have killed a person if I wanted to: I'd killed a werewolf once with nothing but my fangs.

Kyle was up and beside her before she could run out the door. He took her arm in a firm grip.

"If she were a werewolf, you'd be in trouble," Kyle told her. "Never run from a predator. Even the best behaved of them will have a hard time restraining themselves from chasing after prey."

I sat down and yawned away the last of the change-tingles. It also gave her another look at my teeth, which seemed to bother her. Kyle gave me a chiding look, but continued soothing the other lawyer.

"She's not a werewolf; they're a lot bigger and scarier, trust me. She's not fae either. She's something a little different, native to our land, not imported like the fae or were-wolves. The only thing she can do is shift to coyote and back."

Not quite. I could kill vampires — as long as they were helpless, imprisoned by the day.

I swallowed, trying to get moisture to my suddenly dry mouth. I hated this sudden, gut-wrenching fear that assaulted me without warning. Every time I saw the little hitch in Warren's walk, I knew I would destroy the vampires again — but I paid the cost of their elimination with these panic attacks..

Kyle's calm explanation had given Ms. Ryan time to restore her calm facade. Kyle probably couldn't tell how angry she was, but my keener senses weren't fooled by the cool control she'd regained. She was still afraid, but her fear was not as strong as her rage.

Fear usually made me angry, too. Angry and careless. I wondered if showing her what I was had been such a good idea.

I changed back into my human self and ignored the growl of hunger that the two quick changes left me with. I put my clothes back on, taking time to tie my tennis shoes so that the bow was even before I resumed my seat, giving Ms. Ryan time to regain her composure.

She was seated when I looked up, but she'd moved to the other side of the table and taken the chair next to Kyle's.

"Zee is my friend," I told her again in measured tones. "He taught me everything I know about fixing cars and sold me his shop when he was forced to admit he was fae."

She frowned at me. "Are you older than you look? You'd have been a child when the fae came out."

"All of them didn't come out at once," I

told her. Her question settled my nerves. It was Zee whose life was at stake here, not mine. Not just yet. I kept talking so she wouldn't ask why Zee had come out. The one thing I absolutely couldn't tell an outsider was the existence of the Gray Lords. "Zee only admitted what he was a few years ago, seven or eight, maybe. He knew that being a fae would keep people away from the shop. I'd been working for him for a couple of years and he liked me so he sold it to me."

I collected my thoughts, trying to tell her what she needed to know without taking forever about it. "As I told you, he called me yesterday to ask for my help because someone had been killing fae in the reservation. Zee thought my nose might be able to pick out the killer. I gather I was sort of a last resort. When we got to the rez, O'Donnell was at the gate and wrote down my name when we drove through — that is on record. I imagine the police will find it, if they think to look. Zee took me through the murder scenes and I discovered that one man had been present at each house — O'Donnell."

She'd been taking notes in a stenographer's notebook but stopped, set down her pencil, and frowned. "O'Donnell was present at all the murder scenes and you verified that by *smelling* him?"

I raised my eyebrows. "A coyote has a keen sense of smell, Ms. Ryan. I have a very good memory for scents. I caught O'Donnell's when he stopped us as we went in — and his scent was in every one of the murder victims' houses I visited."

She stared at me — but she was no werewolf who might rip my throat out for challenging her — so I met her stare with one of my own.

She dropped her eyes first, ostensibly looking at her notes. People, human people, can be pretty deaf to body language. Maybe she didn't even notice that she'd lost the dominance contest, though her subconscious would.

"I understand O'Donnell was employed by the BFA as security," she said, turning back a few pages. "Couldn't he have been there investigating the deaths?"

"The BFA had no idea there were any murders," I told her. "The fae do their own internal policing. If they had gone to the Feds for help, I'm pretty sure it would be the FBI who would have been called in, not the BFA anyway. And O'Donnell was a guard, not an investigator. I was told that there was no reason O'Donnell should have been in every house that there was a murder in, and I have no reason to doubt that."

She'd started writing again, in shorthand. I'd never actually seen anyone use shorthand before.

"So you told Mr. Adelbertsmiter that O'Donnell was the murderer?"

"I told him that he was the only person whose scent I found in all the scenes."

"How many scenes?"

"Four." I decided not to tell her that there had been others; I didn't want to tell her why I hadn't gone to all the murder scenes. If Zee hadn't wanted to talk about my trip Underhill with me, I thought it would not be something he wanted me discussing with a lawyer.

She paused again. "There were four people murdered in the reservation and they did not ask for help?"

I gave her a thin smile. "The fae are not fond of attracting outside attention. It can be dangerous for everyone. They are also quite aware of the way most humans, including the Feds, feel about them. 'The only good fae is a dead fae' mentality is quite prevalent among the conservatives who make up most of the rank and file in the government whether they be Homeland Security, FBI, BFA, or any of the other alphabet soup agencies."

"You have trouble with the federal government?" she asked.

"As far as I know, none of them are prejudiced against half-Indian mechanics," I told her, matching her blandness with my own, "so why would I have a problem with them? However, I can certainly see why the fae would be reluctant to turn over a series of murders to a government whose record for dealing with the fae is not exactly spotless." I shrugged. "Maybe if they'd realized sooner that their killer wasn't another fae, they might have done so. I don't know."

She looked down at her notes. "So you told Zee that O'Donnell was the killer?"

I nodded. "Then I took Zee's truck and drove home. It was early in the morning, maybe four o'clock, when we parted company. It was my understanding that he was going to go over to O'Donnell's and talk to him."

"Just talk?"

I shrugged, glanced at Kyle, and tried to decide how far I trusted his judgement. All the truth, hmm? I sighed. "That's what he said, but I was pretty sure that if O'Donnell didn't have a good story, he wouldn't wake up this morning."

Her pencil hit the table with a snap.

"You are telling me that Zee went to O'Donnell's house to murder him?"

I took a deep breath. "You aren't going to understand this. You don't know the fae, not really. Imprisoning a fae is . . . impractical. First of all, it's damned difficult. Holding a person is hard enough. Holding a fae for any time at all, if he doesn't want to be held, is near impossible. Even without that, a life sentence is highly impractical when fae can live for hundreds of years." Or a lot more, but the public didn't know that. "And when you let them go, they aren't likely to shrug it off as justice served. The fae are a vengeance-hungry race. If you imprison a fae, for whatever reason, you'd better be dead when he gets out or you'll wish you were. Human justice just isn't equipped to deal with the fae, so they take care of it. A fae who commits a serious crime — like murder — is simply executed on the spot." The werewolves did the same.

She pinched the bridge of her nose as if I were giving her a headache.

"O'Donnell wasn't fae. He was human."

I thought about trying to explain why a people who were used to dealing out their own justice would care less that the perpetrator was human, but decided it was pointless. "The fact remains that Zee did not kill

O'Donnell. Someone got there first."

Her bland face didn't indicate belief, so I asked, "Do you know the story of Thomas the Rhymer?"

"True Thomas? It's a fairy tale," she said. "A prototype of Irving's 'Rip Van Winkle.'"

"Uhm," I said. "Actually, I'm under the impression that it was mostly a true story, Thomas's I mean. Thomas was, at any rate, a real historical person, a noted political entity of the thirteenth century. He claimed that he'd been caught for seven years by the queen of the fairies, then allowed to return. He either asked the fairy queen for a sign that he could show his kin so they would believe him when he told them where he'd been, or he stole a kiss from the fairy queen. Whatever the reason, he was given a gift, and like most fairy gifts, it was more curse than blessing — the fairy queen rendered him incapable of lying. For a diplomat or a lover or a businessman, that was a cruel thing to do, but the fae are often cruel."

"Your point?"

She didn't sound happy. I guess she didn't like thinking any of the fairy tales were true. It was a common attitude.

People could believe in the fae, but fairy tales were fairy tales. Only children would really believe in them.

It was an attitude that the fae themselves promoted. In most folktales, the fae are not exactly friendly. Take Hansel and Gretel, for instance. Zee once told me that there are a lot of fae in the rez, if left to their preferred diets, would happily eat people . . . especially children.

"He was cursed to become like the fae themselves," I told her. "Most fae, including Zee, cannot tell a lie. They are very, very good at making you think they are saying one thing, when they mean another, but they cannot lie."

"Everyone can lie."

I smiled at her tightly. "The fae cannot. I don't know why. They can do the damnedest things with the truth, but they cannot lie. So." I sighed unhappily. I had tried to figure out a way to leave Uncle Mike out, but unfortunately there was no other way to tell this part. Zee and I hadn't talked since his arrest; that was a matter of public record. I had to convince her that Zee was innocent. "I haven't spoken to Zee yet, so I don't know what his story —"

"No one has," she said. "My contact at the police department assured me that he hasn't spoken to anyone since he was arrested — a wise move that allowed me to talk to you before I speak to him."

111

"There was another fae who went with Zee — he's the one who told me Zee didn't kill O'Donnell. He and Zee walked in and found the dead body about the same time the police showed up. The other fae was able to hide himself from the police, but Zee did not."

"Could he have hidden, too?"

I shrugged. "All the fae have glamour which allows them to change their appearance. Some of them can hide themselves entirely. You'll have to ask him — though he probably won't tell you. I think Zee did it so that the police wouldn't look too hard and find his friend."

"Self-sacrifice?" Maybe someone who hadn't been raised with werewolves wouldn't have seen the scorn she felt for my theory. Fae, she apparently thought, weren't capable of self-sacrifice.

"Zee is one of the rare fae who can tolerate metal — his friend is not. Jail would be very painful for most fae."

She tapped the end of her notebook on the table. "So the point of all of this is that you say that a fae who cannot lie told you Zee didn't kill O'Donnell. That won't convince a jury."

"I was hoping to convince you."

She raised her eyebrows. "It doesn't matter what I think, Ms. Thompson."

I don't know what expression was on my face, but she laughed. "A lawyer has to defend the innocent or the guilty, Ms. Thompson. That's how our justice system works."

"He isn't guilty."

She shrugged. "Or so you say. Even if Zee's friend can't lie — you aren't fae, are you? At any rate, no one is guilty until convicted in a court of law. If that's all you have to tell me, I'll go talk to Mr. Adelbertsmiter."

"Can you get me into O'Donnell's house?" I asked. "Maybe I can find out something about the real murderer." I tapped my nose.

She considered it, then shook her head. "You've hired me to be Mr. Adelbertsmiter's attorney, but I feel some obligation to you as well. It would not be in your best interest — nor in Mr. Adelbertsmiter's best interest — to prove yourself something . . . other than human at the moment. You are paying for my services, so the police will look at you. I trust they won't find anything."

"Nothing of interest."

"No one knows that you can . . . change?"

"No one who would tell the police."

She picked up her notebook and set it

down again. "If you have been reading the papers or following the national news, you'll know that there are some legal issues being brought up about the werewolves."

Legal issues. I suppose that was one way to put it. The fae, by accepting the reservation system, had opened up the path for a bill to be introduced in Congress to deny the werewolves full citizenship and all the constitutional rights that came with it. Ironically, it was being proposed as an amendment to the Endangered Species Act.

Ms. Ryan nodded sharply. "If it comes out that you can become a coyote, the court might find your testimony inadmissible, which might have further legal consequences for you." Because they might decide I was an animal and not human, I thought. "Anything you find would be flimsy evidence even if it was admitted. The court is not going to have the same view on your reliability as Zee apparently did. Especially as you will have to declare yourself a separate species — which might be a very dangerous thing for you to do at this time." The werewolf bill wouldn't pass — Bran had too much influence in Congress — but I was neither werewolf nor fae, and the same protection might not cover me.

She frowned and moved her notebook

restlessly. "You should know that I belong to the John Lauren Society."

I looked at Kyle. The John Lauren Society was the largest of the anti-fae groups. Though they maintained a front of respectability, there had been allegations last year that they had funded a small group of college-age kids who had tried to blow up a well-known fae bar in Los Angeles. Luckily their competence hadn't matched their conviction and they'd only managed to do a little minor damage and send a couple of tourists to the hospital for smoke inhalation. The authorities had caught them rather quickly and found an apartment full of expensive explosives. The kids had been convicted, but the authorities hadn't managed to build a case against the larger, wealthier organization.

I had access to information not available to the authorities and I knew that the John Lauren Society was a good deal dirtier than even the FBI suspected.

Kyle had found me a lawyer who not only disliked fae — she'd like to see them eliminated.

Kyle patted my hand. "Jean won't allow her personal beliefs to interfere with her job." Then he smiled at me. "And it will make a point, having someone so active in the anti-fae community defending your friend."

"I'm not doing it because I believe he is innocent," she said.

Kyle turned his smile to her and it became sharklike. He seldom showed anyone that side of him. "And you can tell the newspapers and the jury and the judge that — and it still won't stop them from believing that he must be innocent or you wouldn't have taken the case."

She looked appalled, but she didn't disagree.

I tried to imagine working a job where your convictions were an inconvenience that you learned to ignore — and decided I'd rather turn a wrench no matter how much better her paycheck was than mine.

"I'll stay away from the crime scene, then," I lied. I wasn't a fae. What the police and Ms. Ryan didn't know wouldn't hurt them. The coyote is a sly beastie and no stranger to stealth — and I wasn't about to let Zee's fate depend wholly on this woman.

I'd find out who killed O'Donnell and figure out a way to prove him guilty that didn't involve me telling twelve of my peers that I smelled him.

I picked up a couple of buck burgers and

fries from a fast-food place and drove home. The trailer was looking as spiffy as a seventies single-wide could. New siding had made the porch look tacky, so I'd repainted it gray. Samuel had suggested flower boxes to dress it up, but I don't like living things to suffer unnecessarily — and I have a black thumb.

Samuel's Mercedes was gone from its usual spot so he must still be at Tumbleweed. He'd offered to come with me to meet with the lawyer — so had Adam. Which is how I ended up with just Kyle, whom neither of the werewolves looked upon as a rival.

I opened the front door and the smell of crock pot stew made my stomach rumble its approval.

There was a note next to the crock pot on the kitchen counter. Samuel had learned to write before typewriters and computers rendered penmanship an art practiced by elementary school children. His notes always looked like formal wedding invitations. Hard to believe a doctor actually wrote like that.

Mercy, his note said with lovely flourishes that made the alphabet look like artwork. *Sorry, I am not here. I promised to volunteer at the festival until after tonight's concert. Eat something.*

I followed his advice and got out a bowl. I was hungry, Samuel was a good cook — and it was still a few hours until dark.

O'Donnell's address was in the phone book. He lived in Kennewick just off Olympia in a modest-sized house with a neat yard in the front and an eight-foot white fence that enclosed the backyard. It was one of the cinder block houses that were fairly common in the area. Recently someone had been of the mistaken impression that painting it blue and putting shutters on the windows would make it look less industrial.

I drove past it, taking in the yellow police-line tape that covered the doors — and the darkened houses to either side of it.

It took me a while to find a good parking spot. In a neighborhood like this, people would notice a strange car parked in front of their house. Finally I parked in a lot by a church that was not too far away.

I put on the collar with the tags that gave Adam's phone number and address as my home. One trip to the dog pound had left me grateful for this little precaution. I didn't look anything at all like a dog, but at least in town there wouldn't be angry farmers ready to shoot me before they saw my collar.

Finding a place to change was a little more challenging. The dog pound I could deal with, but I didn't want to get a ticket for indecent exposure. Finally I found an empty house with a realtor's sign out front and an unlocked gardening shed.

From there, I only had to trot a couple of blocks to O'Donnell's house. Happily, O'Donnell's backyard fence ensured his backyard was private, because I had to change back and get out the picks I'd taped to the inside of the collar.

It was still close enough to summer that the night air was pleasant — a good thing since I had to pick the damned lock stark naked and it took me too long. Samuel had taught me to pick locks when I was fourteen. I hadn't done it a lot since then — just a couple of times when I'd locked my keys in my car.

As soon as I had the door open, I replaced the picks inside my collar. Bless duct tape, it was still sticky enough to hold them.

A washer and dryer were just inside, with a dirty towel laid across the dryer. I picked it up and wiped the door, doorknob, lock, and anything else that might have picked up my fingerprints. I didn't know if they had something to check for bare footprints, but I wiped the floor where I had taken a step inside to reach the towel, then tossed it back on the dryer.

I left the door mostly shut but unlatched, then shifted back into coyote, hunching under the gaze of eyes that weren't there. I knew, *knew* that no one had seen me go inside. The gentle, gusty wind would have brought the scent of anyone skulking about. Even so, I could feel someone watching me, almost as if the house was aware of me. Creepy.

With my tail tucked uncomfortably close I turned my attention to the task at hand, the sooner to leave — but unlike the fae houses, this one had seen a lot of people in and out recently. Police, I thought, forensic team, but even before they had come there had been a lot of people in the back hallway.

I hadn't expected an obnoxious boor like O'Donnell to have a lot of friends.

I ducked through the first doorway and into the kitchen, and the heavy traffic of people mostly faded away. Three or four light scents, O'Donnell, and someone who wore a particularly bad male cologne had been in here.

The cupboard doors gaped and the drawers hung open and a little askew. Dish towels were scattered in hasty piles on the counter.

Maybe Cologne Man was a police officer who searched the kitchen — unless O'Donnell was the sort who randomly shoved all of his dishes to one side of a cupboard and stored his cleaning supplies in a pile on the floor instead of tucked neatly in the space under the sink behind the doors that hung open, revealing the empty dark space beneath.

The faint light of the half moon revealed a fine black powder all over the cupboard doors and counter tops that I recognized as the substance the police use to reveal fingerprints — the TV is a good educational tool and Samuel is addicted to those forensic, soap opera–mystery shows.

I glanced at the floor, but there was nothing on it. Maybe I'd been a little paranoid when I'd wiped the place where I'd stood on the linoleum with bare human feet.

The first bedroom, across the hall from the kitchen, was obviously O'Donnell's. Everyone from the kitchen had been in here, including Cologne Man.

Again, it looked like someone had gone through every cranny. It was a mess. Every drawer had been upended on the bed, then the whole dresser had been overturned. All of his pants' pockets had been turned inside out.

I wondered if the police would have left it that way.

I backed out of there and went into the next room. This was a smaller bedroom, and there was no bed. Instead there were three card tables that had been flung helter-skelter. The bedroom window was shattered and covered with police tape. Someone had been angry when they'd come in here, and I was betting it wasn't the police.

Avoiding the glass on the floor as much as I could, I got a closer look at the window frame. It had been one of those newer vinyl ones, and the bottom half had been de-signed to slide up. Whatever had been thrown through the window had pulled most of the framing out of the wall as well.

But I'd known the killer was strong. He had, after all, ripped off a man's head.

I left the window to explore the rest of the room more closely. Despite the apparent mess, there wasn't much to look at: three card tables and eleven folding chairs — I glanced at the window and thought that a folding chair, thrown very hard, might break through a window like that.

A metal machine that looked oddly famil-iar had left a dent in the wall before landing on the ground. I pawed it over and realized it was an old-fashioned mail meter. Someone had been sending out bulk mail from here.

I put my nose down and started to pay attention to what it had been trying to tell me. First, this room was more public than the kitchen or first bedroom, more like the back door and hallway had been.

Most houses have a base scent, mostly a combination of preferred cleaning supplies (or lack thereof) and the body scents of the family who live in it. This room smelled different from the rest of the house. There had been — I looked again at the scattering of chairs — maybe as many as ten or twelve people who came to this room often enough to leave more than a surface scent.

This was good, I thought. Given the way O'Donnell had rubbed me wrong — anyone who knew him was likely to have murdered him. However — I took another look at the window — there hadn't been a fae or any other magical critter in the bunch that I could tell. No human had taken out the window that way — or torn off O'Donnell's head either.

I memorized their scents anyway.

I'd done what I could with this room — which left me with only one more. I'd left the living room for last for two reasons. First, if someone were to see me, it would be where the big picture window looked out onto the street in front of the house. Second, even a human's nose could have told them that the living room was where O'Donnell had been killed and I was growing tired of blood and gore.

I think it was dread of what I'd find in the living room that made me look back into the bedroom, rather than any instinct that I might have missed something.

A coyote, at least this coyote, stands just under two feet at the shoulder. I think that's why I never thought to look up at the pictures on the wall. I'd thought they were only posters; they were the right size and shape, with matching cheap Plexiglas and black plastic frames. The room was dark, too, darker than the kitchen because the moon was on the other side of the house. But from the doorway I got a good look at the framed pictures.

They were indeed posters, very interesting posters for a security guard who worked for the BFA.

The first showed a child dressed in a fluffy Easter Sunday dress sitting on a marble bench in a gardenlike setting. Her hair was pale and curly. She was looking at the flower

124

in her hand. Her face was round with a button nose and rosebud lips. Bold letters across the top of the poster said: PROTECT THE CHILDREN. Across the bottom, in smaller letters, the poster announced that Citizens for a Bright Future was holding a meeting the November eighteenth of two years ago.

Like the John Lauren Society, Bright Future was an anti-fae group. It was a lot smaller organization than the JLS and catered to a different income bracket. Members of the JLS tended to be like Ms. Ryan, the relatively wealthy and educated. The JLS held banquets and golf tournaments to raise money. Bright Future held rallies that mostly resembled the old-fashioned tent revival meetings where the faithful would be entertained and preached at, then passed a hat.

The other posters were similar to the first, though the dates were different. Three of them were for meetings held in the Tri-Cities, but one was in Spokane. They were slick, and professionally laid out. Stock posters, I thought, printed at the headquarters without dates and places, which could be added later in Sharpie black.

They must have been meeting here and sending out their mailings. That's why there had been so many people in O'Donnell's house.

Thoughtfully, I padded into the living room. I think I'd seen so much blood the night before that it wasn't the first thing that struck me, though it was splattered around with impressive abandon.

The first thing I noticed was that, under the blood and death, I caught a familiar scent that was out of place in this room. Something smelled like the forest fae's home. The second thing I noticed was that whatever it was, it packed a tremendous magical punch.

Finding it, though, was more problematical. It was like playing "Find the Thimble" with my nose and the strength of the magic to tell me if I was hot or cold. Finally I stopped in front of a sturdy gray walking stick tucked into the corner behind the front door, next to another taller and intricately carved stick, which smelled of nothing more interesting than polyurethane.

When I first looked at the stick, it appeared unremarkable and plain, though clearly old. Then I realized that the metal cap wasn't stainless steel: it was silver, and very faintly I could see that something was etched into the metal. But it was dark in the room and even my night eyes have limits.

It might as well have had "A Clue" painted in fluorescent orange down the side. I thought long and hard about taking it, but decided it was unlikely to go anyplace, having survived O'Donnell's murderer and the police.

It smelled of wood smoke and pipe tobacco: O'Donnell had stolen it from the forest fae's home.

I left it alone and began quartering the living room.

Built-in bookshelves lined the room, mostly full of DVDs and VHS tapes. One whole bookshelf was devoted to the kind of men's magazines that people read "for the articles" and argue about art versus pornography. The magazines on the bottom shelf had given up any pretense of art — judging by the photos on the covers.

Another bookcase had doors that closed over the bottom half. The open shelves at the top were mostly empty except for a few chunks of . . . rocks. I recognized a good-sized chunk of amethyst and a particularly fine quartz crystal. O'Donnell collected rocks.

There was an open case for *Chitty Chitty Bang Bang* sitting on top of the DVD player under the TV. How could someone like O'Donnell be a Dick Van Dyke fan? I wondered if he'd had a chance to finish watching it before he died.

I think it was because I felt that moment of sorrow that I heard the creak of a board giving way beneath the weight of the house's dead occupant.

Other people, people who are completely, mundanely human, see ghosts, too. Maybe not as often — or in broad daylight — but they do see them. Since there had been no ghosts at the death sites in the reservation, I'd unconsciously assumed that there would be none here as well. I'd been wrong.

O'Donnell's shade walked into the living room from the hallway. As some ghosts do, he grew clearer in bits and pieces as I focused on him. I could see the stitching on his jeans, but his face was a faded blur.

I whined, but he walked by me without a glance.

There are a very few ghosts who can interact with the living, as much a person as they had been in life. I got caught once talking to a ghost without realizing that's what he was until my mother asked me whom I was talking to.

Other ghosts repeat the habits of a lifetime. Sometimes they react, too, though I usually can't talk to them. There is a place near where I was raised where the ghost of a rancher goes out every morning to throw hay to cows who are half a century gone. Sometimes he saw me and waved or nodded his head as he would have responded to anyone who'd approached him in life. But if I tried to converse with him, he'd just go about his business as if I weren't there at all.

The third kind are the ones born in moments of trauma. They relive their deaths until they fade away. Some dissipate in a few days and others are still dying each day even centuries later.

O'Donnell didn't see me standing in front of him so he wasn't the first, most useful kind of ghost.

All I could do was watch as he walked to the shelves that held the rocks and touched something on the top shelf. It clicked against the fake wood shelf. He stood there for a moment, his fingers petting whatever he touched, his whole body focused on that small item.

For a moment I was disappointed. If he was just repeating something he'd done every day, I wouldn't learn anything from him.

Then he jerked upright, responding, I

thought, to a sound I could not hear and he walked briskly to the front door. I heard the door open with his motions, but the door, more real than the apparition, stayed closed.

This was not a habitual ghost. I settled in, prepared to watch O'Donnell die.

He knew the person at the door. He seemed impatient with him, but after a moment of talk, he took a step back in invitation. I couldn't see the person who came in — he wasn't dead — or hear anything except the creaks and groans of the floorboards as they remembered what had happened here.

Following O'Donnell's attention, I watched the path of the murderer as he walked rapidly to a place in front of the bookcase. O'Donnell's body language became increasingly hostile. I saw his chest move forcefully and he made a cutting gesture with one hand before storming over to confront his visitor.

Something grabbed him around the neck and shoulder. I could almost make out the shape of the murderer's hand against the paleness of O'Donnell's form. It looked human to me. But before I could get a good look, whoever it was proved that they were not human at all.

It was so fast. One moment O'Donnell

was whole and the next his body was on the floor, jerking and dancing, and his head was rolling across the floor in a lopsided, spinning gyre that ended not a foot from where I stood. For the first time, I saw O'Donnell's face clearly. His eyes were becoming unfocused, but his mouth moved, forming a word he no longer had breath to say. Anger, not fear, dominated his expression, as if he hadn't had time to realize what had happened.

I'm not a terrific lip reader, but I could tell what he'd tried to say.

Mine.

I stayed where I was and shook for minutes after O'Donnell's specter faded. It wasn't the first death I'd witnessed — murder is one of those things that tend to produce ghosts. I'd even cut someone's head off before — that being one of the few ways you can make sure that a vampire will stay dead. But it hadn't been as violent as this, if only because I'm not strong enough to rip someone's head off.

Eventually, I remembered that I had things to do before someone realized there was a coyote running free in a crime scene. I put my nose down on the carpet to see what it could tell me.

Distinguishing any scents at all here

proved difficult with O'Donnell's blood soaking into couch cushions, walls, and carpet. I caught a hint of Uncle Mike's scent in one corner of the room, but it faded quickly, and though I searched the corner for a while, I never caught it again. The Cologne Man had been in the living room, along with O'Donnell, Zee, and Tony. I hadn't realized Tony had been one of the arresting officers. Someone had been sick just inside the front door, but it had been wiped up and left only a trace.

Other than that, it was like trying to pick up a trail in the Columbia Center Mall. There had simply been too many people in here. If I was trying to pick out a scent, I could do that — but trying to distinguish all the scents . . . it just wasn't going to work.

Giving up, I went back to the corner where I'd scented Uncle Mike just to see if I could pick him up again — or figure out how he managed to leave only the barest trace for me to find.

I don't know how long it was there before I finally looked up and saw the raven.

CHAPTER 5

It watched me from the hall doorway, as if it had simply found the open back door and flown in. But ravens are not night birds despite their color and reputation. If there had been nothing else, that alone would have told me that there was something off about this bird.

But that wasn't the only thing. Or even the first.

As soon as I caught the glitter of the moon's light in the shine of its feathers, I smelled it — as if it hadn't been there until then.

Ravens smell of the carrion they eat overlaying a musty sharp scent they share with crows and magpies. This one smelled of rain, forest, and good black garden soil in the spring. Then there was its size.

The Tri-Cities has some awfully big ravens, but nothing like this bird. It was taller than the coyote I was; easily as big as a golden eagle.

And every hair on my body stood up to attention as a wave of magic swept through the room.

It took a sudden hop forward, which moved its head into the faint light that trickled through the windows. There was a spot of white on its head, like a drop of snow. But what caught most of my attention were its eyes: bloodred, like a white rabbit's, they glittered eerily as it stared right at me . . . and through me, as if it were blind.

For the first time in my life I was afraid to drop my eyes. Werewolves put great value on eye contact — and I'd blithely used that all my life. I have no trouble dropping my eyes, acknowledging anyone's superiority and then doing whatever I please. Among the werewolves, once dominance was acknowledged, the dominant werewolf could, by custom, do no more than cuff me out of his way . . . while I then ignored him or plotted how to get back at him as I chose.

But this wasn't a werewolf, and I was consumed with the conviction that if I moved at all, it would destroy me — though it was not making any sign of aggression.

I value my instincts, so I stayed motionless.

It opened its mouth and gave a rattling cry, like old bones shaken roughly in a wooden box. Then it dismissed me from its notice. It strode to the corner and knocked the walking stick to the floor. The raven took the old thing into its mouth and without so much as a glance over its shoulder took flight through the wall.

Fifteen minutes later, I was well on the way back home — in human shape and driving my car.

Being not exactly human myself and raised by werewolves, I'd thought I'd seen just about everything: witches, vampires, ghosts, and a half dozen other things that aren't supposed to exist. But that bird had been real, as solid as me — I'd seen its ribs rise and fall as it breathed and I'd touched that walking stick myself.

I'd never seen one solid object go through another solid object — not without some pretty impressive CGI graphics or David Copperfield.

Magic, despite *Bewitched* and *I Dream of Jeannie,* just doesn't work like that. If the bird had faded, become immaterial or something before it hit the wall, I might have accepted that as magic.

Maybe, just maybe, I'd been like the rest

of the world, accepting the fae at their face value. Acting like they were something familiar, that they were constrained by rules I could understand and feel comfortable with.

If anyone should have known better, it would be me. After all, I well understood that what the public knew about the were-wolves was just the polished tip of a nasty iceberg. I knew that the fae were, if anything, worse about secrecy than the wolves. Though Zee had been my friend for a decade, I knew very little about the fae side of his life. I knew he was a Steelers fan, that his human wife had died of cancer shortly before I met him, and that he liked tartar sauce on his fries — but I didn't know what he looked like beneath his glamour.

There were lights on at my house when I pulled the Rabbit into the driveway and parked it next to Samuel's Mercedes and a strange Ford Explorer. I'd been hoping Samuel would be home and awake, so I could use him as a sounding board — but the SUV put paid to that idea.

I frowned at it. It was two in the morning, an odd time for visitors. Most visitors.

I took in a deep breath through my nose, but couldn't catch a whiff of vampire — or anything else. Even the night air smelled duller than usual. Probably just a leftover from the shift from coyote to human. My human nose was better than most people's but quite a bit less sensitive than the coyote's, so changing to human was a little like taking out a hearing aid. Still . . .

Vampires could hide their scent from me if they chose to.

I shivered in the warm night air. I think I would have stayed out there all night, except that I heard the murmur of guitar. I couldn't see Samuel playing for Marsilia, the mistress of the vampire seethe, so I climbed up the steps and went in.

Uncle Mike sat on the overstuffed chair Samuel had replaced my old flea-market find with. Samuel was half-stretched out on the couch like a mountain lion. He played idle bits of music on his guitar. He might look relaxed, but I knew him too well. The cat who was purring on the back of the couch, just behind Samuel's head, was the only relaxed person in the room.

"There's hot water for cocoa," said Samuel, without looking away from Uncle Mike. "Why don't you get yourself some, then come tell us about Zee, who put you on the scent of their murderer so they could go kill him. Then tell me what you've been doing tonight that would leave you smelling of blood and magic?"

Yep, Samuel was ticked at Uncle Mike.

I riffled through the cupboards until I found the box of emergency cocoa. Not the milk chocolate with marshmallow kind, but the hard stuff, dark chocolate with a bit of jalapeño pepper for flavor. I wasn't really upset enough now to need it, but it kept me busy while I thought about how I might keep matters peaceable. Real cocoa needs milk, so I put some in a sauce pan and began heating it up.

I'd left Samuel and the other werewolves this morning knowing only that Zee was in jail and needed a lawyer. Obviously, someone had filled Samuel in a bit since then. Almost certainly *not* Uncle Mike.

Probably not Warren, who would know everything from the lawyer's meeting — I'd told Kyle to go ahead and tell him what I'd told the lawyer. Warren could keep secrets.

Ah. Warren wouldn't keep secrets from his pack Alpha, Adam. Adam would see no reason not to tell Samuel the whole story if he asked.

See that's the thing about secrets. All you have to do is tell one person — and suddenly everyone knows. Still, if I disappeared, I'd like to know that the werewolves would come looking for me. Hopefully the fae (in the person of Uncle Mike) understood that, and I wasn't likely to just disappear: if the Gray Lords would arrange a suicide for Zee, one of their own who was of some value, they certainly wouldn't hesitate to arrange something to happen to me as well. The pack would make that a little more difficult.

A cup of liquid doesn't take long to heat. I poured it into a mug; took the first sip, bittersweet and biting; then rejoined the men. My deliberations in the kitchen led me to the couch, where I sat with a whole cushion between me and Samuel so I wouldn't be assumed (by Samuel) to be taking a side in the antagonism that was stirring in my living room like the inky surface of Loch Ness just before the monster erupts. I didn't want any eruptions in my living room, thank you. Eruptions meant repair bills and blood. Growing up with werewolves had left me hyperaware of power struggles and things unspoken.

With another werewolf, a show of support might put the likelihood of violence down a few notches, because he would feel more confident. Samuel didn't need more confidence. He needed to know that I felt that Uncle Mike had done the right thing by calling me in, no matter what Samuel's opinion on the matter was.

"I found a good lawyer for Zee," I told Uncle Mike.

"She is a member of the John Lauren Society." Uncle Mike seemed much more himself than he'd sounded on the phone. That meant that his "cheerful innkeeper" guise was in full swing. I couldn't tell if he was unhappy with my choice of lawyers or not.

"Kyle —" I stopped myself and backed up. "I have a friend who is among the best divorce attorneys in the state. When I called him, he suggested this Jean Ryan from Spokane. He told me she was a barracuda in the courtroom, and says that her membership in a fae hate group will actually help. People will think that she must be absolutely convinced of Zee's innocence to take this case."

"Is that true? She believes him innocent?"

I shrugged. "I don't know, but both Kyle and she say it won't matter. I did my best to convince her." I took a sip of cocoa and told them everything Ms. Ryan had told me, including her warning that I keep my nose out of police business.

Samuel's lips quirked at that. "So how long did you wait before going to O'Donnell's after she told you not to?"

I gave him an indignant look. "I wouldn't

140

have done it before dark. Too many people would have been calling Animal Control if they saw a coyote that far into town, collar or not. I can't do much investigating from the animal shelter, and they've already picked me up once this summer."

I looked at Uncle Mike and wondered how to get him to tell me all the things I needed to know. "Did you know that O'Donnell was involved with Citizens for a Bright Future?"

He sat up straighter. "I'd have thought he would be smarter than that. If the BFA had known, he'd have lost his job."

He didn't say that he'd been unaware of it, I noticed.

"He didn't seem too worried about anyone finding out," I told him. "There were Bright Future posters all over the walls of one of his rooms."

"The BFA doesn't exactly make a habit of searching their employees' houses. Their funding just got cut again and the moneys diverted to that mess in the Middle East." He didn't sound too upset about the BFA's troubles.

I rubbed my tired face. "The search wasn't as much help as I'd hoped. I didn't find a scent, except for O'Donnell himself, of anyone who was in the reservation murder scenes. I don't think that there was anyone with him when he killed the fae." Except maybe Cologne Man, I thought. I had no way of telling what he really smelled like, though I had not the slightest idea why he'd have worn cologne to kill O'Donnell and not for killing the fae. Surely he wouldn't expect a werewolf or someone like me to be tracking down O'Donnell's killer.

"So your visit was uneventful." That was Samuel, his voice just a little more intense than the soft, harplike notes he was calling from the guitar. If he kept playing like that, I was going to be asleep before I finished. "Why then do you smell like blood and magic?"

"I didn't say it was uneventful. The blood is because the living room of O'Donnell's house was covered in it."

Uncle Mike gave a faint grimace, which I didn't believe at all. My experience with immortals might be with werewolves, but the fae aren't a kind and gentle people either. He might have been thrown off his game when Zee was taken into custody, but blood and gore never really bother the old ones.

"The magic . . ." I shrugged. "It could have been a number of things. I saw the murder take place."

"Magic?" Uncle Mike frowned. "I didn't

142

know you were a farseer. I thought that magic didn't work around you."

"That would be terrific," I said. "But no, magic works around me for the most part. I just have some kind of partial immunity to it. Usually the way it works is that the less harmful the magic is, the better the chance it won't work. The really bad stuff usually does just fine."

"She sees ghosts," said Samuel, impatient with my whining.

"I see dead people," I deadpanned back. Oddly, it was Uncle Mike who laughed. I hadn't thought he'd be a moviegoer.

"So did these ghosts tell you anything?"

I shook my head. "No. I just got the playback of the murder with O'Donnell as the only player. I think the killer was after something, though. Did O'Donnell steal from the fae?"

Uncle Mike's face went blank and I knew two things. The answer to my question was yes, and Uncle Mike had no intention of telling me what O'Donnell had taken.

"Just for kicks," I said instead of waiting in vain for his answer, "how many fae are there who can take on the shape of a raven?"

"Here?" Uncle Mike shrugged. "Five or six."

"There was a raven in O'Donnell's house

and it reeked of fae magic."

Uncle Mike gave an abrupt, harsh laugh. "If you're asking if I sent someone to O'Donnell's house, the answer is no. If you're wondering if one of them killed O'Donnell, the answer is still no. None of those with a raven shape have the physical strength to tear off someone's head."

"Could Zee?" I asked. Sometimes if you ask unexpected questions, you get answers.

His eyebrows rose and his brogue grew thicker. "Sure and why would you ask that? Haven't I told you he had naught to do with it?"

I shook my head. "I know Zee didn't kill him. The police have an expert who told them that he could. I have reasons to doubt her ability — and it might help Zee if I know exactly how far off she is."

Uncle Mike took a deep breath and tilted his head to the side. "The Dark Smith of Drontheim might have been able to do what I saw, but that was a long time ago. Most of us have lost a bit of what was once ours over the years of cold iron and Christianity. Zee less than most, though. Maybe he could have. Maybe not."

The Dark Smith of Drontheim. He'd said something like that before. Trying to figure out who Zee had once been was one of my favorite hobbies, but the current situation made the small jewel of information taste like ashes. If Zee lost his life over this, who he had once been was irrelevant.

"Just how many of the fae in the reservation . . ." I thought about that and reworded it a little. ". . . or in the Tri-City area could have done that?"

"A few," Uncle Mike said without taking time to reflect. "I've been racking my head all day. One of the ogres could have, though I'll be a Catholic monk if I know why they would want to. And once they get to that point, they'd not have stopped until they'd had a bite or two. None of the ogres were particularly friendly with any of the victims on the reservation — or anyone else, except maybe Zee. There are a few others who might have been capable of it once, but most of them haven't fared as well as Zee in the modern world."

I remembered the power of the sea man.

"What about the man I met in the selkie's . . ." I glanced at Samuel and bit my tongue. That ocean I knew was a secret, and it could have no impact on Zee's fate. I wouldn't speak of it in front of Samuel, but that left my sentence hanging in the air.

"What man?" Samuel's question was mild, though Uncle Mike's words, coming right over the top of Samuel, were not.

I could smell Uncle Mike's fear, harsh and sudden, like his words. It wasn't an emotion I associated with him.

After a quick, wary look around the room, he continued in an urgent whisper, "I don't know how you managed it, but it will do you no good to speak of the encounter. The one you met could have done it, but he has not bestirred himself this past hundred years." He took a breath and forced himself to relax. "Trust me, it wasn't the Gray Lords who killed O'Donnell, Mercedes. His murder was too clumsy to be their work. Tell me more of this fae raven you encountered."

I stared at him a moment. Was the sea fae one of the Gray Lords?

"The raven?" he prompted gently.

So I told him, backing up a bit to tell him about the staff, then about the raven leaping through the wall with it.

"How did I miss the staff?" Uncle Mike asked himself, looking thoroughly shaken.

"It was tucked in a corner," I told him. "It came from one of the victims' houses, didn't it? The one who smoked a pipe and whose back window looked out over a forest."

Uncle Mike seemed to come back to himself and he stared at me. "You know too many of our secrets, Mercedes."

Samuel set his guitar aside and put himself between us before I had time to register the menace in Uncle Mike's voice.

"Careful," he said, his voice thick with Wales and warning. "Careful, Green Man. She's put her neck out to help you — shame upon you and your house if she comes to harm by't."

"Two," Uncle Mike said. "*Two* of the Gray Lords have seen your face in our business, Mercy. One might have forgotten, but two never will." He waved an impatient hand at Samuel. "Oh, stand down, wolf. *I'll* not harm your kit. I only spoke the truth. There are things not nearly so benign who will not be happy about her knowing what she knows — and two of them already have."

"Two?" I asked in a voice that was smaller than I'd meant it to be.

"That was no raven you met," he said grimly. "It was the great Carrion Crow herself." He gave me a long look. "I wonder why she didn't kill you."

"Maybe she thought I was a coyote," I said in a small voice.

Uncle Mike shook his head. "She might be blind, but she perceives more clearly than I, still."

There was a brief silence. I don't know

what the others were thinking about, but I was contemplating just how many close calls I'd been having lately. If the vampires didn't hurry, the fae or some other monster would kill me before she got a chance. What had happened to all the years of carefully keeping to myself and staying out of trouble?

"You are *sure* that one of the Gray Lords didn't kill O'Donnell?" I asked.

"Yes," he said firmly, then paused. "I hope not. If so, then Zee's arrest was intended and he is doomed — and probably me as well." He ran a hand along his chin and something about the gesture made me wonder if he'd once worn a beard. "No. It was not they. They aren't above a messy kill — but they wouldn't have left the staff for the police to find. The Carrion Crow came to keep the staff out of human hands — though I'm surprised she didn't retrieve it sooner." He gave me a speculative look. "Zee and I weren't in that living room long, but we'd never have overlooked the staff. I wonder . . ."

"What is the staff?" I asked. "I could tell it was magic, but nothing else."

"Naught of interest to you, I trust," said Uncle Mike, coming to his feet. "Naught for you to fuss with when there's the Carrion Crow about. There's money in the briefcase . . ." For the first time I noticed a brown leather case tucked against the arm of his chair. "If it is not enough to cover Zee's expenses, let me know."

He tipped an imaginary hat toward Samuel, then took my hand, bowed, and kissed it. "Mercy, I'd be doing you no favors if I didn't tell you to stop. We appreciate the help you have given us so far, but your usefulness ends here. There are things going on that I'm not at liberty to tell you. If you continue, you are not going to discover anything — and if those Nameless Ones find out how much you know, it will go ill with you. And there are two too many of them about." He nodded sharply at me, then at Samuel. "I'll bid you both good mornin'."

And he was out the door.

"Keep your weather eye on him, Mercy," Samuel said, still standing with his back to me as we watched Uncle Mike's headlights turn on as he backed out of the driveway. "He's not Zee. His loyalties are to himself and his alone."

I rubbed my shoulders and stood up myself. Never have a discussion with a werewolf when he's standing and you're sitting; it puts you at a disadvantage and makes them think they can give you orders.

"I trust him about as far as I can throw him," I agreed. Uncle Mike wouldn't go out of his way to harm me, but . . . "You know, one of the things I learned growing up about you wolves was that sometimes the most interesting part of the conversation with someone who can't lie is the questions they *don't* answer."

Samuel nodded. "I noticed it, too. That staff, whatever it is, was stolen from one of the murder victims — and he didn't want to talk about it."

I yawned twice and heard my jaw pop the second time. "I'm going to bed tonight. I have to go to church in the morning." I hesitated. "What do you know about the Black Smith of Drontheim?"

He gave me a small smile. "Not as much as you do, I expect, if you've worked with him for ten years."

"Samuel Cornick," I snapped.

He laughed.

"Do you know a story about this Black Smith of Drontheim?" I was tired and the heap of my worries was a weight I was staggering under: Zee, the Gray Lords, Adam, and Samuel — and the wait for Marsilia to find out that Andre had not been killed by his helpless victims. However, I'd been searching for stories about Zee for years.

Too many of the fae treated him with awed respect for him not to be in stories somewhere. I just couldn't find them.

"The Dark Smith, Mercy, the Dark Smith."

I tapped my toe and Samuel gave in. "Ever since I saw his knife, I've wondered if he was the Dark Smith. That one was supposed to have forged at least one blade that would cut through anything."

"Drontheim . . ." I muttered. "Trondheim? The old capital of Norway? Zee's German."

Samuel shrugged. "Or he's pretending to be German — or the old story could have it wrong. In the stories I heard, the Dark Smith was a genius and a malicious bastard, a son of the King of Norway. The sword he made had a nasty habit of turning on the man who wielded it."

I thought about it for a moment. "I guess I could believe a villain before I'd believe a story about him being a goody-goody hero."

"People change over the years," said Samuel.

I looked up sharply and met his eyes. He wasn't talking about Zee anymore.

There were only a few feet between us, but the gulf of history was much larger: I'd loved him so much, once. I'd been sixteen

151

and he'd been centuries older. I'd seen in him a gentle protector, a knight who would rescue me and build his world around me. Someone for whom I would not be an obligation, a burden, or a bother. He'd seen in me a mother who could bear his living children.

Werewolves, with one exception, are made, not born. It takes more than a nip or two — or as I read in a comic book once, a scratch of a claw. A human who wants to change must be savaged so badly that he either dies or becomes a werewolf and is saved by the rapid healing that is necessary to surviving as a hot-tempered monster among other such beasts.

Women don't survive the Change as well as the men for some reason. And the women who do cannot bear children. Oh, they're fertile enough, but the monthly change at the full moon is too violent and they abort any pregnancies when they shift from human to werewolf.

Werewolves can mate with humans, and often do. But they have a terribly high miscarriage rate and higher than usual infant mortality. Adam had a daughter born after his Change, but his ex-wife had had three miscarriages while I knew her. The only children who survive are completely human.

But Samuel had a brother who was born a werewolf. The only one that anyone I know had ever heard of. His mother was from a family that was gifted with magic native to this land and not Europe as most of our magic-using humans have. She was able to hold off the change every month until Charles's birth. Weakened by her efforts, she died at his birth — but her experiences had started Samuel thinking.

When I, neither human nor werewolf, was brought to his father for his pack to raise, Samuel had seen his chance. I don't have to change — and even when I do, the change is not violent. Though real wolves in the wild kill any coyotes they find in their territory, they can mate and have viable offspring.

Samuel waited until I was sixteen before he made me fall in love with him.

"We all change," I told him. "I'm going to bed."

Just as I've always known there are monsters in the world, monsters and things even more evil, I've always known that it is God who keeps evil at bay. So I make a point of going to church every Sunday and praying on a regular basis. Since killing Andre and his demon-bearing spawn, church was the only place I felt truly safe.

"You look tired." Pastor Julio Arnez's hands were big-knuckled and battered. Like me, he'd worked with his hands for a living — he'd been a lumberman until he retired and become our pastor.

"A little," I agreed.

"I heard about your friend," he said. "Would he appreciate a visit?"

Zee would like my pastor — everyone liked Pastor Julio. He might even manage to make being in jail more bearable, but getting close to Zee was too dangerous.

So I shook my head. "He's fae," I said apologetically. "They don't think very highly of Christianity. Thank you for offering."

"If there's anything I can do, you tell me," he said sternly. He kissed my forehead and sent me off with his blessing.

Zee on my mind, as soon as I got home I called Tony on his cell phone because I had no idea how to get in to see Zee.

He answered, sounding cheerful and friendly rather than coolly professional, so he must have been home.

"Hey, Mercedes," he said. "It was not nice of you to sic Ms. Ryan on us. Smart, but not nice."

"Hey, Tony," I said. "I'd apologize but Zee matters to me — and he's innocent, so I got the best I could find. However, if it makes you feel any better, I have to deal with her, too."

He laughed. "All right, what's up?"

"This is stupid," I told him, "but I've never had to go visit anyone in jail before now. So how do I go about seeing Zee? Are there visiting hours or what? Should I wait until Monday? And where is he being held?"

There was a short silence. "I think visiting hours are weekends and evenings only. But before you go, you might talk to your lawyer," he said cautiously. Was there something wrong with me seeing Zee?

"Call your lawyer," he said again when I asked him.

So I did. The card she'd given me had her cell on it as well as her office.

"Mr. Adelbertsmiter is not talking to anyone," Jean Ryan told me in a frosty voice, as if it were my fault. "It will be difficult to mount an effective defense unless he talks to me."

I frowned. Zee could be cantankerous but he wasn't stupid. If he wasn't talking, he had a reason.

"I need to see him," I told her. "Maybe I can persuade him to talk to you."

"I don't think you're going to persuade him of anything." There was a bare hint of smugness in her voice. "When he wouldn't respond to me, I told him what I knew about O'Donnell's death — all that you had told me. That was the only time he spoke. He said that you had no business telling his secrets to strangers." She hesitated. "This next part is a threat, and I normally would not pass it on, as it does my client's case no good. But . . . I think you ought to be warned. He said you'd better hope he doesn't get out — and that he's calling the loan due immediately. Do you know what he means?"

Numbly I nodded before realizing that she couldn't see me. "I bought my shop from him. I still owe him money on it." I'd been paying him on a monthly basis, just as I did the bank. It wasn't the money, which I didn't have, that left my throat dry and pressure building behind my eyes.

He thought I'd betrayed him.

Zee was fae; he could not lie.

"Well," she said. "He made it clear that he had no desire to talk to you before he went mute again. Do you still wish to retain my services?" She sounded almost hopeful.

"Yes," I said. It wasn't my money that was paying her — even at her rates there was more than enough in Uncle Mike's briefcase to cover Zee's expenses.

"I'll be honest, Ms. Thompson, if he doesn't talk to me, I can't do him any good at all."

"Do what you can," I told her numbly. "I'm working on a few things myself."

Secrets. I shivered a little, though as soon as I'd gotten home from church, I'd turned up the temperature from the sixty degrees Samuel had set it at this morning before he'd left to go to the last day of Tumbleweed. Werewolves like things a little cooler than I do. It was a balmy eighty in the house, not a reason in the world that I should feel cold.

I wondered which part of what I'd told the lawyer he objected to — the murders in the reservation, or telling Ms. Ryan that there had been another fae with him when he'd found the body.

Damn it, I hadn't told Ms. Ryan anything someone wasn't going to have to tell the police. Come to think of it — I *had* told the police most everything I'd told Ms. Ryan.

However, I should have asked someone before I'd talked to the police or the lawyer. I knew that. It was the first rule of the pack — keep your mouth shut around the mundanes.

I could have asked Uncle Mike how much I could tell the police — and the lawyer — rather than depending upon my own judgement. I hadn't . . . because I knew that if the police were going to look beyond Zee for a murderer, they'd have to know more than Uncle Mike or any other fae would have told them.

It is easier to ask for forgiveness than permission — unless you are dealing with the fae, who aren't much given to forgiveness. They see it as a Christian virtue — and they aren't particularly fond of Christian anything.

I didn't lie to myself that Zee would get over it. I might not know much about his history, but I did know him. He gathered his anger to him and made it as permanent as the tattoo on my belly. He'd never forgive me for betraying his trust.

I needed something to do, something to keep my hands and mind busy, to distract me from the sick feeling that I'd done something terrible. Unfortunately I'd stayed late and finished all the work I had at the shop on Friday, thinking I'd be spending most of Saturday at the music festival. I didn't even have a project car to work on. The current project, an old Karmann Ghia, was out getting the upholstery redone.

After pacing restlessly around the house and making a batch of peanut butter cookies, I went to the small third bedroom that served as my study, turned on the computer, and connected to the Internet before I started on brownies.

I answered e-mail from my sister and my mother and then browsed a bit. The brownie I brought into the room with me sat undisturbed on its plate. Just because I make food when I'm upset doesn't mean I can eat it.

I needed something to do. I ran through the conversation with Uncle Mike and decided that he probably really didn't know who had killed O'Donnell — though he was pretty sure it wasn't the ogres, or he wouldn't have mentioned them at all. I knew it wasn't Zee. Uncle Mike didn't think it was the Gray Lords — and I agreed with him. From the fae point of view, O'Donnell's murder was a screwup — a screwup that the Gray Lords could have easily avoided.

The old staff I'd found in the corner of O'Donnell's living room had something to do with the murder, though. It was important enough that the raven . . . no, what had Uncle Mike called it — the Carrion Crow — had come and taken it, and Uncle Mike hadn't wanted to talk about it.

I looked at the search engine screen that I used as my default page when I surfed the 'Net. Impulsively, I typed *staff* and *fairy* then hit the search button.

I got the results I should have expected had I thought about it. So I substituted *folklore* for *fairy,* but it wasn't until I tried *walking stick* (after *magic staff* and *magic stick*) that I found myself on a website with a small library of old fairy and folklore books scanned online.

I found my walking stick, or at least *a* walking stick.

It was given to a farmer who had the habit of leaving bread and milk on his back porch to feed the fairies. While he held that staff, each of his ewes gave birth to two healthy lambs every year and gave the farmer modest, if growing, prosperity. But (and there is always a "but" in fairy tales) one evening while walking over a bridge, the farmer lost his grip on the staff and it fell into the river and was swept away. When he got home, he found that his fields had flooded and killed most of his sheep — thus all the gain he'd gotten from the staff had left with it. He never found the staff again.

It wasn't likely that a staff that ensured all its owner's ewes had two healthy lambs each year was worth murdering people over —

especially as O'Donnell's killer hadn't taken it. Either the walking stick I'd found wasn't the same one, it wasn't as important as I had thought it might be, or O'Donnell's killer hadn't been after it. The only thing I was certain of was that O'Donnell had taken it from the murdered forest man.

The victims, even though they were mostly names, had been gradually becoming more real to me: Connora, the forest man, the selkie . . . It is a habit of humans to put labels on things, Zee always told me. Usually when I was trying to get him to tell me just who or what he was.

Impulsively, I typed in *dark smith* and *Drontheim* and found the story Samuel had told me about. I read it twice and sat back in my chair.

Somehow it fit. I could see Zee being perverse enough to create a sword that, once swung, would cut through whatever was in its path — including the person who was using it.

Still, there wasn't a Siebold or an Adelbert in the story. Zee's last name was Adelbertsmiter — smiter of Adelbert. I'd once heard a fae introduce him to another in a hushed voice as "*the* Adelbertsmiter."

On a whim I looked up *Adelbert* and laughed involuntarily. The first hit I had was

161

on Saint Adelbert, a Northumbrian missionary who sought to Christianize Norway in the eighth century. All I could find out about him was that he'd died a martyr's death.

Could he be Zee's Adelbert?

The phone rang, interrupting my speculations.

Before I had a chance to say anything, a very British voice said, "Mercy, you'd better get your butt over here."

There was a noise in the background — a roar. It sounded odd and I pulled my ear away from the phone long enough to confirm that I was hearing it from Adam's house as well as through the phone.

"Is that Adam?" I asked.

Ben didn't answer me, just yelped a swearword and hung up the phone.

It was enough to have me sprinting through my house and out my door, the phone still in my hand. I dropped it on the porch.

I was vaulting over the barbed wire fence that separated my three acres from Adam's larger field before it occurred to me to wonder why Ben had called *me* — and not asked for, say Samuel, who had the advantage of being a werewolf, one of the few more dominant than Adam.

CHAPTER 6

I didn't bother going around to the front of Adam's house, just opened the kitchen door and ran in. There was no one in the room.

Adam's kitchen had been built to *cordon bleu* specifications — Adam's daughter, Jesse, had once told me that her father could *really* cook, but mostly they didn't bother.

As in the rest of his house, Adam's ex-wife had chosen the decor. It had always struck me as odd that, except for the formal living room, which was done in shades of white, the colors in the house were much more welcoming and restful than she had ever been. My own house was decorated in parents' castoffs meet rummage sale with just enough nice stuff (courtesy of Samuel) to make everything else look horrible.

Adam's house smelled of lemon cleaner, Windex, and werewolves. But I didn't need my nose or ears to know that Adam was home — and he wasn't happy. The energy of his anger had washed over me even outside the house.

I heard Jesse whisper, "No, Daddy," from the living room.

It was not reassuring that the next sound I heard was a low growl, but then Ben wouldn't have called me if things had been good. I was pretty surprised he'd called me at all; he and I weren't exactly great friends.

I followed Jesse's voice into the living room. The werewolves were scattered all over the big room, but for a moment the Alpha's magic worked on me and all I could pay much attention to was Adam, even though he was facing away from me. The view was nice enough that it took me a moment to remember that this must be a crisis situation.

The only two humans in the room huddled together under Adam's intense regard on Adam's new antique fainting couch that had replaced the broken remains of his old antique fainting couch. If I had been Adam, I wouldn't have wasted money on antiques. Fragile things just don't fare well in the house of an Alpha werewolf.

One of the humans was Adam's daughter, Jesse. The other was Gabriel, the high school boy who worked for me. He had an arm around Jesse's shoulders, and her diminutive stature made him look bigger than he actually was. Sometime since I'd last seen her, Jesse had dyed her hair a cotton candy blue, which was cheerful, if a little odd. Her usual heavy makeup had slid down her face, striping it with metallic silver eye shadow, black mascara, and tearstains.

For a moment I thought the obvious. I'd warned Gabriel to be careful with Jesse and explained the downside of dating the Alpha's daughter. He'd heard me out and solemnly promised me that he'd behave himself.

Then I realized that under the streaks of makeup were the faint marks of new bruises. And part of what I'd thought was more mascara was actually a trickle of dried blood that ran from one nostril to her upper lip. One bare shoulder had a patch of road rash that still had gravel in it. No way that Gabriel had done that — and if he had, he wouldn't be living now.

Damn, I thought, growing cold. Someone was going to die today.

Gabriel's submissive posture must have been a reaction to something Adam had done, because as I watched him, he straightened his shoulders and lifted his gaze to Jesse's father's face. Not a really smart move with an enraged Alpha, but brave.

165

"Did *you* know them, Gabriel?" I couldn't see Adam's face, but his voice told me that his eyes would be bright gold.

I took another step into the room and a wave of his power almost sent me to my knees — as it did all of Adam's wolves, who fell to the floor almost as one. The motion made me actually look at them and realize that there weren't as many as I'd originally thought. Werewolves have a tendency to fill up the spaces in a room.

There were only four. Honey, one of the few women in Adam's pack, and her mate had their heads bowed and were holding each other's hands in a white-knuckled grip.

Darryl kept his face up and expressionless, but there were a few drops of perspiration on the mahogany skin of his forehead. Chinese and African blood ran in his veins and combined in a rather awesome mixture of color and feature. By day he was a researcher at the Pacific Northwest National Laboratory; the rest of the time he was Adam's second.

Next to Darryl, Ben looked as pale as his hair and almost fragile — though that was deceptive because he was tough as nails. Like Honey, he'd been gazing at the floor, but just after he'd dropped to the floor, he looked up and gave me a rather frantic look that I had no idea how to interpret.

Ben had fled England to Adam's pack to avoid questioning in a brutal multiple rape case. I was pretty sure he was innocent . . . but it says something about Ben that he'd have been my first suspect also.

"Daddy, leave Gabriel alone," said Jesse with a shadow of her usual spirit.

But neither Adam nor Gabriel paid attention to her protest.

"If I knew who they were and where to find them, sir, I wouldn't be here now," Gabriel said in a grim voice that made him sound thirty. "I'd have dropped Jesse off with you and gone after them."

Gabriel had grown up the oldest male in a house that had more than a passing acquaintance with abject poverty. It had made him driven, hardworking, and mature for his age. If I thought him reckless for going out with Jesse, I thought Jesse very wise for choosing him.

"Are you all right, Jesse?" I asked, my own voice more of a growl than I'd planned.

She looked up with a gasp. Then jumped up from her seat, where she'd been trying not to lean too close to Gabriel and give her father a target for his anger. She ran to me, burying her face in my shoulder.

Adam turned to look at us. Being a little

better versed in prudence than Gabriel (even if I used it only when it suited me), I dropped my gaze to Jesse's hair almost immediately, but I'd seen enough. His eyes blazed just this side of change, icy yellow, pale like the winter morning sun. White and red lines alternated on his wide cheekbones from the force he was using to clench his jaws.

If a news camera ever captured a shot of him looking like this, it would ruin all the spin-doctoring the werewolves had been doing over the last year. No one would ever mistake Adam in such a fury for anything except a very, very dangerous monster.

He wasn't just angry. I'm not sure there is an English word for just how much rage was in his face.

"You have to stop him," Jesse murmured as quietly as she could in my ear. "He'll kill them."

I could have told her that she couldn't whisper quietly enough that her father wouldn't hear, not when he was in the same room with us.

"You protect them!" he roared in outrage and I saw what little humanity he was clinging to disappear into the anger of the beast. If he hadn't been as dominant, if he hadn't been Alpha, I'm not sure he wouldn't have already changed. As it was, I could see the lines of his face begin to lose their solidity.

That's all we needed.

"No, no, no," Jesse chanted into my shoulder, her whole frame shaking. "They'll kill him if he hurts someone. He can't . . . he can't . . ."

I don't know what my mother intended when she sent me to be fostered with the werewolves on the advice of a cherished great-uncle who was a werewolf. I don't know that I could have given away my child to strangers. But I'm not a teenage single parent working a minimum wage job who'd discovered her baby could change into a coyote pup. It had worked out for me — at least as well as most people's childhoods. And it had left me with a certain skill for managing enraged werewolves, which was a good thing, my foster father had told me often enough, since I sure had a talent for enraging them.

Still, it was easier to deal with them when I wasn't what had set them off. The first step was to get their attention.

"That's enough," I said in firm, quiet tones that carried right over the top of Jesse's voice. I didn't need her warning to know that she was right. Adam would hunt down and kill whoever did this to his

169

daughter, and damned be the consequences. And the damned consequences would be fatal to him, and maybe to every werewolf anywhere.

I raised my eyes to meet Adam's fierce gaze and continued more sharply. "Don't you think you've done enough to her? What are you thinking? How long has she been here and no one has cleaned her wounds? Shame on you."

Guilt is a wonderful and powerful thing.

Then I turned, hauling Jesse, who stumbled in surprise, over to the stairs. If Darryl hadn't been in the room, I couldn't have left Gabriel. But Darryl was smart, Adam's second, and I knew he'd keep the boy out of the line of fire.

Besides, I didn't think Adam would stay in the living room for very long.

We made it only about three steps before I felt Adam's hot breath on the back of my neck. He didn't say anything, just stalked us all the way up to the upstairs bathroom. There seemed to be about a hundred steps more than the last time I'd come up here. Anything feels longer when you have a were-wolf behind you.

I sat Jesse down on the closed lid of the toilet and glanced back at Adam. "Go get me a washcloth."

He stood in the doorway for a moment, then turned and punched the door frame, which buckled. Maybe I should have said "please." I gave a worried glance upward, but other than a little plaster dust, the ceiling seemed unaffected.

Adam stared intently at the splinters that were splattered with blood from his split knuckles, though I don't think he really saw the damage he'd done.

I had to bite my lip to keep from saying something sarcastic like "Now that was helpful" or "Trying to keep the local carpenters in work?" When I get scared, my tongue gets sharp — which is not an asset around werewolves. Especially werewolves who are mad enough to take out doorways.

Jesse and I both waited, frozen, then he screamed, a sound more howl than human, and he hit the door frame again, and this time he took out the whole wall, his fist pushing through the remnants of the frame, the next two wall studs, and all the drywall between.

I risked a glance behind me. Jesse was so scared I could see the whites all the way around her eyes. I suspect she could have seen mine if she were looking at me instead of her father.

"Talk about overprotective fathers," I said

in a suitably amused tone. The lack of fear in my voice surprised me as much as anyone. Who'd have thought I was such a good actor?

Adam straightened and stared at me. I knew he wasn't as large as he looked — he wasn't that much taller than me — but in that hallway he was plenty big.

I met his gaze. "Could you get me a washcloth, please?" I asked as pleasantly as I could manage.

He turned on his heel and stalked silently toward his bedroom. Once he was out of sight, I realized that Darryl had followed us up the stairs. He leaned against the wall and closed his eyes, letting out two long breaths. I tucked my cold hands in my jeans.

"That was too damn close," he said, maybe to me, maybe to himself. But he didn't look at me as he pushed himself upright with a shrug of his shoulders and headed back down the stairs, taking them two at a time in a manner more common among high school boys than doctors of physics.

When I turned back to Jesse, she held a gray washcloth to me with a shaking hand.

"Hide that," I said. "Or he'll think I sent him away just to get rid of him."

She laughed, as I'd meant her to. It was

wobbly, and stopped abruptly when a cut broke open on her lip. But it was a laugh. She'd be all right.

Because I didn't really care if he knew I'd sent him on a useless errand, I took the washcloth and used it to thoroughly clean the scrape on her shoulder. There was another road rash on her back just above the waistline of her jeans.

"You want to tell me what happened?" I asked, rinsing the washcloth to get rid of the gravel on it.

"It was dumb."

I raised an eyebrow. "What? You thought you'd add some more color to your complexion so you punched yourself a couple of times and then skidded on the pavement?"

She rolled her eyes, so I guess I wasn't as funny as all that. "No. I was at Tumbleweed with some friends. Dad brought me over and dropped me off. I was supposed to get a ride back, but there were too many kids to fit in Kayla's car when we got to the parking lot. I'd forgotten my cell phone at home, so I started walking back to find a place to call."

She stopped talking. I handed her the washcloth so she could do her own face. "I've been running cold water over it; it should feel okay on your bruises. I think

173

your dad will feel better if you get cleaned up a bit. You'll look pretty bad tomorrow, but most of the bruising won't show for a couple hours yet."

She looked in the mirror and gave a gasp of dismay that reassured me that most of the damage was surface. She hopped off the toilet and opened the medicine cabinet and pulled out makeup remover.

"I can't believe Gabriel saw me looking like this," she muttered, dismayed, as she scrubbed at the mascara on her cheeks. "I look like a freak."

"Yep," I agreed.

She looked at me, started to laugh, and then her face crumpled again. "Tuesday, I have to go to school with them," she said.

"They were Finley kids?" I asked.

She nodded and went back to cleaning her face. "They said that they didn't want a freak in their school. I've known —"

I cleared my throat rather loudly, interrupting her — and she gave me a little smile. Her father could hear us, so it was better not to give him too many hints about her attackers. If they'd done more to her, I wouldn't be so concerned for them. But the incident wasn't worth people dying over it. What was needed was an education, not a murder. However, those boys needed to understand just how dumb attacking the Alpha's daughter was.

"I didn't expect it at all. Not from them," she said. "I don't know what they'd have done if Gabriel hadn't seen what was happening." She gave me a smile then, a real smile that didn't stop when she pressed the cold cloth against her lip, which was beginning to swell up pretty well. "You should have seen him. We were in that little parking lot behind the art gallery, you know, the one with the giant paintbrushes out front?"

I nodded.

"I guess Gabriel was walking on the little road below us and heard me cry out. He was up the hill and over the fence as fast as my father could have done it."

I doubted that — werewolves are fast. What I didn't doubt was that the effect of being rescued by someone like Gabriel, who, with his velvety brown skin, his black eyes, and his fair share of muscle, was not exactly hard on the eyes at any time.

"You know," I told her with a conspiratorial smile, "it's probably a good thing that he didn't know who they were, either."

"I'll find out," said Gabriel behind my right shoulder.

I'd heard him coming. Maybe I should have warned her, but he deserved to hear the hero worship in her voice. He wasn't the only one in the hall, but the wolves, who'd all followed him up, were keeping out of Jesse's sight.

Gabriel gave me an ice pack and watched Jesse duck behind the washcloth to hide her blush. His face was set. "I could have caught up to them, but I wasn't sure how badly hurt Jesse was. Cowards —" He started to spit, then realized where he was and restrained himself. "Takes a pair of real macho men to pick on a girl half their size."

He looked at me. "On the way home, Jesse said that she thought she'd been set up. Those girls she was with, one of them, the girl with the car, has a thing for one of the boys. And the boys knew where to wait for her. There aren't many places you could beat someone up without people seeing them. They'd pulled her behind one of those big dumpsters. Someone put a lot of planning into this."

Finley High is a small school.

"Do you want to transfer to Kennewick High?" I asked her, knowing that her father was listening from the bedroom. I couldn't hear him, but I could feel his intent and see it in the stiff postures of the wolves. If we weren't very careful, the whole pack would be after those stupid boys.

"Gabriel goes to Kennewick, and I know he has a lot of friends who will watch out for you. Or you could go to Richland, where Aurielle teaches." Aurielle was another of Adam's three female wolves, Darryl's mate, and a high school chemistry teacher.

Jesse whipped the washcloth off her face and gave me a look that reminded me that she was her father's daughter. "I wouldn't give them the satisfaction," she said coldly. "But they won't take me by surprise again. I fought like a girl because I couldn't believe they were really going to hit me. I won't make that mistake again either."

"You'll have to start practicing aikido again, then," said Adam, his voice as quiet and calm as if he hadn't just thrown a hissy fit a few minutes ago. "You're three years out of practice, and if you are only half their weight, you'll have to do better than that."

He walked out of his bedroom, a dark blue washcloth in his hand. If his eyes had been darker, I'd have bought the calm facade. He'd managed somehow to stuff all that anger and Alpha energy down and out of sight. But I'd believe the cold yellow eyes before I believed the quiet voice. He handed me the washcloth, but his gaze was on Jesse.

"Yes," she said with grim determination.

"She hurt them," Gabriel said. "One of

them had a bloody nose and the other was holding on to his side while he ran off." He gave her an assessing look, which I was glad Adam didn't see. "I bet they're more hurt than she is."

Darryl cleared his throat, and when Adam looked at him, he said, "Send her with an escort to and from school." Jesse was a general favorite. If Adam hadn't been so enraged, there would have been a lot more growls from the wolves. Darryl's eyes were lighter than they usually were, too. The gold was eerie in his dark face.

"Send her with a werewolf," I suggested, "in wolf form. For the first few days he can wait for her in front of the school, somewhere very visible."

"No," said Jesse. "I won't be a freak show."

Adam raised an eyebrow. "You'll do as you're told."

"It's a territorial thing," I told Jesse. "Even mundane people play those stupid games. They tried a power play and your father cannot just let it go. If he does, the harassment will get worse — until someone dies." That's what all the werewolf politics and posturing that I complained about so much really did, kept people alive.

"You should call the police and the school and warn them," said Honey. "So no one gets hurt."

"Do a show and tell," suggested Gabriel. "Call Jesse's biology teacher — or aren't you taking a course in Current Affairs? That would be better. You can take your class out and give them an up-close and personal with a werewolf. Same effect but less embarrassing for Jesse."

Adam smiled, showing lots of teeth. "I like that."

Jesse brightened a little. "Maybe I can get extra credit."

"The school will never go for it," Darryl said. "The liability is too great if something happened."

"I'll check into it," Adam said.

Jesse was a little pale, but she wasn't seriously injured. A hot shower would help with the soreness — and she needed to shower before her father calmed down enough to realize that she didn't need to tell him who had attacked her. If I could get their scent, so could he.

I made a dismissive gesture at the whole lot of them, Gabriel, Adam, and werewolves. "Go downstairs and work it out," I told them. "I want to get a better look at some of Jesse's bruises so I can make sure that she doesn't need Samuel to come check her out."

I took Jesse by the hand. "We'll use Adam's bathroom . . ." I couldn't actually remember if he had a bathroom, but I couldn't imagine that this house didn't have a master bedroom suite, and besides, he'd come out of it with a washcloth. "Since Adam has chosen to remodel this one." Sure my tone was a little snide — but if he was irritated with me, he wasn't going to be thinking about finding Jesse's assailants.

Jesse followed me through the crowded hallway and into Adam's bedroom. There was an open door on the far side that could only be a bathroom. I tugged her into it and shut the door.

Then I whispered, very, very quietly, "You need to shower and get rid of their scent before your father thinks of it — if he already hasn't."

Her eyes widened. "Clothes?" she mouthed.

"Everything," I said.

She gave her tennis shoes a rueful glance, but turned on the shower and stepped into the big stall, shoes, clothes, and all.

"I'll go get clean clothes," I told her.

Adam met me at the hall doorway. He jerked his chin toward the bathroom, where anyone could clearly hear that someone was showering. "Scent," he said.

"Her clothes were very dirty," I told him a little smugly. "Even her shoes."

"Sh—" He bit it off before he could complete the word. Adam was a little older than he looked. He'd been raised in the fifties, when a man didn't swear in front of women. "Shoot," he said, the word obviously not giving him the satisfaction to be gotten out of cruder terms.

"Cheeses crusty, got all musty, got damp on the stone of a peach," I agreed. He looked blank, so I repeated it with proper emphasis. "*ChEEZ*-zes crusty. Got *Al*-musty. Got DAMp on the StoneofapeaCH. My foster father used to say those around me all the time. He was an old-fashioned sort of wolf, too. He especially liked the Stoneofapeach. 'Stoneofapeach, Mercedes. You don't have the sense God gave little apples.' "

Adam closed his eyes and leaned his forehead against the door frame.

"Gonna be expensive if you break another wall," I offered helpfully.

He opened his eyes and looked at me.

I threw up my hands. "Fine. You want to support the Carpenters' Union, that's your business. Now move, I told Jesse I'd be back with clothes."

He stepped back with exaggerated courtesy. But when I walked past him, he swatted my rump. Hard enough to sting.

"You need to be more careful," he growled. "Keep interfering in my business and you might get hurt."

I said sweetly as I continued to Jesse's room, "The last man who swatted me like that is rotting in his grave."

"I have no doubt of it." His voice was more satisfied than contrite.

I turned to face him, yellow eyes and all.

"I'm thinking of picking up a parts car for the Syncro. I have plenty of room in the field."

Someone listening in might have thought my last comment was off topic, but Adam knew better. I'd been punishing him with my Rabbit parts car for several years. Clearly visible from his bedroom window, it now sat on three tires and had various pieces missing. The graffiti was Jesse's suggestion.

If Adam hadn't been as uptight, it wouldn't have worked — but he was one of those "everything in its place and a place for everything" kind of people. It bothered him — a lot.

Adam grinned briefly in appreciation, then his face sobered. "Tell me you, at least, had the brains to catch their scent."

I raised an eyebrow. "Why would I do that? Then instead of harassing Jesse, you'd be tormenting me."

One of them had been a stranger to me, but the other . . . there was something about his scent that was ringing a bell, but I'd wait until I was out of here before I tried to work it out.

He gave a bark of fierce laughter.

"Liar," he said.

He took two quick steps forward, wrapped a hand around the back of my neck, and held me for his kiss. I hadn't expected it — not while he was still so close to changing. I'm sure that's why I didn't pull out of his hold.

The first touch of his lips was soft, tentative, asking where his hands had demanded. The man was diabolical. I could have resisted force, but the question of his kiss was an entirely different matter.

I leaned into him because he asked with the light touch and the gentle withdrawal of his lips that begged me to follow where he led. The heat of his body, welcome in the overcooled house, rewarded me as I leaned closer to him, as did the hard planes of his body, so I was drawn to press even tighter against him.

He danced like that, too. Leading instead

of pulling. It had to have been deliberate, something he worked at, because he was as dominant as they came — Alphas are. But Adam was more than just dominant: he was smart, too. And he didn't play fair.

Which is how he ended up against the wall with me plastered all over him when someone . . . Darryl, quietly cleared his throat.

I jerked free and hopped back to the middle of the hallway. "I'll just get Jesse's clothes now," I told the carpet on the floor and then took my red face into Jesse's room and shut the door. I didn't mind getting caught kissing, but that had been a lot more carnal than a kiss.

Sometimes good hearing isn't a blessing.

"Sorry," Darryl said, though his voice carried more amusement than apology.

"I bet," growled Adam. "Damn it. This has got to stop."

Darryl gave a full-throated laugh that lasted quite a while. I'd never heard him laugh like that. Darryl was pretty uptight usually.

"Sorry," he said again, sounding more apologetic this time. "Looked to me like you'd rather it not stop."

"Yeah." Adam sounded suddenly tired. "I should have gone after her a long time ago. But after Christy got through with me, I

184

wasn't sure I wanted another woman ever. And Mercy is more gun-shy than I ever was." Christy was his ex-wife.

"Then Samuel came to compete for the prize," Darryl said.

"I am not a prize," I muttered.

I knew they both heard me, but all he said was, "Samuel has always been the competition. I prefer him here, so at least I'm competing with a flesh-and-blood man, and not a memory."

"If you're going to talk about me behind my back," I told Adam, "at least do it where I can't hear you."

They must have followed my request because I didn't hear any more of their conversation. The shower was still going, so I sat down in the middle of Jesse's room — pulled a bottle of nail polish out from under one hip — and then took the opportunity to pull myself together. Adam was right; this had gone on too long.

Samuel had been behaving himself like an angel, for the most part — and Adam had been likewise. But it seemed to me that Adam had been more restless than usual and his temper more uncertain.

That was troubling news because Adam had a hot temper, worse even than most werewolves. Otherwise, Samuel had told me, the Marrok would have used Adam more heavily as one of the spokesmen for the werewolves. He had the looks and the speaking abilities for it. Adam had attracted some attention from the press anyway because he was doing some consulting and negotiating in Washington, D.C. His control was very, very good, but when he lost it, he went berserk and the Marrok wouldn't risk it.

I was pretty sure that Adam would have exploded over Jesse's bruises anyway — but maybe he'd have regained his control better if he hadn't already been on edge.

Jesse's door opened and Honey came in, shutting the door behind her. Honey was one of those people who can make me feel grubby, even when I'm wearing a perfectly presentable T-shirt. She could have been a recruitment poster model for the trophy wife. She intimidated me in an entirely different way than the werewolves usually did, and it had taken me a long time to get over it.

She stepped gingerly over the usual teenager mess that Jesse had scattered on her floor — Jesse's room looked even worse than mine usually did, which made it pretty bad.

"You've got to do something, Mercedes,"

she told me softly. As long as the rest of the pack was downstairs, they wouldn't hear us. "The whole pack is restless and short-tempered — and Adam almost lost it today. Pick someone, Adam or Samuel, it doesn't matter. But you have to do it soon." She hesitated. "When Adam declared you his mate —"

For my safety, he said, and he was probably right. Timber wolves will kill a coyote in their territory — and werewolves are every bit as territorial as their smaller brethren.

"He didn't ask me," I interrupted her, with heat. "I wasn't there and I didn't find out about it until it was done. It wasn't my fault."

She shook her mane of honey-colored hair and crouched down beside me. If she could have seen the floor, I think she'd have been sitting like I was, because she was technically lower in the pack (thanks to Adam declaring me his mate), but she was too fastidious to sit on a pile of dirty clothes.

"I'm not saying it is anyone's fault," she said. "Fault doesn't change what is. We can all feel it, the weakness in the pack. It is allowed for you to refuse him absolutely, and then things will return to normal. Or accept him, and things will change another way, a better way. But until then . . ." She shrugged.

It was easy, even for someone like me who was around them all the time, to forget that there was more to the magic of the werewolves than their change. I think it's because the change was so spectacular — and the rest of the magic is the pack's business and affects no one else. I didn't consider myself pack — and until Adam had made his claim, no one else had either.

My foster father told me once that he was always aware on some level of all the other pack members. They knew when one of their own was in distress; they knew when one died. When my foster father committed suicide, it took a while for them to find the body, but they'd all known when to go looking. I'd seen Adam call his pack to him with more than the sound of his voice and had seen them heal him of silver damage that should have killed him.

I hadn't realized that there might be more to Adam declaring me his mate than the simple act until I'd been able to help Warren control his wolf when he was too hurt to do it himself. I'd been grateful, but I hadn't looked at it any closer.

I was getting a headache; dread sometimes does that to me. "Tell me that again and be clear, please."

"When he declared you his mate, he offered you an invitation to join us. He opened a place for you that you have not filled. That opening is a weakness. Adam mostly keeps it from us, but he only does it by absorbing all of the effects himself. His wolf knows there is a weakness, a place where harm might come to us, and it leaves him on alert, on edge, all the time. We can feel that, and respond to it." She gave me a tight smile. "That's why I was so unpleasant to you when he sent me to play bodyguard against the vampires. I thought you were playing games and leaving us to pay the price."

No. No game playing. Just a lot of panicking. Whomever I chose in the end, Adam or Samuel, I'd lose the other one — and that was more than I could bear.

"All of us depend upon our Alpha to help us live among the humans," Honey said. "Some of Adam's wolves have human women as mates. It is his willpower that allows us to control ourselves, particularly as the moon nears her zenith."

I put my aching head on my knees. "What was he thinking? Damn it."

She patted me on the shoulder, an awkward touch that managed to convey both comfort and sympathy. "I don't think he was thinking of anything except to place his claim on you before another wolf killed or claimed you."

I gave her a look of disbelief. "What is going on? Is everyone losing their minds? I haven't had so much as a date for ten years and now there's Adam and Samuel and —" I'd have bitten off my tongue before I continued and mentioned Stefan. I hadn't seen the vampire since he and the Wizard had killed two innocents to take the blame for killing Andre so Marsilia didn't kill me. It was just as well as he wasn't my favorite person.

"I know why Samuel wants me," I told her.

"He thinks that the two of you could have children — and you can't forgive him for wanting you for practical reasons." There was something in Honey's voice that told me that she liked Samuel — and maybe it hadn't been just my perceived "game playing" with Adam and her pack that she'd resented. But the expression on her face told me more. She understood Samuel's point from experience; she wanted children, too.

I don't know why I started talking to Honey. I didn't know her that well — and had spent most of that time disliking her.

Maybe it was because there was no one else I knew who was in a position to understand.

"I don't blame Samuel for realizing that a shapeshifter who changed into a coyote and was not bound by the moon might be a good mate," I told her, speaking very quietly. "But he let me love him without telling me exactly why he was so interested. If the Marrok hadn't interfered, I'd probably have been his mate when I was sixteen."

"Sixteen?" she said.

I nodded.

"Peter is a lot older than me," she said, speaking of her husband. "That was hard. But I wasn't sixteen and . . ." She paused, thinking. Finally she shook her head. "I don't recall ever hearing how old Samuel is, but he's older than Charles, and Charles dates back to Lewis and Clark."

The outrage that filtered into her voice, still pitched not to carry to the other werewolves, was like a balm. It gave me the courage to tell her a bit more.

"I am happy with who I am," I told her. "The incident with Samuel let me break with the pack and join the human world. I'm independent and good at my job. It's not glamorous, but I like fixing things."

"And still," she said, voicing the thing I hadn't said.

I nodded. "Exactly. And still . . . what if I'd taken him up on his offer? I tell myself that I'd be a lesser person, but Samuel isn't the kind of man to iron all the personality out of his wife. Half the trouble I got into when I was a teen he got me into — and got me out of the other half."

"So you'd be a doctor's wife, and free to do as you please — because Samuel's not the control freak that most of the dominant males are."

There it was. Oh, not Samuel. She, like most people, saw what he wanted them to see. Gentle, laid-back Samuel. Hah.

But, I'd always wondered why Honey had married her husband, who was so far down in the pack power structure when she was as dominant as all but the top two or three wolves. Since she took her rank from her husband, she was a lot lower than she'd been before she'd taken Peter as her mate. There weren't actually all that many submissive wolves out there. The kind of determination it takes to survive the Change isn't usually found in a person who isn't at least a little dominant.

"Samuel is as much a control freak as any of them. He just hides it better," I said. "The reality of it is that he'd have wrapped me in cotton wool and protected me from the world. I'd never have grown or become the person I am."

She raised an eyebrow. "Like what, a mechanic? You work for less than minimum wage. I saw Gabriel do the paychecks — he clears more than you do."

I'd been wrong. She'd never understand.

"Like owning my own business," I told her, though I knew it was futile to expect her to comprehend what I meant. I'd turned down everything that she'd wanted out of life — status, both in the werewolf world and the human one, and money. "Like being able to take something that doesn't work and fix it. Like being able to hold my own with Adam today instead of falling on my knees and looking at the ground. Like deciding what I'm going to do every day — including going after that demon-riding vampire who almost killed Warren. I'm not all that, especially not compared to the werewolves, but you have to admit that I was uniquely suited to taking him out. The werewolves couldn't. The vampires and fae wouldn't. What would have happened if I hadn't been able to kill him? Samuel would never let his wife risk her life to do something like that."

I realized something then. As scary as it had been (and I had the nightmares and the scars to prove it), as stupidly dangerous as it still was — and possibly deadly — I was proud of killing those two vampires. No one else would have been able to do it. Just me.

Samuel would never let me do something like that.

I could never have Samuel without giving up something I cherished about myself. It was the first time I'd let myself look at that because then I'd have to admit that Samuel could never be for me.

The question was, would Adam be any better? And if I took Adam, Samuel would leave. Part of me still loved Samuel, and I was not ready to give him up.

I was so screwed.

"You think that Adam would have let you go after that thing if you were his mate?" asked Honey in disbelief.

Maybe.

"I didn't mean to walk in on anything," said Jesse in a small voice.

I realized that I hadn't been hearing the water from the shower for a while. I hadn't heard her approach either.

She'd wrapped a towel around herself, but she was still quick at closing the door behind her. She gave Honey a wary look, but then dismissed her.

"I overheard that last part," she told me.

"Dad told me to stay out of his affairs. But I thought you ought to know that he told me not too long ago that if you don't fall out of a plane now and then, you never learn to fly."

"He gave me bodyguards," I told her dryly. Honey had been one of them.

She rolled her eyes at me. "He's not stupid. But if there is something you have to do, he'll be at your back." I gave her an incredulous look and she rolled her eyes again. "Okay, okay, he'll lead the way. But he won't make you stay behind. He doesn't waste his resources that way."

When Jesse had been missing, and Adam too hurt to do anything about it, he'd all but recruited me to find her, knowing that the people who had her had almost killed him. For some reason that recollection let me breathe deeply again.

Knowing that I could not have Samuel hurt. I think giving up Adam might just break me — which didn't mean that I might not have to anyway.

I hopped to my feet.

"I'll keep it in mind," I told her and then changed the subject. "How are you feeling?"

She smiled and held out a rock-steady hand. "I'm fine. You were right; a hot shower really helped. I'll have some bruises, but

I'm all right. Gabriel helped, too. He's right. I did defend myself, better than they expected. I know to watch for them now and . . ." Her smile widened just short of splitting her lip again. "Dad's given me bodyguards." She said it in the same exasperated tones I used.

CHAPTER 7

Sometimes it seems like the distance between Adam's house and mine changes. Just an hour or so earlier, it had taken me only a moment to get from my door to his. It took me a long time to walk back home and I mourned all the way.

I would not choose Samuel. Not because I didn't trust him, but because I could trust him absolutely. He would love me and care for me, until I chewed off my arm to be free — and I wouldn't be the only person I'd hurt. Samuel had been damaged enough without me adding to it.

When I told him how I felt, he would leave.

I hoped he would still be gone, but his car was parked next to my rust-colored Rabbit. I stopped in the driveway, but it was already too late. He'd know I was outside.

I didn't have to tell him today, I thought. I wouldn't have to lose him today. But soon.

Very soon.

Warren and Honey were right. If I didn't do something soon, blood would flow. It was a testament to the control both Adam and Samuel had, that there had been no fighting up until now. I knew in my heart of hearts, if it ever came down to a real fight between them, one of them would die.

I could bear losing Samuel again if I had to, but I could not bear being the cause of his death. And I was certain that it was Samuel who would die in a fight with Adam. Not that Adam was a better fighter. I'd seen Samuel in a fight or ten, and he knew what he was doing. But Adam had an edge of ruthlessness that Samuel lacked. Adam was a soldier, a killer, and Samuel a healer. He would hold back until it was too late.

The screen door of the house creaked and I looked up into Samuel's gray eyes. He wasn't a handsome man, but there was a beauty to his long features and ash brown hair that went bone deep.

"What put that look on your face?" Samuel asked. "Something wrong at Adam's house?"

"A couple of bigoted kids beat up on Jesse," I told him. It wasn't a lie. He wouldn't know that I was just answering his second question, not his first.

For an instant anger flew across his face — he liked Jesse, too. Then his control reasserted itself, and Dr. Cornick was on the spot and ready for action.

"She's all right," I told him before he said anything. "Just bruises and hurt feelings. We were worried for a bit that Adam was going to do murder, but I think we've got him settled down."

He came down off the porch and touched my face. "Just a few rough minutes, eh? I'd better go check Jesse over anyway."

I nodded. "I'll get something on for supper."

"No," he said. "You look like you could use some cheering up. Adam in a rage and Zee locked up, both in one day, is a little much. Why don't you get cleaned up and I'll take you out for pizza and company."

The pizza place was stuffed full of people and musical instrument cases. I took my glass of pop and Samuel's beer and went looking for two empty seats while he paid for our food.

After Tumbleweed shut down on Sunday night, their last night, all the performers and all the people who'd put it on apparently gathered together for one last hurrah

— and they'd invited Samuel, who'd invited me. They made quite an impressive crowd — and didn't leave very many empty seats.

I had to settle for an already occupied table with two empty chairs. I leaned down and put my lips near the ear of the man sitting with his back to me. It was too intimate for a stranger, but there was no choice. A human ear wouldn't have picked up my voice in this din from any farther away.

"Are those seats taken?" I asked.

The man looked up and I realized he wasn't as much of a stranger as I thought . . . on two levels. First, he was the one who had complained about Samuel's Welsh, Tim Someone with a last name that was Central European. Second, he had been one of the men in O'Donnell's house, Cologne Man, in fact.

"No problem," he said loudly.

It could be coincidence. There could be a thousand people in the Tri-Cities who wore that particular cologne; maybe it didn't smell as bad to someone who didn't have my nose.

This was a man who knew Tolkien's Elvish and Welsh (though not as well as he thought he did, if he was critical of Samuel's). Hardly qualifications for a fae-hating bigot. He was more likely one of the fae aficionados who made the owner of the little fae bar in Walla Walla so much money, and had turned the reservation in Nevada into another Las Vegas.

I thanked him and took the seat nearest the wall, leaving the outside one for Samuel. Maybe he wasn't one of O'Donnell's Bright Future crowd. Maybe he was the killer — or a police officer.

I smiled politely and took a good look at him. He wasn't in bad shape, but he was certainly human. He couldn't possibly have beheaded a man without an ax.

So, not a Bright Futurean, nor a killer. He was either just a man who shared poor taste in cologne with someone who was in O'Donnell's house, or a police officer.

"I'm Tim Milanovich," he said, all but shouting to get his voice over the sound of all the other people talking, as he extended his arm carefully around his beer and over his pizza. "And this is my friend Austin. Austin Summers."

"Mercedes Thompson." I shook his hand — and the other young man's hand as well. The second man, Austin Summers, was more interesting than Tim Milanovich.

If he'd been a werewolf, he'd have been on the dominant side. He had the same subtle appeal of a really good politician. Not so handsome that people noticed it, but good-looking in a rugged football player way. Medium brown hair, several shades lighter than mine, and root beer brown eyes completed the picture. He was a few years younger than Tim, I thought, but I could see why Tim was hanging around him.

It was too crowded for me to get a good handle on Austin's scent when he was sitting across the table, but impulsively, I managed to move the hand I'd used to shake his against my nose as if I had an itch — and abruptly the evening turned into something besides an outing to keep my mind off my worries.

This man had been at O'Donnell's house — and I knew why one of Jesse's attackers had smelled familiar.

Scent is a complicated thing. It is both a single identification marker and an amalgam of many scents. Most people use the same shampoo, deodorant, and toothpaste all the time. They clean their houses with the same cleaners; they wash their clothes with the same laundry soap and dry them with the same dryer sheets. All these scents combine with their own personal scent to make up their distinctive smell.

This Austin wasn't the man who'd attacked Jesse. He was too old, a couple of

202

years out of high school at least, and not quite the right scent — but he lived in the same household. A lover or a brother, I thought, and put money on the brother.

Austin Summers. I would remember that name and see if I could come up with an address. Hadn't there been a Summers boy that Jesse had had a crush on last year? Before the werewolves had admitted to their existence. Back when Adam had just been a moderately wealthy businessman. John, Joseph . . . something biblical . . . Jacob Summers. That was it. No wonder she was so upset.

I sipped my pop and glanced up at Tim, who was eating a slice of pizza. I'd have bet my last nickel that he wasn't a police officer — he had none of the usual tells that mark a cop and he wasn't in the habit of carrying a gun. Even if they are unarmed, police officers always smell a little of gunpowder.

The odds of Tim being Cologne Man had just made it near a hundred percent. So what was a man who loved Celtic folk songs and languages doing in the house of a man who hated the largely Celtic fae?

I smiled at Tim and said sincerely, "Actually, Mr. Milanovich, we sort of met this weekend. You were talking to Samuel after his performance."

There were places where my Native American skin and coloring made me memorable, but not in the Tri-Cities, where I blended in nicely with the Hispanic population.

"Call me Tim," he said, while trying frantically to place me.

Samuel saved him from continued embarrassment by his arrival.

"Here you are," he said to me after murmuring an apology to someone trying to walk through the narrow aisle in the opposite direction. "Sorry it took me so long, Mercy, but I took a minute to stop and talk." He set a little red plastic marker with a black *34* on top of the table next to Tim's pizza. "Mr. Milanovich," he said as he sat down next to me. "Good to see you."

Of course Samuel would remember his name; he was like that. Tim was flattered to be recognized; it was written all over his earnest face.

"And this is Austin Summers," I yelled pleasantly, louder than I needed to, since Samuel's hearing was at least as good as mine. "Austin, meet the folksinging physician, Dr. Samuel Cornick." Ever since I heard them introduce him as "the folksinging physician," I'd known he hated it — and I'd known I had to use it.

Samuel gave me an irritated look before turning a blandly smiling expression to the men we shared the table with.

I kept a genial expression on my face to conceal my triumph at irritating him while Samuel and Tim fell into a discussion of common themes in English and Welsh folk songs; Samuel charming and Tim pedantic. Tim spoke less and less as they continued.

I noticed that Austin watched his friend and Samuel with the same pleasantly interested expression that I'd adopted, and I wondered what he was thinking about that he felt he had to conceal.

A tall man stood up on a chair and gave a whistle that would have cut through a bigger crowd than this one. When everyone was silent, he welcomed us, said a few words of thanks to various people responsible for the Tumbleweed.

"Now," he said, "I know that you all know the Scallywags . . ." He bent down and picked up a bodhran. He sprayed the drumhead with a small water bottle and then spread the water around with a hand as he spoke with a studied casualness that drew attention. "Now the Scallywags have been singing here since the very first Tumbleweed — and I happen to know something about them that you all don't."

205

"What's that?" someone shouted from the crowd.

"That their fair singer, Sandra Hennessy, has a birthday today. And it's not just any birthday."

"I'll get you for this," a woman's voice rang out. "You just see if I don't, John Martin."

"Sandra is turning forty today. I think she needs a birthday dirge, whatd'you all think?"

The crowd erupted into applause that quickly settled into anticipatory silence.

"Hap-py birthday." He sang the minor notes of the opening of the "Volga Boatmen" in a gloriously deep bass that needed no mike to carry over the crowd, then hit the bodhran once with a small double-headed mallet. THUMP.

"It's your birthday." THUMP.

"Gloom and doom and dark despair,

"People dying everywhere.

"Happy birthday." THUMP. *"It's your birthday."*

Then the rest of the room, including Samuel, started to sing the mournful tune with great cheer.

There were well over a hundred people in the room, and most of them were professional musicians. The whole restaurant vibrated like a tuning fork as they managed to turn the silly song into a choral piece.

Once the music started, it didn't stop. Instruments came out to join the bodhran: guitars, banjos, a violin, and a pair of Irish penny whistles. As soon as one song finished, someone stood up and started another, with the crowd falling in on the chorus.

Austin had a fine tenor. Tim couldn't sing on pitch if his life depended upon it, but there were enough people singing that it didn't matter. I sang until our pizza arrived, then I ate while everyone else sang.

Finally, I got up to refill my soda, and by the time I returned, Samuel had borrowed a guitar and was at the far end of the room leading a rousing chorus of a ribald drinking song.

The only one left at our table was Tim.

"We've been deserted," he said. "Your Dr. Cornick was summoned to play, and Austin's gone out to the car to get his guitar."

I nodded. "Once you get him singing" — I waved vaguely to indicate Samuel — "you're in for it for a while."

"Are the two of you dating?" he asked, rolling the Parmesan jar between his hands before setting it down.

I turned to look at Samuel, who was singing a verse alone. His fingers flew on the neck of the borrowed guitar and there was a wide grin on his face.

"Yes," I said, though we weren't really. And wouldn't now. It was less complicated just to say yes rather than explain our situation.

"He's a very good musician," Tim said. Then, his voice so quiet I knew I wasn't supposed to hear him, he murmured, "Some people have all the luck."

I turned back to him and said, "What was that?"

"Austin's a pretty good guitarist, too," he said quickly. "He tried to teach me, but I'm all thumbs." He smiled like it didn't matter, but the skin around his eyes was taut with bitterness and envy.

How interesting, I thought. How could I use this to pry information from him?

"I know how you feel," I confided, sipping my pop. "I was practically raised with Samuel." Except that Samuel had been an adult several times over. "I can plunk a bit on the piano if someone forces me. I can even sing on key — but no matter how hard I worked at it" — not very — "I could never sound as good as Samuel. And he never even had to practice." I let a sharp note linger in my voice, a twin to the jealousy he'd revealed. "Everything is so easy for that man."

Zee had told me not to help him.

Uncle Mike told me to stay out of it.

But then I'd never been very good at listening to orders — ask anyone.

Tim looked at me — and I saw him register me as a real person for the first time. "Exactly," he said — and he was mine.

I asked him where he'd learned Welsh, and he visibly expanded as he answered.

Like a lot of people who didn't have many friends, his social skills were a little lacking, but he was smart — and under all that earnest geekiness, funny. Samuel's vast knowledge and charm had made Tim close up and turn into a jerk. With a little encouragement, and maybe the two glasses of beer he'd drunk, Tim relaxed and quit trying to impress me. Before I knew it, I found myself forgetting for a while that I had ulterior motives and got into a spirited argument about the tales of King Arthur.

"The stories came out of the courts of Eleanor of Aquitaine. They were to teach men how to behave in a civilized fashion," Tim said earnestly.

A caller with more volume than tone on the other side of the room called out, *"King Louie was the king of France before the Revolu-shy-un!"*

"Sure," I said. "Cheat on your husband

and your best friend. The only way to find love is through adultery. All good civilized behavior."

Tim smiled at my quip, but had to wait as the whole room responded, *"Weigh haul away, haul away Joe."*

"Not that," he said, "but that people should strive to better themselves and to do the right thing."

"Then he got his head cut off, it spoiled his constitu-shy-un!"

I had to hurry to slip in before the chorus. "Like sleep with your sister and beget your downfall?"

"Weigh haul away, haul away Joe."

He gave a frustrated huff. "Arthur's story isn't the only one in the Arthurian cycle or even the most important. Parcival, Gawain, and half a dozen others were more popular."

"Okay," I said. We were getting our timing down now and I started to tune out the music completely. "I'll give you the urge to do heroic deeds, but the pictures they painted of women were right along the lines the Church held. Women lead men astray, and they will betray you as soon as you give them your trust." He started to say something but I was in the middle of a thought and didn't pause. "But it's not their fault — that's just what women do as a result of their weaker natures." I knew better actually, but it was fun to rant.

"That's a simplification," he said hotly. "Maybe the popular versions that were retold in the middle twentieth century ignore most of the women. But just go read some of the original authors like Hartman von Aue or Wolfram von Eschenbach. Their women are real people, not just reflections of the Church's ideals."

"I'll give you Eschenbach," I conceded. "But von Aue, no. His *Iweine* is about a knight who gave up adventuring because he loved his wife — for which he must atone. So he goes out and rescues women to regain his proper manly state. Ugh. You don't see any of his women rescuing themselves." I waved my hand. "And you can't escape that the central Arthurian story revolves around Arthur, who marries the most beautiful woman in the land. She sleeps with his best friend — thereby ruining the two greatest knights who ever lived and bringing about the downfall of Camelot, just as Eve brought about the downfall of mankind. Robin Hood was much better. Maid Marian saves herself from Sir Guy of Gisbourne, then goes out and slays a deer and fools Robin when she disguises herself as a man."

He laughed, a low attractive sound that

seemed to take him as much by surprise as it did me. "Okay. I give up. Guinevere was a loser." His smile slowly died as he looked behind me.

Samuel put his hand on my shoulder and leaned close. "Everything all right?"

There was a stiffness in his voice that had me turning a little warily to look at him.

"I came to rescue you from boredom," he said, but his eyes were on Tim.

"Not bored," I assured him with a pat. "Go play music."

Then he looked at me.

"Go," I said firmly. "Tim's keeping me entertained. I know you don't get much chance to play with other musicians. Go."

Samuel had never been the kind of person who put on graphic public displays of affection. So it took me by surprise when he bent over me and gave me an open-mouth kiss that started out purely for Tim's benefit. It didn't stay there for very long.

One thing about living a long time, Samuel told me once, it gave you a lot of time to practice.

He smelled like Samuel. Clean and fresh, and though he hadn't been back to Montana for a while, he still smelled of home. Much better than Tim's cologne.

And still . . . and still.

This afternoon, talking to Honey, I'd finally admitted that a relationship between Samuel and I would not work. That admission was making several other things clear.

I loved Samuel. Loved him with all my heart. But I had no desire to tie myself to him for the rest of my life. Even if there had been no Adam, I did not feel that way about him.

So why had it taken me so long to admit it?

Because Samuel needed me. In the fifteen years more or less between the day I'd run away from him and last winter when I'd finally seen him again, something in Samuel had broken.

Old werewolves are oddly fragile. Many of them go berserk and have to be killed. Others pine and starve themselves to death — and a starving werewolf is a very dangerous thing.

Samuel still said and did all the right things, but sometimes it seemed to me that he was following a script. As if he'd think, this should bother me or I should care about that and he'd react, but it was a little off or too late. And when I was coyote, her sharper instincts told me that he was not healthy.

I was deathly afraid that if I told him I

would not take him for a mate and he believed me, he would go off someplace and die.

Despair and desperation made my response to his kiss a little wild.

I couldn't lose Samuel.

He pulled away from me, a hint of surprise in his eyes. He was a werewolf after all; doubtless he'd caught some of the grief I felt. I reached up and touched his cheek.

"Sam," I said.

He mattered to me, and I was going to lose him. Either now, or when I destroyed us both fighting the gentle, thorough care he would surround me with.

His expression had been triumphant despite his surprise, but it faded to something more tender when I said his name. "You know, you are the only one who calls me that — and only when you're feeling particularly mushy about me," he murmured. "What are you thinking?"

Samuel is way too smart sometimes.

"Go play, Sam." I pushed him away. "I'll be fine." I hoped that I was right.

"Okay," he said softly, then ruined it by tossing Tim a smug grin. "We can talk later." Marking his territory in front of another male.

I turned to Tim with an apologetic smile

for Samuel's behavior that died as I saw the betrayed look on his face. He hid it quickly, but I knew what it was.

Damn it all.

I'd started out with an agenda, but the discussion had made me forget entirely what I was doing. Otherwise I'd have been more careful. It's not often I got a chance to pull out my history degree and dust it off. But still I should have realized that the discussion had meant a lot more to him than it had to me.

He thought I'd been flirting when I'd just been enjoying myself. And people like Tim, awkward and unlikable by most standards, don't get flirted with much. They don't know how to tell when to take it seriously or not.

If I'd been beautiful, maybe I'd have noticed sooner or been more careful — or Tim would have been more guarded. But my mongrel mix hadn't resulted as nicely for me as it had for Adam's second Darryl, who was African (his father was a tribesman from Africa) and Chinese to my Anglo-Saxon and Native American. I have my mother's features, which look a little wrong in the brown and darker brown color scheme of my father.

Tim wasn't dumb. Like most people who

don't quite fit in, he'd probably learned in middle school that if a beautiful person paid too much attention to you, like as not, there was another motive.

I'm not bad looking, but I'm not beautiful. I can clean up pretty nice, but mostly I don't bother. Tonight my clothes were clean, but I wasn't wearing any makeup and hadn't taken particular care when I braided my hair to keep it out of my face.

And it had to have been obvious I'd been enjoying the conversation — to the point that I'd forgotten that I was supposed to be gathering information about Bright Future.

All this went through my head in the time it took him to clear his face of the hurt and anger I'd seen. But it didn't matter. I didn't have a clue on how to get out of this without hurting him — which he didn't deserve.

I liked him, darn it. Once he got over himself (which took a little effort on my part), he was funny, smart, and willing to concede a point to me without arguing it into the ground — especially when I thought he was more right than wrong. Which made him a better person than I was.

"A bit possessive, isn't he?" he said. His voice was light, but his eyes were blank.

There was a spill of dry cheese on the table and I played with it a little. "He's usually not bad, but we've known each other a long time. He knows when I'm having fun." There, I thought, a sop for his ego, if nothing else. "I haven't had a debate like that since I got out of college." I could hardly explain that I hadn't flirted on purpose without embarrassing us both, so that was the closest I could come.

He smiled a little, though it didn't go to his eyes. "Most of my friends wouldn't know de Troyes from Malory."

"Actually, I've never read de Troyes." Probably the most famous of the medieval authors of Arthurian tales. "I took a class in German medieval lit and de Troyes was French."

He shrugged . . . then shook his head and took a deep breath. "Look, I'm sorry. I didn't mean to get all moody on you. There was this guy I know. We weren't close or anything, but he was murdered yesterday. You don't expect someone you know to be murdered like that. Austin brought me here because he thought we both needed to get out."

"You knew that guy, the one who was a guard at the reservation?" I asked. I'd have to be careful now. I didn't think that my connection to Zee would have been newsworthy, but I didn't want to lie either. I didn't want to hurt him any more than I already had.

He nodded, "Even though he was pretty much a jerk, he didn't deserve killing."

"I heard they caught some fae they think did it," I said. "Pretty scary stuff. It would bother anyone."

He examined my face, then nodded. "Listen," he said. "I probably ought to collect Austin and go — it's almost eleven and he has to leave for work at six tomorrow. But if you are interested, some friends and I are having a meeting Wednesday night at six. Things are apt to be a bit odd this week — we usually met at O'Donnell's. But we do a lot of discussion about history and folklore. I think you'd enjoy it." He hesitated and then finished in a bit of a rush. "It's the local Citizens for a Bright Future chapter."

I sat back, "I don't know . . ."

"We don't go out and bomb bars, or anything," he said. "We just talk and write to our congressmen" — he smiled suddenly and it lit up his face — "and our congress-women. A lot of it is research."

"Isn't that a little bit of an odd fit for you?" I asked. "I mean, you know Welsh and, obviously, all sorts of folklore. Most of the people I know like that are —"

"Fairy lovers," he said matter-of-factly.

"They go to Nevada on vacation and hang out at the fae bars and pay fae hookers to make them believe for an hour or two that they aren't human either."

I raised my eyebrows. "That's a little harsh, isn't it?"

"They're idiots," he said. "Have you ever read the original Brothers Grimm? The fae aren't big-eyed, gentle-souled gardeners or brownies who sacrifice themselves for the children in their care. They live in the forest in gingerbread houses and *eat* the children they lure in. They entice ships onto rocks and then drown the surviving sailors."

So, I thought, here was my chance. Was I going to investigate this group and see if they knew anything that would help Zee? Or was I going to back out gracefully and avoid hurting this fragile — and well-informed man.

Zee was my friend and he was going to die unless someone did something. As far as I could tell, I was the only someone who was doing anything at all.

"Those are just stories," I said with just the right amount of hesitation.

"So is the Bible," he said solemnly. "So is every history book you read. Those fairy tales were passed down as a warning by people who could neither read nor write.

People who wanted their children to understand that the fae are dangerous."

"There's never been a case of a fae convicted of hurting any human," I said, repeating the official line. "Not in all the years since they officially came out."

"Good lawyers," he said truthfully. "And suspicious suicides by fae 'who could no longer bear being held so near cold-iron bars.' "

He was persuasive — because he was right.

"Look," he said. "The fae don't love humans. We are nothing to them. Until Christianity and good steel came along, we were short-lived playthings with a tendency to breed too fast. Afterward we were short-lived, dangerous playthings. They have power, Mercy, magic that can do things you wouldn't believe — but it's all there in the stories."

"So why haven't they killed us?" I asked. It wasn't really an idle question. I'd wondered about it for a long time. The Gray Lords, according to Zee, were incredibly powerful. If Christianity and iron were such a bane to them, why weren't we all dead?

"They need us," he said. "The pure fae do not breed easily, if at all. They need to intermarry in order to keep their race going." He put both hands on the table. "They hate us for that most of all. They are proud and arrogant and they hate us because they need us. And the minute they don't need us anymore, they will dispose of us like we dispose of cockroaches and mice."

We stared at each other — and he could see I believed him because he pulled a small notebook and a pen out of his back pocket and ripped out a sheet of paper.

"We're holding the meeting at my place on Wednesday. This is the address. I think you ought to come." He took my hand and put the piece of paper in it.

As his hands folded around mine, I felt Samuel approach. His hand closed on my shoulder.

I nodded at Tim. "Thank you for keeping me company," I told him. "This was an interesting evening. Thank you."

Samuel's hand tightened on my shoulder before he released it completely. He stayed behind me as I walked out of the pizza place. He opened the passenger door of his car for me, then got in the driver's side.

His silence was unlike him — and it worried me.

I started to say something, but he held up a hand in a mute request for me to be quiet. He didn't seem angry, which actually surprised me after the display he'd put on for Tim. But he didn't start the car and drive off either.

"I love you," he said finally, and not happily.

"I know." My stomach tightened into knots and I forgot all about Tim and Citizens for a Bright Future. I didn't want to do this now. I didn't want to do this ever. "I love you, too." My voice didn't sound any happier than his did.

He stretched his neck and I heard the vertebrae crack. "So why aren't I tearing that little geeky bastard into pieces right now?"

I swallowed. Was this a trick question? Was there a right answer?

"Uhm. You don't seem too angry," I suggested.

He hit the dash of his very expensive car so fast that I didn't even really see his hand move. If his upholstery hadn't been leather, he'd have cracked it.

I thought about saying something funny, but decided it wasn't quite the moment. I've learned a *little* something since I was sixteen.

"I guess I was mistaken," I said. Nope. Haven't learned a thing.

He turned his head slowly toward me, his

eyes hard chips of ice. "Are you laughing at me?"

I put my hand over my mouth, but I couldn't help it. My shoulders started to shake because I suddenly knew the answer to his question. And that told me why it bothered him that he wasn't in a killing rage. Like me, Samuel had had a revelation tonight — and he wasn't happy about it.

"Sorry," I managed. "Sucks, doesn't it?"

"What?"

"You had this great plan. You'd weasel your way into my house and carefully seduce me. But you don't want to seduce me all that much. What you really want to do is cuddle, play, and tease." I grinned at him, and he must have been able to smell the relief pouring off me. "I'm not the love of your life; I'm your pack — and it's really ticking you off."

He said something really crude as he started the car — a nice Old English word.

I giggled and he swore again.

That he didn't really consider me his mate answered a lot of questions. And it told me that Bran, who was both the Marrok and Samuel's father, didn't know everything, even if he and everyone else thought he did. Bran was the one who told me Samuel's wolf had decided I was his mate. He'd been wrong: I was going to rub his nose in it next time I saw him.

Now I knew why Samuel been able to restrain himself and not attack Adam all these months. I'd been crediting Samuel's control with a dash of the magic that comes from being more dominant than most other wolves on the planet. The real answer was that I *wasn't* Samuel's mate. And since he was more dominant than Adam, if he didn't want to fight, it would make it much easier for Adam to hold off.

Samuel didn't want me any more than I wanted him — not that way. Oh, the physical stuff was there, plenty of spark and fizzle. Which was puzzling.

"Hey, Sam," I asked. "Why is it, if you don't want me as a mate, that when you kiss me, I go up in flames?" Why was it that after the first rush of relief was over — I was starting to feel miffed that he didn't actually want me as a mate?

"If I were human, the heat between us would be enough," he told me. "Damned wolf feels sorry for you and decided to step down."

Now that made no sense at all. "Excuse me?"

He looked at me and I realized he was still angry, his eyes glittering with icy fury. Samuel's wolf has snow-white eyes that are freaking scary in a human face.

"Why are you still angry?"

He pulled over on the shoulder of the highway and stared at the lights of Home Depot. "Look, I know my father spends a lot of time trying to convince the new wolves that the human and wolf are two halves of a whole — but that's not really true. It is just easier to live with and most of the time it's so close to being the truth that it doesn't matter. But we're different, the wolf and the human. We think differently."

"Okay," I said. I could kind of understand that. There were plenty of times when my coyote instincts fought against what I needed to do.

He closed his eyes. "When you were about fourteen and I realized what a gift had been dropped in my lap, I showed you to the wolf and he approved. All I had to do was convince you — and myself." He turned to look me squarely in the eyes and he reached out and touched my face. "For a true mating, it isn't necessary for the human half to even like your mate. Look at my father. He despises his mate, but his wolf decided that he had been alone long enough." He shrugged. "Maybe it was right, because

225

when Charles's mother died, I thought my father would die right along with her."

Everyone knew how much Bran had loved his Indian mate. I think that was part of what made Leah, Bran's current mate, a little crazy.

"So it is the wolf who mates," I said. "Carrying the man along for the ride whether he wants to or not?"

He smiled. "Not quite that bad — except maybe in my father's case, though he's never said anything against Leah. He never would, nor permit anyone else to say anything against her in his hearing either. But we weren't talking about him."

"So you set your wolf on me," I said, "when I was *fourteen*."

"Before anyone else could claim you. I was not the only old wolf in my father's pack. And fourteen was not an uncommon age for marriage in older days. I couldn't chance a prior claim." He rolled down the window to let the cooler night air flush the stuffy car. The noise of the traffic zipping past us increased dramatically. "I waited," he whispered. "I knew you were too young but . . ." He shook his head. "When you left, it was a just punishment. We both knew it, the wolf and I. But one moon I found myself outside of Portland where the wolf had taken us.

The *need* . . . we went all the way to Texas to make sure there was no chance of an accidental meeting. Without distance . . . I don't know that I could have let you leave."

So, Bran had been right about Samuel after all. I couldn't bear the closed-off look on his face and I put my hand over his.

"I'm sorry," I said.

"You shouldn't be. It wasn't your fault." His smile changed to a lopsided grin as his hand gripped mine almost painfully tight. "Usually things work out better. The wolf is patient and adaptable. Mostly he waits until your human half finds someone to love and then he claims her, too. Sometimes years after they marry. I did it backward on purpose and got caught in the backlash. Not your fault. I knew better."

There's something really disturbing about finding out how little you really know about something you felt like you were an expert on. I grew up with the wolves — and this was all news to me.

"But your wolf doesn't want me now?" That came out pretty pathetic sounding. I didn't need his laugh to tell me so.

"Jerk," I said, poking him.

"Here I thought you were above all that girl stuff," he said. "You don't want me as your mate, Mercy, so why are you miffed that my wolf finally admitted defeat?"

If he'd known how much that last statement told me about how hurt he was that I'd rejected him, I think he'd have bitten off his tongue. Was it better to talk about it — or just let it pass by?

Hey, I may be a mechanic and I may not use makeup very often, but I'm still a girl: it was time to talk it out.

I nudged him. "I love you."

He crossed his arms over his chest and leaned sideways so he could see me without twisting his neck. "Yeah?"

"Yeah. And you're hot — and a terrific kisser. And if your father hadn't interfered, I'd have run away with you all those years ago."

The smile slid off his face, and I couldn't tell what he was feeling at all. Not with my eyes or my nose — which is usually a better indicator. Maybe he was feeling as confused as I was.

"But I'm different now, Samuel. I've been taking care of myself too long to be happy letting anyone else do it. The girl you knew was sure that you would make a place for her to belong — and you would have." I had to say this right. "Instead I made a place for myself and the process changed me into who I am now. I'm not the kind of person you'd be happy with, Samuel."

"I'm happy with you," he said stubbornly.

"As a roommate," I told him. "As a pack-mate. As a mate mate you'd be unhappy."

He laughed then. "A mate mate?"

I waved an airy hand. "You know what I mean."

"And you're in love with Adam," he said quietly, then a little humor crept into his voice. "You'd better not flirt with that geek in front of Adam."

I raised my chin; I was *not* going to feel guilty. Nor did I understand my feelings for Adam well enough to discuss them tonight.

"And you're not *in* love with me." I realized something more and it made me grin at Samuel. "Wolf or not, you aren't in love with me — otherwise you wouldn't have been getting such a charge out of teasing Adam all this time."

"I was *not* teasing Adam," he said, offended. "I was courting you."

"Nope," I said, settling back in my chair. "You were tormenting Adam."

"I was not." He started the car and pulled out aggressively into the traffic.

"You're speeding," I told him smugly.

He turned his head to say something to put me in my place, but just then the cop behind us lit up.

■ ■ ■ ■

We were almost home when he decided to quit being offended.

"All right," he said, relaxing his hands on the steering wheel. "All right."

"I don't know what you were so mad about," I said. "You didn't even get a ticket. Twenty miles an hour over the speed limit and all you got was a warning. Must be nice being a doctor."

Once the cop had recognized him, she'd been all kinds of nice. He'd apparently treated her brother after a car wreck.

"There are a couple of cops whose cars I take care of," I murmured. "Maybe if I flirted with them, they'd —"

"I was *not* flirting with her," he ground out.

He wasn't usually so easy. I settled in for some real fun.

"She was certainly flirting with you, Dr. Cornick," I said, even though she hadn't been. Still . . .

"She was *not* flirting with me either."

"You're speeding again."

He growled.

I patted his leg. "See, you didn't want to be stuck with me for a mate."

He slowed as the highway dumped us in Kennewick and we had to travel on city streets for a while.

"You are horrible," he said.

I smirked. "You accused me of flirting with Tim."

He snorted. "You were flirting. Just because I didn't take him apart doesn't mean you aren't fishing in dangerous waters, Mercy. If it had been Adam with you tonight, that boy would be feeding the fishes — or the wolves. And I am not kidding."

I patted his leg again and took a deep breath. "I didn't mean to let it be a flirtation, I just got caught up in the conversation. I should have been more careful with a vulnerable boy like him."

"He isn't a boy. If he's five years younger than you, I'd be surprised."

"Some people are boys longer than others," I told him. "And that boy and his friend were both in O'Donnell's house not too long before he was killed."

I told Samuel the whole story, from the time Zee picked me up until I'd taken the paper from Tim. If I left anything out, it was because I didn't think it was important. Except, I didn't tell him that Austin Summers was probably the brother of one of the boys who beat up on Jesse. Samuel's temper might be easier than Adam's — but he'd kill both boys without a shred of remorse. In his world, you didn't beat up girls. I'd come up with a suitable punishment, but I didn't think anyone needed to die over it. Not as long as they quit bothering Jesse.

That was the only thing I left out. Both Zee and Uncle Mike had left me to my own devices in this investigation. Okay, they'd told me not to investigate, which amounted to the same thing. Proceeding without any help from the fae made investigating riskier than it would have otherwise been, and Zee was already mad at me for sharing what I had. More wouldn't make him any madder. The time for keeping their secrets strictly to myself was over.

If there was one thing I'd learned over the past few interesting (in the sense of the old Chinese curse, "May you live in interesting times") months, it was that when things started to get dangerous, it was important to have people who knew as much as you did. That way, when I stupidly got myself killed — someone would have a starting place to look for my murderer.

By the time I was finished telling him everything, we were sitting in the living room drinking hot chocolate.

The first thing Samuel said was, "You

have a real gift for getting into trouble, don't you? That was one thing I forgot when you left the pack."

"How is any of this my fault?" I asked hotly.

He sighed. "I don't know. Does it matter whose fault it is once you're sitting in the middle of the frying pan?" He gave me a despairing look. "And as my father used to point out, you find your way into that frying pan way too often for it to be purely accidental."

I put aside the urge to defend myself. For over a decade I'd managed to keep to myself, living as a human on the fringe of werewolf society (and that only because, at the Marrok's request, Adam decided to interfere with my life even before he built a house behind mine). It was *Adam's* trouble that had started everything. Then I'd owed the vampires for helping me with Adam's problems. Clearing *that* up had left me indebted to the fae.

But I was tired, I had to get up and work tomorrow — and if I started explaining myself, it would be hours before we got back to a useful discussion.

"So, finding myself in the frying pan once again, I came to you for advice," I prodded him. "Like maybe you can tell me why neither Uncle Mike nor Zee wanted to talk about the sea man or how there happened to be a forest and an ocean — a whole ocean — tucked neatly into a backyard and a bathroom. And if any of that could have something to do with O'Donnell's death."

He looked at me.

"Oh, come on," I said. "I saw your face when I told you about the funny things that happened in the rez. You're Welsh, for heaven's sake. You know about the fae."

"You're Indian," he said in a falsetto that I think was supposed to be an imitation of me. "You know how to track animals and build fires with nothing but sticks and twigs."

I gave him a haughty stare. "Actually, I do. Charles — another Indian — taught me."

He waved his hand at me; I recognized the gesture as one of mine. Then he laughed. "All right. All right. But I'm not an expert on the fae just because I'm Welsh."

"So explain that 'ah-ha' expression on your face when I told you about the forest."

"If you went Underhill, you just confirmed one of Da's theories about what the fae are doing with their reservations."

"What do you mean?"

"When the fae first proposed that the

234

government put them on reservations, my father told me he thought that they might be trying to set up territories like they once had in Great Britain and parts of Europe, before the Christians came and started ruining their places of power by building chapels and cathedrals. The fae didn't value their anchors in this world because their magic works so much better Underhill. They didn't defend their places until it was too late. Da believes the last gate to Underhill disappeared in the middle of the sixteenth century, cutting them off from a great deal of their power."

"So they've made new anchors," I said.

"And found Underhill again." He shrugged. "As for not talking about the sea fae . . . well, if he were dangerous and powerful . . . you're not supposed to speak about things like that, or name them — it may attract their attention."

I thought about it a moment. "I can see why they'd want to keep it quiet if they've found some way to regain some of their power. So does it have anything to do with figuring out who killed O'Donnell? Did he find out about it? Or was he stealing? And if so, what did he steal?"

He gave me a considering look. "You're still trying to find the killer, even though

Zee is being a bastard?"

"What would you do if, in order to defend you from some trumped-up charge, I told a lawyer that you were the Marrok's son?"

He raised his eyebrows. "Surely telling her that there were killings in the reservation doesn't compare?"

I shrugged unhappily. "I don't know. I should have checked with him, or with Uncle Mike, before I told anyone anything."

He frowned at me, but didn't argue anymore.

"Hey," I said with a sigh, "since we're friends and pack now, instead of potential mates, do you suppose you could loan me enough to pay Zee what I owe him for the garage?" Zee didn't make threats. If he told his lawyer to tell me that he expected repayment, he was serious. "I can pay you back on the same schedule I was paying him. That will get you paid off, with interest, in about ten years."

"I'm sure we can arrange something," Samuel said kindly, as if he understood that my change of subject was because I couldn't stand to talk about Zee and my stupidity anymore. "You've got a pretty solid line of credit with me — and Da, for that matter, whose pockets are a lot deeper. You look beat. Why don't you go to sleep?"

"All right," I said. Sleep sounded good. I stood up and groaned as the thigh muscle I'd abused at karate practice yesterday made its protest.

"I'm going out for a minute or two," he said a little too casually — and I stopped walking toward my bedroom.

"Oh, no, you're not."

His eyebrows met his hairline. "What?"

"You are *not* going to tell Adam that I'm his for the taking."

"Mercy." He stood up, strode over to me, and kissed me on the forehead. "You can't do a damned thing about what I do or don't do. It's between me and Adam."

He left, closing the door gently behind him. Leaving me with the sudden, frightening knowledge that I'd just lost my best defense against Adam.

CHAPTER 8

My bedroom was dark, but I didn't bother to turn on the light. I had worse things to worry about than the dark.

I headed for the bathroom and took a hot shower. By the time the water had cooled and I got out, I knew a couple of things. First, I was going to have just a little time before I had to face Adam. Otherwise he'd already have been waiting for me and my bedroom was empty. Second, I couldn't do anything about Adam or Zee until tomorrow, so I might as well go to sleep.

I combed out my hair and blow-dried it until it was only damp. Then I braided it so I could comb it out in the morning.

I pulled back my covers, knocking the stick that had been resting on top of them to the ground. Before Samuel moved in, I used to sleep without covers in the summer. But he kept the air-conditioning turned down until there was a real chill in the air, especially at night.

I climbed into bed, pulled the covers up under my chin, and closed my eyes.

Why was there a stick on my bed?

I sat up and looked at the walking stick lying on the floor. Even in the dark I knew it was the same stick I'd found at O'Donnell's. Careful not to step on it, I got out of bed and turned on the light.

The gray twisty wood lay innocuously on the floor on top of a gray sock and a dirty T-shirt. I crouched down and touched it gingerly. The wood lay hard and cool under my fingertips, without the wash of magic it had held in O'Donnell's house. For a moment it felt like any other stick, then a faint trace of magic pulsed and disappeared.

I searched out my cell phone and called the number Uncle Mike had been calling me from. It rang a long time before someone picked it up.

"Uncle Mike's," a not so cheerful stranger's voice answered, barely understandable amid a cacophony of heavy metal music, voices, and a sudden loud crash, as if someone had dropped a stack of dishes. "*Merde.* Clean that up. What do you want?"

I assumed that only the last sentence was directed at me.

"Is Uncle Mike there?" I asked. "Tell him

it's Mercy and that I have something he might be interested in."

"Hold on."

Someone barked out a few sharp words in French and then yelled, "Uncle Mike, phone!"

Someone shouted, "Get the troll out of here."

Followed by someone with a very deep voice muttering, "I'd like to see you try to get this troll out of here. I'll eat your face and spit out your teeth."

Then Uncle Mike's cheerful Irish voice said, "This is Uncle Mike. May I help you?"

"I don't know," I answered. "I've got a certain walking stick that someone left on my bed tonight."

"Do you now?" he said very quietly. "Do you?"

"What should I do with it?" I asked.

"Whatever it will allow you to do," he said in an odd tone. Then he cleared his voice and sounded his usual amused self again. "No, I know what you are asking. I think I'll give someone a call and see what they'd like. Probably they'll come and get it this time, too. It's too late for you to be awaiting for them to come callin'. Why don't you put it outside? Just lean it against your house. It'll come to no harm if no one collects it.

And if they do, well, then they'll not be disturbing you or the wolf, eh?"

"You're sure?"

"Aye, lass. Now I've got a troll to deal with. Put it outside." He hung up.

I put my clothes back on and took the stick outside. Samuel wasn't back yet, and the lights were still on at Adam's house. I stared at the walking stick for a few minutes, wondering who had put it on my bed and what they wanted. Finally I leaned it against the mobile home's new siding and went back to bed.

The stick was gone and Samuel was asleep when I got up the next morning. I almost woke him up to see what he'd told Adam, or if he'd noticed who'd gotten the stick, but as an emergency room doctor, his hours could be pretty brutal. If my staring at him hadn't woken him up, then he needed his sleep. I'd find out what had happened soon enough.

Adam's SUV was waiting next to the front door of my office when I drove up. I parked as far from it as I could, on the far side of the parking lot — which was where I usually parked.

He got out when I drove up, and was leaning against his door when I came up to him.

I've never seen a werewolf that was out of shape or fat; the wolf is too restless for that. Even so, Adam was a step harder, though not bulky. His coloring was a bit lighter than mine — which still left him with a deep tan and dark brown hair that he kept trimmed just a little longer than military standards. His wide cheekbones made his mouth look a little narrow, but that didn't detract from his beauty. He didn't look like a Greek god . . . but if there were Slavic gods, he'd be in strong contention. Right now that narrow mouth was flattened into a grim line.

I approached a little warily, and wished I knew what Samuel had told him. I started to say something when I noticed that there was something different about the door. My deadbolt was still there, but next to it was a new black keypad. He waited in silence as I checked out the shiny silver buttons.

I crossed my arms and turned back to him.

After a few minutes Adam gave me a half smile of appreciation though his eyes were too intent to carry off real amusement. "You complained about the guards," he explained.

"So why did you set up an alarm without asking me?" I asked stiffly.

"It's not just an alarm," he told me, the smile gone as if it had never been there. "Security is my bread and butter. There are

242

cameras in the lot and inside your garage, too."

I didn't ask him how he'd gotten in. As he said, security was his business. "Don't you usually work on government contracts and things a little more important than a VW shop? I suppose someone might break in and steal all the money in the safe. Maybe five hundred bucks if they're lucky. Or maybe they'll steal a transmission for their '72 Beetle? What do you think?"

He didn't bother to answer my sarcastic question.

"If you open the door without using the key code, a physical alarm will sound and one of my people will be tagged that the alarm has gone off." He spoke in a rapid, no-nonsense voice as if I hadn't said anything. "You have two minutes to reset it. If you do, my people will call your shop number to confirm it was you or Gabriel who reset it. If you don't reset it, they'll notify both the police and me."

He paused as if waiting for a response. So I raised an eyebrow. Werewolves are pushy. I've had a long time to get used to it, but I didn't have to like it.

"The key code is four numbers," he said. "If you punch in Jesse's birthday, month-month-day-day, it deactivates the alarm."

He didn't ask if I knew her birthday, which I did. "If you punch in your birthday, it will alert my people and they'll call me — and I'll assume you're in the kind of trouble you don't want the police to attend."

I gritted my teeth. "I don't need a security system."

"There are cameras," he said, ignoring my words. "Five in the lot, four in your shop, and two in the office. From six at night until six in the morning, the cameras are on motion sensors and will only record when there's something moving. From six in the morning to six at night the cameras are off — though I can change that for you if you'd like. The cameras record onto DVDs. You should change them out every week. I'll send someone over this afternoon to show you and Gabriel how that all works."

"You can send them over to take it out," I told him.

"Mercedes," he said. "I'm not happy with you right now — don't push me."

What did he have to be unhappy with me about?

"Well, isn't that just convenient?" I snapped. "I'm not happy with you either. I don't need this." I waved my hand to take in the cameras and keypad.

He pushed himself off his SUV and

stalked over to me. I knew he wasn't angry enough to hurt me, but I still backed up until I hit the outer wall of the garage. He put one hand on either side of me and leaned in until I could feel his breath on my face.

No one could ever say that Adam didn't know how to intimidate people.

"Maybe I'm mistaken," he began coolly. "Perhaps Samuel was misinformed and you aren't engaged in investigating the fae without their cooperation or the approval of either Zee or Uncle Mike, who might otherwise be reasonably expected to keep an eye out for you."

The warmth of his body shouldn't have felt good. He was angry and every muscle was tense. It was like being leaned on by a very heavy, warm brick. A sexy brick.

"Perhaps, Mercedes," he bit out in a voice like ice, "you didn't set out last night to join up with Bright Future, a group that has been tied into enough violent incidents that the fae, who *are* watching you, are going to be somewhat concerned — especially since you have ferreted out a number of things they'd rather be kept secret. I'm sure they'll be extremely happy when they find out you've told the son of the Marrok everything you know about the reservation — that you were supposed to keep secret." The coolness was gone from his voice by the time he'd finished, and he was all but snarling in my face.

"Uhm," I said.

"The fae aren't exactly cooperative at the best of times, but even they just might hesitate to do something to you if Samuel or I show up. I trust you to be able to survive until one of us gets here." He leaned down and kissed me forcefully once, a quick kiss that was over almost before it began. Possessive and almost punitive. Nothing that should have sent my pulse racing. "And don't think I've forgotten that the vampires have a good reason not to be happy with you, too." Then he kissed me again.

As soon as his lips touched mine the second time, I knew that Samuel, in addition to telling Adam everything I'd told him last night, had also informed Adam that he was no longer interested in being my mate.

I hadn't realized how much restraint Adam had been using until it was gone.

When he pulled back, his face was flushed and he was breathing as hard as I was. He reached over and punched in four numbers with his left hand.

"There's an instruction booklet, if you'd like to read it, next to your cash register.

Otherwise my man will answer any questions you have when he comes." His voice was too deep and I knew he was a hairsbreadth away from losing control. When he pushed away and climbed back into his SUV, I should have been relieved.

I stayed where I was, leaning against the building until I could no longer hear his engine.

If he'd wanted to take me right then and there, I would have let him. I'd have done anything for his touch, anything to please him.

Adam scared me more than the vampires, more than the fae. Because Adam could steal more from me than my life. Adam was the only Alpha I'd ever been around, including the Marrok himself, who could make me do his bidding against my will.

It took me three tries before I was able to slide the key into the deadbolt.

Monday was my busiest day, and this was no exception. It might be Labor Day, but my clients knew I was usually unofficially open on most Saturdays and holidays. Adam's security man, who was not one of the wolves, came in shortly after lunch. He showed Gabriel and me how to change out the DVDs.

"These are better than the tapes," he told me with more childlike enthusiasm than I expected out of a fifty-year-old man with Marine tattoos on his arms. "People don't usually change tapes often enough, so the saved footage is too grainy to be much help, or else they record over an important incident without realizing it. DVDs are better. These can't be written over. When they fill up, they'll automatically switch to a secondary disc. Since you're only activating them when you are not here, they probably won't fill the first disc in a week. So you just change them once a week — most people do it on Monday or Friday. Then you store them for a few months before you throw them out. If something happens to your system here, the boss is recording remotely as well." He obviously loved his job.

After some additional instructions and a little bit of a sales pitch to make sure we were happy with what we had, Adam's man left with a cheery wave.

"Don't worry," Gabriel told me. "I'll change them for you."

He'd been as happy to play with the new toys as the tech had been.

"Thanks," I told him sourly, unhappy about *the boss is recording remotely* part.

248

"You do that. I'll go take my temper out on that Passat's shift linkage problem."

When there was a lull in customers about two, Gabriel came back to the garage. I was teaching him a little here and there. He was going on to college rather than becoming a mechanic, but he wanted to learn.

"So, for a person who just shelled out a lot of money for a security system, you don't seem too happy," he said. "Is there some trouble I should know about?"

I pushed a strand of hair out of my eyes, doubtlessly leaving a trail of the sludge that covered every inch of the thirty-year-old engine I was working on and had gotten a good start on covering every inch of me, too.

"Not much trouble that you need to worry about," I told him after a moment. "If I thought there'd be a problem, I'd have warned you. Mostly it's just Adam over-reacting."

And it was overreacting, I'd decided after thinking things over all morning. Only a moron would believe that I was joining Bright Future in order to protest the fae — and somehow I was pretty sure that stupid fae didn't last long. If they talked to Uncle Mike — or Zee (even if he was still angry)

— they'd know that I was still trying to clear Zee.

I might know a few things that made the fae uncomfortable, but if they wanted me dead for it, I'd already be dead.

Gabriel whistled. "Jesse's father installed the whole security system without asking you? I guess that's pretty aggressive." He gave me a concerned look. "I like him, Mercy. But if he's stalking you —"

"No." He'd go away if I told him to. "He feels he has reason." I sighed. Things just got more and more complicated. I couldn't involve Gabriel in this mess.

"Something to do with Zee's arrest?" Gabriel laughed at my look. "Jesse warned me yesterday that you'd be preoccupied. Zee didn't do it, of course." The confidence in his voice showed how innocent Gabriel still was: it would never occur to him that the only reason Zee hadn't killed O'Donnell was because someone else had gotten there first.

"Adam's afraid I'm stirring up a hornet's nest," I said. "And he's probably right." I wasn't really mad about the security system. It was more than I could afford — and it was a good idea.

I always get angry when I'm afraid — and Adam terrified me. When he was around, it was all I could do not to follow him around and wait for orders like a good sheep dog. But I didn't want to be a sheep dog. Nor, to his credit, did Adam want me to be one.

Which was something I didn't need to tell Gabriel. "I'm sorry to be such a grouch. I'm worried about Zee, and the security system gave me something to fuss about."

"All right," Gabriel said.

"Did you come back to help me with this engine or just to talk?"

Gabriel looked at the car I was working on. "There's an engine in there?"

"Somewhere." I sighed. "Go do some paperwork. I'll call you in if I need a second hand, but there's no reason for both of us to get dirty if I don't need you."

"I don't mind," he said.

He never complained about work, no matter what I asked him to do.

"It's all right. I can get this."

My cell phone rang about fifteen minutes later, but my hands were too greasy to pick it up so I let it take a message while I worked on cleaning up the engine well enough that I could figure out where all the oil was leaking from.

It was almost quitting time and I'd already sent Gabriel home when Tony walked into the open garage bay.

"Hey, Mercy," he said.

Tony is half-Italian, half-Venezuelan, and all whatever he decides to be for the moment. He does most of his work undercover because he's a chameleon. He'd worked a stint in Kennewick High School posing as a student ten or fifteen years younger, and Gabriel, who knew Tony pretty well because Gabriel's mother worked as a police dispatcher, hadn't recognized him.

Today Tony was all cop. The controlled expression on his face meant he was here on business. And he had company. A tall woman in jeans and a T-shirt had one hand tucked under his elbow and the other holding firmly to the leather harness of a golden retriever. Dogs are sometimes troublesome for me. I suppose they smell the coyote — but retrievers are too friendly and cheerful to be a problem. It wagged its tail at me and gave a soft woof.

The woman's hair was seal brown and hung in soft curls to just below her shoulders. Her face was unremarkable except for the opaque glasses.

She was blind, and she was fae. Guess what fae I'd run into lately that was blind? She didn't look like someone who could turn into a crow, but then I didn't look much like a coyote, either.

I waited for the sense of power I'd sensed from the crow to sweep over me, but nothing happened. To all of my senses she was just what she appeared to be.

I wiped the sweat off my forehead onto the shoulder of my work overalls. "Hey, Tony, what's up?"

"Mercedes Thompson, I'd like you to meet Dr. Stacy Altman from the University of Oregon's folklore department. She is consulting with us on this case. Dr. Altman, this is Mercedes Thompson, who would doubtless shake your hand except hers is covered in grease."

"Nice to meet you." *Again.*

"Ms. Thompson," she said. "I asked Tony if he would introduce us." She patted his arm when she said his name. "I understand you don't think the fae the police are holding is guilty: though he had motive, means, and opportunity — *and* he was found next to the freshly killed dead body."

I pursed my lips. I wasn't sure what her game was, but I wasn't going to let her railroad Zee. "That's right. I heard it from the fae who was with him at the time. Zee is not incompetent. If he'd killed O'Donnell, no one would have known it."

"The police surprised him." Her voice was

cool and precise without a trace of accent. "A neighbor heard fighting and called the police."

I raised an eyebrow. "If it had been Zee, they would have heard nothing, and if they had, Zee would have been gone long before the police showed up. Zee doesn't make stupid mistakes."

"Actually," Tony told me with a small smile, "the neighbor who called said he saw the vehicle Zee was driving pull up to the house after he called the police having heard someone scream."

The doctor who was a Gray Lord hadn't known about the neighbor before he told us both. I saw her lips tighten in anger. Tony must not like her, since he'd never play a trick like that on someone he liked.

"So why are you trying so hard to pin this on Zee?" I asked her. "Isn't it up to the police to find the guilty party?"

"Why are you trying so hard to defend him?" she countered. "Because he used to be your friend? He doesn't appear to be appreciative of your efforts."

"Because he didn't do it," I said, as if I were surprised she'd asked such a stupid question. From the way she stiffened, she was as easy to get a rise out of as Adam. "What are you worried about? It's no skin off your nose if the police do a little more work. Do you think a fae in the hand is better than searching the reservation for the guilty one?"

Her face tightened and magic swelled in the air. It was searching the reservation that she was here to prevent, I thought. She wanted a quick execution — maybe Zee was supposed to hang himself and save everyone the publicity of a trial and the inconvenience of an investigation that put intruders' noses into the reservation. She was here to make sure there were no screwups.

Like me.

I considered her and then turned to Tony. "Did you put Zee on a suicide watch? Fae don't do well in iron cages."

He shook his head while Dr. Altman's mouth tightened. "Dr. Altman said that as a gremlin, Mr. Adelbertsmiter would be fine with the metal. But if you think I ought to, I will."

"Please," I said. "I'm very concerned." It wouldn't be foolproof, but it would make it harder to kill him.

Tony's eyes were sharp as they looked from me to Dr. Altman. He was too good a cop not to notice the undercurrents between the two of us. He probably even knew it wasn't suicide I was worried about.

"Didn't you tell me you had some questions to ask Mercedes, Dr. Altman?" he suggested with deceptive mildness.

"Of course," she said. "The police here seem to respect your opinion about the fae, but they don't know what your credentials are — other than the fact you once worked with Mr. Adelbertsmiter."

Ah, an attempt to discredit me. If she'd expected to fluster me, she didn't know me very well. Any female mechanic knows how to respond to that kind of attack.

I gave her a genial smile. "I've a degree in history and I read, Dr. Altman. For instance, I know that there was no such thing as a gremlin until Zee decided to call himself one. If you'd excuse me, I'd better get back to work. I promised that this car would be finished today." I turned to do just that and tripped on a stick that was lying on the ground.

Tony was there with a hand under my elbow to help me back to my feet. "Did you twist an ankle?" he asked.

"No, I'm fine," I told him, frowning at the fae walking stick that had appeared on the floor of my garage. "You'd better let go or you'll get covered with grease."

"I'm fine. A little dirt just impresses the rookies."

"What happened?" Dr. Altman asked, as if her blindness was something that would keep her from knowing what was happening around her. Which I was certain it did not. I noticed that her dog was staring intently at the stick. Maybe she really did use it to help her see.

"She tripped on a walking stick." Tony, who'd disengaged himself from Dr. Altman to catch me when I'd stumbled, bent down, picked it up, and put the stick down on my counter. "This is pretty cool workmanship, Mercy. What are you doing with an antique walking stick on the floor of your garage?"

Darned if I knew.

"It's not mine. Someone left it at the shop. I've been trying to give it back to its rightful owner."

Tony looked at it again. "It looks pretty old. The owner should be happy to get it back." There was a question in his voice — I don't think Dr. Altman heard it.

I don't know how sensitive Tony is to magic, but he was quick and his fingers lingered on the Celtic designs on the silver.

I met his eyes and gave him a brief nod. Otherwise he'd pick at it until even the blind fae noticed he'd seen more than he ought.

"You'd think so," I said ruefully. "But here it is."

He smiled thoughtfully. "If Dr. Altman is through, we'll just get out of your way," he said. "I'm sorry Zee is unhappy with the way you chose to defend him. But I'll see to it he doesn't get railroaded."

Or killed.

"Take care," I told him seriously. *Don't do anything stupid.*

He raised an eyebrow. "I'm as careful as you are."

I smiled at him and went back to work. No matter what I'd told its owner, this car wasn't going to be done until tomorrow. I buttoned it up, then cleaned up and checked my phone. I'd actually missed two calls. The second one was from Tony, before he'd brought the department's fae consultant. The first one was a number I didn't know with a long-distance area code.

When I dialed it, Zee's son, Tad, answered the phone.

Tad had been my first tool rustler, but then he'd gone on to college and deserted me — just as Gabriel would do in a year or two. He'd actually been the one to hire me. He'd been working alone when I'd come needing a belt for my Rabbit (having just blown an interview at Pasco High; they wanted a coach and I thought they should be more concerned that their history teachers could teach history) and I'd helped him out with a customer. I think he'd been nine years old. His mother had just passed away and Zee wasn't dealing well with it. Tad had had to rehire me three more times in the next month before Zee resigned himself to me — a woman and, he thought at first, a human.

"Mercy, where have you been? I've been trying to get you since Saturday morning." He didn't give me a chance to answer. "Uncle Mike told me that Dad had been arrested for murder. All I could get out of him was that it was related to the deaths on the reservation and that I was, under the Gray Lords' edict, to stay where I am."

Tad and I share a certain disregard and distaste for authority. He probably had a plane ticket in his hand.

"Don't come," I said after a moment's fierce thought. The Gray Lords wanted someone guilty and they didn't care who it was. They wanted a quick end to this mess and anyone who stood between them and what they wanted would be in danger.

"What the hell happened? I can't find out anything." I heard in his voice the frustration I was feeling, too.

I told him as much as I knew, from when Zee asked me to sniff out the murderer to the blind woman who had just come with Tony — including Zee's unhappiness with me because I had told the police and his lawyer too much. My gaze fell on the walking stick, so I added it into the mix.

"It was a *human* killing the fae? Wait a minute. Wait a minute. The guard who was killed, this O'Donnell, was he a swarthy man, about five-ten or thereabouts? His first name was Thomas?"

"That's what he looked like. I don't know what his first name was."

"I told her that she was playing with fire," Tad said. "Damn it. She thought it was funny because he thought he was doing her such a favor and she was just stringing him along. He amused her."

"She who?" I asked.

"Connora . . . the reservation's librarian. She didn't like humans much, and O'Donnell was a real turkey. She liked playing with them."

"He killed her because she was playing games?" I asked. "Why'd he kill the others?"

"That's why they quit looking at him as the killer. He had no connection to the second guy murdered. Besides, Connora didn't have much magic. A human could have killed her. But Hendrick —"

"Hendrick?"

"The guy with the forest in his backyard. He was one of the Hunters. His death pretty much eliminated all the human suspects. He was pretty tough." There was a crashing sound. "Sorry. Stupid corded phone — I pulled it off the table. Wait a minute. Wait a minute. A walking stick, huh? It just keeps showing up?"

"That's right."

"Can you describe it to me?"

"It's about four feet long, made of some sort of twisty wood with a gray finish. It's got a ring of silver on the bottom and a silver cap with Celtic designs on the top. I can't think why someone would keep bringing it back to me."

"I don't think anyone is bringing it to you. I think it is following you around on its own."

"What?"

"Some of the older things develop a few quirks. Power begets power and all that. Some of the things made when our power was more than it is now, they can become a little unpredictable. Do things they weren't meant to."

"Like follow me around. Do you think it

followed O'Donnell to his house?"

"No. Oh, no. I don't think it did that at all. The walking stick was created to be of use to humans who help the fae. It's probably following you around because you are trying to help Dad when everyone else has their fingers up their noses."

"So O'Donnell stole it."

"Mercy . . ." There was a choking sound. "Damn it. Mercy, I can't tell you. I am forbidden. A geas, Uncle Mike said, for the protection of the fae, of me, and of you."

"It has something to do with your father's situation?" I thought. "With the walking stick? Were other things stolen? Is there anyone who can talk to me? Someone you could call and ask?"

"Look," he said slowly, as if he was waiting for the geas to stop him again, "there's an antiquarian bookstore in the Uptown Mall in Richland. You might go talk to the man who runs it. He might be able to help you find out more about that stick. Make sure you tell him that I sent you to him — but wait until he's alone in the store."

"Thank you."

"No, Mercy, thank you." He paused, and then for a moment sounding a bit like the nine-year-old I'd first met, he said, "I'm scared, Mercy. They mean to let him take the fall, don't they?"

"They were," I said. "But I think it might be too late. The police are not accepting his guilt at face value and we found Zee a terrific lawyer. I'm doing a little nosing about in O'Donnell's other doings."

"Mercy," he said quietly. "Jeez, Mercy, are you setting yourself up against the Gray Lords? You know that's what the blind woman is, right? Sent to make sure they get the outcome they want."

"The fae don't care who did it," I told him. "Once it's been established that it was a fae who killed O'Donnell, they don't care if they get the murderer. They need someone to take the fall quickly and then they can hunt down the real culprit out of sight of the world."

"And even though my father has done everything he can think of to dissuade you, you're not going to back down," he said.

Of course. *Of course.*

"He's trying to keep me out of it," I whispered.

There was a short pause. "Don't tell me you thought he was really mad at you?"

"He's calling in his loan," I told him as a knot of pain slowly unknotted. Zee knew what the fae would do and he'd been trying to keep me out of danger.

How had he put it? *She'd better hope I don't get out.* Because if I got him out, the Gray Lords would be unhappy with me.

"Of course he is. My father is brilliant and older than dirt, but he has this unreasoning fear of the Gray Lords. He thinks they can't be stopped. Once he realized how the wind was blowing, he would do his best to keep everyone else out of it."

"Tad, stay at school," I told him. "There's nothing you can do here except get into trouble. The Gray Lords don't have jurisdiction over me."

He snorted. "I'd like to see you tell them that — except that I like you just as you are: alive."

"If you come here, they will kill you — how is that going to help your father? Tear up that ticket and I'll do my best. I'm not alone. Adam knows what's up."

Tad really respected Adam. As I hoped, it was the right touch.

"All right, I'll stay here. For now. Let me see if I can give you a little more help — and how far this damned geas Uncle Mike set on me goes."

There was a long pause as he worked through things.

"Okay. I think I can talk about Nemane."

"Who?"

"Uncle Mike said the Carrion Crow, right? And I assume he wasn't talking about the smallish crow that lives in the British Isles, but the Carrion Crow."

"Yes. The three white feathers on her head seemed to be important."

"It must be Nemane then." There was satisfaction in his voice.

"This is a good thing?"

"Very good," he said. "There are some of the Gray Lords who would just as soon kill everyone until the problems go away. Nemane is different."

"She doesn't like to kill."

Tad sighed. "Sometimes you are so innocent. I don't know of any fae who doesn't enjoy spilling blood at some level — and Nemane was one of the Morrigan, the battle goddesses of the Celts. One of her jobs was delivering the killing blow to the heroes dying in the aftermath of a battle to end their suffering."

"That doesn't sound promising," I muttered.

Tad heard. "The thing about the old warriors is that they have a sense of honor, Mercy. Pointless death or wrongful death is an anathema to them."

"She won't want to kill your father," I said.

He corrected me gently. "She won't want

to kill you. I'm afraid that, except to you, my father is an acceptable loss."

"I'll see what I can do to change that."

"Go get that book," he said, then coughed a bit. "Stupid geas." There was real rage in his voice. "If it cost me my father, I'm going to have a talk with Uncle Mike. Get that book, Mercy, and see if you can't find something that will give you some bargaining room."

"You'll stay there?"

"Until Friday. If nothing breaks by then, I'm coming home."

I almost protested, but said good-bye instead. Zee was Tad's father — I was lucky he agreed to wait until Friday.

The Uptown Mall is a conglomeration of buildings cobbled together into a strip mall. The stores range from a doughnut bakery to a thrift store, plus bars, restaurants, and even a pet store. The bookstore wasn't hard to find.

I'd been there a time or two, but since my reading tastes run more to sleazy paperbacks than collectibles, it wasn't one of my regular haunts. I was able to park in front of the store, next to a handicapped space.

I thought for a moment it had already closed. It was after six and the store looked deserted from the outside. But the door opened easily with a jingle of mellow cowbells.

"A minute, a minute," someone called from the back.

"No trouble," I said. I took in a deep breath to see what my nose could tell me, but there were too many smells to separate much out: nothing holds smells like paper. I could detect cigarettes and various pipe tobaccos, and stale perfume.

The man who emerged from the stacks of bookcases was taller than me and somewhere between thirty-five and fifty. He had fine hair that was easing gracefully from gold to gray. His expression was cheerful and shifted smoothly into professional when he saw that I was a stranger.

"What can I help you with?" he asked.

"Tad Adelbertsmiter, a friend of mine, told me you could help me with a problem I have," I told him and showed him the stick I was carrying.

He took a good look at it and paled, losing the amiable expression. "Just a moment," he said. He locked the front door, changing the old-fashioned paper sign to CLOSED and pulling down the shades over the window.

"Who are you?" he asked.

"Mercedes Thompson."

He gave me a sharp-eyed look. "You're not fae."

I shook my head. "I'm a VW mechanic."

Comprehension lit his face. "You're Zee's protégé?"

"That's right."

"May I see it?" he asked, holding out his hand for the stick.

I didn't give it to him. "Are you fae?"

His expression went blank and cold — which was an answer in itself, wasn't it?

"The fae don't consider me one of them," he said in an abrupt voice. "But my mother's grandfather was. I've just enough fae in me to do a little touch magic."

"Touch magic?"

"You know, I can touch something and have a pretty good idea how old it is, and who it belonged to. That kind of thing."

I held up the staff to him.

He took it and examined it for a long time. At last he shook his head and gave it back. "I've never seen it before — though I've heard of it. One of the fairy treasures."

"If you're a sheep farmer, maybe," I said dryly.

He laughed. "That's the one, all right — though sometimes those old things can do unexpected things. Anyway, it's a magic they can't work anymore, enchanting objects permanently, and they hold those things precious."

"What did Tad think you could tell me about it?"

He shook his head. "If you already know the story about it, I suppose you know as much as I do."

"So what did touching it tell you?"

He laughed. "Not a darn thing. My magic only works on mundane things. I just wanted to hold it for a bit." He paused. "He told you I could find you information on it?" He looked me over keenly. "Now this wouldn't have any bearing on that trouble his father is in, could it? No, of course not." His eyes smiled slyly. "Oh, I expect that I know just exactly what Tad wants me to find for you, clever boy. Come back here with me."

He led me to a small alcove where the books were all in locking barrister's bookcases. "This is where I keep the more valuable stuff — signed books and older oddities." He pulled up a bench and climbed on it to unlock the topmost shelf, which was mostly empty — probably because it was difficult to reach.

He pulled out a book bound in pale leather and embossed in gold. "I don't suppose you have fourteen hundred dollars you'd like to pay for this with?"

I swallowed. "Not at the moment — I might be able to scrape it up in a few days."

He shook his head as he handed the book down to me. "Don't bother. Just take care of it and give it back when you're finished. It's been here for five or six years. I don't expect that I'll have a buyer for it this week."

I took it gingerly, not being used to handling books that were worth more than my car (not that *that* was saying very much). The title was embossed on front and spine: *Magic Made.*

"I'm loaning this to you," he said slowly, considering his words carefully, "because it talks a little about that walking stick . . ." He paused and added in a "pay attention to this part" voice, "*And* a few other interesting things."

If the walking stick had been stolen, maybe more things had disappeared, too. I clutched the book tighter.

"Zee is a friend of mine." He locked the bookcase again and then got off the bench and put it back where it had been. Then in an apparent *non sequitur* he said casually, "You know, of course, that there are things that we are forbidden to discuss. But I know that the story of the walking stick is in there.

You might start with that story. I believe it is in Chapter Five."

"I understand." He was giving me all the help he could without breaking the rules.

He led the way back through the store. "Take care of that staff."

"I keep trying to give it back," I said.

He turned and walked backward a few steps, his eyes on the staff. "Do you now?" Then he gave a small laugh, shook his head, and continued to the front door. "Those old things sometimes have a mind of their own."

He opened the door for me and I hesitated on the threshold. If he hadn't told me that he was part fae, I'd have thanked him. But acknowledging a debt to a fae could have unexpected consequences. Instead I took out one of the cards that Gabriel had printed up for me and gave it to him. "If you ever have trouble with your car, why don't you stop by? I work mostly on German cars, but I can usually make the others purr pretty well, too."

He smiled. "I might do that. Good luck."

Samuel was gone when I got back, but he'd left a note to tell me he had gone to work — and there was food in the fridge.

I opened it and found a foil-covered glass

pan with a couple of enchiladas in it. I ate dinner, fed Medea, then washed my hands and took the book into the living room to read.

I hadn't expected a page that said, "This is who killed O'Donnell," but it might have been nice if each page of the six-hundred-page book hadn't been covered with tiny, handwritten words in old faded ink. At least it was in English.

An hour and a half later I had to stop because my eyes wouldn't focus anymore.

I'd turned to Chapter Five and gotten through maybe ten pages of the impossible text and three stories. The first story had been about the walking stick, a little more complete than the story I'd read off the Internet. It also had a detailed description of the stick. The author was obviously fae, which made it the first book I'd ever knowingly read from a fae viewpoint.

All of Chapter Five seemed to be about things like the walking stick: gifts of the fae. If O'Donnell had stolen the walking stick, maybe he'd stolen other things, too. Maybe the murderer had stolen them in return.

I took the book to the gun safe in my room and locked it in. It wasn't the best hiding place, but a casual thief was a little less likely to run off with it.

I washed dishes and mused about the book. Not so much about the contents, but what Tad had been trying to tell me about it.

The man at the bookstore had told me that the fae treasure things like the walking stick, no matter how useless they are in our modern world.

I could see that. For a fae, having something that held the remnant of magic lost to them was power. And power in the fae world meant safety. If they had a record of all the fairy-magicked items, then the Gray Lords could keep track of them — and apportion them as they chose. But the fae are a secretive people. I just couldn't see them making up a list of their items of power and handing it over.

I grew up in Montana, where an old, unregistered rifle was worth a lot more than a new gun whose ownership could be traced. Not that the gun owners in Montana are planning on committing crimes with their unregistered guns — they just don't like the federal government knowing their every move.

So what if . . . what if O'Donnell stole several magic items and no one knew what they were, or maybe what all of them were. Then some fae figured out it was

O'Donnell. Someone who had a nose like mine — or who saw him, or maybe tracked him back to his house. That fae could have killed O'Donnell to steal for himself the things O'Donnell had taken.

Maybe the murderer had timed it so Zee would be caught, knowing the Gray Lords would be happy to have a suspect wrapped up in a bow.

If I could find the killer and the things O'Donnell had stolen, I could hold those things hostage for Zee's acquittal and safety.

I could see why a fae would want the walking stick, but what about O'Donnell? Maybe he hadn't known exactly what it was? He'd had to have known something about it, or else why take it? Maybe he'd intended to sell it back to the fae. You'd think that anyone who'd been around them for very long would know better than to think you'd survive long selling back stolen items to the fae.

Of course, O'Donnell was dead, wasn't he?

Someone knocked on my door — and I hadn't heard anyone drive up. It might have been one of the werewolves, walking over from Adam's house. I took a deep breath, but the door effectively blocked anything my nose might have told me.

I opened the door and Dr. Altman was standing on the porch. The seeing eye dog was gone — and there was no extra car in the driveway. Maybe she'd flown here.

"You've come for the walking stick?" I asked. "You're welcome to it."

"May I come in?"

I hesitated. I was pretty sure the threshold thing only worked on vampires, but if not . . .

She smiled tightly and took a step forward until she was standing on the carpet.

"Fine," I said. "Come in." I got the old stick and handed it to her.

"Why are you doing this?" she asked.

I deliberately misunderstood. "Because it's not my stick — and that sheep thing won't do me any good."

She gave me an irritated look. "I don't mean the stick. I mean why are you pushing your nose into fae business? You are undermining my standing with the police — and that may be dangerous for them in the long run. My job is to keep the humans safe. You don't know what is going on and you're going to cause more trouble than you can handle."

I laughed. I couldn't help it. "You and I both know that Zee didn't kill O'Donnell. I just made sure that the police were aware that someone else might be involved. I don't leave my friends out to swing in the wind."

"The Gray Lords will not allow someone like you to know so much about us." The aggressive tension she'd been carrying in her shoulders relaxed and she strode confidently across my living room and sat in Samuel's big, overstuffed chair.

When she spoke again, her voice had a trace of a Celtic lilt. "Zee's a cantankerous bastard, and I love him, too. Moreover, there are not so many of the iron kissed left that we can lightly lose them. At any other time I would be free to do what I could to save him. But when the werewolves announced themselves to the public, they caused a resurgence of fear that we cannot afford to make worse. An open-and-shut case, with the police willing to keep mum about the condition of the murder victim, won't cause too much fuss. Zee understands that. If you know as much as you think you do, you should know that sometimes sacrifices are necessary for the majority to survive."

Zee had offered himself up as a sacrifice. He wanted me to get mad enough I'd leave him to rot because he knew that otherwise I'd never give up, I'd never agree to leave him as a sacrifice no matter what the cost to the fae.

"I came here tonight for Zee," she told me earnestly, her blind eyes staring through me. "Don't make this harder on him than it already is. Don't let this cost you your life, too."

"I know who you are, more or less, Nemane," I told her.

"Then you should know that not many get a warning before I strike."

"I know that you prefer justice to slaughter," I told her.

"I prefer," she said, "that my people survive. If I have to eliminate a few innocents or — stupidly obtuse people — in the meantime, that will not live long on my conscience."

I didn't say anything. I wouldn't give up on Zee, couldn't give up on Zee. If I told her that, she'd kill me right now. I could feel her power gathering around her like a spring thunderstorm. Layer upon layer it built as I stared at her.

I wouldn't lie and the truth would get me killed — and leave no one to help Zee.

Just then a car turned into the gravel of the driveway. Samuel's car.

I knew then what I could do, but would it be enough? What would it cost?

"I know who you are, Nemane," I whispered. "But you don't know who I am."

"You're a walker," she told me. "A shape-shifter. Zee explained it to me. There aren't many of the native preternatural species left — so you belong nowhere. Neither fae nor wolf, vampire or anything else. You are all alone." Her expression didn't change, but I could smell her sorrow, her sympathy. She was alone, too. I don't know if she meant me to understand that, or if she was unaware how much I could glean from her scent. "I don't want to have to kill you, but I will."

"I don't think so." Thank goodness, I thought, thank goodness that I had told everything to Samuel. He wouldn't have to play catch-up. "Zee told you part of who I am." Maybe because he thought it would make her hesitate to kill me, knowing that I was alone. "You're right, I don't know any other people like me, but I'm not alone."

Samuel opened the door on cue. His eyes were bloodshot and he looked tired and grumpy. I could smell the blood and disinfectant on him. He paused with the door open, taking in Dr. Altman's appearance.

"Dr. Altman," I said pleasantly, "may I introduce you to Dr. Samuel Cornick, my roommate. Samuel, I'd like you to meet Dr. Stacy Altman, police consultant, the Carrion Crow. The fae know her as Nemane."

Samuel's eyes narrowed.

"You're a werewolf," said Nemane. "Samuel Cornick." There was a pause. "The Marrok is Bran Cornick."

I kept my gaze on Samuel. "I was just explaining to Dr. Altman why it would be inadvisable for them to eliminate me even though I'm sticking my nose in their business."

Comprehension lit his eyes, which he narrowed at the fae.

"Killing Mercy would be a mistake," he growled. "My da had Mercy raised in our pack and he couldn't love Mercy more if she were his daughter. For her he would declare open war with the fae and damned be the consequences. You can call him and ask, if you doubt my word."

I'd expected Samuel to defend me — and the fae could not afford to hurt the son of the Marrok, not unless the stakes were a lot higher. I'd counted on that to keep Samuel safe or I'd have found some way to keep him out of it. But the Marrok . . .

I'd always thought I was an annoyance, the only one Bran couldn't count on for instant obedience. He'd been protective, still was — but his protective instinct was one of the things that made him dominant.

I'd thought I was just one more person he had to take care of. But it was as impossible to doubt the truth in Samuel's voice as it was to believe that he'd be mistaken about Bran.

I was glad that Samuel was focused on Nemane, who had risen to her feet when Samuel began speaking. While I blinked back stupid tears, she leaned on the walking stick and said, "Is that so?"

"Adam Hauptman, the Columbia Basin Pack's Alpha, has named Mercy his mate," continued Samuel grimly.

Nemane smiled suddenly, the expression flowing across her face, giving it a delicate beauty I hadn't noticed before.

"I like you," she said to me. "You play an underhanded and subtle game — and like Coyote, you shake up the order of the world." She laughed. "Coyote indeed. Good for you. Good for you. I don't know what else you'll run into — but I'll let the Others know what they are dealing with." She tapped the walking stick on the floor twice. Then, almost to herself, she murmured, "Perhaps . . . perhaps this won't be a disaster after all."

She raised the staff up and touched the top end to her forehead in a salute. Then she took a step forward and disappeared from the reach of any of my senses between one moment and the next.

CHAPTER 9

Wednesday night I ate dinner at my favorite Chinese place in Richland then drove out to Tim's house. Since O'Donnell's killer was almost certainly fae, I didn't know how much good it would do me to attend a Bright Future meeting — but maybe someone would know something important. I only had until Friday to prove Zee innocent or Tad would be putting his life on the line, too.

The more time I had to think about it, though, the more sense it made for Tad to come back. I certainly wasn't getting any nearer to figuring out anything. Tad, being fae, could go to the reservation and ask questions — if the Gray Lords didn't kill him for his disobedience. Maybe I could persuade Nemane that it was in the fae's best interest that Zee's son come home to help me save his father. Maybe.

Tim's address was in West Richland, a few

miles from Kyle's. It was in a block so new that several houses didn't have lawns yet, and I could see two buildings under construction on the next block over.

Half of the front was beige brick and the rest was adobe the color of oatmeal. It looked upscale and expensive, but it was missing the touches that made Kyle's house a mansion rather than a house. No stained glass, no marble or oak garage doors.

Which meant that it was still several orders of magnitude nicer than my old trailer even with its new siding.

There were four cars parked in the driveway and a '72 once-red Mustang with a lime green left fender parked on the street in front. I pulled in behind it because it's not often I find a car that makes the Rabbit look good.

As I got out of the car, I waved at the woman who was peering out at me from behind a sheer curtain in the house across the street. She jerked a window shade down.

I rang the doorbell and waited for the stocking-footed person who was hopping down a carpeted staircase to open the door. When it opened, I wasn't surprised to see a girl in her late teens or very early twenties. Her footsteps had sounded like a woman — men tend to clomp, thunder, or like Adam, move so silently you can barely hear them.

She was dressed in a thin T-shirt that sported crossed bones, like a pirate flag, but instead of a human skull it boasted a faded panda head with exes for eyes. She was a little overweight, but the extra pounds suited her, rounding her face and softening her strong features. Under the distinctive aura of Juicy Fruit, I recognized her scent from O'Donnell's house.

"I'm Mercy Thompson," I told her. "Tim invited me."

She looked me over with sharp eyes and then gave me a welcoming smile. "I'm Courtney. He said you might be coming. We're not started yet — still waiting for Tim and Austin to get back with goodies. Come on in."

She was one of those women cursed with a little girl's voice. When she was fifty, she'd still sound like she was thirteen.

As I followed her up the stairs, I did the polite thing. "I'm sorry to intrude on this meeting. Tim told me that one of your members was just killed."

"Couldn't have happened to a nicer man," she said airily, but then stopped on the stair landing. "All right, that didn't need to be said, sorry. I don't mean to make you uncomfortable."

I shook my head. "I didn't know him."

"Well, he started our chapter of Bright Future and he was all right to the guys, but he only had one use for women and I was getting tired of fighting him off all the time." Her eyes really focused on me for the first time, "Hey, Tim said you were Hispanic, but you aren't, are you?"

I shook my head. "My father was an Indian rodeo rider."

"Yeah?" Her voice was mildly inquiring. She wanted to know more, but didn't want to pry.

I was starting to like her. Somewhere under all the bubbles, I was pretty sure she was hiding a sharp brain. "Yeah."

"A rodeo rider? That's pretty cool. Is he still?"

I shook my head. "Nope. He died before I was born. Left my mother a pregnant unwed teenager. I was raised w—" I'd been spending too much time with Adam's pack and not enough with real people, I thought as I hastily replaced *werewolf* with *white-bread American.* Happily she *wasn't* a were-wolf, and didn't sense my lie.

"Wish I was Native American," she said a little wistfully as she started back up the stairs. "Then all the guys would go for me

— it's that mysterious Indian thing, you know?"

Not really, but I laughed because she meant me to. "Nothing mysterious about me."

She shook her head. "Maybe not, but if I were an Indian, I'd be mysterious."

She led me into a large room already occupied with five men who were tucked into a circle of chairs in the far corner of the room. They were evidently deep into a very involved conversation because they didn't even look up when we came in. Four of them were young, even younger than Austin and Tim. The fifth looked very university professorish, complete with goatee and brown sport coat.

Even with people in it, there was an unused air to the room. As if everything had just come fresh from a furniture store. The walls and Berber carpet were in the same color scheme as the house.

I thought of the vivid colors in Kyle's house and the pair of life-sized, Greek-inspired, stone statues in the foyer. Kyle called them Dick and Jane and was quite fond of them, though they'd been commissioned by the house's former owner.

One was male, the other female, and both of their faces had a dreamy, romantic expression as they looked up toward heaven — an expression that somehow didn't quite go with the spectacular evidence that the male statue wasn't thinking heavenly thoughts.

Kyle dressed Jane's naked body in a short plaid skirt and an orange halter top. Dick generally wore only a hat — and not on his head. At first it was a top hat — but then Warren went to a thrift store and found a knitted ski cap that hung down about two feet with a six-inch tassel on the end.

In contrast, Tim's house had no more personality than an apartment, as if he didn't have enough confidence in his taste to make the house his own. Even as little as I had talked to him, I knew there was more to him than beige and brown. I don't know what someone else would think, but to me, his house all but screamed with his desire to fit in.

It made me like him more: I know what it's like to not quite fit in.

The room might have been uninspired, but it was still nice. Everything was good quality without being excessive. One corner of the room had been set up as an office. There was a dorm-sized fridge next to a well-made, but not extravagant, oak computer desk. The long wall opposite the door was dominated by a TV large enough to please Samuel with waist-high speakers on either side of it. Comfy-looking chairs and a couch, all upholstered with a medium brown microfiber designed to look like suede, were scattered in a manner appropriate to a home theater.

"Sarah couldn't make it tonight," Courtney told me as if I should know who Sarah was. "I'm glad *you* did, otherwise I'd have been the lone woman out. Hey, guys, this is Mercy Thompson, the woman Tim told us might be coming, you know, the one he met at the music festival last weekend."

Her voice penetrated where our entrance had not and the men all looked up. Courtney walked me up to them.

"This is Mr. Fideal," she said, indicating the older man.

Close up, his face looked younger than his iron gray hair made him appear. His skin was tanned and healthy and his eyes were a bright blue with the intensity of a six-year-old.

I didn't remember his scent from O'Donnell's house, but it was obvious that he was comfortable in this group — so he must be a regular attendee . . .

"Aiden," he corrected her kindly.

She laughed and told him, "I just can't do

it." To me, she explained, "He was my econ teacher — and so he's forever enshrined upon my heart as Mr. Fideal."

If I hadn't shaken his hand, I don't know if I would have noticed anything odd about his scent. Though brine is not usually a fragrance I associate with people, he might have had a saltwater aquarium hobby or something.

But his grip made my skin buzz with the faint touch of magic. There are things other than fae that carry a feel of magic: witches, vampires, and a few others. But fae magic had a certain feel to it — I was willing to bet that Mr. Fideal was as fae as Zee . . . or at least as fae as Tad's bookstore guy.

I wondered what he was doing at a Bright Future meeting. It might be that he was here to keep track of what they were doing. Or maybe he was a part-breed and didn't even know what he was. A drop of fae blood could account for those young eyes in the older face and for the faintness of the magic I felt.

"Good to meet you," I told him.

"So you know what I do to earn my bread," he said in a gruffly friendly voice. "What is it that you do?"

"I'm a mechanic," I said.

"Righteous," declared Courtney. "My

Mustang's been making odd noises for the last couple of days. Do you think you could take a look at it? I don't have any money right now — just paid for this semester of school."

"I do mostly VWs," I told her, taking a card out of my purse and handing it to her. "You'd be better off taking it to a Ford mechanic, but you can bring it by my shop if you want. I can't do it for free. My hourly rates are better than most places, but since I don't work on a lot of Fords, it'll probably take me longer to fix."

I heard the front door open. A moment later Tim and Austin arrived with a case of beer and a couple of white plastic grocery bags filled with chips. They were greeted with cheers and mobbed for food and beer.

Tim set his burdens down on a small table next to the door and escaped being buried by foraging young men. He looked at me for a moment without smiling. "I thought you might bring your boyfriend."

"He's not my boyfriend anymore," I said — and the relief of that made me smile.

Courtney saw my relief and misread it. "Oh, honey," she said. "One of those, eh? Better off without them. Here, have a beer."

I shook my head, softening my refusal with a smile. "I never learned to like the stuff." And I intended to keep my wits about me to catch any clues that came my way, though my already-not-high hopes of that had been falling by the minute. I'd thought I was going to infiltrate an organized hate group, not a bunch of beer-swilling college kids and their teacher.

I was willing to swear there wasn't a murdering bastard among them.

"How about a Diet Coke," Tim said in a friendly voice. "I used to have a six-pack of ginger ale and another of root beer in the fridge, but I bet these turkeys have already finished them off."

He got a bunch of denying catcalls back that seemed to please him. Good for you, I thought, and quit feeling sorry for him because he didn't have a purple wall or a statue wearing a hat. *Find your own group to fit in with.*

"Diet Coke would be great," I told him. "Your house is pretty impressive."

That pleased him even more than the catcalls had. "I had it built after my parents died. I couldn't stand to stay in that old empty place alone."

Since Tim stayed to talk, Courtney was actually the one who got the pop for me. She handed it over and then patted Tim on the head. "What Tim isn't telling you is that his parents were rich. They died in a freak car accident a few years back and gave Tim an estate and life insurance that left him set for life."

His face tightened in embarrassment at her rather bold announcement in front of a relative stranger. "I'd rather have had my parents," he said stiffly, though he must have gotten over whatever grief he'd felt, because all he smelled of was irritation.

She laughed. "I knew your father, honey. No one would rather have had him than money. Your mother was a sweetie, though."

He thought about getting mad, then shrugged it off. "Courtney and I are kissing cousins," he told me. "It makes her pushy — and I've learned to tolerate her."

She grinned at me and took a long pull of her beer.

Over her shoulder I could see that the others had pulled the chairs around into a loose semicircle and were starting to get settled down with munchies propped on a couple of small, strategically placed tables.

Tim took a seat that someone else had moved and motioned to me to sit beside him, while Courtney went to scrounge her own chair.

Since it was his house, I'd kind of expected him to take the lead, but it was Austin Summers who stood in front and let out a loud whistle.

I wish he'd warned me. My ears were still ringing when he began talking.

"Let's get started. Who has business to address?"

It only took a very few minutes to discern that Austin was the leader. I'd seen the possibilities of his dominance at the pizza party, but I'd been talking to Tim instead of watching Austin. Here his role was as established as Adam's was in his pack.

Aiden Fideal, the fae teacher, was either second in line or third behind Courtney. I had a hard time deciding — because so did they. From the uncertainness of their placement, I was pretty sure that O'Donnell had occupied that spot previously. A petty tyrant like O'Donnell wouldn't have accepted Austin's leadership easily. If Austin had been fae, I'd have put him on the top of my suspect list — but he was more human than I.

Tim faded into the background as the meeting continued. Not because he didn't say anything, but because no one listened to him unless his remarks were repeated by either Courtney or Austin.

After a while I started to put some things together from chance remarks.

O'Donnell might have started Bright Future in the Tri-Cities, but he hadn't had much luck until he'd found Austin. They had met in a class at the community college a couple of years earlier. O'Donnell was taking advantage of the BFA program that paid for continuing education for the reservation guards. Austin divided his time between Washington State University and CBC and was almost through with a computer degree.

Tim, who had no need to find work, was older than most of them.

"Tim has a masters in computer science from Washington State," Courtney whispered to me. "That's how he met Austin, in a computer class. Tim still takes a couple of classes from CBC or WSU every semester. It keeps him busy."

Austin, Tim, and most of the students had belonged to a college club — which seemed to have had something to do with writing computer games. Mr. Fideal had been the faculty advisor for that club. When Austin got interested in Bright Future, he'd preempted the club. CBC had dissociated itself with the group when it became obvious the nature of their business had changed — but Mr. Fideal had kept the privilege of dropping in occasionally.

The first bit of business for Bright Future

this meeting was to send a bouquet to O'Donnell's funeral as soon as the time for it was arranged by his family. Tim accepted the assumption that he would pay for the flowers without comment.

Business concluded, one young man got up and presented methods sure to protect you from the fae, among them salt, steel, nails in your shoes, and putting your underwear on inside out.

In the question-and-answer session that followed, I finally couldn't keep my mouth shut anymore. "You talk as if all the fae are the same. I know that there are some fae that can handle iron and it would seem to me that the sea fae, like selkies, wouldn't have a problem with salt."

The presenter, a shy giant of a young man, gave me a smile, and answered with far more articulation than he'd managed during his presentation. "You're right, of course. Part of the problem is that we know that some of the stories have been embellished past all recognition. And the fae aren't exactly jumping up and down to tell us just what kind of fae are left — the registration process is a joke. O'Donnell, who had access to all the paperwork on the fae in the reservation, said that he knew for a fact that at least one in three lied when answering what they were. But part of what we're trying to do is sift through the garbage for the gold."

"I thought the fae couldn't lie," I said.

He shrugged. "I don't know about that, exactly."

Tim spoke up. "A lot of them made up a Gaelic- or German-sounding word and used that to fill out the form. If I said I was a Heeberskeeter, I wouldn't be lying since I just invented the word. The treaties that set up the reservation system didn't allow any questions asked about the way the registration forms were filled out."

By the time the meeting was wrapping up, I was convinced that none of these kids had anything to do with O'Donnell's killing spree and subsequent murder. I'd never attended the meeting of any hate group — being half-Indian and not quite human, I'd have been pretty out of place. But I hadn't been expecting a meeting conducted with all the passion and violence of a chess club. Okay, *less* passion and violence than a chess club.

I even agreed with most of what they said. I might like a few individual fae, but I knew enough to be afraid. Hard to blame these kids for seeing through the fae politicians and speech making. As Tim had told me, all they had to do was read the stories.

Tim walked me to my car after the meeting.

"Thanks for coming," he said, opening my door for me. "What did you think?"

I smiled tightly to disguise my dislike of the way he'd grabbed my door before I had. It felt intrusive — though Samuel and Adam, both products of an earlier era, opened doors for me, too, and they didn't bother me.

I didn't want to hurt his feelings, though, so all I said was, "I like your friends . . . and I hope you aren't right about the threat the fae present."

"You don't think we're a bunch of over-educated, under-socialized geeks running around yelling *the sky is falling?*"

"That sounds like a quote."

He smiled a little. "Directly from the *Herald.*"

"Ouch. And no, I don't."

I bent to get in the car and noticed that the walking stick was back, lying across the two front seats. I had to move it so I could sit down.

I glanced at Tim after I moved it, but he didn't seem to recognize the stick. Maybe O'Donnell had kept it out of sight during the Bright Future meetings; maybe it had kept itself out of sight. Nor did Tim seem to see anything odd about a person who had a walking stick in the front seat of their car. People tend to expect VW mechanics to be a little odd.

"Listen," he said. "I've had a little time to brush up on my Arthurian myths — read a little de Troyes and Malory after we got through talking. I wonder if you'd like to come over for dinner tomorrow?"

Tim was a nice man. I wouldn't have to worry about him practicing undue influence via some werewolf mojo or turning control freak on me. He'd never get mad and rip out someone's throat. He wouldn't kill two innocent victims in order to protect me or anyone else from the mistress of the vampires. I hadn't seen Stefan since then, but I often went months without seeing the vampire.

For a bare instant I thought about how nice it would be to go out with a normal person like Tim.

Of course, there was the small problem of telling him what I was. And the little fact that I wasn't interested in getting into his bed at all.

Mostly, though, I was more than half in love with Adam, no matter how much he scared me.

"Sorry, no," I said, shaking my head. "I just got out of one relationship. I'm not about to start another."

His smile widened a little and grew pained. "Funny, me, too. We'd been dating for three years and I'd just gone to Seattle to buy a ring. I took her to our favorite restaurant, the ring in my pocket, and she told me she was getting married in two weeks to her boss. She was sure I would understand."

I hissed in sympathy. "Ouch."

"She was married in June, so it's been a couple of months, but I don't really feel like getting involved again either." Evidently tiring of bending down, he crouched beside the car, putting his head just a little below mine. He reached out and touched me on the shoulder. He wore a plain silver ring, the once smooth surface scratched and worn. I wondered what it meant to him because he didn't seem to be the kind of man who normally wore rings.

"So why invite me to dinner?" I asked.

"Because I don't intend to turn into a hermit. In the spirit of 'Don't let the bastards get you down.' Why shouldn't we sit down and have a nice meal and a little conversation? No strings and I don't intend us to end up in bed. Just a conversation.

You, me, and Malory's *Le Morte d' Arthur.*" He gave me a twisted smile. "As an added bonus, one of the things I've taken a lot of classes in is cooking."

Another evening of arguing about Arthurian writers of the Middle Ages sounded like a lot of fun. I opened my mouth to accept but stopped without speaking the words. It might be fun, but it wasn't a good idea.

"How about seven thirty," he was saying. "I know it's late, but I have a class until six and I'd like to have dinner ready when you come."

He stood up and shut my door, giving it a pat before he strolled back to his house.

Had I just accepted a date with him?

Dazed, I started the Rabbit and headed for the highway home. I thought of all the things I should have said. I'd call him as soon as I got home and could look up his number. I'd tell him thanks but no thanks.

My refusal would hurt his feelings — but going might hurt him more: Adam would *not* like me having dinner with Tim. Not at all.

I'd just passed the exit for the Columbia Center Mall when I realized that Aiden Fideal was behind me. He'd pulled out of Tim's house at the same time as I — and about three other people. I'd only noticed him because he was driving the Porsche, a 911 wide-body like the ones I'd always lusted after — though I preferred black or red (clichéd as that was) to bright yellow. Someone around town drove a purple one that was just mouthwatering.

A Buick passed me and my headlights caught his bumper sticker: *Some people are like Slinkies. They aren't really good for anything, but they still bring a smile to my face when I push them down a flight of stairs.*

It made me laugh and broke the odd worry that seeing the Porsche just behind me had caused. Fideal probably lived in Kennewick and was just driving home.

But it wasn't long before the nagging feeling that I was being hunted came back to settle on the nerves in the back of my neck. He was still behind me.

Fideal was a fae — but Dr. Altman was the fae's hit man and she knew they couldn't attack me without retaliation. There was no reason for me to be nervous.

Calling Adam for help would be overkill. If Zee hadn't been in jail and if we'd been on speaking terms, I'd have called him, though. He wouldn't overreact like Adam might.

I could call Uncle Mike — assuming he

301

didn't share Zee's reaction and that he would take my phone call.

Uncle Mike might know if I was being stupid to let Fideal panic me unnecessarily. I took out my phone and flipped it open, but there was no welcoming light. The screen on the phone was blank. I must have forgotten to charge it.

I risked a speeding ticket and took the Rabbit up a notch. The speed limit was fifty-five here, and the police patrolled this stretch of highway often, so most of the traffic was actually traveling only sixty or thereabouts. I did a little weaving and breathed a sigh of relief when Fideal's distinctive headlights slipped out of sight behind a minivan.

The highway dropped me off on Canal Street, and I slowed to city speeds. *This must be my night to be stupid,* I thought.

First, I'd accepted an invitation to eat with Tim — or at least I hadn't refused — and then I'd panicked when I saw Fideal's car. Dumb.

I knew better than to accept an offer to dinner from Tim. No matter how good the conversation might be, it wasn't worth dealing with Adam about it. I should just have said no right then. Now it was going to be harder.

Oddly enough, it wasn't the thought of Adam's temper that dismayed me — knowing he was going to be angry if I did something usually just encouraged me to do it. I provoked him on a regular basis if I could. There was something about that man when he was all angry and dangerous that got my blood up. Sometimes my survival instincts are not what they should be.

If I went to Tim's house for a dinner for two — and whatever Tim had said, dinner alone with a man was a date — Adam would be hurt. Angry was fine, but I didn't want Adam hurt, ever.

The Washington Street light was red. I stopped next to a semi. His big diesel shook the Rabbit as we waited for a flood of nonexistent traffic. I passed him as we started up again and glanced in my rearview mirror to make sure he was far enough behind me before I pulled into the right-hand lane in preparation for my turn onto Chemical Drive. He was far enough back — and right next to him was the Porsche, which gleamed like a buttercup in the streetlights.

Sudden, unreasoning fear clenched my stomach until I regretted the Diet Coke. That I had no real reason for the fear didn't lessen its impact. The coyote had decided I was ignoring her and insisted that he was a threat.

I breathed through my teeth as the reaction settled down to an alert readiness.

I'd been willing to believe that we might have the same path home. That little stretch of highway was the fastest way to the eastern half of Kennewick — and you could get to Pasco and Burbank that way, too, though the interstate on the other side of the river was faster.

But as I turned onto Chemical Drive, which led only to Finley, he followed me — and I'd have noticed if there were a 911 yellow wide-body in Finley. He was following me.

Instinctively I reached for the cell phone again — and when I grabbed it out of the passenger seat, it dripped water all over my hand. I realized then that the smell of brine had been getting stronger and stronger for a while. I dropped the useless phone and brought my hand to my mouth. It tasted of swamp and salt, like a salt marsh rather than seawater.

Although Adam's house and my house share a back fence, his street turns off a quarter mile before mine does. I couldn't remember if Samuel was at work tonight or not — but even if Adam wasn't at his house, there was bound to be someone there. Someone who was a werewolf.

Of course, Jesse was likely to be there, too, and Jesse could protect herself even less than I could.

I took the turn onto Finley Road to give myself a chance to think. It was the long way around and I'd have to get back onto Chemical before I went home, but I'd made so many stupid moves tonight, I had to take time to make sure bringing this fae, whatever his intentions were, to Adam's house was a smart idea.

I shouldn't have worried. Just as I was passing Two Rivers Park, where the road was nice and deserted and the houses far away, the Rabbit coughed, sputtered, and choked before it died.

There was no shoulder to the road, so I guided the car off the blacktop and hoped for the best. If I left it on the road, some poor person, coming home late, could hit it and kill himself. The Rabbit bounced over some rocks, which didn't do my undercarriage any good, and came to rest in a relatively flat spot.

The car felt like a trap, so I got out as soon as the wheels quit turning. The Porsche had stopped on the highway and sat growling its throaty song.

Full dark had fallen while I was driving back, and the lights were hard on my sensitive eyes, one of the downsides of good night vision. I turned my head away from the headlights so when Fideal got out of his car, I heard it rather than saw it.

"Odd seeing a fae drive a Porsche," I told him coolly. "They might have an aluminum block, but the body is steel."

The car made a hollow sound, as if it had been patted. "Porsche puts many coats of good paint on their cars. I have an additional four coats of wax and I find that it doesn't trouble me at all," he said.

Like the water in my phone, he smelled of rotting vegetation and salt. Not being able to see him bothered me; I needed to get away from the headlights.

I could have run, but running from something that might be faster is more of a last resort than a first action. Maybe all he wanted was that stupid walking stick. So I got onto the road and walked a big semicircle around the car until I was facing the side of his car rather than the lights in front.

As my shoes hit the blacktop, I felt a well of magic that seemed to be spreading out through the asphalt. Strong magic usually is almost painful, like touching my tongue to both sides of a nine-volt battery. Tonight there was something more, something . . . predatory about it.

Fideal was not as weak as he'd appeared at Tim's party.

I hissed between my teeth as sharp pains shot up my legs. I stopped on the far side of the road. My eyes were still burning, but at least I could see him standing by the driver's side door. He looked a little different than he had at Tim's. I couldn't see him well enough for fine details, but it seemed to me that he was taller and broader than he'd been.

Courteously he'd waited until I stopped moving before speaking. It is generally a bad thing when someone hunting you is polite. It means they are sure they can take you anytime they want to.

"So you are the little dog with the curious nose," he said. "You should have kept your nose to your own kind."

"Zee is my friend," I told him. For some reason the "dog" part of that offended me. It would sound stupid to say, "I'm not a dog," though. "You fae were going to let him die for someone else's crime. I was the only one willing to look elsewhere for a murderer." I thought of a reason he might be upset with me. "Am I looking at a murderer now?"

He threw his head back and laughed, a full-throated barrel-chested laugh. When he spoke again, his voice acquired a Scot's brogue and had dropped half an octave. "I didn't kill O'Donnell," he said, which wasn't quite an answer.

"I have protection," I told him quietly, careful not to put a challenge in my voice. "Killing me will start a war with the were-wolves," I told him. "Nemane knows all about it."

He shook his head from side to side, like an athlete stretching out the muscles of his neck. His hair was longer, I thought, and rustled wetly when he moved.

"Nemane is not what she once was," he said. "She is weak and blind and troubles herself overmuch with humans." He inhaled and he grew. When he finished breathing in, the outline of his form was larger than any human male I'd ever seen by about a foot, and he was almost as wide as he was tall. My eyes were adjusting and I could see that size wasn't the only change.

"The call for your death has been set," he said. "It is too bad that no one told me until too late that the orders had been recalled."

He laughed again and it shook the froth of dark strands that covered him like a tattered overcoat. His lips were larger than they had been and there were long, pale shapes in the dark cavern of his mouth. "It has been so long." His voice was wet and sloppy. "Human flesh is sweet to my tongue and I have not partaken for so long that my very bowels cry out for sustenance." He roared like a winter wind as he leaped across the road in a single jump.

I was in coyote form and hightailing it at top speed down the road before he landed. Bits of clothing scattered behind me as I ran. I tripped once when my foot caught in my bra, but I rolled with it and shed the bra in my fall.

He could have had me then, but I think he was enjoying the chase. It must have been the reason he didn't just go back and get the Porsche. It might take him a minute to shrink down so he could get into it, but the car was a lot faster than I was, and it could run forever.

I had to stay on the road until it crossed the canal. Otherwise it was too far for me to jump across and I wasn't swimming anything with a water fae of some kind after me.

As soon as I was past it, I dodged down the road that paralleled the canal, running toward the river. I jumped through the fence behind the first house and tore through the field. By the time their dog noticed me and began barking an alarm, I was in the next field over and running through grass taller than I was. After a half mile of running, I slowed to a trot.

The ground was soft and there were horses and cows in the fields. A donkey chased me through its paddock with murderous intent, but I just picked up the pace until I could jump out of its paddock. Horses mostly don't care about coyotes, nor do cows. Chickens run, but donkeys hate us every one.

When I heard hoofbeats behind me, I thought maybe the donkey had jumped its fence — until the horse I'd just passed let out a terrified squeal.

Kelpies could take on the form of a horse, I thought as I moved back into top gear.

I learned that whatever Fideal was, he didn't like railroad tracks. Though he could cross them, they slowed him down and made him shriek with evident pain. Finley has lots of railroad tracks and, after that, I crossed them wherever I could without slowing down my headlong run for Adam's house.

On the flats Fideal was faster than I was, but he couldn't get through or over obstacles as quickly as I could. I scrambled over a twelve-foot-high chain-link fence that surrounded one of the big industrial compounds and wished it were iron. The barbed wire at the top made it a little interesting, but I managed.

The fence bent down under his weight and I heard the metal groan as the fence collapsed. It slowed him down. So I avoided the open gate and scrambled over the fence on the other side of the compound, too.

Though I hadn't turned, the river had, and I had to run about a half mile along the shore past several old barges that had been tied up along the shoreline. He gained on me until I found the big hedge of blackberries.

This was part of one of my usual trails and over the years I'd built a path under the bushes and so I could run almost unhindered. Fideal, being a lot bigger, didn't have that luxury.

When I cleared Adam's fence, I couldn't hear Fideal behind me so I changed as I ran. I mistimed it a bit and stumbled painfully to my knees in Adam's gravel driveway. Darryl's car was there, and Honey's Toyota. The little red Chevy truck belonged to Ben.

"Adam!" I yelled. "Trouble on the way!" My legs didn't want to work right as a single pair instead of two pairs, and I stumbled as

I tried to regain my feet and run at the same time.

By the time I was on the porch, Darryl had the front door open. I fell again and this time I just rolled until I hit the outside of the house, just under the big picture window.

"Some kind of water fae," I told him, panting hard and coughing with the force of my breathing. "Might look sort of like a horse or some hooved animal. Or it could be a swamp thingy as big as Adam's SUV. A monster with fangs."

I must have sounded like a ninny, but it didn't faze Darryl.

"You keep bothering the monsters, Mercy, and someday something's going to eat you." He sounded calm and cool as he kept his eyes on the fence I'd jumped over. He had a big automatic in one hand — he must carry concealed because I hadn't noticed him holding one when he opened the door.

"Oh, I hope not," I said in between gasps. "I don't want to be eaten. I've been counting on the vampires to kill me first."

He laughed, though it wasn't that funny. "Everyone else is changing," he told me, and he didn't mean clothes. But I could feel them, so he didn't need to tell me. "How far behind you is this thing?"

I shook my head. "Not far. I led it into the blackberries, but — *There! There!* From the river."

Darryl shifted his aim and began firing at the thing that emerged from the black water and trailed over Adam's groomed gravel beach.

I hastily plugged my ears in an attempt to save my hearing. Even with Adam's porch light and my own night vision, I couldn't really focus on the thing that Fideal had become. It was as though his body swallowed the light and left me with an impression of marsh grasses and water.

The bullets slowed him a little, but I didn't think they were doing enough damage to stop him. I'd caught my breath, even if my legs felt like they were made of rubber, and I had no intention of sitting here like bait.

I started to get up and Darryl grabbed my arm and jerked me down as the big plate glass window over me shattered and a werewolf leaped over my head and landed on the porch railing ten feet away. He paused there, examining Fideal.

"Careful, Ben," I said. "It's as fast as I am and it has great big teeth."

The lanky red werewolf glanced back and the porch gave a warning creak. Ben sneered at me, an expression infinitely more impressive with gleaming white fangs than it was when he did it as a human. He jumped off the porch and barreled silently into Fideal.

A black wolf, tipped with silver like a reverse Siamese cat, jumped out behind him. He turned Adam's eyes to me, where I sat covered in glass shards, and then looked at Darryl.

"Right," said Darryl, though I know Adam couldn't talk to his pack while he was in wolf shape the way the Marrok could.

Darryl dropped the gun he'd been firing continuously and picked me up gingerly. "Let's get you off the glass. If you bleed to death, Adam's going to make mincemeat out of Ben."

I looked down and realized that I was bleeding from small cuts all over my bare skin. I let Darryl carry me out of the glass and into the house before wriggling free.

He let me go and started tearing off his own clothes.

Another werewolf, this one tawny and beautiful, streaked by me, knocking me a step sideways. Honey. She was followed by another pair of wolves; one was brindled and the other gray. More of Adam's pack, though I couldn't have named either of them.

"Mercy, what is that thing?" Honey's husband, Peter, was still in human form. He saw my look and said, "Adam told me to stay human. I'm to get Jesse away if things go badly."

I quit paying attention to him when I heard a yelp from outside. It would have taken a lot of pain to wring a sound out of a wolf this close to the pack's den. They were trained to fight silently so as not to attract undue attention. That yelp meant someone was badly hurt.

I'd brought it here. I had to help fight.

"Cold iron." My voice jittered with adrenaline. "Salt won't work on that one, I don't think — and I'm a little short of underwear to turn inside out. No shoes. I need something steel."

"Steel?" asked Peter.

I ignored him and ran into the kitchen and grabbed a French chef's knife and a butcher knife out of the set of Henckels that Adam had paid a large fortune for. They weren't stainless steel because regular, high-carbon steel holds a better edge. It also works better on fae.

As I charged out of the kitchen, Honey's husband landed at the base of the stairs, right in front of me. I think he'd just jumped down the whole thing — werewolves can do things like that. He held a sword in his hand.

"Mercy," he said. His voice sounded different than I'd ever heard it. His pleasant Midwest accent disappeared and he sounded vaguely German, not like Zee exactly, but close. "Adam bound me to watch over Jesse and not help."

Something hit the side of the house hard.

A sword was better than two little knives. "Can you use that thing?"

"*Ja.*"

As Adam's declared mate, I could change his orders — though I'd have to answer for it if he got ticked off.

"Go help. I'll stay out of it and get Jesse out of here if it looks like it's going badly."

He was gone before the last words left my mouth.

I tried to look out the living room window, but the wraparound porch hid too much. Jesse's room would have a better view — and she might have clothes that would fit me.

I started up the stairs at a run, but by the time I hit the top, I was lucky to be walking. In coyote form, I can trot for hours, but sprinting is different. I just didn't have any more running in me.

Jesse must have heard me because she

stuck her head out of her bedroom and then rushed over. "Can I help?"

I looked down to see what caused the consternation in her face. It wasn't my nakedness. She'd grown up with werewolves, and shapeshifters can't afford too much modesty. For the wolves, the change is a slow process and it hurts; if they are tearing up clothing as they change, it just hurts that much worse. Makes them even grumpier than usual — so mostly they take their clothes off first.

No, it wasn't my nakedness; it was the blood. I was covered with it.

Appalled, I looked behind me at the carpet that was stained with my blood all the way up the stairs. "Darn it," I said. "That's going to be expensive to clean."

I heard a roar that shook the house and quit worrying about the carpet. I let go of the railing that I'd been using to hold me up and stumbled over to Jesse's window, which was opened wide. She'd pulled the screen off the window already. With the knives still in each hand, I crawled out and down onto the roof of the porch, where I could see what was going on.

The werewolves were badly battered. Ben was crumpled against Adam's SUV and there was a huge dent in the quarter panel just above him.

Darryl circled the fae, his brindled coat fading into the shadows. If he hadn't been moving, I don't know that I'd have seen him at all. Adam perched on the fae's back, his front paws raking through the fronds like a giant cat's, but I couldn't tell how much damage he was doing. Honey and her husband were working as a team. She'd harry the fae with quick leaping nips until he turned to her and her husband would take advantage of its inattention to dive in and rake it with his sword.

From my vantage point, I could hear Peter mutter, "Can't find flesh in all this seaweed."

"I can't tell if they're winning or losing," Jesse said as she climbed through the window. She threw her comforter over me and knelt near the edge of the roof.

"I can't either," I started to say, but I stopped halfway through the last word as a wave of magic brushed painfully over me and dumped me on my rump.

"Careful," I yelled to the wolves below. I was up and on the edge of the roof as quickly as I could manage — which was just in time to see the fae make an incredibly quick move across the stretch of beach and into the inky river. Adam was still on his back.

Werewolves can't swim. Like chimpanzees, they have too little fat: they are too dense to float. My foster father had committed suicide by walking into a river.

I started to jump off the roof. I could have changed in midair, and on four legs I'd have been in the water in seconds — but I'd promised to watch Jesse. Just because a promise becomes desperately inconvenient doesn't mean you don't have to keep it.

Peter dropped his sword and waded into the river without wasting an instant. The porch light showed me his head as it disappeared under the water.

Jesse's hand closed over mine in a bone-crushing grip.

"Come on, come on," she muttered, then let out a yip of joy as Peter reemerged, towing a coughing and sputtering wolf in his wake.

I sat down and buried my face in my hands in relief.

CHAPTER 10

"You are covered with blood and glass," Jesse snapped at me as she helped me drag my tired bones over the windowsill. "All that blood isn't going to do anything to help the wolves calm down."

"I have to go down and check," I insisted doggedly, not for the first time. "Some of them are hurt and it's my fault."

"They enjoyed every minute of that fight and you know it. It'll take them a bit to calm enough to be safe anyway. Dad'll come up when he's fit to talk. You get in the shower before you ruin the carpet."

I looked down and saw that I was still trailing blood. My feet started to throb as soon as I noticed.

With a little more prodding on Jesse's part, I shuffled off to the shower (in Adam's bedroom, since the hall shower was still exposed to the world). Jesse stuffed a pair of old sweats and a T-shirt that told everyone that I loved New York into my arms and shut the bathroom door behind me.

With the excitement done, I was so tired I could hardly move. Adam's bathroom was decorated in tasteful browns that somehow managed to escape being bland. His ex-wife, whatever her other faults — and they were many — had excellent taste.

While I waited for the shower to warm up, I glanced in the full-length mirror that covered the wall between the shower and the his-and-her sinks — and despite the guilt of bringing the fae down upon Adam's unsuspecting pack — I had to grin.

I looked like something out of a bad horror flick. Naked, I was covered from fingertip to elbow and toe to knee with marsh muck: it always amazes me how much swamp there is in the Tri-Cities, which is pretty much a desert. The rest of me sparkled, as though I'd covered myself with some glitter lotion instead of having a window broken over my sweat-covered body. Here and there were larger chunks of glass that dripped off me every time I moved — my hair was littered with them.

And everywhere, I was covered with tiny cuts that oozed blood. I picked up my foot and removed a largish splinter that was responsible for the small pool of blood that was growing around me. All the cuts were really going to hurt tomorrow. Not for the first time, I wished I healed like the werewolves did.

Steam began to rise from the shower and I trudged in and shut the glass door behind me. The water stung and I hissed as it hit tender bits — then swore when I stepped on another shard of glass, probably one of the ones that had fallen out of my hair as soon as the water hit me.

Too tired to fish the glass out, I leaned against the wall and let the water pour over my head and relief rolled over me with it, robbing my knees of their last bit of starch. Only the fear that I'd sit on glass and cut something more dear than my feet kept me from sinking to the tiled shower floor.

I took inventory.

I was still alive, and with the possible exception of Ben, so were the werewolves. I closed my eyes and tried not to think of the red wolf lying in the grass. Ben would probably be all right. Werewolves can take a lot of damage and there had been the others to keep the fae off him while he was helpless. He'd be all right, I reassured myself — but it didn't matter. Somehow I was going to have to work up the energy to get out of the shower and check.

The bathroom door opened, and I felt the wash of Adam's power.

"There's a Porsche sitting in the middle of Finley Road, right in front of Two Rivers Park," I said, though I hadn't remembered it until just that moment. "Someone's going to hit it and get killed if it doesn't get moved."

The door opened again and there was a quiet murmur of voices.

Even over the drowning spray of the water, I heard someone say, "I'll take care of it." Honey's husband again, I thought, because the werewolves can't talk in their wolf shape and he was the only one who had stayed human. Some of the wolves could have changed back by now — but without a good reason to do so, they'd probably just stay wolves for the night. Except for Adam.

Changing so quickly to fight the fae I'd brought him, the actual fight, then changing back in under an hour weren't going to leave him in a cheerful mood. I hoped he'd eaten something before he came up here — changing cost a lot of energy and I'd rather he not be hungry. I was bleeding too much for that to be good.

Telling Adam to take care of Fideal's car was supposed to have given me enough time to get out of the shower and wrap up in a towel, but I couldn't work up the energy to do anything but stand in the shower stall.

The big glass door swung open, but I didn't look up. Adam didn't say anything, but turned me with his hands on my shoulders so I was facing the showerhead. I bowed my head farther and took a step forward so the spray hit the top of my head rather than my face.

He must have picked up a comb, because he started to comb my hair free of glass. He was being very careful not to touch me anywhere else.

"Watch it," I said. "There's glass all over the floor."

The comb hesitated and then resumed its task. "I have my shoes on," he said. The rumble of his growl told me that the wolf wasn't far away no matter how human or gentle the hands that worked through my hair were.

"Is everyone all right?" I asked, though I knew he needed quiet now.

"Ben's hurt, but nothing that won't heal by morning — and nothing he doesn't deserve after jumping through the window. Glass is heavy and sharper than a guillotine's blade. He's lucky he didn't cut his own throat — and luckier still that all you have are cuts."

I could feel the anger vibrate through him. Werewolves, in their wolf form, are not always angry — just as a grizzly bear is not always angry: it only seems like it. If what Honey had told me was correct, Adam's temper was even more uncertain than usual. The fight wouldn't have helped it.

All that meant I couldn't cover my own uncertain state by pricking his temper — it wouldn't be fair to him. Damn it.

I was too tired to be playing the kind of games that kept werewolves calm — and keep him from knowing just how scared I had been at the same time.

"I'm not hurt," I said. "Just tired. That fae could run."

He growled at the mention of his recent opponent, and it wasn't a human sound.

I swore, though I usually tried not to do that in front of Adam, as he had the sensibilities of a man raised in the nineteen fifties when nice women didn't swear. "I'm too tired for this. I'm going to shut up now."

He resumed combing my hair and I waited patiently until he was satisfied that he'd gotten all the glass out. He shut off the water and got out of the shower stall to grab a towel out of a cabinet beside the door. I looked at him then, while his head was turned away so there was no chance of catching his gaze. Though he'd taken his shirt off, he was dressed in a very wet pair of jeans and tennis shoes.

As soon as he shifted his weight to turn, I dropped my eyes. He came back to the shower stall and dried me with a fluffy, sweet-smelling towel. It had spent too much time with a dryer sheet, so it wasn't very absorbent, despite the thick nap. I bit my lip so I wouldn't tell him so.

This close to him, I could smell how near his temper was to the surface, so I kept my gaze on our feet and made myself stand submissively while he worked off his temper by taking care of me.

I can fake submissive with the best of them. It's a survival technique around were-wolves.

He paused when he came to my belly. He let the towel drop away and dropped to one knee until his face was on level with my navel. He closed his brilliant eyes and pressed his forehead against the vulnerable softness under my rib cage.

The flesh of the belly is soft and sweet, unprotected. But my nose told me that he was definitely not thinking of food. For a breathless moment we both waited.

"Samuel told me about your tattoo," he

said, his breath warm against my skin.

Hadn't he seen it before? Being very careful not to tease him meant that I kept my clothes on around him — so maybe not.

"It's a coyote paw print," I told him. "I had it done when I was in college."

He raised his face until he was looking up at me. "It looks like a wolf print to me."

"Is that what Samuel said?" I asked. I wasn't unaffected by the close contact — I couldn't help but let the fingers of one hand slide through his hair. "What did he say? That I'd marked myself his property?" Oh, he wouldn't lie, not to another werewolf; it doesn't work. But a hint here and there was just as effective.

Adam pressed his head against me until all I could see was the top of his head. His cheek and chin were prickly, which should have tickled or hurt, but that wasn't the sensation that I was feeling. His hands slid up my legs to my rump, where they tightened, pulling me harder against his face.

His lips were soft, but not as soft as his tongue.

This was about to go one step further than I was ready for — and for a long moment I considered it. I closed my eyes. Maybe if it had been someone other than Adam, I'd have let him. But one of the things that the

Marrok had taught me is that with were-wolves you are always dealing with two sets of instincts. The first belonged to the beast, but the second belonged to the man. Adam wasn't a modern man, content to hop from bed to bed. In his era you didn't have sex unless you were married or getting married and I knew that he believed that.

Having been the result of a casual night of sex and grown up belonging to no one — I believed that, too. Oh, I'd fooled around a bit, but I didn't much anymore.

Would it be so bad to be Adam's mate? All that I had to do to let this relationship go one step more was nothing.

"My college roommate had grown up helping her parents run their tattoo shop and she put herself through college by doing tattoos. I tutored her in a few subjects and she offered to give me the tattoo in return," I told him, trying to distract one of us.

"Still scared of me?" he asked.

I didn't know how to answer him because that wasn't it, really. I was scared of the person I became around him.

He sighed and leaned back until none of his skin touched mine before coming back to his feet. He tossed the damp towel on the floor and stepped back out of the stall.

I started to get out, too.

"Stay there."

He grabbed another towel and wrapped me in it. Then he picked me up and set me on the counter between the sinks.

"I'm going to change out of this wet stuff and find something for your feet. There's glass scattered all over downstairs and everywhere you walked. You stay on this counter until I get back."

He didn't wait for my agreement, which was probably for the best as I would have choked on it. That last sentence would have made me bristle even if his tone of voice hadn't been military-sharp. Why was it that I was always trying to handle the werewolves instead of the other way around?

Maybe because Adam's other form had big claws and great big teeth.

I could reach Jesse's clothes without leaving the counter and so I ditched the towel and scrambled into the sweatpants and then the T-shirt. My T-shirts were the old-fashioned thick cotton kind, but Jesse wore fashionably thin ones that clung to every curve. Since my skin was still damp and the shirt was tight, I looked like a refugee from a wet T-shirt contest.

I snagged the towel and used it to cover my assets just as Adam strode back in. He was wearing clean, dry jeans and a different pair of tennis shoes. He hadn't bothered putting on a shirt: after two changes in under an hour, his skin must feel raw, like a bad sunburn. The shower wouldn't have helped that.

I focused on his feet and clutched the towel a little closer to my chest.

To my surprise, he took a good look at me and laughed abruptly. "You look so meek. I don't think I've ever seen you meek before."

"Looks are deceiving," I said. "What I am is exhausted, scared, and stupid. I'm sorry I brought it here and endangered Jesse."

I watched his shoes as they approached the counter. He leaned close, enveloping me in his power and in his scent. His face rubbed against my hair, and the faint trace of stubble caught on the wet strands.

"You have a few cuts on your scalp," he said.

"I'm sorry I brought him here," I told Adam again. "I thought I could lose him in the chase, but he was too fast. He has another form, some kind of horse, I think, though I was too busy running to look."

His head stilled and he took a deep breath, assessing my mood.

"Exhausted, scared, and stupid, you said." He paused as if he were evaluating what I'd said. "Exhausted, yes." If he could smell exhaustion, his nose was a lot better than mine, which I didn't believe. "And I can catch a faint trace of fear, though the shower took care of most of that. But stupid I don't believe. What else could you have done but bring it here where we could handle it?"

"I could have led it somewhere else."

He tipped my chin back and forced me to look into his bright gold eyes. "You'd have died."

His voice was soft, but the wolf's eyes were hot with the fire of battle.

"Jesse could have died . . . *you* almost did." For a moment I felt the gut-wrenching twist of seeing him disappear under the water.

He let me hide my face against his shoulder so he couldn't read my expression — but I felt the power that had been buzzing against my skin drop a notch. My reaction to his near-drowning pleased him.

"Shh," he said and one of his big, calloused hands slid under my hair and around the back of my neck to hold me against him. "I coughed up a gallon or two of river and am as good as new. Much better than I'd have been if you'd gotten yourself killed because you didn't trust me to take care of one lone fae."

Leaving my head tucked against him was as dangerous as anything I'd done tonight, and I knew it. I just couldn't seem to care. He smelled so good and his skin was so warm.

"All right," he said at last. "Let me take a look at your feet."

He did more than that. He washed them in hot water in the sink and scrubbed them with a brush he pulled out of a drawer that would have been uncomfortable even if my feet hadn't been all cut up.

To my yips, he purred a little, but it didn't slow down his scrub brush. Nor did I have a chance of pulling a foot out of his hand because he kept a firm grip on my ankle as he worked. He doused my feet in hydrogen peroxide and then dried them off with a dark towel.

"You're going to end up with bleached spots on the towel," I told him, pulling my feet away.

"Shut up, Mercy," he said, catching an ankle and dragging me over until he could hold the foot with one hand and use the towel to wipe my foot off with the other.

"Dad?" Jesse peered carefully around the door. When she got a good look at us, she trotted through the door and held out a cordless phone. "You have a phone call from

Uncle Mike."

"Thanks," he said and took the phone and tucked it against his ear. "Could you finish up here, Jesse? She just needs drying off, bandaging, and something on her feet before we let her out of here."

I waited until he took the phone out of the room and down the stairs before I grabbed the towel from Jesse, who was giggling.

"If you could just see your face," she told me. "You look like a cat in a bathtub."

I dried my feet and then opened the box of bandages Adam had set on the counter next to me. "I can dry my own damn feet," I snarled. "Sit here, stay here."

I was sitting between the sinks so there was room on the far side of the one nearest the door for Jesse to hitch a hip on it and half sit. "So why did you listen to his orders?"

"Because he just saved my bacon and I don't need to rile him more than he already is." There were only three cuts that needed bandages, all of them on my left foot.

"Come on," she said. "Admit it, you enjoyed him fussing over you just a little bit."

I gave her a look. When she didn't back down, I turned my attention to peeling the paper off a bandage so I could stick it on my foot. I wasn't going to admit to anything. Not with Adam just downstairs where he might overhear something I didn't want him to hear.

"How come you're wearing a towel?" she asked.

I showed her and she giggled. "Whoops. I forgot you wouldn't have a bra. I'll get a sweatshirt for you to wear over that."

When she was safely gone, I smiled to myself. She was right. There is something about having someone take care of you, even when you don't need it — maybe especially when you don't need it.

Something else made me happier, though. Even though Adam was on edge, even though he'd been issuing orders left and right, I hadn't felt that desire to do whatever he asked me that was part of his magic as the Alpha. If he could manage that under these circumstances . . . Perhaps I could be his mate and keep myself at the same time.

Jesse's shoes, which Adam had brought in for me, were too small, but in addition to the sweatshirt, she managed to scrounge up a pair of flip-flops that worked.

Honey's husband walked in the door as I came down the stairs, Honey, as gorgeous in wolf form as she was in human, at his side. He gave me a friendly smile when he saw me.

"I didn't find the Porsche, but your Rabbit was off the side of the road with the keys in the ignition. I couldn't start it, so I locked it up." He handed me the keys.

"Thanks, Peter. Fideal must have gone back for his car. That means he wasn't badly hurt." I'd been going to head over to my house, but with Fideal running around, it didn't sound like such a good idea.

Peter obviously shared my displeasure at the fae's state of health. "I'm sorry," he said. "The steel would have done it, I think, but I couldn't find his body under all the fronds."

"How is it that you're so comfortable with the sword?" I asked. "And why did Adam have a sword here anyway?"

"It's my sword," Jesse said. "I got it at the Renaissance Faire last year and Peter's been teaching me how to use it."

He smiled. "I was a calvary officer before I Changed," he explained. "We used guns, of course, but they weren't accurate. The sword was still our first weapon." He sounded as he always had, his Midwest accent firmly back in place.

He'd been Changed during the Revolutionary War era or a little before, I thought,

335

to use guns but rely on swords. That would make him, other than maybe Samuel and the Marrok himself, the oldest werewolf I'd ever met. Werewolves might not die of old age, but violence was part and parcel of their way of life.

He saw my surprise. "I'm not a dominant, Mercy. We tend to last a little longer." Honey pushed her face under his hand and he rubbed her gently behind her ears.

"Cool," I said.

"Fideal is in safe hands," said Adam from behind me.

I turned to see him replacing the phone in its base on the kitchen counter.

"Uncle Mike assures me that it was a mistake — an overeagerness on the part of Fideal to carry out the Gray Lords' orders."

I raised my eyebrows. "He told me he was hungry for human flesh. I guess that could be overeagerness."

He looked at me and I couldn't read his face or his scent. "I talked to Samuel earlier. He's sorry to have missed the excitement, but he's at home now. If Fideal follows you home, he'll have Samuel to contend with." He waved his hand around. "And there are plenty of us here to come to your aid."

"Are you sending me home?" Was I flirting? Damn it, I was.

He smiled, first with his eyes and then his lips, just a little, just enough to turn his face into something that made my pulse pick up. "You can stay if you'd like," he said, flirting right back. Then, a wicked light gleaming in his eyes, he went one step too far. "But I think there are too many people around for what I'd like you to stay for."

I dodged around Honey's husband and out the door, the flip-flops making little snapping sounds that didn't cover up Adam's final comment. "I like your tattoo, Mercy."

I made sure that my shoulders were stiff as I stalked away. He couldn't see the grin on my face . . . and it faded soon enough.

From the porch I could see the damage the fight had done to both the house and the SUV. That dent in the side of the shiny black vehicle was going to be expensive to fix. The side of the house had taken some damage, too, and I didn't know how much it would cost to repair. When I'd had to have the siding replaced on my trailer, the vampires had picked up the tab.

I started adding up the cost of the fight. I didn't know exactly what Fideal had done to my car, but it was going to take hours to fix, even if I could scrounge all the parts off the dead Rabbit presently annoying Adam in my back field. And somewhere I was going to have to come up with money to pay off Zee (and I really didn't want to borrow it from Samuel) — unless Zee had been playing some elaborate game to keep me from investigating the murder.

I rubbed my face, suddenly tired. I'd kept mostly to myself since I left the Marrok's pack when I was sixteen. The only problems I'd stuck my nose into had been my own. I stayed out of werewolf business and Zee kept me out of his. Somehow in the past year all that careful management had gone to hell.

I wasn't sure that there was a way back to my old peaceful existence, or if I even wanted it. But my new lifestyle was starting to get expensive.

A piece of gravel slid between the flip-flop and my sore foot and I yelped. It was getting painful, too.

Samuel was waiting for me on the porch with a mug of hot chocolate and an expert glance that checked for wounds.

"I'm fine," I told him, scooting past the open screen door and snagging the cocoa on the way. It was instant, but the marshmallows were just what I needed. "Ben's the one who got hurt, and I think I saw Darryl limping."

"Adam didn't ask me to come over, so neither of them must have been hurt very badly," he said, shutting the door. When I sat on a chair in the living room, he sat on the couch across from me. "Why don't you tell me about tonight. Like how you happened to get chased by the Fideal."

"*The* Fideal?"

"It used to live in a bog and eat straying children," he told me. "You're a little older than its usual fare. So what did you do to tick it off?"

"Nothing. Not a darn thing."

He made one of those sounds he used to let me know he wasn't buying my story.

I took a long drink. Maybe another viewpoint would notice something I had missed. So I told him most of it — leaving out only what had gone on between Adam and me after I'd gotten into the shower.

As I talked, I noticed that Samuel looked tired. He loved working in the emergency room, but it took a toll. Not just the odd hours, though they could be bad enough. Mostly it was the stress of keeping control when surrounded by blood and fear and death.

By the time I finished my story, he looked better. "So you went to a Bright Future meeting, hoping to find someone else who might have killed this guard, and ran into a bunch of college kids — and a fae who decided that eating you would be fun."

I nodded. "That's about it."

"Could the fae have been the killer?"

I closed my eyes and pictured Fideal's fight with the werewolves. Could he have ripped a man's head off his shoulders? "Maybe. But he didn't seem concerned about the investigation."

"You said that he was angry you were at the meeting. Could he have been worried that you were closing in on him?"

"That might have been it," I said. "I'll call Uncle Mike and see if there's any reason Fideal might have wanted the other fae dead. He certainly knew O'Donnell — and the more I find out about him, the odder it seems that someone hadn't killed him years ago."

Samuel smiled a little. "But you're not convinced the Fideal did it."

I shook my head. "He's put himself on the top of my list, but . . ."

"But what?"

"He was so hungry. Not for sustenance, though that was part of it, but for the hunt." Samuel the werewolf would understand what I meant. "I think that if Fideal had killed the guard, O'Donnell's death would have been different. He'd have been found drowned, or eaten, or never found at all." Putting it into words made it more than a suspicion. "I'll call Uncle Mike and see what he thinks, but I don't believe it was Fideal."

I remembered that I had something else to talk to Uncle Mike about, too. "And that walking stick showed up in my car tonight, again."

I started to get up to get the phone, but my legs had had enough and I fell back. "Darn it."

"What's wrong?" The tired relaxation left Samuel between one heartbeat and the next — I gave him an exasperated glance.

"I told you, I'm fine. Nothing some stretches, Icy Hot, and a good night of sleep won't cure." I thought of all the little cuts and decided to do without the Icy Hot. "Can you throw me the phone?"

He plucked it off its base on the table next to the couch and tossed it to me.

"Thanks." I'd been calling him so often the past few days that I had Uncle Mike's number memorized. It took me a few minutes of wading through minions before Uncle Mike himself got on the phone.

"Could Fideal have killed O'Donnell?" I

asked without ceremony.

"Could have, but didn't," answered Uncle Mike. "O'Donnell's body was still twitching when Zee and I found him. Whoever killed him did it while we were still standing on the doorstep. The Fideal's glamour isn't good enough to hide himself from me if he were that close. And he'd have bitten O'Donnell's head off and eaten it, not just torn it off."

I swallowed. "So what was Fideal doing at the Bright Future meeting and why wasn't his scent at O'Donnell's?"

"The Fideal went to a couple of meetings so he could keep an eye on them. He told us that they were more talk than action and mostly quit attending meetings. When O'Donnell was killed, he was asked to take another look. And he found himself a nosy coyote with a death sentence on her head — a nice evening snack." Uncle Mike sounded irritated, and not with Fideal.

"And when did the coyote end up with a price on her head and why didn't you warn me?" I asked, feeling indignant.

"I told you to leave it alone," he said, his voice suddenly cold with power. "You know too much and you talk too much. You need to do as you are told."

Maybe if he'd been in the room, I'd have

felt intimidated. But he wasn't, so I said, "And Zee would be convicted of murder."

There was a long pause, which I broke. "And then he'd be summarily executed as called for by the fae laws."

Samuel, whose sharp ears had no trouble hearing both sides of the phone conversation, growled. "Don't try throwing this on Mercy, Uncle Mike. You knew she wouldn't leave it alone — especially if you told her to. *Contrary* is her middle name and you played her into looking further than you could. What did the Gray Lords do? Did they order you and the rest of the fae to stop looking for the real killer? Excepting only Zee's capture, they really have no quarrel with the person who killed O'Donnell, do they? He was the one killing the fae and got killed in return. Justice is served."

"Zee was cooperating with the Gray Lords," said Uncle Mike. The apology that had replaced the anger told me not only was Samuel right — Uncle Mike had wanted me to continue investigating — but also Uncle Mike's ears were as sharp as the werewolf's. "I didn't think they would send anyone else to enforce the punishment and the fae here I have some control over. If I'd known they were sending Nemane, I'd have warned you. But she's issued a stay of execution."

"She's an assassin," growled Samuel.

"You wolves have your own assassin, don't they, Samuel Marrokson?" snapped Uncle Mike. "How many wolves has your brother killed to keep your people safe? Do you begrudge us the same necessity?"

"When they come after Mercy, I do. And Charles only kills the guilty, not the inconvenient."

I cleared my throat. "Let's not get diverted from the point. Could Nemane have killed O'Donnell?"

"She's better than that," Uncle Mike said. "If she'd killed O'Donnell, no one would have known it wasn't an accident."

Once more I was left without a suspect.

Any of the werewolves could have done it, I thought, remembering the speed that ripped O'Donnell's head from his body. But they had no reason to, and I hadn't smelled them at O'Donnell's house. The vampires? I didn't know enough about them — though I knew more than I wanted to. I knew they could hide their scents from me if they thought about it. No, O'Donnell's killer had been one of the fae.

Well, if Uncle Mike wanted me to investigate, maybe he'd answer some questions.

"O'Donnell was taking things from the

people he killed, wasn't he?" I asked. "The walking stick — which is in my Rabbit, parked off Finley Road over by Two Rivers, Uncle Mike — was one of those. But there were others, weren't there? The first fae killed, Connora, she was a librarian — she'd have had some of the artifacts, wouldn't she? Small things because she was not powerful enough to keep anything anyone else wanted. The walking stick came from the house of the fae with a forest for a backyard. I could smell him on it. What else was stolen?"

I'd been reading Tad's friend's book. There were a lot of things that I wouldn't want in just anyone's hands. There were some things I wouldn't want in *anyone's* hands.

There was a long pause, then Uncle Mike said, "I'll be over in a few minutes. Stay there."

I tossed Samuel the phone and he hung it up. Then I got to my feet, and retrieved the book I'd borrowed out of the gun safe in my room.

There were actually several walking sticks — one that would lead you home no matter where you roamed, one that allowed you to see people for what they were, and the third, the one that had been following me, was the stick that multiplied the farmer's sheep. None of them sounded bad until you read the stories. No matter how good they seemed, fae artifacts had a way of making their human owners miserable.

I'd found Zee's knife, too. The book called it a sword, but the hand-drawn illustration certainly depicted the weapon I'd twice borrowed from Zee.

Samuel, who'd left the couch to kneel beside my chair as I paged through the section I'd read, hissed between his teeth and touched the illustration: He'd seen Zee's knife, too.

Uncle Mike came in without knocking on the door.

I knew it was him by the deliberate sound of his footsteps and by his scent — spice and old beer — but I didn't look up from the book when I asked, "Was there something that allows the murderer to hide from magic? Is that why you had to call me in to identify the murderer?"

There were a couple of things in the book that would protect someone from the fae's anger or make them invisible.

Uncle Mike shut the door, but stayed just in front of it. "We retrieved seven artifacts from O'Donnell's house. That's why Zee didn't have time to hide from the police —

and why I left him to take the blame alone. The things we found were items of small power, nothing important except that they existed — and fae power in human hands is not usually a good thing."

"You missed the walking stick," I said, looking up. Uncle Mike looked more wrinkled and tired than his T-shirt and jeans.

He nodded. "And there was nothing we found that could have prevented us from finding O'Donnell — so we have to believe that the murderer left with at least one more item."

Samuel, like me, had refrained from looking at Uncle Mike when he'd entered — a small power play that subtly put us in charge. That Samuel had done it told me that he, too, didn't entirely believe Uncle Mike was on our side. Samuel came to his feet before he turned his attention from the book to the fae. He used his extra inches of height to stare down at Uncle Mike.

"You don't know what O'Donnell took?" he asked.

"Our librarian was trying to compile a list of everything our people had. Since she was the first one to die . . ." He shrugged. "He stole the list and there are no copies that I know of. Maybe Connora gave one to the Gray Lords."

"Was O'Donnell looking for the artifacts when he started to date her?" I asked.

He frowned at me. "How did you know they were dating?" He shook his head. "No. Don't tell me. It's best I don't know if you've fae who are talking to you."

He was trying to keep Tad out of it, I thought.

Uncle Mike flopped on the couch, closing his eyes, giving in to the exhaustion that he was obviously feeling — and giving Samuel the upper hand without a fight.

"I don't think he planned the thefts to start with. We've talked to her friends. Connora chose him. He thought he was doing her a favor — she thought he deserved what she planned to do with him." He looked at me. "Our Connora could be kind, but she despised humans, especially anyone connected to the BFA. She played with him awhile before tiring of her game. The day before she died, she told one of her friends she was dropping him."

"So why did you need Mercy?" Samuel asked. "He was the obvious suspect."

Uncle Mike sighed. "We had just set our sights on him when the second victim turned up dead. It took a while before anyone would talk to us about her affair. For a fae to take up with a human is encouraged. Half-breeds are better than no children at all. But O'Donnell — all the guards really are the enemy. And a fae doesn't consort with the enemy . . . especially when they are someone like O'Donnell."

"She was slumming," I said.

He considered it. "If one of your friends was consorting with a dog, would it be considered slumming?"

"So he thinks he's doing her a favor and she tells him what she really thinks of him — and he kills her."

"That's what we think. When the second victim was found — we thought it was unlikely that a human could have killed her so we didn't look at O'Donnell again. It wasn't until the third murder that we realized that the motive was theft. Connora had a few items, but no one thought to check if any were missing. She also must have had something else, something that allowed him to hide from our magic. Something much more powerful than anything someone like her should have had."

He looked at me and gave me a tired smile. "We are a secretive people, and even the risk of disobeying the Gray Lords' orders is not worth giving up all of our secrets. If something you possess is too powerful, They will confiscate it. If They had known that she had something of power, she'd have been forced to give it to someone who could take care of it."

"So O'Donnell gets it instead." I closed the book and set it beside me.

"And the list she had compiled for the Gray Lords, of the items they wanted recorded." He spread his hands. "We aren't sure that she had a copy in her house. One of her friends saw it, but Connora might have turned it over to the Gray Lords without keeping a copy."

That didn't sound like the woman whose house I'd searched. A woman like that would have kept a copy of everything. She loved the storage of knowledge.

"So O'Donnell takes that list," I said. "After playing with whatever toys he stole from Connora, he decided he wanted more. He looks at the list and goes after the things he wants." My sample size was limited, but — "It seemed to me that he was killing the least powerful, Connora, to the most, the forest fae who was last killed. Is that right?"

"Yes. She might have told him or maybe she had the list organized that way. He didn't get it quite right, by the way, but close enough. I suppose whatever items he stole allowed him to kill people he would otherwise never have been able to touch."

"Do you have any idea at all what things O'Donnell's killer might have?" Samuel growled.

Uncle Mike sighed. "No. But he doesn't either. The list said things like 'one walking stick' or 'a silver bracelet,' but it didn't explain what they were. Mercy, the walking stick wasn't in your car. The Fideal says that he didn't touch it. I suspect it will show up again — it has been persistent in following you."

"It *is* the walking stick that would make all my ewes have twins, isn't it?" I asked, though I was almost certain. The stories about the others had worried me enough to be grateful the stick was useless to me.

He laughed. It started from his belly and worked its way to his eyes, until they twinkled merrily. "You have some ewes you plan on breeding?"

"No, but I'd like to be able to travel more than five miles from home without finding myself on my own doorstep — or worse, be able to see all the faults in the people around me without any of the goodness." Not that any of that had been happening, but for all I knew, the stick had to be activated somehow in order to work.

"Not to worry," he said, still grinning. "If you decide to be a sheep farmer, all of your sheep would have healthy twins until the stick decided to roam again."

I let out a sigh of relief and turned back to what I needed to know. "When O'Donnell was killed, were you and Zee the only ones who knew he was the killer?"

"We hadn't told anyone else."

"Were you the only ones who knew the murderer was stealing artifacts?" I caught a whiff of something magical and tried to keep my face from showing my sudden alertness.

"No. It wasn't talked about, but as soon as we discovered that Connora's list had been taken, we started asking around. Anyone would have made the obvious connection."

Beside me, Samuel nodded in happy agreement. Not that he should have objected to anything Uncle Mike said but . . .

"Quit that," I told Uncle Mike. I noticed that the tiredness I'd seen in him when he came was gone and he once more appeared to be a kindly man who made his living making people happy.

"What?"

I narrowed my gaze at him. "I don't like you right now, and no fae magic is going to change that." Samuel jerked his head toward me. Maybe he hadn't caught that Uncle

Mike was using some kind of charisma magic — or maybe he smelled that I was lying. I did like Uncle Mike, but Uncle Mike didn't need to know that. He'd be easier to pry information out of as long as I could keep him feeling guilty.

"My apologies, lass," he said, sounding as appalled as he looked. "I'm tired and it's a reflex thing."

That might be true, it might be reflex, but he didn't say he wasn't doing it deliberately either.

"I'm tired, too," I said.

"All right," he said. "Let me tell you what we are going to do right now. It is agreed among us that the Fideal offered first offense. It is agreed among us that your death would cost the fae more than it would gain us — you can thank Samuel and Nemane for that."

He leaned forward. "So here is what we can offer you. As it seems important to you that Zee be proven innocent, we can work on that — so you don't cause even greater problems for us. We are allowed to aid the police — except that we cannot tell them about the stolen things. They are powerful, some of them, and it is better if the mortals don't have any idea that they might exist."

Cool relief flowed down my spine. If the

Gray Lords were willing to accept the time and notoriety of an investigation, then Zee's chances had risen exponentially. But Uncle Mike hadn't finished speaking.

". . . So you may leave the investigation to us and to the police."

"Good," said Samuel.

Now it was true I had no idea where to look for O'Donnell's killer. Perhaps it had been Fideal, or another of the fae, maybe someone who cared for one of the victims, who had somehow discovered O'Donnell was the killer. If it were one of the fae, which at this point was probable, I didn't have a chance of finding out anything. So maybe if Samuel hadn't said "Good," my response to Uncle Mike would have been different — but probably not.

"I'll make sure and keep you informed when I find out anything interesting," I told them gently.

"It is too dangerous," Uncle Mike said, "even for heroes, Mercy. I don't know what relics the killer has, but the things we recovered were lesser items, and I know that Herrick — the forest lord — was a guardian of some greater items."

"Zee is my friend. I'm not going to leave his life in the hands of people who were willing for him to die for this because it was more convenient for them."

Uncle Mike's eyes glittered with some strong emotion, but I couldn't tell what it was. "Zee seldom forgives trespasses, Mercy. I have heard he was so angry that you betrayed his trust that he will not speak to you."

I paid close attention to that "I have heard." "I have heard" wasn't the same thing as "Zee is angry with you."

"I've heard the same," I told him. "But I am Zee's friend anyway. If you'll excuse me, I need to get to bed now. Work starts bright and early."

I heaved myself out of the chair, tucked the book under my arm, and waved at both of the disapproving males as I limped out of the living room on my sore feet. I closed the bedroom door on them and did my best not to listen to them discussing me behind my back. They weren't very polite. And Samuel, at least, should know me better than to think I could be persuaded to sit back and leave Zee to fae hands.

CHAPTER 11

I called Tim the next morning before I went to work. It was early, but I didn't want to miss him. He'd caught me off guard last night, but I had no business dragging a human into my mess of a love life — even if I liked him that way, which I didn't.

Maybe I couldn't live with Adam — but it looked like I was going to try. If I went to Tim's, it would hurt Adam and give Tim the wrong impression. It had been stupid not to just refuse yesterday . . .

"Hey, Mercy," he said as he picked up the phone. "Listen, Fideal called me last night — what did you do to tick him off? Anyway he told me that you came to our meeting to do some investigating into O'Donnell's death. He said you knew the suspect they have in custody."

There was absolutely no anger in his voice, which pretty much meant that he must have been speaking the truth when he said he wasn't interested in a romantic entanglement. If he'd been interested in me, he'd have felt used.

Good. He wouldn't feel bad when I told him I couldn't go.

"Yes," I said cautiously. "He's an old friend. I know that he didn't do it, which is more than anyone else investigating can say." Zee's name was still being withheld from the press, as well as his being a fae. "Since no one else was doing anything, I've been poking around."

"I suppose we're on the top of the list of suspects," said Tim matter-of-factly. "O'Donnell wasn't exactly rolling in friends."

"On top of my list until I attended one of your meetings," I told him.

He laughed. "Yeah, none of us is exactly murderer material."

I didn't agree with him — anyone can be driven to kill, given the right cause. Except for Fideal, though, none of them were capable of killing someone the way O'Donnell had been killed.

"I didn't think of it at the time," he said. "But after Fideal talked to me, I started thinking. That walking stick in your car was O'Donnell's, wasn't it? He'd just bought it off of eBay a couple of days before he died."

"Yes."

"Do you think it had something to do with his death? I know the police say they don't think that robbery was the motive, but O'Donnell started collecting Celtic stuff a couple of months ago. He claimed it was pretty valuable."

"Did he say where he got it?" I asked.

"He said he inherited some of it and the rest he picked up on eBay." He paused. "You know, he said that it was all magical fae stuff, but he couldn't get any of it to do anything. I assumed that he was just being conned . . . but do you suppose he actually got something that really belonged to the fae and they decided to take it back?"

"I don't know. Did you get a good look at his collection?"

"I recognized that staff," he said slowly. "But not until Fideal told me that you had a connection with O'Donnell. There was a stone with some writing on it, a few battered pieces of jewelry that might have been silver — or silver plate . . . If I took a look at his collection, I might be able to tell you what is missing."

"I think the whole collection is missing. Except for the walking stick." I saw no need to tell him that the fae had gotten some of it back.

He whistled. "So it was a robbery."

"That's what it looks like. If I can prove that, then my friend is no longer a good suspect."

The Gray Lords didn't want any mortals knowing that they had magical artifacts, and I could see their point. The problem was that the Gray Lords could be ruthless in making sure that no word got out. Tim already knew too much.

"Did Fideal know about the collection?" I asked.

Tim considered it. "No. I don't think so. O'Donnell didn't like him, and Fideal never went to O'Donnell's house. I think the only ones he showed it to were Austin and me."

"Okay." I took a deep breath. "Look, it might be dangerous to know about that collection. If he did manage to find something that belonged to the fae, they wouldn't want that known. And you, of all people, know how ruthless they are. Don't talk to the police or anyone else about it for now."

"You do think it was a fae who killed him," Tim said, sounding a little taken aback.

"The collection is gone," I said. "Maybe one of the fae sent someone after it, or maybe someone else believed O'Donnell's stories and wanted it. I might be able to figure out more, if I knew what he had. Could you make a list of what you remember?"

"Maybe," he said. "I only saw it the once. How about I do my best to write it down and we can take a look at them tonight?"

I remembered that I'd called him to cancel our dinner.

He didn't give me a chance to say anything. "If I have all day to think about it, I should be able to put together most of it. I'll see Austin at school; we usually do lunch together. He saw O'Donnell's collection, too, and he's a pretty decent artist." He gave a rueful laugh. "Yes, I know. Good looks, intelligence, and talented, too. He can do anything. If he wasn't so nice, I'd hate him, too."

"Drawings would be terrific," I said. I could compare them to the drawings in Tad's friend's book. "Just remember that this is dangerous stuff."

"I will. See you tonight."

I hung up the phone.

I ought to call Adam and tell him what I was doing. I dialed the first number and then hung it up. It was easier to get forgiveness than permission — not that I should need permission. Getting a list of what O'Donnell had stolen was a good enough reason that Adam would understand why I went to Tim's house. He might get mad, but he wouldn't be hurt.

And Adam angry was really an awesome sight. Was I a bad person that I enjoyed it?

Laughing to myself, I went to work.

Tim opened his own door this time, and the house smelled of garlic, oregano, basil, and fresh-baked bread.

"Hi," I said. "Sorry I'm late. It took me a while to get the grease out from under my nails." I'd taken Gabriel and some chains out to the Rabbit after work and towed it home with my Vanagon. It had taken a little longer than I'd expected. "I forgot to ask what to bring so I stopped and picked up some chocolate for dessert."

He took the paper bag and smiled. "You didn't have to bring anything, but chocolate is —"

I sighed. "A girl thing, I know."

His smile widened. "I was going to say, it is always good. Come in."

He led me through the house and into the kitchen, where he had a small bowl of Caesar salad.

"I like your kitchen." It was the only room that seemed to have a personality. I'd been expecting oak cabinets and granite counter tops and I'd been right about the counters. But the cabinets were cherry, and contrasted nicely with the dark gray counters. Nothing too daring, but at least it wasn't bland.

He looked around with a frown. "Do you think it looks all right? My fiancée — *ex-*fiancée — told me I needed a decorator for the kitchen."

"It's lovely," I assured him.

A bell chimed and he opened the oven door and pulled out a small pizza. My oven's timer buzzes like an angry bee.

The smell of the pizza distracted me from my oven-envy.

"Now that smells marvelous," I told him, closing my eyes to get a better sniff.

A red flush tinted his cheeks at my compliment as he slid it onto a stone round and cut it with expert speed. "If you'll get the salad and follow me, we can eat."

Obediently I took the wooden bowl of greens and followed him through the house.

"This is the dining room," he told me unnecessarily, since the big mahogany table gave it away. "But when I eat alone or with just a couple of people, I eat out here."

"Out here" was a small circular room surrounded by windows. The shape of the room was innovative, but it was out-blanded by beige tiles and window treatments. His architect would be sad to know his artistic vision had been swallowed by insipidness.

Tim set the pizza on the small oak table and opened the roman blinds so we had a view of his backyard.

"I keep the curtains down most of the time, or it gets like an oven in here," he said. "I suppose it will be nice in the winter."

He'd already set the table, and like the kitchen, his tableware was a surprise. Handmade stoneware plates that didn't match exactly, either in size or color, but somehow complemented each other, and handmade pottery goblets. His was blue with a cracked glaze finish and mine brown and aged-looking. There was a pitcher on the table, but he'd already filled the glasses.

I thought of Adam's house and wondered if he still used his ex-wife's china the way Tim obviously used the stuff his ex-fiancée or maybe the decorator had chosen.

"Sit, sit," he said, following his own advice. He put a piece of pizza on my plate, but allowed me to get my own salad and a generous helping of some kind of baked pear dish.

I took a cautious sip of the contents of my glass. "What is this?" I asked. It wasn't alcoholic, which surprised me, but something both sweet and tart.

He grinned. "It's a secret. Maybe I'll show you how to make it after dinner."

I sipped again. "Yes, please."

"I noticed you're limping."

I smiled. "I stepped on some glass. Nothing to worry about."

We both quit talking as we dug into the meal with appetite.

"Tell me about your friend," he said as he ate. "The one the police think killed O'Donnell."

"He's a grumpy, fussy old man," I said. "And I love him." The pears had some sort of brown sugar glaze. I expected them to be too sweet, but they were tart and melted in my mouth. "Mmm. This is good. Anyway, right now he's ticked off at me for poking my nose into this investigation." I took a deep drink. "Or else he thinks it's dangerous and I'll quit investigating if he makes me think he's angry with me." Zee was right, I talked too much. Time to shift the conversation Tim's way. "You know, I'd have thought you would be angry with me when you found out I had an ulterior motive for attending your meeting."

"I always wanted to be a private investigator," Tim confided. He'd finished his food and was watching me eat with a pleased expression. "Maybe if I liked O'Donnell, I'd have been angrier."

"Were you able to come up with a list?" I asked.

"Oh, yes," he lied.

I frowned at him and put down my fork. I'm not as good at smelling a lie as some of the wolves. Maybe I'd misread his response. It seemed like an odd thing to lie about.

"Did you make sure that Austin wouldn't talk about it to anyone?"

He nodded and his smile widened. "Austin won't tell anyone. Finish up your pears, Mercy."

I had eaten two bites before I realized something was wrong. Maybe if I hadn't been fighting this kind of compulsion with Adam, I wouldn't have noticed anything at all. I took a deep breath and concentrated, but couldn't smell any magic in the air.

"This was terrific," I told him. "But I'm absolutely full."

"Take another drink," he said.

The juice or whatever it was tasted better with every sip — but . . . I wasn't thirsty. Still, I'd swallowed twice before I thought. It wasn't like me to do anything someone told me to do, let alone everything. Maybe it was the juice.

As soon as the doubt touched my mind, I could feel it. The sweet liquid burned with magic and the goblet throbbed under my hand — so hot that I was surprised my hand wasn't smoking.

I set the old thing down on the table and wished the stupid book had included a picture of Orfino's Bane — the goblet that the fairy had used to rob Roland's knights of their ability to resist her will. I'd bet it would match the rustic goblet beside my plate.

"It was you," I whispered.

"Yes, of course," he said. "Tell me about your friend. Why do the police think he killed O'Donnell?"

"They found him there," I told him. "Zee could have run, but he and Uncle Mike were trying to gather all the fae artifacts so the police wouldn't find them."

"I thought I got all the artifacts," said Tim. "The bastard must have been taking more things than the ones I sent him for. Probably thought that he might get more money for them somewhere else. The ring isn't as good as the goblet."

"The ring?"

He showed me the worn silver ring I'd noticed last night.

"And it makes the tongue of the wearer sweeter than honey. It's a politician's ring — or will be," he said. "But the goblet works better. If I'd made him drink before he went out, he wouldn't have been able to take more. I told him if we took too much, the fae would start looking outside Fairyland for their murderer. He should have listened to me. I suppose your friend is a fae and was going to talk to O'Donnell about the murders."

"Yes." I had to answer him, but I could hold back information if I tried. "You hired O'Donnell to get magic artifacts and kill the fae?"

He laughed. "Killing the fae was his thing, Mercy. I just gave him the means to do it."

"How?"

"I went over to his house to talk to him about the next Bright Future meeting, and he had this ring and a pair of bracers sitting on his bookcase. He offered to sell them to me for fifty bucks." Tim sneered. "Dumb putz. He had no idea what he had, but I did. I put on the ring and persuaded him to tell me what he'd done. That's when he told me about the real treasure — though he didn't know what he had."

"The list," I said.

He licked his finger and pointed at me. "Score a point for the bright girl. Yes, the list. With names. O'Donnell knew where they lived and I knew what they were and what they had. He was scared of the fae, you know. Hated them. So I loaned him back the bracers and a couple of other things and told him how to use them. He fetched artifacts for me — for which I paid him — and he got to kill the fae. It was easier than I'd thought it would be. You'd think a dumbshit like O'Donnell would have a little more trouble with a thousand-year-old Guardian of the Hunt, wouldn't you? The fae have gotten complacent."

"Why did you kill him?" I asked.

"I thought the Hunter would take care of it, actually. O'Donnell was a weakness. He wanted to keep the ring — and threatened to blackmail me for it. I told him 'sure' and had him steal a couple more things. Once I had enough that I could do my own stealing without much danger, I sent O'Donnell after the Hunter. When that didn't work . . . well." He shrugged.

I looked at the silver ring. "A politician can't afford to hang out with stupid men who know too much."

"Take another drink, Mercy."

The goblet was full again though it had only been half-full when I'd set it down. I drank. It was harder to think, almost like being drunk.

Tim couldn't afford to let me live.

"Are you a fae?"

"Oh, no." I shook my head.

"That's right," he said. "You're Native American, aren't you? You won't find any Native American fae."

"No." I wouldn't look for fae among the Indians; the fae with their glamour were a European people. Indians had their own magical folk. But Tim hadn't asked, so I didn't need to tell him. I didn't think it was going to save me, him thinking I was a defenseless human instead of a defenseless walker. But I was going to try to keep any advantages that I could.

He picked up his fork and played with it. "So how did you end up with the walking stick? I looked all over for it and couldn't find the darn thing. Where was it?"

"In O'Donnell's living room," I told him. "Uncle Mike and Zee overlooked it, too." It must have been the extra drink, but I couldn't stop before I said, "Some of the old things have a will of their own."

"How did you get into O'Donnell's living room? Do you have friends on the police force? I thought you were just a mechanic."

I considered what he'd asked me and answered with the absolute truth. The way a fae would have. I held up a finger for the first question. "I walked in." Two fingers.

"Yes, as a matter of fact, I do have a friend on the police force." Three fingers. "I'm a damn good mechanic — though not as good as Zee."

"I thought Zee was a fae; how can he be a mechanic?"

"He's iron kissed." If he wanted information, maybe I could stall him and babble. "I like that term better than gremlin because he can't be a gremlin if they just made up that word in the last century, can he? He's a lot older than that. In fact, I finally found a story —"

"Stop," he said.

I did.

He frowned at me. "Drink. Take two drinks."

Damn. When I set the goblet down, my hands tingled with fae magic and my lips were numb.

"Where is the walking stick?" he asked.

I sighed. That stupid stick followed me around even when it wasn't in the room. "Wherever it wants to be."

"What?"

"Probably in my office," I told him. It liked to show up where I was going to come upon it unexpectedly. But the need to answer him made me continue to feed him information. "Though it was in my car. It's not now. Uncle Mike didn't take it."

"Mercy," he said. "What is the thing you least wanted me to know when you came here?"

I thought about that. I'd been so worried about hurting his feelings yesterday, and standing on his doorstep I'd been a little worried still. I leaned forward and said in a low voice, "I am not attracted to you at all. I don't find you sexy or handsome. You look like an upscale geek without the intelligence to make it work for you."

He surged to his feet and his face whitened, then flushed with anger.

But he'd asked and so I continued, "Your house is bland and has no personality at all. Maybe you should try some naked statues —"

"Stop it! Stop it!"

I sat back and watched him. He was still a boy who thought he was smarter than he really was. His anger didn't scare me, or intimidate me. He saw that and it made him angrier.

"You wanted to know what O'Donnell had? Come with me."

I would have, but he grabbed my arm in a grip and his hand bit down. I heard a crack but it was a moment before the pain registered.

He'd broken my wrist.

He pulled me through the doorway, through the dining room, and into his bedroom. When he pushed me onto his bed, I heard a second bone pop in my arm — this time the pain cleared my head just a little. Mostly, though, it just hurt.

He threw open a large oak entertainment center, but there was no TV on the shelf. Instead there were two shoe boxes sitting on a bulky fur of some sort that looked almost like yak hide, except it was gray.

Tim set the boxes on the ground and pulled out the hide, shaking it out so I could see it was a cloak. He pulled it around himself, and once it settled over him, it disappeared. He didn't look any different from when he'd put it on.

"Do you know what this is?"

And I did, because I'd been reading my borrowed book and because the strange-looking hide smelled of horse, not yak.

"It's the Druid's Hide," I told him, breathing through my teeth so I didn't whimper. At least it wasn't the same arm I'd broken last winter. "The druid had been cursed to wear the form of a horse, but when he was skinned, he regained his human form. But the horse's skin did something . . ." I tried to remember the wording, because it was important. "It kept his enemies from finding or harming him."

I looked up and realized that he hadn't wanted me to answer him. He'd wanted to know more than I did. I think it was the "not intelligent enough" comment still bothering him. But part of me wanted to please him, and as the pain subsided, that compulsion grew stronger.

"You are much stronger than I thought," I said to distract myself from this new facet of the goblet's effect. Or maybe I said it to please him.

He stared at me. I couldn't tell if he liked hearing that or not. Finally he drew up the sleeves of his dress shirt to show me that he wore a silver band around each wrist. "Bracers of giant strength," he said.

I shook my head. "Those aren't bracers. Those are bracelets or maybe wristlets. Bracers are longer. They were used —"

"Shut up," he gritted. He closed the wardrobe and kept his back to me for a moment. "You love me," he said. "You think I'm the handsomest man you've ever seen."

I fought it. I did. I fought his voice as hard as I've ever fought anything.

But it's hard to fight your own heart, especially when he was so handsome. Until that moment, no man had competed with

Adam for sheer breathtaking male beauty — but his face and form palled beside Tim.

Tim turned to me and stared into my eyes. "You want me," he said. "More than you wanted that ugly doctor you were dating."

Of course I did. Desire made my body go languid and I arched my back a little. The pain in my arm was nothing to the desire I felt.

"The walking stick makes you rich," I told him as he put a knee on the bed. "The fae know I have it and they want it back." I tried to brace up on my elbow so I could kiss him, but my arm didn't work right. My other hand did, but it was already reaching up to caress the soft skin of his neck. "They'll get it, too. They have someone who knows how to find it."

He pulled my hand away.

"It's at your work?"

"It should be." After all, it followed me wherever I went. And I was going to go to my office. This beautiful man would take me.

He ran a hand over my breast, squeezed too hard, then released it and stood up. "This can wait. Come with me."

My love had me drink some more from the

goblet before we took his car to go to my office. I couldn't remember what it was that we were looking for there, but he'd tell me when we got there. That's what he told me. We were on 395 headed toward East Kennewick when he unzipped his jeans.

A trucker, passing us, honked his horn. So did the car in the other lane when Tim swerved too much and almost had a wreck.

He swore and pulled me off him. "We'll do that where there aren't so many cars," he said, sounding breathless and almost giddy. He had me zip his pants again, because he couldn't manage. It was hard with only one hand, so I used the other one, too, ignoring the pain it caused.

When I'd finished, I looked out the window and wondered why my arm hurt so badly and why I was sick to my stomach. Then he picked the cup off the floor where it had fallen and gave it to me.

"Here, drink this."

There was dirt on the outside of the cup, but the inside was full — which didn't make sense. It had been on its side on the floor mat under my feet. There shouldn't be any liquid there at all.

Then I remembered it was a fairy thing.

"Drink," he said again.

I quit worrying about how it had happened, and took a sip.

"Not like that," he said. "Drink the whole glass. Austin took two sips this morning and did exactly what I told him to do. You sure you aren't fae?"

I upended the goblet, drinking as fast as I could, though some of it spilled over and poured stickily down my neck. When it was empty, I looked for a place to set it. It didn't seem right to put it on the floor. Finally I managed to make the cup holder on my door fit around it.

"No," I told him. "I'm not fae."

I set my hands on my lap and watched them clench into fists. When the highway dropped us into east Kennewick, I told him how to find my shop.

"Would you shut up?" he said. "That noise is getting on my nerves. Take another drink."

I hadn't realized I was making noise. I reached up and felt my vocal cords, which were indeed vibrating. The growl I'd been hearing must be me. It stopped as soon as I became aware of it. The cup was full again when I reached for it.

"That's better."

He pulled into the parking lot and parked in front of the office.

I was so jittery that I had trouble opening the door of the car, and even when I was out, I was shaking like a junkie.

"What's the code?" he asked, standing in front of the door.

"One, one, two, zero," I told him through the chattering of my teeth. "It's my birthday."

The little light on the top switched from red to green: something in me relaxed and my jitters settled down.

He took my keys and opened the door, then locked it behind us. He looked through the office for a while, even pulling the step ladder over so he could get up high on the parts shelves. After a few minutes he started pulling things off the shelves and dumping them on the floor. A thermostat housing hit the cement floor and cracked. I would have to remember to reorder it, I thought. Maybe Gabriel could go through the parts and see what we could salvage. If I had to repay Zee, I couldn't afford to lose too much inventory.

"Mercy!" Suddenly Tim's face replaced the thermostat housing in my view. He looked angry, but I didn't think it had anything to do with the housing.

He hit me, so it must have been my fault that he was angry. He obviously wasn't used to fighting. Even with his borrowed strength, he only managed to knock me back a couple of steps. It hurt to breathe afterward; I recognized the feeling. One of my ribs was cracked or broken.

"What?" he asked.

I cleared my throat and told him again, "You need to get your thumb out of your fist before you hit someone or you'll break it."

He swore and stormed out of the office and out to the car. When he came back, he had the goblet.

"Drink," he said. "Drink it all."

I did and the jitters got worse.

"I want you to focus," he said. "Where is the walking stick?"

"It wouldn't be in here," I told him solemnly. "It only stays places where I live. Like the Rabbit or my bed."

"What?"

"It will be in the garage." I let him into the heart of home.

The bay nearest the office was empty, but so was the other bay — which worried me until I remembered that the Karmann Ghia I'd been restoring was out getting more work done. Upholstery.

"I'm glad to hear it," he said dryly. "Whoever Carmine is. Now where's the walking stick?"

It was lying across the top of my second

biggest tool chest as if I'd set it down casually when I got some other tool. Clever stick. It hadn't been there when we walked into the garage, but I doubt Tim had noticed.

Tim picked it up and ran his hands over it. "Gotcha," he said.

Not for long. I must not have said it out loud — or else maybe he didn't hear me. I was babbling again, so maybe it just had bled in with the rest of the words that were leaving my mouth. I took a breath and tried to direct what I said.

"Was it worth killing O'Donnell for?" I asked him. A dumb question but maybe it could keep my thoughts focused. He'd told me that, that I needed to focus.

As soon as the thought occurred to me, my head quit feeling so muzzy.

He caressed the stick. "I'd have killed O'Donnell for pleasure," he said. "Like I did my father. The walking stick, the cup, they were gravy." He laughed a little. "Very nice gravy."

He leaned it against the tool chest and then turned to me.

"I think this is the perfect place," he said.

He might have been handsome, but the expression on his face wasn't.

"So it was all a game," he said. "All the

talk of King Arthur and the flirting. Was that guy even your boyfriend?"

He was talking about Samuel. "No," I said.

It was the truth. But I could have said it in a way that wouldn't make him angry. Why did I want my love angry with me?

Because I liked it when he was angry. But the picture that ran through my head was Adam, punching the bathroom door frame. So angry. Magnificent. And I knew to the bottom of my soul that he'd never turn that great strength against anyone he loved.

"So you were just using the doctor to shake up the situation, huh? And you invaded" — he liked the sound of that, so he said it again — "*invaded* my home. What did you think? Poor geek, he never gets any. What a loser. He'll be grateful for a few crumbs, eh?" He grabbed me by the shoulders. "What did you think? Flirt with the geek a little and he'll fall in love?"

I had worried that he'd take it too seriously — once I realized I'd been flirting. "Yes," I said.

He shoved me with an inhuman sound and I stumbled back, then fell hard, knocking into a rolling tool tray that spilled a few tools on the ground.

"You'll do it with me," he said, breathing hard. "You'll do it with the poor pathetic

380

loser — and you'll like it . . . no, be grateful to me." He looked around frantically, then noticed I was carrying the cup. "You drink. Drink it all."

It was hard. My stomach was so full. I wasn't thirsty, but with his words ringing in my ear, I couldn't do anything else. And the magic in it burned.

He took the cup from me and set it on the ground, next to the walking stick.

"You'll be so grateful to me and you'll know that you'll never feel anything like it again." He dropped to his knees beside me. His beautiful skin was flushed an ugly red. "When I finish . . . when I leave — you won't be able to stand it all alone, because you know that no one will ever love you after I'm done. No one. You'll go to the river and swim until you can't swim anymore. Just like Austin did."

He unzipped his jeans, and I knew with bleak certainty that he was right. No one would love me after this. Adam would never love me after this. I might as well drown myself when I lost my love, just as my foster father had.

"Quit crying," he said. "What do you have to cry about? You want this. Say it. You want me."

"I want you," I said.

"Not like that. *Not* like that." He reached out and grabbed the end of the walking stick and used it to knock the cup over, so it rolled toward him. He dropped the stick and grabbed the cup.

"Drink," he said.

I don't remember exactly what happened from there. The next remotely clear thought I had was when my hand touched something smooth and old, something that spread its coolness up my arm when I closed my hand over it.

I stared at Tim's face. His eyes were closed as he made animal grunts, but almost as if he felt the intensity of my gaze, they opened.

The angle was bad, so I didn't try anything fancy. I just shoved the silver end of the walking stick into his face, visualizing it going through his eye and out the back of his skull.

It didn't, of course. I didn't have the strength of giants, or even of werewolves. There is only so much force you can gather when you are flat on your back hitting someone who is on top of you. But I hurt him.

He reared back and I scrambled away, dropping the stick as I moved. I knew where there was a better weapon. I ran to the counter, where my big crowbar sat right where I'd put it after prying the engine I was replacing this afternoon that extra quarter of an inch.

I could have run away. I could have shifted into my coyote form and run while he was distracted. But I had nowhere to run. No one could love me after tonight. I was all alone.

I'd learned to make the strange noises that seem to go along with all the martial arts — though part of me had always winced away at the stupid sounds. As I raised the crowbar as if it were a spear, the sound I made came from the depths of my anger and despair. Somehow it didn't sound stupid at all.

He was strong, but I was faster. When I closed with him, he grabbed my right arm, the one he'd already injured, and squeezed.

I screamed, but not in pain. I was too far gone to feel something as finite as physical pain. I shoved the end of the pry bar into his stomach with my left hand.

He dropped, vomiting and wheezing, to the ground. Even with only my left hand to guide it, the pry bar was heavy enough to crush his skull when I brought it down on his head.

Part of me wanted to beat his head in until there was nothing left but splinters of bone. Part of me knew I loved him. But I didn't give in to love. Not with Samuel so long ago, not with Adam, and not with Tim.

I didn't bring the pry bar back down on his head — I had something more important to do.

But no matter how hard I hit it, the iron bar did nothing to the cup. It didn't make sense because the cup was clearly made of pottery and iron broke through most fae enchantments. I chipped up cement, but I couldn't so much as put a smudge on that damned cup with the pry bar.

I was searching for a sledgehammer, tracking blood and other stuff all over my garage, when I heard a car engine being revved hard as it peeled around a corner.

I knew that engine.

It was Adam, but he was too late. He couldn't love me anymore.

He would be so angry with me.

I had to hide. He didn't love me so he might hurt me when he was angry. When he calmed down, that would hurt him. I didn't want him hurting because of me.

There was nowhere for a person to hide. So I wouldn't be a person. My eyes fell on the shelves that lined the far back corner. A coyote could hide there.

I changed, and on three legs scrambled up the shelves and slipped behind a couple of big boxes of belts. The shadows were dark.

There was a crash from the office as Adam proved that a deadbolt lock is no protection against an angry werewolf. I cowered a little lower.

"Mercy." He didn't shout. He didn't need to.

The voice carried and swept me up in its liquid rage. It didn't sound like Adam, but it was. I pulled back from the boxes just a little so that they would quit shaking.

What came through the door into the garage was like nothing I'd ever seen before. The closest I'd seen was one of the between forms a werewolf takes on when he's changing. But this one was more complete than that, as if the between form had become finished and useful. He was covered from top to tail with black fur and his hands looked very functional — as did his teeth-laden muzzle. He stood upright, but not like a man. His legs were caught halfway between human and wolf.

Adam.

I had only an instant to take it in, because Adam caught sight of Tim's body. With a roar that hurt my ears, he was upon him, ripping and tearing with those huge claws. It was horrifying, terrifying . . . and part of me wished it was I who was being torn to shreds.

It would only hurt for an instant and then it would be over. I panted with pain and fear, but stayed where I was because Tim had told me that I was to find the river instead. And I didn't want to hurt Adam.

Werewolves filtered in cautiously from the office. Ben and Honey, both still in human form — I wondered how they did that with Adam in a frenzy. Maybe something about this halfway form protected them . . . but then Darryl followed. He had a grimace on his face and sweat glistened on his forehead and darkened his rib-knit shirt. His control was allowing the others to keep from being caught up in Adam's rage.

They looked around the garage though they stayed near the door and away from Adam.

"Do you see her?" Darryl asked softly.

"No," said Ben. "I'm not sure she's still here — do you smell . . ."

His voice stopped because Adam dropped an arm (not one of his) and focused on Ben.

"Obviously," Darryl said in a strained voice, "we all smell her terror." He knelt on one knee, like a man proposing to his beloved.

Ben dropped to both knees and bowed his

head. Honey did the same, and their attention was all for Adam.

"Where is she?" His voice was guttural and oddly accented from speaking out of a mouth meant for howling rather than talking.

"We will look, sir." Darryl's voice was very quiet.

"She's here," said Ben in a rush. "She's hiding from us."

Adam's great mouth opened and he roared, more like a bear at that moment than a wolf. He dropped to all fours — and I expected him to complete the change, to become all wolf. But he didn't. I could feel him pull on the power of the pack and they gave it to him. Either it was easier to change from a transitional stage, or the pack sped his way, but it wasn't five minutes before Adam stood naked and human in the harsh fluorescent light.

He took a deep breath and stretched out his neck, the crack of his vertebrae loud in the silent garage. When he was finished, all that was left of the wolf was the scent of his anger and the amber of his eyes.

"She's still here?" he asked. "You can tell?"

"Her scent is all over," Ben answered. "I can't track her. But she'd have found a corner to hide in. She wouldn't have run."

He said the last sentence absently as his eyes drifted over the shop.

"Why not?" asked Darryl, his voice surprisingly gentle.

Ben inhaled as if the question startled him. "Because you only run if you have hope. You saw what he did, heard what he told her. She's here."

They'd watched, I thought, remembering the technician telling me that Adam was recording from the cameras, too. They'd seen it: I was so ashamed I wanted to die. Then I remembered that I was going to and took comfort from the thought of the river, so cool and inviting.

"Mercy?" Adam turned in a slow circle. I tucked my nose into my tail and held very still, closing my eyes and trusting my ears to tell me if they got too close. "Everything is all right, now. You can come out."

He was wrong. Nothing was all right. He didn't love me, nobody loved me, and I would be all alone.

"You could *call* her," suggested Darryl.

There was a thud and a choking sound. Unable to resist, I looked.

Adam held Darryl against the wall, his forearm across his throat.

"You saw," he whispered. "You saw what he did to her. And now you suggest I do the

388

same? Bring her to me with magic that she cannot resist?"

I knew the drink from the fae goblet was still affecting me: my stomach was burning, my body shaking like a meth addict's. But something bothered me. I still should have been able to understand Adam's reactions, right? He'd been so concerned . . . angry for me. But if he'd seen . . .

He'd know I'd been unfaithful.

Adam had declared me his mate before his pack. And if I was just learning that there were other, paranormal results, I did understand the politics involved.

A werewolf whose mate is unfaithful is seen as weak. If it is the Alpha . . . well, I knew that there had been one Alpha whose mate had slept around, but she did it with his permission. By not accepting Adam, I had already weakened him. If his pack knew that Tim had . . . that I'd let Tim . . .

Adam dropped his arm, freeing Darryl. "Did you hear that?"

I'd quit whining as soon as I realized I was making noise. But it was too late.

"It came from over there," said Honey. She stepped over a few pieces of Tim on her way to my side of the garage, followed by Darryl and Ben. Adam stayed where he was, his back to me, his hands braced

389

shoulder high against the wall.

So it was him that the fae attacked when she came through my office door.

Nemane looked very little like the woman who had come to my office with Tony. Her dark hair glowed with silver and red highlights and floated about her as if held away from her body by the power of her magic. She blasted Adam with a wave of magic that knocked him halfway across the garage to land flat on his back in a puddle of dark blood. He rolled to his feet as soon as he hit and went for her.

War, I thought. If he killed her or she him, it would be war.

I was off my shelf and sprinting as fast as my three legs could manage before the thought had completed itself.

Though there was no uncertainty in his movement, she must have hurt him because I reached her before he did.

I shifted so I could talk, but I didn't get a chance because Adam hit me like a football player, his shoulder in my stomach. I don't think he meant to hit me, because he rolled under me, jerking me down with him. I never hit the ground.

Diaphragm spasming, I sprawled all over him in an awkward position that left one of my knees in his armpit and my good arm caught under his opposite shoulder. In another instant he was on his feet and I was cradled against him, all three of the other werewolves between us and the enraged fae.

I tried to talk, but he'd knocked the wind out of me.

"Shh," Adam said, never taking his eyes off the enemy. "Shh, Mercy. You'll be all right now. I've got you safe."

I swallowed against the bleak sorrow. He was wrong. I would always be alone now. Tim had told me so. He had had me, and now I would be alone forever. No, not forever because there was the river flowing nearby, almost a mile wide and so deep that it could appear black. My shop was close enough that sometimes I could catch a scent of the water from the Columbia.

Thoughts of the river calmed me, and I could think a little better.

The werewolves were waiting for Nemane to attack again. I don't know why Nemane waited, but the pause gave me a chance to talk before anyone got hurt.

"Wait," I said, getting my wind back. "Wait. Adam, this is Nemane, the fae who was sent here to deal with the guard's death."

"The one who was willing to let Zee die rather than find the real murderer?" He lifted his upper lip in contempt as he spoke.

"Adam?" Nemane said coolly. "As in Adam Hauptman? What is the werewolf Alpha doing with our stolen property?"

"They came to help me," I said.

"And who are you?" She cocked her head to the side and I realized that I didn't sound like myself. My voice was hoarse, as if I'd been smoking for a dozen years — or screaming all night. And Nemane was blind.

"Mercedes Thompson," I said.

"Coyote," she said. "What mischief have you been making tonight?" She took a step forward, into the room, and all the werewolves stiffened. "And whose blood is feeding the night?"

"I found your murderer," I told her tiredly, resting my face against Adam's bare skin. His scent washed over me in a falsely comforting wave: he didn't love me. I was so weary that I accepted the comfort while I could. I would be alone soon enough. "And he brought his own death upon himself."

The tension in the air went down noticeably as Nemane's magic quit scenting the air. But the wolves waited for Adam to tell them the danger was over.

"Darryl, call Samuel and see if he can come," Adam said quietly. "Then call

Mercy's policeman. Honey, there's a blanket and some spare clothes in the back of the truck. Fetch them."

"Should we call Warren, too?" asked Ben, looking away from Nemane so he could see Adam, but his eyes stopped on my arm. "Bloody hell. Look at her wrist."

I didn't want to, so I watched Nemane, because she was the only one who didn't look horrified. It takes a bit to horrify a werewolf. I'd certainly never managed it before.

"It's crushed," said Nemane, in her cool professorial voice. "And her arm broken above it, too."

"How can you tell that?" said Honey, returning with the blankets and clothes. "You're blind."

The fae smiled. Not a happy expression. "There are other ways of seeing."

"How can they fix that?" said Ben, looking at my arm. He sounded a lot more shaken up than I expected from Ben. Werewolves are used to violence and its results.

Nemane walked past Adam like a wolf on a scent. She bent and picked up the druid horse's skin. It must have fallen off Tim when Adam ripped him to pieces.

Those pieces might haunt my dreams for a good long time, but I was too numb to be horrified by them now.

Nemane caressed the cloak and shook her head. "No wonder we couldn't find him. Here, this is what she needs." She'd found the goblet where it had rolled under my tool chest.

"What is that?" asked Adam.

"Orfino's Bane, it was once called, Huon's cup, or Manannan's gift. It has a few uses and one of those is healing."

"That's not what it does," I told Adam in a horrified whisper.

Nemane looked at me.

"He made her drink from it," Adam said. "I thought it contained some kind of drug — but it's fairy magic?"

She nodded. "In the hands of a human thief, it allows him to enslave another, given as a gift it will heal as well, and in the hands of the fae it will testify to truth."

"I won't drink it," I told Adam's shoulder, shifting in his arms until I'd gotten as far from the cup as I could.

"It will heal her?" he asked.

We all heard a car drive up.

"It's one of mine," Adam said — I assumed he was talking to the fae because the rest of us could all recognize the sound of Samuel's car. To get here so fast he must have come from work. The hospital was only a few blocks away. "He's a doctor. I'd like to get his opinion."

When he came in, Samuel's single, awed swearword took in the whole garage: bits of Tim scattered wherever Adam had deposited them, blood all over the place, a couple of naked people (Adam and I), and Nemane in her full fae glory.

"I need you to check out Mercy's arm," Adam said.

I didn't want him to touch it. It was numb right now, but I knew that could change at any time. It looked more like a pretzel than an arm, bending in places that it shouldn't. It had been working when we came into the office. Sort of. Tim must have damaged it more while I was killing him.

No one cared what I wanted.

At first Samuel just knelt so he could look at it lying across my thighs. He whistled between his teeth. "You need to pick out new friends, Mercy. The crowd you hang out with is awfully hard on you. If things keep going this way, you're going to be dead before the year is out."

He was so relentlessly cheerful, I knew it was bad. His hands were light on my arm, but the searing pain made odd flashes of light dance in front of my eyes. If Adam hadn't been holding me, I'd have jerked away, but he held me steady, murmuring soft, comforting things I couldn't hear over the buzzing in my ears.

"Samuel?" It was Ben who asked, his voice sharp and clear.

Samuel quit touching my arm and stood up. "Her arm feels like a tube of toothpaste filled with marbles. I don't think it's something that can be tacked back together with a hundred pins or bolts."

I am not a fainting kind of person, but the imagery Samuel used was too horrible and black things swam in front of my vision. It felt like I blinked twice and someone jumped events forward a minute or two. If I'd remembered about the river sooner, Samuel's prognosis wouldn't have made me faint.

I knew I'd been out because gathering the amount of power that Adam was amassing didn't just suddenly happen. I didn't realize why he was doing it until it was too late.

"You don't have to worry anymore, Mercy," Adam murmured, his head bent so that he whispered it into my ears.

I stiffened. I tried. But tired, hurt, and terrified, I didn't have the slightest chance to fight his voice. I didn't really want to. Adam wasn't angry. He wouldn't hurt me.

I let him pull the power of his pack over

me like a warm blanket and relaxed against him. My arm still hurt, but the feeling of peace that wove over me separated me from the pain just as it did from the terror. I was so tired of being afraid.

"That's it," he said. "Take a deep breath, Mercy. I won't let you do anything that will harm you, all right? You can trust me that far."

It wasn't a question, but I said "yes" anyway.

In a very quiet voice I don't think even the other werewolves could hear, he said, "Please don't hate me too much when this is over." There was no push to his voice when he said it.

"I don't like this," I told him.

He ran his chin and cheek over the side of my face in a quick caress. "I know. We're going to give you something that will heal you."

That information broke through the peace he'd given me. He was going to make me drink from the cup again. "No," I said. "I won't. I won't."

"Shh." His power rolled over me and smothered my resistance.

"I know the fae," said Samuel harshly. "Why are you so eager to help?"

"Whatever you might think, wolf" — Nemane's voice was chill — "the fae don't forget our friends or our debts. This happened because she was trying to help one of us. I can heal only her body, but it looks to me as if it is the least of the hurts she took tonight. The debt is still owed."

A cup was pressed against my lips, and as soon as I recognized the smell of it, my stomach rebelled and I retched helplessly as Adam shifted me in his arms until I wasn't throwing up on either of us. When I was finished, he tipped me back where I'd been.

"Plug her nose," suggested Darryl and Samuel pinched my nostrils together.

"Swallow fast," Adam told me. "Get it over with quickly."

I did.

"Enough," said Nemane. "It will take an hour or so, but I swear that it will heal her."

"I just hope we didn't break her doing it." Adam's voice rumbled under my ear and I sighed in contentment. I wasn't all alone yet. His arms shook and I worried that holding me was tiring him.

"No," he told me, so I must have said something. "You aren't heavy."

Samuel, used to emergencies, took control. "Honey, give me the blanket and the clothes. Go grab a chair from the office — something with a back. Darryl, take Mercy, so that —" Adam's arm tightened around my legs and he growled, making Samuel change his mind. "All right, all right, we'll wait for Honey to get back with the chair. Here she is. We'll wrap Mercy in the blanket, you send her to sleep, and then go wash up and change before the police get here."

Adam didn't move.

"Adam . . ." Samuel's tone was wary, his posture carefully neutral. A truck drove up and the tension in the garage dropped appreciatively. No one said anything, though, until Warren came in to the garage. He looked pale and strained, and he slowed down as he got a good look around him.

He walked into the center of the garage and nudged a piece of meat with the toe of his boot. Then he looked at Adam. "Good job, boss."

His eyes went to Samuel and the blanket he was holding. Then he looked at the chair resting on the floor in front of Honey.

Samuel's body language told Warren what had been going on and what he wanted without saying a word.

Warren strolled over to us and snagged the blanket from Samuel, snapping it out. "Let's get her warm and covered up."

Adam let Warren take me without argument. Instead of setting me in the chair, though, Warren sat in it and pulled me snugly against him. Adam watched us for a moment — I couldn't read his face at all. Then he leaned forward and kissed me on the forehead.

"If you called the police, they will be here shortly," said Nemane as soon as Adam had gone to the bathroom to wash up. "I need to be gone with these before the police come."

"There's a ring," I told her, still basking in the peace that Adam had gifted me with.

"What?"

"A silver ring on his finger." I yawned. "I think there are a few more things in Tim's house. He keeps them in a cabinet in his bedroom."

"The Mac Owen ring," Nemane said. "Would you all help me to look for it?"

"Maybe Adam swallowed it," I suggested and Warren laughed.

"No more horror movies for you," he murmured. "But Adam didn't eat any of him."

"Here it is," Honey said, bending down to pick something up. Instead of giving it to Nemane, she closed her hand over it. "If you go and take that cup, they're going to prosecute Mercy for murder."

"Give it to me." The temperature in the

room dropped appreciatively with the ice in Nemane's voice.

"We have the video," Darryl said. "It should be enough."

Honey laughed and turned on him. "Why? All it shows is that Mercy was drunk. She drank more every time he asked her to. She might have said no, but he never appeared to force her to drink. From the video, a prosecutor could argue that her judgement was impaired by alcohol — but that's not enough to get her freed from a murder charge. She had him incapacitated and she deliberately got up and took a crowbar and hit him with it."

"Then that is what may be," Nemane said. "It is too dangerous for humans to know we have these things."

"Not everything," said Honey. "Just the cup."

"By itself it would answer most of the police's questions," said Samuel. "Though you might have to explain how a human managed to rip a man's head off."

"He had bracelets," I told him. "Called them bracers of giant strength — but they weren't bracers. They'll be around some-place, too."

"Ben," said Adam, sounding cool and controlled as he came back into the garage bay. "Go get my laptop." He was wearing jeans and a long-sleeved gray shirt. His hair was damp. "Nemane, I will make you a deal. If you watch what happened tonight, I will let you take your toys and run away — if that's what you still want to do."

"I am the Carrion Crow," Nemane said. "I've seen more death and rape than you can imagine."

Shame slipped through the warm peace Adam had given to me. I didn't want anyone to watch. "She's blind," I said. "She can't see anything."

"She can use my eyes," Samuel said.

I saw Nemane stiffen.

"My father is a Welsh bard as well as the Marrok," Samuel told her. "He knows things. You can use my eyes, if Adam thinks it's important to see this."

Ben brought Adam's laptop and handed it to him. Adam set it up on the counter.

I buried my head against Warren and tried to ignore the sounds coming from Adam's laptop. The speakers weren't very good so I pretended I couldn't hear the helpless noises I made or the wet sounds . . .

He let it play until the moment Nemane walked in and turned it off.

"She should be dead," Nemane said flatly when he was finished. "If I'd seen it first,

I'd never have given her another drink so soon."

"Will she be all right?" Warren asked sharply.

"If she hasn't gone into convulsions and died yet, I don't suppose she's going to." Nemane stroked the cloak she held on her arm, sounding troubled. "I don't know how she managed to kill him while he was wearing this. It should have kept her from touching him."

"It only protected him from his enemies," I told Warren's shirt. "I wasn't his enemy because he told me not to be."

A storm of police sirens was brewing up outside.

"All right," Nemane said. "You may have the bracelets to explain how a human killed O'Donnell. And the cup. Adam Hauptman, Alpha of the Columbia Basin Pack, you will take possession of them on your honor and return them to Uncle Mike when they are of no further use."

"Samuel," said Warren, and I realized I was starting to shiver helplessly.

"She needs to sleep," Nemane told them.

Adam knelt beside us and looked me in the eye. "Mercedes, go to sleep."

I was too tired to fight the compulsion, even if I had wanted to.

CHAPTER 12

I woke up with the smell of Adam in my nose and my stomach cramping. I didn't have time to wonder about my surroundings. I dove off the bed and made it to the bathroom just in time to throw up in the toilet.

Fairy brew tastes a lot worse the second time around.

Gentle hands pulled my hair out of the way — though it was too late for that — and wiped my face with a damp washcloth. Someone had put a pair of underwear and one of Adam's T-shirts on me.

"At least you made it to the loo this time," Ben said prosaically. And then, just so I could be absolutely sure it was really him and not some kinder, nicer clone, he said, without affection, "Good thing, too. We are almost out of sheets."

"Happy to oblige," I managed before heaving up some more — so hard it came burning out my nose as well as my mouth. By the time I finished, I'd have been crying on the floor if the idea of doing that in front of Ben hadn't been so repugnant.

He waited until it became apparent that getting to the bathroom was as good as I was going to manage before he sighed and heaved me up with more effort than I knew he felt. He was a werewolf; he could probably pick up a piano. My weight wasn't enough to make him sweat.

He tucked me back in the sheets with surprising efficiency. "The fae told us you'd sleep a lot for a while. The vomiting surprised her, though. Probably something to do with your resistance to magic and how much of the stuff you had. Best thing for you is sleep." He paused. "Unless you're hungry."

I turned my head out from the pillow far enough that he could see my face.

He smirked. "Yeah, well, I'm not excited about cleaning up another mess either."

It was still dark out the next time I woke up so it wasn't too much later. I lay unmoving as long as I could. I knew Ben was still in the room and I didn't want to attract his attention. I didn't want anyone to look at me.

Without nausea to distract me, the events

of the evening, those that I remembered clearly anyway, rolled through my head like an Ed Wood movie: so horrible that you can't force yourself to stop watching. Worse, I could smell it on me. The fairy liquor, blood . . . and Tim. The worst was knowing what I had done . . . and what I hadn't.

In the end, I crawled out of bed and slunk on my hands and knees to the bathroom door. I kept my eyes lowered so Ben would know that I understood what I'd done.

He got to the door before me and held it open. I hesitated. Protocol would have me roll over and give him my throat and underbelly . . . but I couldn't stand to be that vulnerable again. Not right now. Maybe if it were Adam.

"Poor little bitch," he said softly. "Go get cleaned up. I'll keep the villains at bay for that long."

He shut the door behind me.

I stood on shaky feet and turned the water to hot. I stripped off the clothing and scrubbed and scrubbed, but I couldn't get rid of the smells. Finally I came out and searched through Adam's cabinets. I found three bottles of cologne, but none of them smelled like him.

Finally I splashed his aftershave on instead. It burned on the healing cuts and scrapes I'd picked up off the cement floor of the garage, but it covered up Tim's scent at last.

I couldn't put on the clothes I'd just taken off because they still smelled like . . . everything. Even though the shirt smelled only of Adam and the underwear was a clean pair of mine and I was pretty sure that someone had scrubbed me up before they put me in them since I remember being covered with blood . . .

As soon as the thought occurred, I remembered standing in Adam's shower and Honey's voice in my ear. *You'll be fine. Let me just get this stuff off you —*

I began to hyperventilate so I grabbed a towel and breathed through it until the panicky feeling went away.

So, no clothes, and I couldn't stay in here much longer before someone came in to check.

No one would ask the coyote questions she couldn't answer.

For a frightening moment I wasn't sure I could shift, when shifting had always been second nature.

You need to stay human, Mercy. We're in the hospital and you need to stay with us just a little longer. Samuel's voice.

I didn't care about police and this wasn't

the hospital. Fur slid over my skin at last and my fingernails turned to claws. It took longer than it ever had, but in the end I stood on four paws. I whined to myself because I still didn't want to go out.

The door opened before I could figure out any alternative, which was just as well as there were no good hiding places in the bathroom — not even for a coyote.

Ben sniffed. "Aftershave? Good enough. Someone had time to run some sheets through the wash, and I put them on the bed. So the sheets are clean."

I realized I was looking up into his face and dropped my gaze and tucked my tail.

"Like that, eh?" he said. "Mercy . . ." He sighed. "Never mind. Come on, then. Get back to bed."

I didn't need to sleep, but I curled up in the clean sheets and waited for Ben to leave so I could go . . . somewhere. I couldn't go home because Samuel was there and he knew.

Everyone knew and Tim was right: I was going to be alone.

I should go swimming . . . but that wasn't right. My foster father had done that. No, I would never kill myself, never do to someone else what he had done to me.

After a while the door opened and Adam

came in. He must not have had time to wash properly, because he still smelled faintly of Tim's blood and the stuff Tim had made me drink. I'd thrown up on him, I remembered with regrettable clarity.

"Zee's being released as soon as they can get the paperwork through," Adam said. He must have been talking to Ben because I was pretending very hard to be asleep. He didn't say anything more for a minute, as if he were waiting for some response. Then he sighed. "I'm going to shower. When I come out, you can take a break."

Ben waited for the shower to start before he began talking. "I don't know how much you remember. That fae, Nemane, was going to take her fairy things and leave before the police got there, but Adam thought that her part of the story was necessary to prove beyond a shadow of a doubt that the gremlin was innocent. And that you had reason to kill Tim. So he showed her the video the security cameras caught and she changed her mind and gave us a couple of things to prove your innocence. She was very impressed that you fought your way free of the goblet's influence."

I pulled my tail tighter over my face. I hadn't fought, not until the very last. I'd let Tim . . . I'd wanted him. For a moment I felt the pull of his beauty, just as I had then.

"Shh," Ben said with a nervous look at the bathroom. "You have to be quiet. He's on edge right now and we don't want to send him over."

I didn't want to hear any more. Zee was free. Tomorrow I'd be very happy for it. He could take the shop back in lieu of my payment. I'd find somewhere else to go. Mexico, maybe. They had lots of Volkswagens in Mexico. Lots of coyotes, too. Maybe I'd just stay a coyote.

Unaffected by my attitude, Ben continued. "Turns out your Tim killed his best buddy yesterday before you went to his house. At least that's what we think." Even in my current state I realized that his speech was missing its usual heavy dosing of foul language. Maybe he was worried about Adam, who disapproved of swearing in front of women. I lost my curiosity about it, though, when I understood what he was saying. "Austin Summers walked into the river and drowned himself. Some old man saw him do it and said he was smiling. He tried to save him, but Austin just kept swimming and then dove. Never came up. They found his body a few miles downstream. No one knew why until the fae showed them how the cup worked and they watched the video. It was nice of Timmy-boy to confess."

Austin knew too much, I thought. He must have known something about the artifacts, and once Tim learned that I knew about them, and might have told other people, Austin was too much of a liability. It hadn't been all my fault, though.

Tim was jealous of Austin and hated him for being so good at everything. He would have killed Austin sooner or later. It wasn't my fault. Not completely.

Ben pulled the edge of the blanket over me and sat on the edge of the mattress. "We showed the cops the video, too. Don't worry, your change was off camera. No one knows you're a coyote. Adam also picked the camera shots that didn't show any of us werewolves except for him. He's pretty fast with that computer of his." I heard professional approval in his voice: Ben was employed as a hotshot computer geek and he was apparently good at his job.

"Adam was going to go with the police anyway," he continued. "He had to since Nemane put him in charge of the artifacts — but the police were kinda freaked out about the condition of old Tim's body. There was no danger they'd keep him — not with the clear evidence that you killed him. But Adam didn't fuss. Truth to tell, I think that Adam was freaked, too. They, ah" — a sudden, satisfied smile was in his voice — "*requested* very nicely that he come with them to the police station with the video. Warren went, too, just in case the police decided to give Adam a bad time. All in all, it's a good thing that Tim was already dead when we happened on the scene, or Adam might have been kept more than a few hours."

"Not so," Adam said from the bathroom. He turned off the shower. "I'd rather have gotten there a lot sooner and taken the consequences with the police."

Ben stilled on the bed, but when Adam didn't say any more, he relaxed a little.

I shouldn't have taken Tim to my garage. Surely I could have figured out some other way. I'd been running to Adam for help again, just as if I hadn't brought Fideal to his door yesterday and endangered his home, his pack, and his daughter. If it hadn't been for Peter, Honey's sword-wielding husband, they might not have been able to drive him off. Adam might have been killed.

If Adam had been closer to my shop when I used my birthday on the keypad to call for help, if he'd killed Tim . . . I hadn't even considered the risks. I'd just known that Adam would come and save me from my own stupidity. Again.

Adam came out of the bathroom dressed in clean jeans and nothing else, rubbing his short-cropped hair with a towel. He dropped it on the floor and knelt beside the bed. Ben slipped off and went to stand by the window.

Adam's face was drawn with worry and weariness.

"I'm sorry," he said tiredly. "I'm so sorry that I forced you. I told you I'd try not to do that and I broke my word."

He reached out to touch me and I couldn't bear it. Couldn't bear that he'd apologize to me when I'd endangered him. When I'd betrayed him.

I slid out from under his hand before he could touch me and cowered on the far side of the bed. His face was very still as he let his hand drop to his side.

"I see," he said. "I'm sorry, Ben, you'll have to stay here a few more minutes. I'll find Warren and send him up."

"Don't be stupid, Adam."

Adam came to his feet and took two long strides to the door. "She's afraid of me. I'll send someone else up."

He shut the door very quietly behind him. Ben stood in the middle of the room and

413

used all the words he'd left out when he'd been speaking to me earlier. With a jerky motion, he pulled his cell phone out of the front pocket of his jeans and hit a button.

"Warren," he said, his voice tight, "would you tell our lord and master to get his arse back up here? I have a few things to tell him."

He closed his phone without waiting for an answer and began to pace restlessly back and forth muttering swearwords to himself. He'd begun to sweat and it smelled of anxiety and anger.

The door swung open and Adam loomed in the open doorway. He was so angry I came to my feet.

"Come in and shut the door," Ben said harshly, in a voice he really shouldn't have used to his Alpha.

Without glancing in my direction, Adam came in and shut the door with awful precision that was a strong indication of how close he was to losing control — if the way the brass doorknob deformed in his hand hadn't already been a clue.

As Adam walked to the middle of the room, I sank on the bed, not so much lying down as gathering my feet underneath me in preparation for running.

Ben didn't seem to notice how much

trouble he was in. Or maybe he didn't care. "How much do you want her?" Unable to meet Adam's hot glare, he turned and stared out the window. "Do you want her enough to put aside your worries and hurt?"

There was something in Ben's voice . . . Adam heard it, too. He didn't exactly cool down, but he was paying attention. A different Alpha, one less sure of himself, would have already put Ben in his place.

Ben hadn't paused as he continued to talk in a quick, nervous voice. "If you handle this right, tomorrow, next week . . . she's probably going to be all pissy by then about how you forced her to drink that fairy shit. She'll take off a door from that old car out there — that old car that makes sure you always think about her even when you're cursing at her for spoiling your view." He looked at me and I dropped my ears. Adam's eyes weren't the only ones that had gone wolf. Before I could back away from him, Ben turned his attention to Adam.

As if they were equals, Ben took two steps forward and I saw that he was actually taller than Adam. "An hour and a half ago she was still puking that fairy shit that you and Mr. Wonderful poured down her throat. You heard Nemane. She said it would be a while before the effects wore off completely. And you are *still* holding her responsible for what she does."

Adam growled, but I could tell he was trying to hold on to his control and listen. After a moment he asked, "What do you mean?" in a fairly civilized voice.

"You're treating her like a rational being and she's still off in Fairyland." Ben was breathing hard and that stink of fear was growing — making it more difficult for Adam to control himself. But that didn't slow Ben down. "Do you love her?"

"Yes." There was no hesitation in his voice. None at all. And yet he'd seen . . . he must not have seen, must not have realized . . .

"Then put aside your *goddamned* self-loathing and look at her."

Golden eyes settled on me, and unable to meet Adam's gaze, I turned my own eyes to the wall as my stomach twisted uneasily.

"She's afraid of me."

"That stupid bitch has never had the brains to be afraid of you, me, or anyone else," Ben snapped with more force than truth. "Forget yourself and take another fucking look. You're supposed to be able to read body posture."

I didn't see it, but I heard Adam quit breathing for a moment.

"Damn," he said in an arrested voice.

"She crawled," Ben said. There were tears in his voice. That was wrong. Ben barely even tolerated me on the best of days. "She crawled to the bathroom to clean herself again. If it weren't for the two subs in the pack, I'd be on the bottom. And *she* wouldn't stand up in my presence for guilt."

Unable to take the scrutiny anymore, I slunk off the bed entirely and hid between the wall and the mattress.

"No, wait. Leave her alone for a minute and listen to me. She's safe enough there."

"I'm listening." All that anger had been swallowed until the only emotion I could smell in the room was Ben's.

"A rape victim . . . a rape victim who fights . . . They've been violated, made helpless and afraid. It breaks their confidence in the safety of their little world. It makes them afraid." Terror and anger and something else pushed Ben until he paced all the way to the bathroom and then back to the bed in quick, frantic steps.

"All right," agreed Adam in a gentle voice, as if he understood something I'd missed. Not surprising. After Ben pointed it out, I realized that I wasn't exactly firing on all four cylinders.

"If — if you don't fight. If the rapist is someone you're supposed to obey so you can't fight or don't think you can fight or they've drugged you so you . . ." Ben stuttered to a halt and then swore. "I'm making a muddle of this."

"I understand." Adam's voice was a caress.

"Fine then." Ben stopped pacing. "Fine. If you don't fight, it's not quite the same. If they make you help, make you cooperate, then it's not clear to you anymore. Is it rape? You feel dirty, violated, and guilty. Most of all guilty because you should have fought. Especially if you're Mercy and you fight everything." Ben's breathing was rough, his voice pleading. "You've got to see it from her point of view."

I crawled all the way under the bed until, still hidden in a fall of blankets, I could see their faces.

"Tell me."

"Samuel told you . . . told us that she'd flirted with that one. She hadn't meant to, but you don't always see it until it happens. Right?"

"Right," Adam agreed.

"Samuel said he told her that she better not do that in front of you."

He waited for Adam's nod to continue. "But she needs to help her friend and that means going to this man's house. It's all right, though, because there will be a lot of other people and she won't flirt because she knows that it's a danger. And she doesn't flirt. She behaves just like an interested guest — which is going to piss him off at her."

"How do you know she didn't flirt?" Adam asked, then in response to something I hadn't caught, he moved a hand in a negating manner. "No, I don't doubt you. But how do you know?"

"It's Mercy," Ben said simply. "She wouldn't know how to betray someone she cared about. Once she noticed, she'd stop and not start again."

He kept his gaze on Adam's face, but his head was canted so he was looking up into the Alpha's eyes rather than challenging him. "But she knows that she's skirting the line. She knows that you wouldn't like it that she went to his house . . . not that she's done anything wrong . . . but it feels that way." He started pacing again, but he'd calmed down. Now that he was talking about me. "I don't know why she went back again. Maybe he tells her that he knows who killed Zee, or that he knows something about O'Donnell or the stuff that was stolen. He would know, wouldn't he? He lured her to his house because he thought she posed a danger to him — or maybe just because he knew she had that damned walking stick that followed her around and he wanted it. Or maybe he just wanted to get even with her for rejecting him."

"Right."

"Right. So she knows that you won't like it if she goes back. She knows that you'll be all territorial about her going to a man's home even if she's just trying to keep Zee safe. Did you know that until a couple of days ago, she thought that your declaring her your mate was just politics? Just a way to keep her safe from the pack?"

There was a little silence.

"Honey told me that last night. She explained to Mercy that it was a little more. So Mercy learned more than you intended her to."

"Pressure makes her run in the other direction," Adam said dryly. "I thought I'd wait to explain until matters became critical."

"So she knows that it's more than words. She knows that your declaration makes you vulnerable."

"Make your point."

"So, she knew she should call you and tell you that she was going to the bastard's house. But she also knows that you'll tell her no and she feels like she needs to go for

Zee's sake — or whatever reason Tim found to persuade her."

"Okay."

"And maybe she doesn't like checking in with you for every move she makes. In any case, she knows she should call you and she doesn't. She chooses to go to Tim's house, but she also feels on some level that it's the wrong thing to do. Her choice. Her fault. Her fault when she drinks from that bloody fairy cup. Her fault that he —"

Just that fast Adam had Ben on the ground underneath him while he snarled. "It's not her fault she was raped," he growled.

Ben lay limp and gave Adam his throat, but he didn't quit talking, even though a tear slid down his cheek. "She thinks so."

Adam stilled.

"What's more," he continued hoarsely. "I bet she wonders if she was raped at all."

Adam sat back, releasing Ben entirely. "Explain it to me." His voice was very soft.

Ben shook his head and put an arm over his eyes. "You saw it. You *heard* him. That drink took away her ability to resist, but he didn't just make her take off her clothes. He made her feel, made her want."

Adam shook his head. "And you heard her . . . You saw her. She told him, 'No.' He made this friend of his drown himself with a smile on his face — and he couldn't keep Mercy under control while he was with her. He had to pour the frickin' stuff down her throat." Was that *pride* in his voice?

"But she took off her clothes and she touched him."

"She fought it," Adam snarled. "You saw. You heard her. You saw Nemane's shock when she saw Mercy's resistance. She couldn't believe it when Mercy hit him with the walking stick."

Ben whispered, "When he told her that she wanted him, that she loved him — she *felt* it. Did you see her face? It was real to her. That's why she could kill him while he was wearing that fucking fairy horse pelt. Wasn't that what she said? In that moment Mercy loved him so she couldn't be his enemy — otherwise she wouldn't have been able to kill him while he was wearing it."

Adam believed it. I saw his face change and heard the growl that rumbled in his chest. Now, he understood. Now, he'd hate me for betraying him.

The floor creaked as Ben rolled suddenly to his feet. He dusted off his pant legs, a nervous gesture because the floor was clean. Adam had covered his face with a hand.

"So was it rape?" Ben asked lightly as he rubbed his face briskly, cleaning it of any evidence of tears. It was a good performance. If the other two people in the room had been human, they might have believed in this nonchalant Ben and not the tormented one he'd let peek out. "You'll have to decide for yourself. If you blame her for how he made her feel, then go back down those stairs and send Warren up. He'll take care of her, and when she can, she'll leave and you won't ever have to worry about her again. She won't blame you because she knows it was her fault. Everything was her fault. She'll be sorry that she hurt you and she'll leave us all so we can forget about her."

Startled, I stared at Ben. How did he know I planned to leave?

Adam stood up with slow deliberation. "You live," he rasped, "you live because I know how you really feel. Of course it was rape." He stared at Ben's bowed head and I could feel the sudden rise in power that told me he was using some touch of the power that was his as Ben's Alpha. He waited until the other werewolf raised his eyes and even I felt the sudden sizzle of that connection. Then slowly he said, "Just as it is rape when an adult coerces or cajoles a child. No matter if the child cooperates or not. Whether it feels good or not. Because that child is not able to do anything else."

Something changed in Ben's face, a subtle shift that Adam saw, too, because he dropped the magic. "And now you know that I understand and believe that."

Ben was abused as a child. It wasn't surprising given his warm and cheery personality, really. I'd just never given much thought about why he was the way he was.

"Thank you for sharing your understanding," Adam said formally.

Ben dropped to his knees as if they had suddenly turned to water. It was a supremely graceful move. "I am sorry that I did not do it . . . better. More respectfully."

Adam cuffed him gently. "I wouldn't have listened. Get up and go get some rest." But when Ben stood, Adam pulled him into a hug that proved that werewolves aren't people. Two men, heterosexual and human, would never have touched after a revelation like that.

"Being a werewolf gives you time to get over your childhood," Adam whispered into Ben's ear. "Or it gives you time to destroy yourself with it. I'd rather you be one of the survivors, do you hear me?" He stepped back. "Now go downstairs."

He waited until the door closed behind Ben, and then shook his head. "I owe you," he told the door. "I won't forget."

He dropped down beside the bed as if he were too tired to stand. With the same suddenness, though I thought I was more than adequately hidden, he reached out and grabbed me by the scruff of the neck and pulled me out from under the bed and onto his lap.

I shivered, torn between the knowledge that I didn't deserve his touch and the tentative understanding that he didn't blame me, no matter how much I thought he should.

"My father always told me that when I heard good advice, I needed to listen to it," he said.

He continued to hold me firmly by the scruff of the neck with one hand, but the other caressed my face. "We're going to wait for a talk until that stuff has worn off completely." His caress stopped. "Don't misunderstand me, Mercedes Thompson. I am mad at you."

He bit my nose once, hard. Wolves do that to discipline their young — or misbehaving members of the pack. Then he tipped his head so it rested on mine and sighed.

"Not your fault," he told me. "But I'm still mad as . . . mad as heck that you scared me like that.

"Darn it, Mercy, who would have thought that a pair of humans caused all this misery? Even if you had called me, I wouldn't have objected to you going . . . at least not because I thought it was dangerous. I wouldn't have sent a guard with you just to go talk to some human." He put his face against my neck then gave a half laugh. "You smell like my aftershave."

Hard arms pulled me tightly against him as he said in a quiet voice, "It's only fair to warn you that you sealed your fate tonight. When you knew you were in trouble, you came to me. That makes twice, Mercy, and twice is almost as good as a declaration. You are mine now."

His hands, which had been moving in circles in my fur, stopped and took a good hold. "Ben says you might run. If you do, I will find you and bring you back. Every time you run, Mercy. I won't force you, but . . . I won't leave or let you leave either. If you can fight that cursed fairy drink, you can certainly overcome any advantage being an Alpha gives me if you really want to. No more excuses, Mercy. You are mine, and I am keeping you."

My independent nature, which would doubtless reassert itself soon, would be outraged by this possessive, arrogant, and medieval concept. But . . .

Tim's wish that I would always be alone had hit me particularly hard . . . because it was something I already knew. Nothing like being a coyote raised among werewolves to make you understand that different means not belonging. I didn't belong with my human family either, though I loved them and they loved me.

Under the weight of the unvarnished, possessive intent that began in Adam's words and carried through to his body, my whole world shook on its axis.

He slept eventually, curled up around me as if he were in wolf form, but the lines of strain stayed behind, making him look older — as if he were thirty, say. With Adam surrounding me, I watched as the sky lightened and the new day began.

Somewhere in the house a phone rang.

Adam heard it, too. Jesse's door opened and she ran down the stairs and picked up the phone.

I couldn't quite hear what she said as she was downstairs in the kitchen, but the tone of her voice went from polite to carefully respectful.

Adam stood with me in his arms, then set me on the bed. "You stay there."

"Dad? It's Bran on the phone."

He opened the door. "Thanks, Jesse."

She handed him the phone and peered around the door to look at me. Her eyes were puffy. Had she been crying?

"You go get ready for school," Adam told her. "Mercy's going to be fine."

Today was Thursday morning. The thought galvanized me — I had to get to work . . . Then I settled back into the bed. I wasn't going back to my garage, not with stray bits of Tim scattered here and there. I should call Gabriel and tell him not to show up after school. I should . . .

". . . someone sent them the video of you tearing Mercy's rapist apart. While I appreciate the sentiment, and doubtless would have done the same thing, it leaves us in an awkward position. That bill cannot pass." Bran's voice wafted over me like a cool breeze of calm that had nothing to do with what he was saying, and everything to do with his being Bran.

"How much of the video did they get?" Adam growled.

"Not enough, apparently. Whoever sent it represented it as an Alpha werewolf attacking a human without provocation. I would like you to take the whole video — I trust it doesn't show our Mercy changing shape?"

"No. But it shows her without clothes."

"Mercy won't care, but perhaps it might be possible to add those black rectangles the news reporters use."

"Yeah. I'm sure Ben can do it." Adam sounded tired. "You want me to go with it, don't you?"

"I'm sending Charles with you. I'm sure that once they have seen the entire video, most of the men on the committee will be ready to cheer you on. The others will keep their mouths shut."

"I don't want that video getting on the Internet," Adam growled. "Not Mercy's —"

"I think we can make sure that doesn't happen. The congressman was very clear about who sent him the tape. I'll see that it is taken care of."

Adam wasn't looking at me. I hopped off the bed and slipped through the still open door.

I didn't want to hear any more. I didn't want to think about people watching a video of last night. I wanted to go home.

Warren was standing at the foot of the stairs talking to Ben, so I dodged into Jesse's room before he looked up.

"Mercy?" Jesse was sitting on her bed with her homework scattered in front of her.

I'd hopped onto the sill of her open window, which was still screenless, but something in her voice made me pause. I jumped onto her bed and nuzzled her neck. She gave me a quick hug before I wriggled free and darted out the window.

I'd forgotten that Tim had mangled my arm — foreleg in coyote form — but it held up just fine when I jumped off a low spot of the roof onto the ground. Nemane had been as good as her word about the other things the goblet could do.

I ran all the way home and stopped on the front porch. I couldn't open the door as I was, but I didn't want to change to human anytime in the next decade.

Before I had time to worry too much, Samuel opened the door for me. He closed the door and followed me to my room, opening that door as well.

I jumped on my bed and curled up with my chin on my pillow. Samuel sat down on the foot, giving me plenty of room.

"I have, entirely illegally, snooped into the medical records of one Timothy Milanovich," he told me. "His doctor is a friend of mine and agreed to leave me in his office for a few minutes. When Milanovich's fiancée left him, he had himself tested and was negative for any disease that you might worry about."

And I didn't have to worry about pregnancy either. As soon as I'd realized that there was a possibility of ending up in either Adam or Samuel's bed, I'd started on the pill. Being illegitimate makes you sensitive about things like that.

I sighed and closed my eyes, and Samuel got off the bed. He closed my door behind him.

It opened again after only a few minutes, but it wasn't Samuel. Warren in his wolf form lurked solemnly behind his Alpha.

"I meant what I said, Mercy," Adam told me. "No running. I have to go to Washington and you'd better be here when I get back. Until then, one of my pack will stay with you."

The bed sank heavily under Warren's weight as the huge wolf tucked himself beside me. He licked my face with a rough tongue.

I lifted my head and met Adam's gaze.

He knew. He knew it all and he still wanted me. Maybe he'd change his mind, but I'd known him for a long time and he was as changeable as a boulder. You might move him with a bulldozer, but that was about it.

He nodded once, and was gone.

CHAPTER 13

For a whole day I indulged myself. I slept on my bed with whatever wolf had been sent to stay with me. Whenever I started to have a nightmare, someone was always there. Samuel, Warren, Honey, and Darryl's mate, Aurielle. Samuel dragged one of the kitchen chairs into my room and played his guitar for hours.

The next morning I woke up and knew I had to do something or all this pity and guilt was going to make me go stir crazy. If I let them all treat me like I was broken, then how was I going to convince myself I wasn't?

It was Friday. I should be at work . . . My lungs froze at the thought of going back into my shop. I breathed my way through the panic attack.

So I wouldn't go to work. Not today at least.

What to do . . .

I lifted my head to the pile of wolves that

were threatening to make my twin bed collapse under their weight and considered my minions. Darryl wouldn't work. He wouldn't twitch without Adam's say-so — and Aurielle wouldn't go against her mate. She opened her eyes to look at me. Like me, both of them should have been at work: Aurielle at her high school and Darryl at his high-price think tank. Neither of them would do for the main project, but for now it didn't matter. Today would be reconnaissance.

It was actually Warren who came with me, shifting to his human form so he could play "walk the coyote" while Darryl and Aurielle stayed at Adam's house to play guardians for Jesse.

"So how far are we going to walk?" Warren asked.

I staggered a few steps, fell on my side, and then dragged myself forward weakly before hopping back up and continuing to walk briskly down the shoulder of the highway.

"If things get that bad, I'll give Kyle a call and tell him he needs to come pick us up," Warren said dryly.

I gave him a canine grin and turned off the highway and onto a secondary road. The

Summers' house was a nice two-story house built in the past decade on a two-acre parcel. They had a dog who took one look at me and came at us in a silent rush that stopped dead as soon as Warren growled — or maybe it just smelled the werewolf on him.

I put my nose to the ground and searched for the trail I'd hoped was there. It was summer and just a quarter mile away was the river. Most self-respecting boys would . . . yes. Here it was.

I'd thought about finding Jacob Summers at home, but it would be hard to explain why I needed to talk to him alone. I wasn't even quite sure what I was going to tell him — or if I was going to say anything at all.

The road continued most of the way to the river, sort of petering out just after it crossed the canal. I found Jacob's favorite place by following his trail. There was a pretty good sized boulder right on the edge of the river.

I hopped on it and stared out at the river, just as Jacob must.

"You aren't thinking of jumping in, are you, Mercy?" Warren asked. "I wasn't much of a swimmer when I was human and matters haven't improved over the years."

I gave him a scornful look, then remembered that Tim had told me to drown myself for love of him.

"Glad to hear it," he said and sat on the rocky shore beside me.

He leaned over and picked up a tangle of fishing line complete with hook and sinker and a couple of old beer cans. He put the hook in the cans. Suddenly he straightened and looked around.

"Do you feel that?" he asked me. "Temperature just dropped about ten degrees. Do you suppose your Fideal friend is about?"

I knew why it was colder. Austin Summers stood beside me and petted me with his cool, dead hand. When I looked up at him, he was just staring at the river, as I had been.

Warren paced back and forth along the shoreline, looking for Fideal, unaware that we'd been joined by someone else.

"Tell my brother." Austin didn't look away from the deep blue water. "Not my parents, they wouldn't understand. They'd rather believe that I committed suicide than hear that I'd succumbed to Tim's magical potion. They get that kind of stuff mixed up with Satanism." He smiled faintly with a hint of contempt in his voice. "But my brother needs to know I didn't abandon him, all right? And you're right. Here is a good place. It's his thinking place."

I leaned into his hand a little.

"Good," he said.

We sat there a long time before he faded away. I lost his scent soon after, but I felt his fingers in my fur until I hopped off the rock and headed back home, with Warren walking beside me, two crumpled beer cans in his hand.

"So did you have something you wanted to do?" Warren asked. "Or did you just want to stare at the river — which you could have done without coming all of this way."

I wagged my tail, but made no effort to answer him any other way.

The next step required me to be human. It took me twenty minutes in the bathroom with the door shut before I managed it. It was stupid, but for some reason I felt more vulnerable as a human than I did as a coyote.

Warren knocked on the door to tell me that he was going home to catch some shut-eye and that Samuel was home for the night.

"Okay," I said.

I could hear the smile in his voice. "You're going to be just fine, girl." He banged his knuckles one more time on the door and left.

I stared at my human face in the mirror and hoped he was right. Life would be simpler as a coyote.

"You wuss," I told myself and got in the shower without warming it up first.

I showered until the water was cold again, which took a while. One of the upgrades Samuel had put in was a huge hot water tank, even though there hadn't been anything wrong with the old one.

With goose bumps on my skin, I braided my hair without looking in the mirror. I'd forgotten to bring in clothes so I wrapped myself in a towel. But the bedroom was empty, and I dressed in peace.

Safely covered in a sweatshirt with a picture of the two-masted sailing vessel, *Lady Washington,* on the front and black jeans, I headed into the kitchen to look for a newspaper to see when Austin Summer's funeral was going to be — if they hadn't already held it. I figured after the funeral was as good a time as any for Jacob Summers to head for the river.

I found yesterday's newspaper on a counter in the kitchen and made myself a cup of chocolate from the water that was already hot in the teakettle. It was the instant kind, but I didn't feel like doing the work to make the good stuff. So I dumped a handful of stale minimarshmallows on top.

I took the paper and my mug and sat down at the table next to Samuel. Unfolding the paper, I began to read.

"Feeling better?" he said.

Politely I said, "Yes, thank you." And went back to reading, ignoring him when he tugged at my braid.

I'd made the front page. I hadn't expected that. When you run with werewolves and other things that people aren't supposed to know too much about, you get used to fake news. MAN DIES IN MYSTERIOUS FIRE, ARSONIST SOUGHT, or WOMAN FOUND STABBED TO DEATH. Things like that.

LOCAL MECHANIC KILLS RAPIST was just above STUDENT DROWNS IN COLUMBIA. I read my story first. When I finished, I put down the newspaper and took a thoughtful sip of cocoa in which the marshmallows had softened to chewy.

"Now that you can talk, tell me how you are," Samuel said.

I looked at him. He appeared composed and self-contained, but that wasn't how he smelled.

"I think Tim Milanovich is dead. I killed him and Adam ripped him into pieces small

438

enough that not even Elizaveta Arkadyevna is witch enough to call back to unlife if she decided to make zombies instead of money." I took another sip of cocoa, chewed on a marshmallow, and said reflectively, "I wonder if killing your rapist will ever become a recognized therapy practice. Worked for me."

"Really?"

"Honest to Pete," I said, slamming my cup down on the table. "Really. That is, if everyone else quits running around here like their best friend died and it was their fault."

He smiled, just a little and only with his lips. "Message received. No victims in this house?"

"Damn straight." I picked up the newspaper.

Thursday. Today was Friday. Tad was going to fly down Friday if his father was still in danger.

"Did someone call Tad?" I asked.

He nodded. "You asked us to do that. Adam called him when he got back from the police station. But apparently Uncle Mike had gotten the word to him first."

I didn't remember asking. There were a few hazy bits from Wednesday, but I didn't like having things I didn't remember doing.

It made me feel helpless. So I changed the subject.

"So are we going to blame Tim for O'Donnell's murder?"

"Tomorrow," he said. "The police and the fae want to tie up some loose ends and make sure everyone has their story straight. Since Milanovich is dead, there won't be a trial. Objects found in his house will be linked to O'Donnell and some robberies in the reservation. Officials will conclude that O'Donnell and Milanovich were working together and Milanovich got greedy and offed O'Donnell. Zee connected O'Donnell to the robberies and went to his house to talk, finding O'Donnell already dead. He was taken in for questioning, but released when the evidence proved that he didn't do it. They are being vague on the evidence. Milanovich decided to try out one of the things he and O'Donnell stole on you but you killed him defending yourself."

He grinned faintly. "You'll be happy to know that the newspaper is going to report that the magical objects they stole were obviously not as powerful as the thieves thought, which is why you were able to kill Milanovich."

"Weak magical objects being considerably less frightening than powerful ones," I observed. "And Austin Summers?"

"They're going to try and keep him out of it — but his connection to both Milanovich and O'Donnell is too close to just leave the family wondering. The police will gently tell them that there is some evidence that he was involved, but no one knows exactly how — and never will since everyone is dead."

"Have you heard from Adam?"

"No, but Bran called. The policeman who sent the shortened version of the video has been reprimanded and the copy he made confiscated. Bran seems to think that Adam and Charles are making an impression. Adam should be home Monday."

I didn't want to think about what was going to happen when Adam came home. Today I was going to be very good at only thinking about what I wanted to.

I pulled the paper up and read the article about Austin. "Funeral's tomorrow morning. I think I'll go visit Austin's brother afterward. Do you want to come?"

"I have to work tomorrow — I had last weekend off." He sighed. "Do I want to know why you're going to visit Austin's brother?"

I smiled at him. "I think I'll take Ben."

Samuel's eyebrows shot up. "Ben? Adam won't like that."

I waved him off. "Adam won't care, and Ben's the only one I trust to take things just far enough. Warren may sound like a pussy-cat, but some things hit his hot buttons. Besides, Ben will enjoy this."

Samuel closed his eyes. "You enjoy doing this. Fine, be mysterious. Ben might be a creep, but he's Adam's creep." He may have sounded exasperated but I saw the relief in his body. He was willing to play along that everything was normal if that's what I wanted. He was even beginning to believe it. I could see it in the way his shoulder muscles were relaxing and in the fading of the scent of his protective anger.

I needed to leave before I blew it. Besides, I needed to clean up. "I think I'll just go take a shower," I said.

It wasn't until Samuel stiffened that I remembered I'd just come out of the shower. So much for playing normal.

On Saturday, I took Ben for a walk. He'd been pretty wary when I let myself into Adam's house and told him he was going to be my escort today.

Aurielle, who had been my assigned guard this morning, had tried to invite herself along, but I knew her too well. She had no soft spots for people who hurt the ones she cared about. If she knew that Jacob Summers was one of the boys who'd tried to assault Jesse, she'd have his head. Really.

Me, I believe in revenge — but I also believe in redemption.

So I told Aurielle she couldn't come — and since the pack had decided to treat me as if I had already agreed to be Adam's mate, there was nothing she could do.

At my request, Ben changed, so I went walking with a werewolf by my side.

You'd think that we'd have attracted more attention. Only recently, I'd begun to notice that mostly people don't see the werewolves when they are out and about. I used to think it was just that people didn't know about the wolves, but now they do — and they still don't see them. It's probably some sort of pack magic that keeps them unseen. Not invisible exactly, but easily overlooked.

There was no one at Jacob's rock and I went hunting with Ben for a place we could see it and still stay out of sight. We found a nice place in some bushes near the canal and settled in to wait. At least Ben did. I fell asleep. I'd been sleeping a lot more than usual. Samuel told me he thought it was a result of the forced healing, but I saw the concern in his eyes.

Yes, I'd had moments of black depression

— but I treated them the way I always treated things that bothered me. My freezer was full of cookies and there were brownies in Adam's fridge. *My* fridge sparkled and the main bathroom would have sparkled if the years hadn't worn the shiny finish off the linoleum floor.

Someday I was going to get new fixtures for that bathroom, if Samuel didn't beat me to it. I was really tired of avocado green. My bathroom had been done in mustard yellow when I moved in. Who would put a mustard yellow toilet in a bathroom? Now it sported a boring white sink, shower, and commode — but boring is better than yellow.

Under my head, Ben moved, waking me up.

I rolled over and looked up. Sure enough, there was a young man walking down the road who looked quite a bit like Austin. He was limping a little. I guess Jesse had done some damage. The satisfaction I felt meant I wasn't as nice a person as I liked to pretend.

I stayed where I was until he'd made it all the way to his rock and sat down. Then I got up and dusted myself off until I looked relatively normal.

"You wait here until I call you," I told Ben.

■ ■ ■ ■

"Hello, Jacob," I said when I was still a little ways off.

He rubbed his face quickly before he turned. Once his initial panic at being found crying was over, he frowned at me.

"You're the girl who was raped. The one who killed my brother's friend."

I changed my friendly approach between one breath and the next. "Mercedes Thompson. The one who was raped and the one who killed Tim Milanovich. And you are Jacob Summers, the bastard who decided to get together with his friend and see how easy it would be to beat up my good friend Jesse."

His face paled and I smelled the guilt on him. Guilt was good.

"She wouldn't tell anyone who you were because she knew her father would kill you both." I waited for fear, but had to settle for the guilt. I suppose he thought I was speaking figuratively.

"That's not why I came, though," I told him. "Or at least it's not the only reason I came. I thought you ought to know the truth of how your brother died. This is the story that is not going to get into the newspapers." And I told him what Tim had done to his brother and how.

"So this fairy thing made my brother kill himself? I thought those things were supposed to be playtoys."

"Even playtoys can be dangerous in the wrong hands," I told him. "But no. Tim murdered your brother just as he did O'Donnell. If he hadn't had the cup, he'd have used a gun."

"Why did you tell me this? Aren't you afraid I'll tell people that those artifacts are dangerous?"

It was a good question and it would require a little smooth talking interspaced with truth. "The police know the real story. The newspapers aren't going to take you seriously. How did you find out? Mercy Thompson told me. Then I can say, well, no, sir, I've never met him in my life. That's quite a story, but that's not how it happened. Your parents . . ." I sighed. "I think your parents would be happier thinking he committed suicide, don't you?"

I saw from his face that he agreed with his brother on that. I don't understand some people. If you've brushed up against evil, you don't mistake it for anything else, not werewolves, not teenagers dressed in black with piercings on their piercings, and not fae magic, however powerful.

"The real reason I almost didn't tell you about this is that the people who will believe you are the fae. And if they think that you are making real trouble for them, you might have a convenient accident some dark night. To their credit, they don't want to do that. None of us, not the fae, not me, and not you, want that. It would be better if you just kept it to yourself."

"So why did you tell me?"

I looked at him and then looked at Austin, who stood just behind him. Jacob had goose bumps on his arms, but he wasn't paying attention.

"Because once, when I was a kid, someone I cared about committed suicide," I told him. "I thought it was important that you knew that your brother wasn't that selfish, that he didn't desert you." I turned my face to the river. "If it helps, Tim didn't get away with it."

His response told me I'd been right to believe that anyone Jesse had once liked wasn't irredeemable.

"Does it help you to know that he's dead?" he asked.

I showed him the answer in my face. "Sometimes. Most times. Sometimes not at all."

"I think . . . I think I believe you. Austin had too much to live for — and you have no reason to lie to me." He sniffed, then wiped his runny nose on his shoulder, trying to pretend he wasn't crying. "It does help. Thank you."

I shook my head. "Don't thank me yet. That wasn't the only reason I came. You need to know why you don't want to hurt Jesse. Ben? Could you come here a moment?"

I threw the stick and Ben tore off after it. I'd been right. He'd had a great time. Scaring teenage bullies was right down his alley.

We'd been gentle with Jacob. Ben had played it just right. Scary enough to convince Jacob that Jesse had a reason to worry that her father would kill anyone who hurt her, but just gentle enough that Jacob had asked to touch.

Ben, like Honey, was beautiful — and he was vain enough to enjoy the attention. Jacob, I thought, was entirely redeemable — and he was ashamed that he'd hurt Jesse. He wouldn't do it again.

I'd gotten the name of his friend . . . and his friend's girlfriend who had thought the whole thing up. We'd visited them, too. Ben made a really, really scary boogeyman —

not that any werewolf wasn't scary. I don't know if they'd ever be people I'd care to know, but at least neither of them would go near Jesse ever again.

Sometimes I am not a nice person. Neither is Ben.

Sunday I went to church and tried to pretend that all the looks were directed at Warren and Kyle, who had come to church with me. But Pastor Julio stopped me at the door.

"Are you all right?" he asked.

I liked him so I didn't growl or snap or do any of the things I felt like doing. "If one more person asks me that, I'm going to drop to the floor and start foaming at the mouth," I told him.

He grinned. "Call me if you need something. I know a good counselor or two."

"Thanks, I will."

We were in the car before Kyle started laughing. "Foam at the mouth?"

"You remember," I said. "We watched *The Exorcist* a couple of months ago."

"I know a few good counselors, too," he said, and being smart, he continued without giving me a chance to respond. "So what are we doing this afternoon?"

"I don't know what we're doing," I told

him. "I'm going to see if I can get my Rabbit running again."

The pole barn that served as my home garage was twenty degrees cooler than the sun-scorched outside air. I stood in the dark for a minute, dealing with the momentary panic that the scent of oil and grease brought on. This was the first panic attack of the day, which was exactly one third the number of panic attacks I'd had yesterday.

Warren didn't say anything; not when I was fighting for breath and not when I'd recovered — which is one of the reasons I love him.

I hit the lights as soon as the sweat began drying on my shirt.

"I'm not too optimistic about the Rabbit's chances," I told Warren. "When Gabriel and I brought it home, I checked it out a little. Looks like Fideal turned my diesel to saltwater — and it's been sitting in my tank and lines since Tuesday."

"And that's bad." Warren knew about as much about cars as I did about cows. Which is to say, not a thing. Kyle was better, but given the choice, he'd opted for the air-conditioned house and chocolate chip cookies.

I popped the hood and stared down at the

450

old diesel engine. "It'd probably be as cheap to go find another one in a junkyard and use this for parts as it would be to fix it."

Problem was I had a lot more places to put money than I had money to put there. I owed Adam for the damage to his house and car. He hadn't said anything, but I owed him. And I hadn't been to work since Wednesday.

Tomorrow was Monday.

"Do you want to try this later?" Warren's sharp glance lingered on my face.

"No, I'm all right."

"You taste of fear." It wasn't Warren's voice.

I jerked my head out from under the hood hard enough to kink my neck. "Did you hear that?" I asked. I'd never run into a ghost at my home, but there was a first time for everything.

But even before he said anything, I saw the answer in Warren's body posture. He'd heard it all right.

"Do you smell anything unusual?" I asked.

Something laughed, but Warren ignored it. "No."

Let's see. We were in a brightly lit building with no hiding places and neither Warren nor I could see or smell anything. That left two things it could be, and since it was still daylight outside, vampires were out.

451

"Fae," I said.

Warren must have had the same thought because he picked up the digging bar I kept just inside the door. It was five feet long and weighed eighteen pounds and he picked it up in one hand like I'd grab a knife.

Me, I picked up the walking stick that was lying by my feet where a moment ago there had been nothing but cement. It wasn't cold iron, but it had saved my life once already. Then we waited, senses alert . . . and nothing happened.

"Call Adam's house," Warren told me.

"Can't. My cell phone's still dead."

Warren threw back his head and howled.

"That won't work," the intruder whispered. I cocked my head. The voice was different, bigger and had a distinct Scots accent. It was Fideal, but I couldn't tell where he was. "No one can hear you, wolf. She is my prey and so are you."

Warren shook his head at me; he couldn't tell where the voice was coming from either.

I heard a pop and saw a spark out of the corner of my eye just before the lights went out.

"Damn it," I growled. "I cannot afford an electrician."

I don't have windows in my pole barn, but it was still bright afternoon and the light leaked in around the RV-sized garage doors. I could still see just fine, but there were a lot more shadows for Fideal to hide in.

"Why are you here?" Warren growled. "She is safe from your kind now. Ask your precious Gray Lords."

Fideal emerged from hiding to hit him. For a moment I saw him, a darker form vaguely horse shaped, the size of a large donkey. His front hooves connected with Warren's chest, knocking him off his feet.

I hit the fae with the walking stick and it throbbed in my hands like a cattle prod. Fideal bugled like a stallion, twisted away from the stick's touch, and vanished into the shadows again.

Warren used the distraction to regain his feet. "I'm fine, Mercy. Get out of the way."

I couldn't see Fideal, but Warren held the digging bar like a baseball bat, took two steps to his right, then swung and connected with something.

Warren could perceive the Fideal, but I still couldn't. He was right — I needed to get out of the way before I blundered and got Warren hurt.

I put the Rabbit between me and the fight and then started looking around for something that would be a better weapon against the fae.

There were lots of aluminum fencing supplies and old copper pipes for plumbing. All my pry bars and good steel tools were on the other side of the garage.

Fideal shrieked, a nasty ear-splitting sound that echoed wildly. It was followed by a ringing clank, like a digging bar being flung across a cement floor.

Then there was no sound at all and Warren lay unmoving on the floor.

"Warren?"

Not even the sound of breathing. I ran across the garage to stand over his body, still armed with the walking stick. There was no sign of Fideal.

Something cut my face. I swiped blindly and this time the stick vibrated like a rattlesnake's tail when I connected. Fideal hissed and ran, tripping over a jack stand and into a small tool chest. I still couldn't see him, but he made a mess of my garage.

I jumped over the fallen jack stand, knowing that Fideal couldn't be too far away. As I rounded the tool chest, something big hit me.

I landed on the cement chin-, elbow-, and knee-first. Helpless. It took me a full second to understand that the buzzing in my head was someone snapping nasty phrases in German.

Even dazed and facedown on the floor, I knew who'd come to my rescue. I only knew one man who snarled in German.

Whatever he said, it made Fideal lose control of whatever magic he'd been doing to block my nose. The whole building suddenly reeked of swamp. But it stank more in one place than any other.

I ran for the place where the shadows were the darkest.

"Mercy, *halt*," Zee said.

I swung the walking stick as hard as I could. It connected with something and stuck for a moment, then blazed as brightly as the sun.

Fideal shrieked again and made one of those impossible leaps, jumping over the Rabbit and up against the far wall, knocking the walking stick from my hand as he leapt past me. He wasn't down or even hurt. He just crouched in a manner no horse could ever adopt and stared at Zee.

Zee didn't look like someone worthy of the wariness of a monster. He looked as he always had, a man past middle age, lanky and rawboned, except for his small pot belly. He bent over Warren, who started coughing as soon as Zee touched him. He didn't look at me when he spoke. "He's all right. Let me handle this, please, Mercy. I owe you at least this."

"All right." But I picked up the walking stick.

"Fideal," Zee said. "This one is under my protection."

Fideal hissed something in Gaelic.

"You grow old, Fideal. You forget who I am."

"My prey. She is mine. They said. They said I could eat her and I will. Barnyard animals they give me. That the Fideal should be reduced to eating cow or pig like a dog." Fideal spat on the ground, showing fangs blacker than the grayish slime that coated his body. "The Fideal takes its tribute from the humans who come into its territory to harvest the rich peat to heat their houses or the children who venture too close. Pig, faugh!"

Zee stood up. The area around him lightened oddly, as if someone were slowly turning up a spotlight on him. And he changed, dropping his glamour. This Zee was a good ten inches taller than mine and his skin was polished teak instead of age-spotted German pale. Glistening hair that could have been gold or gray in better light was braided in a tail that hung down over one shoulder and reached past his waist. Zee's ears were pointed and decorated with small white slivers of bone threaded through piercings that ran all the way around them. In one dark hand he held a blade that was identical to the one he'd let me borrow except that it was at least twice as long.

Shadows pulled away from Fideal, too. For a moment I saw the monster that Adam and his pack had fought, but that gave way to a creature that looked like a small draft pony, except that ponies don't have gills in their necks — or fangs. Finally he became the man I'd first met at the Bright Future meeting. He was crying.

"Go home, Fideal," Zee said. "And leave this one. Leave my child alone and your blood will not feed my sword. It, too, hungers and it feeds best on things less helpless than a human child." He waved a hand and a motor spun to life, lifting the garage door next to Fideal.

The fae scrambled out of the pole barn and disappeared around the corner.

"He won't bother you again," said Zee, who once more looked like himself. The knife was gone, too. "I'll speak to Uncle Mike and we'll make certain of it." He held out a hand and Warren used it to pull himself to his feet.

Warren was pale and his clothes were wet as if he'd been immersed in water, seawater from the smell of him. He straightened himself slowly, as if he hurt.

"Are you all right?"

Warren nodded, but he was still leaning on Zee.

The walking stick was just in front of Zee's foot — the blackened silver knob had smoke gently rising from it.

I picked it up gingerly, but it was as inert to my touch as the stick I'd thrown for Ben on Saturday. "I thought this was only good for making ewes have twins."

"It's very old," said Zee. "And old things can have a mind of their own."

"So," I said, still looking at the smoking stick. "Are you still mad at me?"

Zee's jaw stiffened. "I want you to know this. I would rather have died in that cell than have you suffer that madman's attack."

I pursed my lips and gave him my truth in exchange for his. "I'm alive. You're alive. Warren's alive. Our enemies are dead or vanquished. That makes this a good day."

I went to work on Monday morning and learned that Elizaveta, the pack's very expensive witch, had been by and done cleanup. The only trace of my run-in with Tim were the scars I'd left on the cement while I was trying to destroy the cup. Even the door Adam broke had been replaced.

Zee had come in on Friday and Saturday, so all my work was caught up. I had a few bad moments, which I had to hide from Honey, who was Monday's guard, but by lunch I'd reclaimed the shop as mine. Even Gabriel's hovering (after school was out) and Honey camped in my office didn't disturb me as much as I'd expected. I finished at five sharp and sent Gabriel home. Honey followed me to my driveway before going home herself.

Samuel and I ate take-out Chinese and watched an old action flick from the eighties. About halfway through, Samuel got a call from the hospital and had to leave.

I turned off the TV as soon as he was gone and took a long hot shower. I shaved my legs in the sink and took my time blow-drying my hair. I braided it, reconsidered, and wore it loose.

"If you keep fussing, you'll make me come in and get you," Adam told me.

I knew he was there, of course. Even if I hadn't heard him drive up or come in, I would have known he was there. There was only one reason that Samuel wouldn't have called for a replacement. He'd known Adam would be over soon.

I stared at my reflection in the mirror. My

skin was darker on my arms and face from the summer sun than it was on the rest of my body, but at least I'd never be pasty pale. Aside from the cut on my chin that Samuel had put two stitches in and a nice bruise on my shoulder that I didn't remember getting, there was nothing wrong with my body. Karate and mechanicking kept me in good shape.

My face wasn't pretty, but my hair was thick and brushed my shoulders.

Adam wouldn't force me. Wouldn't do anything I didn't want him to do — and had wanted him to do for a long time.

I could ask him to leave. To give me more time. I stared at the woman in the mirror, but all she did was stare back.

Was I going to let Tim have the last victory?

"Mercy."

"Careful," I told him, pulling on clean underwear and an old T-shirt. "I have an ancient walking stick and I know how to use it."

"The walking stick is lying across your bed," he said.

When I came out of the bathroom, Adam was lying across my bed, too.

"When Samuel makes it back from the hospital, he's going to spend the rest of the night at my house," Adam said. "We have time to talk."

His eyes were closed and he had dark circles under them. He hadn't been getting much sleep.

"You look horrible. Don't they have beds in D.C.?"

He looked at me, his eyes so dark they were almost black in this light, but I knew they were a shade lighter than mine.

"So have you made up your mind?" he asked.

I thought of his rage when he'd broken down the door to my garage, of his despair when he persuaded me to drink out of the goblet again, of the way he'd pulled me out from under the bed and bitten my nose — then held me all night long.

Tim was dead. And he'd always been a loser.

"Mercy?"

In answer, I pulled the T-shirt over my head and dropped it on the floor.

ABOUT THE AUTHOR

Patricia Briggs lives in Montana with her husband, children, and six horses. Visit her website at www.patriciabriggs.com.